OCEAN'S BLOOD

THE DROWNING | BOOK ONE

THELMA MANTEY

Cover design: Thelma Mantey
Copyeditor: Toby Selwyn

ISBN: 978-3-00-076765-4 (paperback)
ISBN: 978-3-00-076766-1 (e-book)

First Edition: January 2024

Published by: Thelma Mantey

For inquiries, contact the author on her website: https:/thelmamantey.com

CONTENT NOTE

This is a book of dark fantasy that comes with the usual tropes of the genre. Some scenes may be upsetting for some readers. This is a non-exhaustive list of potentially upsetting themes: blood-drinking, mild body-horror, on page sex with dub con, mention of torture in dream-like flashbacks, mention of past suicide attempt, extreme physical violence.

Note that this book has **a glossary** at the end which you are welcome to refer to should you get confused by unfamiliar names and concepts.

CONTENTS

PART I
ASCENSION

CHAPTER 1

Vindt waited for the song to rise, for the killing to start.

He would have to wait some more. Down in the valley, the battle had barely begun. In the clear air, the clang of clashing weapons, curses and screams carried unfiltered up to his vantage point on the hill. A choir of death. But the killing he waited for was of a different kind.

He watched the fighting with dull detachment. Another war that was not his, its outcome none of his concern. He had seen it so many times. As always, a part of him longed to push his heels into the horse's flanks and plunge into the frenzy, draw his sword and fight, honestly, steel on steel, man on man. The idea was childish, but it suggested relief from being an idle spectator, a servant of a dark force that killed from a cowardly distance.

As always, Vindt stayed where he was.

The "dark force," however, had not deigned to raise its lethal voice yet. Silhorveen stood immobile, watching the spectacle in the valley, his crimson robes with their twisted dark lines flowing down his body. No breeze was blowing, his long dark hair a still mass.

The seething hatred the Singer's tall lean figure used to incite in Vindt had dulled into a sense of inevitability, like facing a natural calamity humans had no choice but to endure. These days, laying eyes on Silhorveen mainly triggered a fierce desire to protect him. The feeling was not Vindt's own, but imposed upon him by the magic embedded in the bracelet around his right wrist. It made the sensation no less real. As real as the disgust in its wake, the awareness of his impotence.

Their contractor, the Guzzar general, had deployed a dozen of his soldiers as Silhorveen's personal guard, reinforcing the Singer's own small retinue. The men didn't look happy either. Vindt pitied them. The Singer might win their war for them, but that did nothing for their feelings toward him.

No, he envied them. They surely had something that bound them, money, a contract, loyalty, love for their country. But they had a choice. Vindt did not, ever since Singers sung his own people to death a decade ago and forced him into their service.

An empty sky hung above, the sun at its zenith, strident, blinding. Vindt hated the sun. It abolished every shadow, annihilating possible refuge for body or mind. It sharpened the contours of the men in the valley, glinting off spear points and sword blades, off armor and metal on horses' bridles. No room for ambiguity. The landscape reflected the sky's bleakness, earth and rocks. A few scrawny plants defied the arid climate.

Sweat trickled from Vindt's armpits and down his back. It was too hot for his liking, always was. The long-sleeved red tunic didn't help with the heat. At least his arms wouldn't get sunburned.

Come on now, get it over with.

Vindt's horse stamped its feet and shook its head against the flies. He patted its neck. Poor thing; it suffered from the heat too. In the valley, ranks had broken by now. The two armies were penetrating each other like eager lovers.

Vindt wondered what the Sylians were thinking. It wasn't the first clash of the two armies; they must be aware that their doom stood here on this hill. He didn't know, though, if the Sylians had been aware of the existence of Singers before Silhorveen had begun diminishing their numbers, or if the Singer was the first embodiment of their dark legends and nightmares come to life—as it had been for Vindt on his homeland's battlefield a decade ago.

In any case, the Sylians had reacted as anyone with a working mind would: they'd split their forces and limited their attacks to raids and skirmishes. That, and sending people to the Guzzar camp at night, trying to murder Silhorveen in his sleep. The first party had been taken down by the Guzzar guards. The second by Silhorveen's own retinue.

In a way, they had been lucky not to have gotten to him. They were dead, of course, but the Singer would have done worse than just kill them. Vindt had witnessed it only once in the past decade, enough not to want to experience it again.

Now that the Guzzar general had cornered the Sylian army in this valley, their last chance was trying to bring the Singer down in plain daylight.

Only, it wasn't a chance.

As if on cue, shouting at his back made Vindt turn in the saddle. Behind them, the hill sloped down into a thicket of thorny shrubs. Silhorveen's guard turned too, taking bows from their shoulders or drawing swords. Vindt carried a bow like theirs; a sword dangled from his waist. He touched neither.

The clash of weapons from the thicket added to the shouting, occasionally cresting into a scream. Shadows moved between the branches. Vindt had no idea how many of his men the Guzzar general had stationed there. Enough, for sure. An arrow suddenly soared from the bushes in an almost vertical line, its slim shape cutting through the sky's perfect blue, slowing. The split second it hung suspended in the air seemed unnaturally long. Vindt wondered what it would feel like to be that arrow, finding one's glorious soar coming to a halt, the surprise, then shock, as gravity pulled you back to the ground.

Silhorveen had not bothered to turn around. Vindt's gaze narrowing down to the back of the Singer's red robes, his hand did now rise to his bow. Old habits. He felt Fora's eyes on him, a futile warning. Fora knew about the bracelet, knew that Vindt couldn't point an arrow at Silhorveen ever again. That the Singer wanted him to carry a bow during battle was a reminder, an act of humiliation. For the task Vindt was bound to do, he needed no weapon.

The Singer's rising song jerked his hand away from the bow and put his attention back on the battlefield below.

Finally.

He didn't want to watch. Yet, he did, drawn by the song's dark gravitation and the inexplicable allure of the horrific. The song drifted across the battlefield, weaving through the ranks of soldiers, untouchable, unstoppable, defying weapons and shields and armor, seizing people's bodies and creeping into their minds. Killing.

The fighting stalled. Even the Guzzar soldiers couldn't escape the song's allure. It wouldn't kill them, only the enemy, only the ones who didn't want to resort to the help of a Singer. Or couldn't afford it.

Inevitable memories stirred, of a day a decade ago when Vindt was no mere spectator on a distant hill but part of the action, the song's very aim, when the men dying around him *were* of his concern. But he had learned not to let those memories in. After years of practice, he could even now switch off, dissolve into the present, turn into a being without a past or future. Safe emptiness.

He closed his eyes—from the killing, from Silhorveen, from the sun. No one would blame him. For his task, he didn't need to see. He would feel a Verdur approaching, but the strange sense inside him was still. Vindt was not surprised. The demonic creatures had never attacked them during a battle. As if Verdurs shunned the presence of too many humans.

Even after ten years of countless encounters with the creature, Vindt didn't fully understand what a Verdur was. "A demon," a Singer had once told him, but Vindt was pretty sure that he had been mocking him. Demons were something else.

Whatever Verdurs were, they killed Singers. The idea would have cheered Vindt up had he not become the creature's target by proxy when they magically bound him to Silhorveen. For whatever reason, Singers couldn't fight Verdurs on their own; their otherwise omnipotent voice simply failed against them. So they bound people like Vindt, rare humans with a special trait, Thyds, and used *their* voice to—

As if fate had listened, the sense inside Vindt buzzed in

sudden alarm. At the same second, all sounds vanished, and silence descended on him like a dead weight.

The cold taste of fear had coated his gums before his mind processed what was happening, before he even opened his eyes again and saw the Verdur. The creature moved as erratically as ever, jumping, running, flying, hovering in one place for a second, gone the next. Its semi-translucent body blurred and morphed, disturbingly human and yet not, parts appearing and disappearing, horns, wings, claws, tendrils, a tail. The eyes changed too, sometimes huge and lidless, sometimes tiny marbles fringed with lashes. Their expression prevailed: hatred. Dark, menacing energy poured from the shape-shifting body, the threat to kill.

What? But we've never encountered a Ver—

Silhorveen spun around. In a split second, his expression changed from surprise to determination. He dropped his killing song and switched to defense. Which meant he turned to Vindt. Silhorveen's voice entered Vindt's body with insubstantial tendrils. As always, Vindt's mind fought the intrusion, the alien pull trying to take over his voice, *him*. The resistance broke in an instant, and his voice rose, entwining with Silhorveen's, filling the gaps in the Singer's own song.

Vindt couldn't hear the creature, yet it had a voice too, an antagonistic flow of something impalpable, negated screams which wiped out other noises like a jealous lover. It aimed to drain all life from him. Silhorveen and his combined voices remained the only sounds defying the acoustic mire.

From the corners of his eyes, Vindt saw the contorted faces of the Guzzar soldiers around them. Their hands had risen to their ears as if trying to get rid of the impenetrable cloth that suddenly clogged them. Horses grew skittish.

Vindt's fear mingled with his helplessness into a scalding broth. He had no way to fight the Verdur on his own. His voice was no longer his but a tool in the Singer's hands. The creature's power, its determination, was stronger than any they had fought before. Sticky silence forced its way into him through ears, mouth, nose and pores.

He sensed Fora's gaze on him again, like a bough held out to a drowning man. Their voices wavered. Something reflected in Silhorveen's face that Vindt had never seen in it before: fear. His own anxiety changed its quality. The Verdur was so close, Vindt felt the drafts of air at its staccato movements, the greed in its eyes, the anticipation.

Silhorveen staggered. Their song fractured.

No.

Vindt's vision blurred; his surroundings vanished. Aural void spread through his body like a disease.

No, Vindt thought again.

Then silence swallowed his thoughts as it dragged him down into oblivion.

CHAPTER 2

The chirping of a bird accompanied Vindt on his slow return to consciousness. *Finch*, his mind claimed, without embellishing the word with meaning. Other noises faded in, the distant banging of hammer on steel, faint voices. He lay for some time, eyes closed, limited to hearing, reluctant to focus on other senses.

His lids rose to reveal the reddish twilight of their tent. The crimson canvas with its twisted lines above him was familiar and at the same time not. He pondered what was different about it compared to every other morning, but thinking felt like dragging rocks through a viscous liquid. When he finally realized, he sat up with a jolt.

The abrupt movement caused the world around him to sway. He clutched the side of his pallet. It took a few deep breaths until his surroundings went still again. The pounding in his temples prevailed.

Bright daylight—that was the difference. Through the fabric, he even saw the sun at its zenith. Impossible. Silhorveen would never tolerate his Thyd sleeping into the day. The unease trickling through him became more prominent when he noticed that instead of wearing his sleeping shirt, he was fully dressed in his official crimson tunic and leather jerkin. At least that would explain why he was drenched in sweat. It didn't explain his aching head.

Hangover. That was how it felt. But it couldn't be. He was not allowed to drink, had not touched alcohol in a decade. Also, his entire body was strangely heavy and sore, as if he had fought a battle the day before. Pain accompanied the weariness, a shadow of it, like a memory. It lingered in every bone, nerve and cell.

Vindt massaged his temples as he tried to remember what he had done yesterday. But only fragmented images appeared and faded, Guzzar's vast, cloudless sky, Silhorveen talking to the Guzzar commander, Silhorveen singing. They refused to form a coherent line of events.

Vindt gave up. It didn't matter. He needed to get up now if he wanted to survive the day. That the Singer had not killed him yet was a miracle.

He had barely swung his legs over the pallet's edge when a sudden groan made him stall. Something about it caused the hairs on the back of his neck to rise. He turned in the direction of the sound, toward Silhorveen's part of the tent. The fabric usually separating their sections was gone. Another oddity. Vindt could look straight onto the bed and the body lying in it. However, from his place on the pallet, he couldn't see a face.

If it was unlikely for Vindt to sleep in, for the Singer it was impossible. Not once in the decade Vindt had spent as his Thyd had Silhorveen gotten up after him. He hardly slept at all.

Another groan made Vindt flinch. The agony it held

resonated through his own body, where it triggered something, a memory, sensations. He gasped as he braced himself for claws to wrench at his organs and shatter his bones, for knives to cut and fire to burn him.

But nothing happened.

Of course not. Vindt had no idea where those thoughts had come from. He shook them away irritably.

As he looked at the body on the bed again, his skin sizzled with a sudden, strange foreboding.

Dead.

The idea was so abstract, it didn't even trigger a feeling. But no, Silhorveen couldn't be dead. One of the few things they had told Vindt back at The Haven, the Singers' capital, was that the blood Bond would take him down too if his Singer was killed. Besides, dead men didn't groan. And why should Silhorveen die? That Vindt's wishful thinking had finally led to the actual event was... unlikely.

Silhorveen being sick was equally impossible. Singers didn't get sick. If they were wounded, their song magic healed them in no time. They didn't even age.

A tart, metallic smell hit him as he warily approached the bed. Silhorveen sometimes smelled like that when the use of his preternatural skills exhausted him. But the faint whiff then was a far cry from the current suffocating stench. It pooled on Vindt's tongue, a sharp, burning taste, as if someone had shoved a bar of rusty iron into his mouth.

He didn't scream when he finally reached the bed. He only would in the years to come, waking up from his nightmares, haunted by the image of Silhorveen's face. Or what remained of it.

It was hard to distinguish any features. If he had not known the person on the bed, he wouldn't have recognized him. All liquid was drained, the flesh gone; the skin clung directly to the skull, stripped of all color, translucent, showing the bone underneath. At least the few parts not covered by winding black-and-silver lines which looked almost organic. The pattern descended to the neck and further down, out of sight. Vindt recognized the shapes—how could he not?—sinuous, intertwining, defying logic and aesthetics, something no human mind could fathom. He saw them every day, on the walls of their tent, on the hilt of the knife and goblet used in the Binding, on dozens of other things in the Singer's possession, on inanimate matter, not on skin, not on a person.

The Singer's shriveled lips were drawn upward, showing snow-white teeth. His eyes were the worst. They stood open, so wide they seemed on the verge of popping out of his head at any moment. Brown once, they now looked as if the color had been a mere layer which someone had removed, revealing what lay underneath, a grayish tissue, sunk deep into iris and pupil. Still, the eyes held an expression—terror.

Vindt doubled over and vomited beside the bed. Only a thin, sour liquid left his mouth, yet the convulsions went on and on, as if his mind wanted to get rid of the image of Silhorveen's face by turning his body inside out.

At that moment, the entrance flap was lifted and Fora's broad figure walked in. After two strides, he stalled. All color left his face; his eyes widened in disbelief. His gaze went from Vindt to the pallet he had just risen from and back. "What...?"

"Fora, what in all the demons' names is wrong with him?" was what Vindt wanted to say, but only an inarticulate noise left his throat. He felt as if he had not spoken in ages.

Fora opened his mouth, but before he could speak, a high-pitched male voice from the tent's entrance asked, "What's going on in there?"

Without taking his gaze off Vindt, Fora bellowed in the voice's direction, "Get Ehlan."

"Ehlan? Why?" The voice of the man outside was imbued with fear. "What happened? I told you I heard something. Can you not—"

"*Now.*" Fora's voice was sharp.

A huff and then receding footsteps.

Vindt cleared his throat and made a new attempt to speak. What came out sounded like the squealing of unoiled hinges, but it was words. "What happened?" He made a vague gesture toward Silhorveen, careful not to look at him.

"A good question. Seems like you're the one with the answers," Fora said.

"Me? I just woke up and—"

"You just *woke up.* Do you take me for a fool?" Something else darkened Fora's gaze now, hostility, almost anger. He took a step back and made the universal sign against demons.

Vindt's jaw dropped. He wasn't sure if he considered Fora a friend, but the man had been his closest form of social contact during the past decade. They had trained together and spent countless nights by the fire in different countries on their journeys from war to war. Vindt had told no one else about his past, the tranquil life as a lord's youngest son he had led before his homeland fell in the war, before he was captured and then spared the life of a slave, only to become a slave of another kind. Fora was the only person who had ever *asked* him about his life.

Before Vindt could react, footsteps approached, and a moment later, Ehlan strode into the tent.

The Singer's seneschal was a tall lean man with the same dirty-blond hair as Vindt's, but whereas Vindt's fell in an intricate braid down his back, Ehlan's was closely cropped. They were of the same age, mid-thirties. However, since Vindt's aging process had come to a near halt when he was bound to Silhorveen a decade ago, Ehlan looked considerably older.

The incredulity in his face matched Fora's. "What happened? How did you...?" Ehlan was only slowly awakening from the stupor he had fallen into at laying eyes on Vindt.

Vindt was unnerved. Waking up with aching limbs, a mortal headache and no memories was what had happened. He pointed at Silhorveen again. "Would someone be so kind as to explain what... *this* is? Is he...? He doesn't seem... He's not... dead?"

Ehlan studied him, an expression on his face Vindt couldn't place. "Tie him up," he bellowed, looking at Fora.

"What?" Vindt and Fora snapped at the same time.

"I wouldn't touch him if you gave me gold," Fora added.

"Don't be ridiculous," Ehlan snarled.

"Ridiculous, eh? Tie him up yourself then."

"Why, in Gaal's name, do you want to tie me up?"

"I don't want to bind you in the name of your stupid dead goddess, Vindt," Ehlan growled. "But I don't have a clue what this is all about. Someone from The Haven's on his way, and another Singer. Until one of them arrives... I certainly won't take any risks."

Someone from The Haven, another Singer... "What fucking risks?"

For a moment Ehlan continued to stare at him, then with two quick strides came over and grabbed Vindt by the arm. "Look at him." He pointed his chin in Silhorveen's direction.

"But I—"

"Look. At. Him."

Reluctantly, Vindt did as he was told. Silhorveen's face was no less horrific than it had been a few minutes ago. Immediately, his stomach tightened, and he choked again.

"You really have no clue what it is you're seeing? No? Fine. I'll tell you. This is what happens to a Singer when his Thyd fails him, when he's bested, when he falls. Singers don't die like humans do. What awaits them is far worse than death. It's this, Thrithid, the demons' world, trapped forever, no coming back."

Ehlan tightened his grip. "Now tell me you, the Thyd, knew nothing about this, nor that the very same fate awaits you. No Singer falls without his Thyd. Thrithid. No coming back. Look and listen carefully." He pulled at Vindt's arm, forcing him to turn toward the Singer's body. "This is what *you* looked like; those are the sounds *you* made the last time I came into this tent, which was yesterday. And now here you are, alive and kicking. Tell me again you've no clue what you did, or how."

For a moment, nothing happened, then the wall holding back Vindt's memories crumbled. A torrent of images flooded his mind and dragged him along like a piece of driftwood. The sun, the battle. The Verdur. The suffocating silence as it entered his body. As it killed him.

No.

He let out a small cry. His knees gave way. Were it not for Ehlan's grip on his arm, he would have dropped to the floor.

Killed—they were killed. And he was...

Not dead.

As much as he had avoided looking at Silhorveen's face before, now his eyes fixed on it as if at the mere mention of the place, Thrithid had broken through its boundaries, extended its fingers, caught his gaze and kept it trapped.

I looked like this?

Vindt lifted a hand to his face. Skin, flesh, stubble on chin and cheeks, normal, intact. The idea that Ehlan was lying, or at least exaggerating, crossed his mind, but the proof lay groaning and twitching before them. Thrithid. Although he had never heard the word before, its meaning revealed itself to him like all the words of the Singers' language did. *Demon's world*—no. It meant *place of the purified mind*. It didn't make sense.

He forced his gaze away from Silhorveen's face. "How long?" His throat was dry.

"How long what?" Ehlan barked.

"Have we... have I..."

"Lain here? Two weeks."

"Two weeks?" Vindt swallowed as he gazed helplessly at the seneschal.

Ehlan let go of his arm. The anger dissipated from his face. He looked lost. "Tell me, Vindt, what would you do in my place now?"

But Vindt had no answer.

CHAPTER 3

The voices didn't talk. He could still hear them. A constant whisper, barely audible, screaming into his ears until his eardrums burst. Mocking him.

His name was gone. They had taken it from him, eaten it, burned it.

Here you don't need a name.

Blazing darkness and deafening silence. Void. Claws riving his organs. His body was bent, his arms broken, his legs, his spine cracked, his skull split open. The voices laughed.

There was no pain. Pain he could describe. This was beyond the realm of words. He was the pain. All that prevailed.

He prayed and pleaded and vomited blood. He was lifted. Into the depths. They pulled him under until his mouth opened and water filled his lungs.

Sometimes he was alone. Hours. Days. Years. Perhaps centuries. Time had expanded into vast, eternal nothingness. When he screamed, no one answered.

Suddenly, there was a different voice. A whisper. Faint.

Very faint. No words, just... music. Song.

Gone.

It came back, soft, beckoning. So sweet.

No, no, go away. He's ours.

The song seemed familiar. He strained his ears to listen.

The voices raged. You have no right. You're violating the law. Get lost.

He fell again, faster, deeper, reeling. The song followed, lingered, unfolded. A word. Repeated. It made no sense.

Nonsense! *the voices roared.*

Their rage bored through his skin. They laughed and dug into the song. It wavered. It screamed. They pulled at it. More and more of them, reinforcements, shapeless, the inversion of color, the shadow of shadows, the shape of agony. They would not give him up.

That word again. Urgent now, like a plea, no, an order. Irresistible.

Vindt, his name.

Suddenly, the song was all around him, shrouding him, taking him into its embrace, holding him, gently, like a baby.

The other voices drifted to the background, muffled shrieks of fury and frustration.

Impossible. You'll pay.

And then the song lifted him, faster and faster, into the light, into soothing blackness.

Vindt woke with a start, panting. The crepuscular light of dusk filled the tent before his blinking eyes. Familiar. Safe. Vindt forced his clenched muscles to relax. He was not surprised to find himself drenched in sweat.

Gaal. Another nightmare.

The images were gone; they always were. Only a weird

sensation prevailed, a shadow of something he had no name for. And the faint memory of a voice calling his—

A wail snapped him back to the present.

Good evening to you, too, Vindt thought, flinching. Even after two weeks, each of the Singer's harrowed sounds twisted his guts. The tart, metallic stench didn't improve things. At least Vindt didn't need to look at the twitching body anymore. As hard as Ehlan had tried, he couldn't find any arguments against putting the fabric separating their sections back up.

Vindt had wished Silhorveen to hell so many times, he should rejoice that his wish had unexpectedly been granted. But whatever spark of glee he had felt in the beginning, the past two weeks in this tent had eradicated it.

Wearily, he rose from the pallet. Sleeping during the day still didn't work as well as he wished. Flipping his sleep-wake rhythm had become the only way to escape the confines of the tent, at least for a few hours. Despite his continuous pleas, Ehlan would not let him spend the days outside. Not to keep him from escaping but to hide him from prying eyes.

As if anybody cared. If even Vindt had not known about Thrithid, how would the Guzzar soldiers? Besides, the camp was half a mile away. Before, their tents had been located at its very heart, surrounded by rows of other tents, other men, by a wall of bodies and weapons, shielded from potential attacks like a newborn baby. If a commander could afford a Singer to fight his wars, he made sure to protect his investment.

Vindt didn't know if Plotliw, the Guzzar general, had cast the half-dead Singer and his retinue out from their midst, or if their move was Ehlan's decision. In any case, no soldier had come near in the two weeks since Vindt had woken up. And no one would. Though the Guzzar were hardly keen on losing this war, he was sure Silhorveen's fall had provoked as much relief as regret. The soldiers *did* think he was a demon.

The idea made Vindt chuckle, though he himself had not fully discarded it. Until his twenty-fifth birthday he had not even known Singers existed. Dark magicians, humans in league with demons who received dark gifts in return—tales Vindt had grown up with. But people who could wipe out an entire army with their song—what else could they be but demons in human disguise?

They weren't demons, though, just a different species, born with a magical voice and an obnoxious personality.

A few meager drops fell from the darkening sky, but it was the first rain in ages. After the heat holding them in its suffocating embrace ever since they had come to this part of the world, it was a more than welcome change. Most of the countries they had traveled through over the past ten years had been warmer than Pel, Vindt's homeland, or at least warmer than Kärö, the wind-swept, weather-beaten island he grew up on. Still, his body stubbornly refused to adjust to the temperatures.

He had not bothered to look for a dry place among the scarce pine trees, but simply dropped onto his usual spot on the carpet of needles and turned his face to the sky. His skin drank the rain just like the surrounding trees did; his lungs swallowed the fresh, damp air in grateful gulps.

Were it not for the shackles around his ankles, he would be almost comfortable. The price of freedom. Absurd. As if running away would not lead to sure and painful death.

Ehlan knew that very well. What did he fear? That Vindt had miraculously gained superpowers to escape Thrithid? That he was in league with demons? But he wouldn't complain. Anything was better than Silhorveen's tent.

From where he sat, he could see the torch marking its entrance, as well as Fora's flickering shadow beside it, keeping watch. It caused a tug in his chest. Even after two weeks, Fora didn't talk to him more than was necessary. The anti-demon sign was his daily greeting. The others behaved the same.

As much as Vindt believed they were acting ridiculously and told himself he didn't care, he was... hurt. Hurt and alone. He had never been close to the others, a group of people tied to the same Singer, forced to travel from war to war together. Never had he felt attachment or belonging. Only now, with the others avoiding him, the loss stung.

Vindt lowered his gaze to his right wrist, which he was again inadvertently stroking. A broad, pale trace marked the place where the bracelet had been, a stark contrast to the tanned skin surrounding it. He kept his sleeve down to cover it and had told no one about its absence.

When he had woken up from hell, it was gone; Vindt had no clue why. Now that its purpose had vanished, it might have simply dissolved. That Ehlan or any of the others had taken it off was unlikely. The golden band didn't have a lock. It had been put in place by Silhorveen after Vindt's attempt to kill the Singer. And could be removed by a Singer's song alone. Its magic had prevented him from ever trying again.

To this day, Vindt didn't know why his shot on that fatal day a decade ago had missed. He was a skilled archer. The Singer stood immobile on the battlefield only a few feet away, back turned to him, absorbed in his favorite pastime: singing people to death. No target could be easier. Yet, Vindt's arrow missed his heart by a hand's width.

It had always baffled Vindt that Silhorveen placed him fully armored at his back in every battle. The Singer knew about his feelings, his hatred. Universal arrogance, impeccable self-confidence, his belief in his own invulnerability. But of course, neither Silhorveen nor anyone in his retinue would ever have suspected *him*, the Thyd, the human whose sole purpose in life was to protect the Singer he was bound to, to raise his hand against his master.

Now, a Verdur had succeeded where Vindt had failed, and the bracelet had vanished.

No one seemed to know what was going to happen to him, not even Ehlan. The seneschal had sent for someone from The Haven, not because of Vindt's miraculous resurrection but because of Silhorveen's fall. The new Singer he had mentioned had not been called by him, but by Plotliw as a replacement. Both men had received an answer telling them someone was on their way, without mentioning a date of arrival.

The confinement in Silhorveen's tent and the idleness were taking their toll on Vindt's nerves. He was not sure, though, if whatever the new Singer decided to do with him would be an improvement. Kill him—an option with uncomfortably high odds. A Thyd outliving his master— how else would they take this than as a blow to their superiority?

On the other hand, humans with his predisposition, Thyds, were rare. Since every Singer needed one to defend himself against a Verdur, there might be hope.

Vindt gave a mirthless laugh as he picked up a pinecone and started plucking off the scales. Hope... Letting him live meant binding him to another Singer, a seamless continuation of the wretched life he had been leading since Pel's fall. Even so, he didn't want to die, and not only because he had recently learned that it wasn't Gaal's eternal hunting grounds that awaited him but hell. Not anymore.

A sudden tugging beneath his skin made him drop the cone. He groaned.

And this. Of course.

The feeling was not painful. A tiny creature nibbling at his flesh, tentatively, playfully. Unfortunately, it would soon cease to be playful; Vindt knew that all too well. The feeling would spread and burrow into every part of his body, as if he was burning alive.

He didn't need the reminder; he was fucking aware of his dependency on the Singer's blood. The last Binding, the ceremony forging the magical Bond between a Thyd and a Singer, had taken place four weeks ago. It was the usual time a Singer allowed to pass, before which Vindt didn't feel anything. *Usually* didn't feel anything. Why it had started already, Vindt had no clue. Withdrawal. The Singer's blood was a drug without exit. No matter how long the abstinence went, how much he suffered, it wouldn't leave his system. If the new Singer didn't arrive soon, Vindt would die, slowly and painfully.

Clamping down on the rearing fear, he stood and grabbed a twig. Then he did what he did every night: exercise as much as the shackles between his ankles allowed. It kept him from thinking. And from what was even worse: waiting.

* * *

To Vindt's dismay, the first to arrive was not the new Singer but the emissary from The Haven. Vaan woke him from one of his shallow slumbers as she entered the tent one afternoon, Ehlan in tow.

The woman had hardly changed since Vindt had seen her last ten years ago, a few more wrinkles in her stern face, some gray strands in the black braid falling down her back. Her age had been hard to estimate back then. It was no more obvious now. Early fifties, if he had to guess.

A slave like Ehlan, Fora and the others, like most of the Singers' servants, she had not been bought but was the offspring of a family who had been in the Singers' service for generations. Were it not for the golden earring she wore in the upper part of her left ear, nothing about her would betray her status, not her riding clothes, which were of better quality than those of some of Plotliw's knights, and least of all her demeanor.

Vindt couldn't claim he was glad to see her. She was the one who had "cared" for him during his two withdrawals back at The Haven. The second time was necessity, when he had passed from Shahen, the Singer who trained him, to Silhorveen, the only way to remove the blood of the first from his system. Apart from food and water, Vaan also gave him a drug to ease the symptoms. It was hard, but bearable; he mostly slept.

The first time, however, was a punishment for his attempted escape, and food and water were all he received from her hands. She might have sympathized with his agony, but he was sure she believed he deserved what he went through.

"I don't understand you," she told him back then. "Why are you fighting this? Everyone here would give their right hand to have your condition. It's an honor; you're blessed."

In this, she was right. The servants' veneration for their masters at The Haven shone out of their every glance and gesture. Even though they were slaves, Vaan and the others considered themselves superior to other human beings. They wore their earrings with pride that bordered on arrogance. And yes, they would have given everything to be in Vindt's place.

"So it's true," she said in lieu of a greeting upon entering the tent. The expression with which she studied Vindt was hard to read. At least she didn't make the anti-demon sign.

She walked over to Silhorveen's bed. Vindt wondered how many times she had seen this. Could you get used to it? If the stench bothered her, she didn't let it show.

However, Vindt had more imminent concerns than the half-dead Singer. "What's going to happen to me? Are you taking me to The Haven?"

"That's not for me to decide."

"No? Who'll decide then?"

"The Singer, who's on his way. Asche."

"Asche?" Ehlan repeated, before Vindt could ask further questions, his voice high-pitched with incredulity. "Asche Ke'Thad? *He* answered Plotliw's call?"

"Apparently. It's not for us to question their decisions."

"No, no, of course not," Ehlan hastened to say. "But it's... unexpected."

"What's so special about this Asche?" Vindt had never heard the name before.

"He's a member of the High Council." Ehlan sounded like Vindt should have known this.

Vindt didn't even know what the High Council was. Even though he was a Thyd, he was almost as oblivious to the Singers' rules and laws as any human being. Apart from giving him orders or insulting him, Silhorveen had virtually never talked to him. In the year Vindt spent at The Haven, he had closed his ears to anything they tried to teach him. Wretched demons and their world. He wanted to know as little about it as possible.

He didn't care if this Asche was a member of some council. All that mattered was that he was a Singer and would get here soon.

"When will he arrive?" Vindt failed to keep the desperation out of his voice.

"I don't know," Vaan said. "But it certainly won't be for a few more—"

"No." A cool voice cut her short. "He's here already."

CHAPTER 4

Vindt hadn't noticed another person enter the tent, and apparently neither had Ehlan nor Vaan. All three turned at the same time. The next moment, everyone was on their knees, including Vindt himself, and not because he had decided to be.

Vindt had come across only a few Singers in his life. Even in their capital, where he had spent the first year of his captivity, the vast majority of the denizens were humans. He didn't have to meet more of them to understand that they were all arrogant bastards, oozing the belief in their superiority from every pore, treating humans with either indifference or cruelty. As if to make up for their shitty personalities, the gods had gifted them with stunning beauty.

It might be strange to call a man beautiful. Before he had laid eyes on a Singer for the first time, Vindt would never have used the term for a male, less one who looked androgynous, almost female, like all Singers he had met. Female Singers didn't seem to exist. However, merely saying handsome missed the point.

Apart from a face that looked chiseled by some divine artist, they were tall and lean, and their movements bore a grace mesmerizing to watch. At the beginning, at The Haven, despite his deep-rooted hatred, Vindt had hardly been able to take his eyes off Shahen, the resident Singer at the time. The effect of Silhorveen's presence was no different.

After a decade of spending day and night at the latter's side, however, though from time to time still captivated by the Singer's looks or the way he moved, the effect had worn off. Or Silhorveen's character had ended up cracking the delusive mask.

The Singer standing before them now was no exception to the rule. Long black hair framed a face whose features were the epitome of perfection: elegantly arched eyebrows, high cheekbones, smooth skin as pale as bone despite the height of summer. He might have looked fragile were it not for his dark eyes, which grazed over the kneeling people with cold indifference. Instead of Singers' robes he wore ordinary riding clothes: boots, leather breeches, a loose tunic.

Under normal circumstances, seeing another of those masks of menacing perfection would have engendered the fierce urge in Vindt to punch it, smear it with mud or taint it in any other way. But besides the familiar uncanny beauty, an aura of overwhelming power radiated from Asche, invisible yet tangible. It bloated the tent's walls and ceiling, pressed down onto Vindt's body and mind, reducing all his desires to one of subjecting himself to the intensity of this being before him. He fought the urge to throw himself at the Singer's feet.

Once, Ehlan had told him of places where people didn't fear or hate Singers but worshipped them like gods, even erected temples in their names. He had taken this for a tale, or those people for superstitious idiots. Now he considered, for the first time, that the words Silhorveen had spat at him so often weren't just an insult but something holding a deeper meaning, even truth: *You're nothing but human.* Yes, he was, and the man before him was not.

Ehlan and Vaan hastened to bow and mutter an awestruck "Kvahad-thed," the title Singers required to be addressed with. Usually, Vindt too performed the movements and said the words without thinking. Only in this case, he was too captivated to react.

Vaan and Ehlan held their heads down, their eyes on the ground. Asche's position as a Singer of the High Council probably called for such conduct. But even if Vindt had wanted to, he wouldn't have been able to withdraw his gaze from the man in front of him, less when Asche's cold stare came to rest upon him. The eyes were not just dark but black, two pits, cold and fathomless, pulling Vindt into their depths. His nerves sizzled in a mixture of fear and fascination.

He expected the Singer to speak to him, but after only a moment he averted his attention. In response, something else stirred in the sea of awe Vindt's soul was drowning in: defiance. He shot Vaan and Ehlan an impatient glance. How much longer were they supposed to kneel? Though Asche's strange aura still pressed down on him, he thought himself well capable of rising. Did they need the Singer's explicit leave? It didn't come.

Asche strolled over to Silhorveen. Vindt wondered whether the disfigured body frightened him, a preview of his own inevitable fate. If so, the Singer's face didn't give it away. He reached out and brushed Silhorveen's skull-like forehead with his fingertips. He also said something; at least, his lips moved, though Vindt couldn't hear the words. Vindt half expected Silhorveen to rise or perhaps just stir or moan or show some other reaction to the touch. He didn't.

Half enthralled, half annoyed, Vindt observed the easy grace of the Singer's movements as he made his way back. His knees ached from the unaccustomed position. The cool black gaze landed on him again. Something about it felt familiar. The sliver of a memory flicked through his mind, but dissolved before he could grasp it.

"So, you're the Thyd who miraculously returned from Thrithid." Asche's voice was as cold as his gaze, devoid of emotion yet soft and melodic. It was a strange contrast.

Vindt didn't know what to say, so he kept quiet; it wasn't a question, anyway. Out of the corner of his eye, he noticed Ehlan shooting him an anxious look. Probably a warning.

"Tell me then, how did you accomplish something no one has ever accomplished before, neither Thyd nor Singer?" Though the tone of Asche's voice had not changed, a sudden threat hung in the air, palpable like mist.

Vindt licked his lips. Why was he nervous? He had done nothing wrong, and he had no secrets. "I... I don't know. I remember the battle and the Verdur and how he... overcame us. And then... nothing. Really, that's all I can tell you. It's... the truth."

"The truth... maybe." Asche sauntered over to him.

The intensity of the Singer's presence right in front of him was overwhelming. Vindt's own existence diminished to insignificance, merely human, nothing. He stared up at the tall slender figure with weary eyes.

Asche placed his fingertips lightly on both of Vindt's temples. Then he sang.

In his years at Silhorveen's side, Vindt had heard countless... well, songs. Singers themselves used the word, and Vindt could think of nothing to better describe what came out of their mouths. It was sound, yet not—more than that, the contrary, tunes, a melody or their inversion. It eluded any concept, defied structure and logic and harmony. Yet, it was not dissonant but beautiful, captivating, and cruel and sickening. It made people stop whatever they were doing and surrender to the sensations it evoked, paralyzed, bound. It sang of agony or ecstasy, gave birth or killed. It built and destroyed. It was audible, yet its perception was not limited to the ears. It resonated throughout one's body, pulsing, floating. Vindt believed it was not made for humans to hear.

Searing pain roiled through his head, as if the Singer was forcing his hands inside, cracking his skull open. Vindt screamed, and then again. His body twitched from the neck down. His head rested immobile, trapped between the touch of Asche's fingertips and the dark, penetrating stare. Withdrawing was impossible.

He failed to judge how long this went on until the Singer let go of him. He slumped to the floor, panting.

"It's true; he doesn't know." Asche watched him with indifference.

Vindt jerked his head up. "What? That was what that was about? You read my mind? Are you mad? I told you I don't know a thing."

Out of the corner of his eye, he saw Ehlan shooting him a horrified glance. Part of Vindt was surprised too. After ten years with Silhorveen, he believed he had if not accepted then at least gotten used to the Singers' arbitrary cruelty, that he was in control.

Apparently he was not, or his recalcitrance had undergone a sudden resurgence with Asche's appearance. He yearned to slit the Singer's throat.

Asche's chill gaze remained unperturbed. He sang again.

Vindt's throat clamped shut. He tried to breathe, but an iron claw had closed around his chest, squeezing his lungs to the size of an apple. His hands rose to his throat as panic chased his pulse into staggering flight.

Asche crouched in front of him. Even amid his agony, Vindt had to admire the unearthly beauty of the Singer's face, so close now, the image of a pale, merciless god within reach of his hand. Vindt retched in a desperate yet vain attempt to fill his lungs with air. His eyes bulged out of his face. His chest burned like fire. He needed air. Now.

Asche watched him with perfect calmness. He didn't smile, but a subtle glint shone from the bottom of his dark eyes. "Mad?" he said, so quietly Vindt was sure the others couldn't hear him. "Funny. You are not the first to say that." Louder, he added, "You need my blood, Thyd. If I were you, I would think before speaking."

With that, he rose and left the tent.

* * *

Over the next few days, Vaan went back and forth between the camp and their own tents. On one occasion, Ehlan accompanied her on Asche's orders because the Singer wanted to question him.

Question him, exactly. Like asking and waiting for an answer, not like "read his mind."

Vindt was curious what Asche wanted to find out from the seneschal, but knew Ehlan would never tell him.

"How're things at the camp?" he asked instead when the seneschal returned from his visit.

"Being forced to stay put for over a month—what do you think? Food shortage, brawls, desertions, the usual. Dysentery's got quite a few killed as well. Plotliw's on the edge."

Dysentery aside, Vindt had imagined the situation would be this way. "What about the Sylians?"

Three months ago, they had outnumbered Plotliw's men three to one. During the following weeks—thanks in no small part to Silhorveen—their ranks had thinned notably. By now, they must have heard about the Singer's demise.

"Seems like they went north and then further into Guzzar territory. Plotliw's sent a few troops out, but of course they haven't been able to do much."

"So he won't move without a Singer."

"Oh, Plotliw would alright; in fact, he'd love to. Just as much as his generals. But his empress won't let him."

"Don't want to risk losing."

"She seems to have a fondness for Singers."

Vindt snorted. Who could be fond of Singers?

"Well, Plotliw isn't," Ehlan continued. "Wasn't before, and is less so now since he met... Asche."

"Something happened?"

"He asked ten times the payment agreed upon with Silhorveen."

"*What?* That's a joke."

Ehlan shook his head. "He said he'll be ten times as effective."

Vindt didn't know whether to laugh or cry. He vividly recalled the aura of power engulfing the Singer. But even if... "Arrogant bastard."

"Watch yourself, Vindt. I mean it. You depend on him."

"Don't need you to tell me that."

"Given your performance last time, apparently you do. Listen to me for once. Asche isn't Silhorveen. You've never met a Singer from the High Council. They're... different. And Asche, he's old. You felt him, his power."

Vindt rolled his eyes. "Old" could mean anything. Singers didn't age. They could theoretically live forever. Five hundred years? A thousand? However many years Asche had walked the earth, it had done nothing to improve his personality.

"Seems like his ancient superpowers don't keep him from needing a Thyd."

"No."

A spark of glee warmed Vindt's insides, directed at Asche and all the other Singers, so full of themselves and their powers yet unable to survive without a human. Every Singer needed a Thyd. Due to the constant threat of a Verdur attack, they couldn't take so much as a step without one.

Twenty-five years Vindt had lived his life oblivious to the strange predisposition that would make him a Thyd. He had not felt it, nor had it manifested in any way. Instead, it lay dormant until Thyds drank a Singer's blood for the first time. Then, it turned them into a tool ready for a Singer to use. Or an instrument, for the Singer raised their voice with his own, combining them into a weapon capable of fighting Verdurs. What else was that but a joke?

Vindt's laughter had died long ago.

He didn't know how Singers found Thyds, but they usually did it shortly after their birth. They stole them right from the cradle and raised them at The Haven, where they were turned into obedient servants. That Vindt had only been found as an adult, picked up half dead from among the actual dead on Pel's battlefield, was an exception.

"What's this High Council, anyway?" Ehlan was in an unusually talkative mood, so Vindt might as well take advantage and pry information out of him for a change. "How many are they? Who decides who gets in?"

"Seven, and no one. It's automatic. They're the oldest Singers."

"And what does this Council do? Rule over the others?" Vindt had never been under the impression Silhorveen answered to anyone or received orders. He could be wrong, of course. The Singer could simply not have let them in on things he considered none of his servants' concern.

"No, not rule. They are their ultimate authority, though. I can't tell you what they do. I think no one knows apart from the Singers themselves." He paused, then asked, "You don't remember him, do you?"

"Remember who?"

"Asche."

"What do you mean, *remember*? My head might be a mess at times, but I'm positive I wouldn't have forgotten *him*."

"One year ago, in Neir Darin."

Neir Darin. Vindt racked his brain. They had passed through so many towns in different countries, Vindt had given up paying attention to their names long ago. "Was that—"

"The town where you tried to get your hands on the

innkeeper's daughter. Or, well, your cock into her."

Ah, that one.

They had been staying in the town for almost a month, an eternity considering they usually moved on from a place after only a few days. Why they had stayed in Neir Darin for so long, or came to the city at all, Vindt had no idea. Singers' business. But yes, one night, another Singer had visited them at the inn where they were staying. However, head covered by a hood, Vindt never saw the man's face. At the time, he didn't wonder. In towns, Silhorveen always walked around with the hood of his cloak up, tired of people's stares.

Vindt had forgotten about the encounter, but now he remembered the feeling when, in the dark corridor outside Silhorveen's room, the Singer's unseen eyes rested on him, the air around him growing denser, the hairs on the back of his neck rising.

Yes, the other day, in Asche's presence, he'd had a similar feeling, only stronger. Back then it must have left an impression, for in the night he even dreamed of the hooded Singer, one of those dreams where images and feelings blurred into one another, incoherent, feverish. Something about blood. He woke up in the middle of it, heart racing.

Ehlan interrupted his reminiscence. "Asche is, well, famous. Or infamous, if you will."

"For what?"

"Affronting people, being his own law."

"People? You mean other Singers?"

Ehlan nodded.

Interesting. Vindt had always perceived Singers as a harmonious entity. The existence of conflicts among them had never occurred to him. The idea cheered him up.

As if to punish him for his happy thoughts, a giant hand clenched into a fist inside him. It squashed his organs and pulled at all his nerves at once. Pain—there it was. Vindt doubled over and took a sharp breath. Little pearls of sweat formed on his forehead.

Ehlan frowned. "How bad is it?"

Okay, Vindt was about to lie, but huffed, "Not as bad as last time." The truth—for the time being.

"He'll give you his blood. Don't worry."

Perhaps. But even if Asche did, the question remained: When?

CHAPTER 5

Looking around the camp, nothing betrayed the chaos Ehlan had described to Vindt the other day.

Plotliw's soldiers were a wild mixture of Guzzar's nobility and their hosts, mercenaries, and commoners detached or forced into military service. Yet, the camp gave an impression of unity and order. Rows of tents stretched along the riverbank, the empress' green-and-yellow banners fluttering. Given the light breeze, even the smell was bearable. Despite the dysentery.

On a nearby field, men were training beneath the blazing sun. The clang of clashing weapons filled the air, metal on metal, metal on wood, underpinned with shouts and curses. It was the sound of battle; yet it always seemed strangely peaceful to Vindt when there was no actual battle, no enemy to fight other than one's own shortcomings. His body yearned to grab a sword and join them.

But it also yearned for something else, a craving which by now thwarted any other. Sharp-edged pebbles seemed to have formed in his blood, chafing the insides of his veins as they passed. He was feverish, his skin covered with a layer of sweat, which had nothing to do with the temperature. His sleep got worse by the day. As did the nightmares.

"You look horrible," Ehlan had said by way of greeting when he came into the tent this morning to deliver the "good news" of Asche's call.

Vindt's first reaction was relief. As soon as they started toward the camp, it gave way to apprehension. What if Asche had not called him to give him his blood? What if he simply wanted to raise Vindt's hopes and crush them, to punish him for his insolent behavior? By now, he fiercely regretted his words at Asche's arrival. But what could he do? Nothing. He was at the Singer's mercy, as he had been for the past ten years.

Asche's tent was pitched in the same place as Silhorveen's, the camp's heart. As soon as it came into view, Vindt's eyes widened. Apart from the twisting lines covering its surface, it looked nothing like Silhorveen's. It had a different shape and was dark blue instead of crimson. Silhorveen's tent had already dwarfed the surrounding ones used by Plotliw's soldiers. This was at least twice as big; it was larger than Plotliw's. Vindt tried to imagine the general's reaction, his first impression of the new Singer, before he even met Asche in person.

The distance from the surrounding tents was also greater than it had been from Silhorveen's. A moat shielding its castle, only in this case, the direction of the potential danger was reversed. Vindt knew the soldiers who slept closest had tried to trade places with others lucky enough to pitch their tents farther away. Or fought for it. It was always like that.

Two guards flanked the entrance. They resembled one another to the point of ridiculousness, the strange clothing and armor they wore, the blond hair braided on top of their heads while shaved at the sides. They also had very similar features, standing out among them a pair of green eyes which curved upwards at the outer edges. Vindt had no clue which part of the world they might be from. The most curious thing about the pair, however, was that one of them was a woman.

After nodding to Ehlan, their gazes fastened on Vindt with undisguised curiosity.

"We've come to—" Ehlan started.

"We know," the woman said in heavily accented Lyskú, the Singers' language. "Wait here."

She went into the tent, only to reemerge a moment later, and nodded for them to go in.

Vindt's eyes adjusted only slowly to the dim light inside. From the tent's dimensions, he had expected to be greeted by exuberant luxury, but the interior was rather sparse. The most prominent piece of furniture was a chair, not because it was of any special size or make but because Asche sat on it. Unlike last time, the Singer *was* wearing his formal robes. They were not crimson, as Silhorveen's had been, but dark blue, like the tent's walls, embroidered with the same sinuous lines, which sometimes appeared silver, at other times black or without any color humans could even fathom.

The effect Silhorveen's robes had had on Vindt had never failed to stun him, as if they were a magical garment wrapping the Singer in an extra layer of power and dignity. Given Asche surpassed Silhorveen in beauty and power, the effect was multiplied. He sat with his legs crossed, his arms resting on the chair's arms, leisurely, indifferent, graceful. The dark blue robes contrasted perfectly with the pale skin of his face. A king on his throne, a god of arrogance and beauty.

Asche's aura of power was weaker than last time, but its flow still enveloped Vindt in its invisible, suffocating embrace. Though he believed himself prepared, a mixture of apprehension and awe again overcame him, the urge to express his veneration, to prostrate himself. He fought the feeling with stubborn defiance. Unless it was unavoidable, he wouldn't kneel before him again. Asche was neither king nor god, only a bloody Singer.

Two men flanked him. Vindt had forgotten the name, but he recognized Asche's Thyd from the night at the inn in Nair Darin. They had spent the several hours of the Singers' meeting outside the room, guarding the door, and exchanged a few polite words. Then, the man's age had already struck Vindt. He looked to be in his forties. Since Thyds hardly aged, that was extremely old.

The elderly man on Asche's left was probably the Singer's seneschal. Unlike the Thyd, who had nodded at Vindt in recognition, even smiled, the man nodded toward Ehlan but gave Vindt only a hard glance.

Ehlan bowed. "Kvahad-thed."

Vindt rushed to do the same.

A sudden commotion outside the tent caught everyone's attention. The female guard entered. "I'm sorry, Kvahad-thed, the Guzzar commander's here to see you."

Asche gave no sign of annoyance. "Send him in."

Plotliw entered accompanied by two of his generals. All three had the coppery skin and dark hair typical of the Guzzar people and, as far as Vindt knew, the population of the entire continent.

He felt a certain sympathy for the man, or rather, his

country. In all the wars Silhorveen had been involved in, the *aggressor* had hired him, people who strove to extend their territory, their power, who had laid a greedy eye on another country's resources or thought it was about time their god ruled the world. Or people who didn't need further reason to start a war but the pursuit of fame and fortune, or didn't know what else to do with their lives. Vindt had seen it all.

The Sylians had invaded Guzzar, though, and he couldn't help but be reminded of Pel, his homeland, which the Kallejdi had stampeded over a decade ago.

Upon the delegation's entry, the aura of Asche's presence grew denser, weighing down on Vindt with new might. He struggled not to drop to his knees.

Plotliw and his two generals were apparently fighting the same battle. Shoulders stiff, hands clenched into fists, the commander's eyes shot daggers at the Singer. The other two men stared at Asche with wide eyes. Vindt wondered if they were meeting him for the first time. One of them wavered, and Plotliw's hand shot out and grabbed him by the arm to keep him from sinking down. His gaze threatened to kill him.

Asche watched the scene, seemingly unimpressed. That was when Vindt realized the Singer could not only control his aura of power; had he wanted to, he would have brought them all to their knees again. Only this time, he preferred to contemplate the struggle.

Plotliw nodded curtly. "Kvahad-thed." His pronunciation of the words was atrocious. Combined with the mocking tone, it sounded not like a tribute but an insult.

Asche returned the nod and the mocking tone. "Commander."

The weight of his aura ebbed somewhat, and Vindt relaxed. A moment later, it regained strength, then fell away, only to rise again. This was repeated several times. It felt like being swept along by a tide, washed to shore and pulled back into the ocean. Except for Asche's Thyd and the elderly servant, all the people in the tent reacted visibly.

The Singer's face remained mask-like, as if nothing was happening. Vindt was sure he was enjoying the spectacle. Despite his sympathy for Plotliw and his aversion to Asche, he couldn't help but let out a small laugh.

At the sound, the general turned to him, brows furrowed in fury. A second later, his eyes widened. "*You? But you… you're dead.*"

"He was," Asche said before Vindt could react. "I brought him back."

Vindt failed to quell the violent laughter that rose in his chest at this, but he turned it into an equally violent cough. Was Asche making fun of Plotliw, or did he really want him to believe he had the power to return the dead to this world?

"He's still a bit weak," Asche continued, as if in response to Vindt's cough or alluding to his general, wretched condition. "But he will make a full recovery soon."

Plotliw's gaze moved from Vindt to Asche and back, taking in Ehlan as it went. His expression grew darker and darker. "I see. I assume you'd charge extra if I asked you to raise my fallen soldiers?"

The faint glitter in Asche's dark eyes from their first encounter made its reappearance. "So I would. But I'm afraid that's beyond even your empress' purse."

The bones in Plotliw's knuckles made a cracking noise.

"But let's not waste time on futile matters," Asche continued placidly. "I take it your unexpected visit means you have reached a decision?"

Plotliw gave Vindt a final dark look before saying, "I've come to negotiate."

"I told you I don't."

"Do you know how much fifty thousand crowns is?" Plotliw almost shouted. "I didn't call for... *you*, I just called for a Singer."

"We've discussed that before. You said you needed someone urgently. I was the one closest to you. So here I am. I told you, you're welcome to make another call. Even if someone answers, they won't be here for another month."

"I don't have the money."

"But your empress does. I assume you sent a messenger?"

Plotliw just glowered at Asche.

"So you've received an answer. Let me guess. She said, 'Try to negotiate, and if he won't, give the bastard the fucking money.' Am I wrong?"

Vindt's breath caught. Plotliw shot the Singer an irritated look, but after a moment he smiled darkly. "She didn't say 'fucking.'"

But "bastard..."

For the first time, the corners of Asche's mouth lifted into something like a smile. It was a scary sight. "Look, Commander. For fifty thousand crowns, I'll wipe out the Sylians for you, get rid of the dysentery and heal the wounded who haven't recovered from the last battle. Seems like a pretty good deal to me."

Get rid of the dysentery and heal the wounded? Ehlan had not mentioned that. And even if he had, Vindt would not have believed him. Heal? A Singer? Silhorveen had healed his servants when one of them was injured. Never had he offered anything similar to the men of his employer.

Plotliw shook his head, then exchanged glances with his two generals. They too shook their heads. "Your offer's of no use to me. The men... They won't want to be treated by..." He hesitated.

"A demon?" Asche finished lightly. "You're the commander. If you gave them the order, they wouldn't have much of a choice, would they?" He shrugged, then leaned back in his chair. "It might help you in your decision to know that the Sylians have also called for a Singer."

"What?" the three delegates bellowed in unison.

Even Asche's Thyd and the older servant cast the Singer surprised looks.

"I suppose that's a joke," Plotliw said.

Or a lie...

In his ten years with Silhorveen and the many battles they had been involved in, the other side never had a Singer too. Vindt had always thought it strange. Anyone who could afford it could hire one. Singers didn't care who they fought for. Why shouldn't both sides have one?

"But... That's... What does that mean?"

"What should it mean? They have a Singer, and you've got one as well."

"Then... What will you... Will you fight one another?"

"Depends."

"On what does that bloody depend?" Plotliw *was* shouting now.

"The other Singer might back off as soon as he finds out the other party has a Singer as well." Asche paused, then added, "And who this Singer is."

Plotliw snorted. "Or *you* choose to back off."

Asche lowered his long lashes, and for a moment the

shadow of a smile broke the surface of his otherwise impassive features. When he looked up again, it was gone. "I won't."

"Even if it turns out he's someone from the High Council as well?"

"It *is* someone from the High Council."

At this, the expressions of both Asche's Thyd and the seneschal changed to alertness. The latter even looked as if he wanted to say something, but eventually refrained.

"So you know who he is."

"Even if I didn't, it doesn't matter; it wouldn't change anything."

"And if he doesn't retract, and you lose, against the odds, then what?" Sarcasm laced the "against the odds" so thickly it dripped from the words.

"Your army gets bested and you save your empress fifty thousand crowns. That, by the way, is the same outcome in the event that you don't accept my terms and I don't engage in the fight at all. I tell you again, Commander, don't waste my time. What's your decision?"

Plotliw exchanged glances with his two generals. They were all very pale. "Can we have some time to discuss... *this*?"

"Until tonight. No longer."

Already halfway out of the tent, Plotliw turned once more, smiling. "If you fight the other Singer, does that mean to the death?"

Asche looked at him for a long moment before saying, his words ice, "Of course not, Commander. We're not humans."

CHAPTER 6

As soon as the three men left the tent, Vindt took a breath. He had not noticed it, but his entire body was tense. Relaxing his muscles, however, only reminded him of the momentarily forgotten withdrawal symptoms. And the reason for being here. He cast Asche a wary look.

Before the Singer could address him, though, the older servant spoke up. "Kvahad-thed, who...?" He didn't finish the sentence. Concern tinged his voice and shadowed his face.

"Ru," said the Thyd before Asche could answer.

Both servants looked at the Singer as if waiting for confirmation. Asche merely stared into the air in front of him, eyes half closed. "Not Ru," he said eventually. "A pity, though. I would have... enjoyed that."

"Kvahad-thed, don't say—"

"That's enough." Asche's voice was quiet, but the two men immediately fell silent and also seemed to remember they were not alone. Their bodies went back to a more formal posture, their faces to a neutral expression.

Asche's dark, heavy gaze came to rest on Vindt. "I think we had business before we were interrupted."

Like last time, everything in Vindt wanted to escape that gaze. At the same time, the eyes sucked him into their depth.

I will not look away.

Asche raised a long-fingered hand. "Leave us."

The Thyd and Ehlan bowed and did as told. The elder servant, however, stayed behind, looking at Asche with a puzzled expression. "Kvahad-thed?"

"You too, Calveen." Asche's voice was firm but gentle.

The man looked as if he wanted to say something, but then he merely frowned at Vindt, bowed and left as well.

As soon as Vindt was alone with the Singer, the atmosphere in the tent changed completely. Asche's aura of power, which had settled into a palpable but not overwhelming draft some time ago, didn't increase, nor did Asche's expression change; yet Vindt felt like he was locked into a pit with a hungry predator. His instincts crackled.

"May I ask what was so funny earlier?" Asche's tone was casual.

"W... what do you mean?" Vindt knew very well what he meant.

"You were laughing, so something I said must have amused you."

Of course Asche would not allow that to pass. Of course Vindt's poorly concealed fit of laughter would have consequences. Ehlan's warnings rang in his ears. He had wanted to heed them. But what else should he have done, hearing Asche claiming publicly he could raise the dead, but laugh?

"Does it mean you put raising the dead beyond my powers?" Asche asked.

Warnings or not, the old anger reared its head, pushing through the fear. What was this? A game? "What do you want me to say?"

"What you think."

As if.

Vindt's anger grew into a sizzling ball. It didn't matter what he said. This was a game. If he said yes, Asche would punish him. If he said no, this would go on until eventually they reached the same point. Impotence—the feeling he hated most, an acid liquid scalding his soul.

A sudden cold tremor ran through his body. He clenched his teeth to suppress a cry of pain. The withdrawal, of course. Instantly, his wrath became imbued with desperation. Indestructible remnants of his pride throbbed against the inside of his scalp, but he forced them down. "Forgive me, Kvahad-thed, I've offended you. It wasn't my intention."

"I assumed that much. That doesn't answer my question. Do you put it beyond my powers to raise the dead, yes or no? I won't punish you. Just give me an answer." Asche's voice was devoid of emotion, but not cold.

Give him an answer, play along, whatever.

He had the "Yes" on his lips when he hesitated. His gaze fastened on Asche, carelessly draped in his chair, the epitome of confidence and power, the pale face of unearthly beauty, the eyes a sea of blackness. "No." He didn't put raising the dead beyond his powers. It was the truth.

Asche watched him for a long, taut moment before his lips curled into a smile, and then... he laughed. The light, sparkling sound caught Vindt completely off guard. He had never heard a Singer laugh.

"Humans," Asche said, his voice suffused with

amusement. "You're surprisingly entertaining at times. Raising the dead—surely a handy skill to have. Unfortunately, I don't possess it. Yet. But who knows what I may be capable of in the future?"

Vindt forbade himself any reaction, least of all anger. He was sure it was what the Singer wanted. Of course, this was all designed to taunt him.

Asche rose from his chair. Apprehensively, Vindt watched him approach, blue robes flowing down his body. It took all his willpower not to take a step back. He tried to brace himself for what was to come, punishment for nothing, pain simply because Asche *could* inflict it.

But when Asche reached him, he merely stretched out his hand and lifted Vindt's left arm. "What's that?" The Singer was looking at the bracelet around his left wrist, a twin of the one which had vanished, though its dark magic held a different purpose. This one had unfortunately not fallen off.

"That's..."

The reminder of the last exit he had eventually seen to escape his fate: taking his life. Ehlan had thwarted his suicide attempt in time. Apart from punishing him to the point of almost letting him die for real, Silhorveen had put the bracelet on him. It prevented him from trying again. He could think about killing himself, he could even take a knife and put it to his throat, but then he couldn't finish the movement. The same held true for every other method he came up with, jumping off a cliff, drowning, poisoning himself.

Asche didn't seem to need an answer. He closed his pale fingers around the bracelet, shut his eyes and sang quietly. The metal on Vindt's skin grew warm while the patterns began to twist. But something else caught his attention. A faint smell wafted over to him from the Singer, more than familiar after weeks of confinement in a tent together with Silhorveen's half-dead body, acidic, metallic. Looking closely now, signs of fatigue did indeed streak the unearthly perfection of Asche's features, a grayish tinge to the pale skin, the shadow of shadows under his eyes. Exhaustion from using his preternatural skills. Vindt had seen this in Silhorveen often enough.

Ten times as powerful, perhaps. But not invincible.

He stifled a satisfied smile.

Asche let go of his arm. "I see."

"You can take it off," Vindt hurried to say. "It's no longer necessary."

"Then why didn't Silhorveen take it off? Seems like he didn't trust you. So why should I?"

Asche walked over to a table. When Vindt saw what was on it, his breath caught, and he forgot all about the bracelet. Goblet and knife of the Binding. How come he hadn't noticed them before? Was Asche merely teasing him or...?

"Don't get me wrong, Thyd," Asche said. "I'm not giving you my blood out of mercy. We cannot afford to lose Thyds. The High Council will decide your fate. This is nothing but a quick remedy for the time being."

Whatever feelings might have sparked at this, fury, even hatred, the flood of relief gushing through Vindt drowned them out. He almost groaned. "And when will the Council decide?"

"As soon as I finish *this*." Asche made a sweeping gesture, probably meant to encompass the camp. "And we reach the next Door."

The next Door... The Haven was so far away, it would

take them months to get there. Singers, however, had some magical way of shortening a trip. They weren't actual doors; they were... well, nothing, at least nothing humans could perceive with their senses. At one moment they were one place, the next, hundreds of miles elsewhere. Vindt had gone through one for the first time when they brought him to The Haven—though feverish as he was at the time he had no memories—and again when he left one year later with Silhorveen.

It was as uncanny as everything else involving Singers and their dark skills. He was not in the slightest keen to have the experience again, but at this very moment, all he could think of was the blood.

"Turn," Asche commanded.

"What? Why?"

"Now."

Reluctantly, Vindt obeyed. Why should he not watch?

But it didn't matter, as long as he got what he wanted. Needed. The realization it was about to happen had his body trembling with anticipation, his need a glowing blaze. His tongue licked over his incisors, which had grown into canines. He had no clue why this happened, but it always did when he was about to drink a Singer's blood. It was pointless, and even after ten years, he found it annoying. The teeth got in the way when drinking from the goblet. It had taken him months to figure out how to do it without spilling blood all over himself.

Normally, getting the Singer's blood was a sacred ritual, strictly regulated, the people present, the words spoken. The seneschal cut the Singer's veins, not the Singer. However, Asche had sent the old man away, so apparently he was going to do it himself. No wonder the man was confused.

Then again, this was no Binding, but about giving him the drug he needed to stay alive.

He was not sure if his mind was playing tricks on him, but he picked up on every sound, Asche rolling up the sleeve on his left arm, taking off the bracelet, picking up the knife from the table and a moment later cutting his flesh. The thick liquid hitting the metallic insides of the goblet.

Definitely not a trick of his mind was the smell.

No human could detect the scent of blood at this distance, but Vindt had ceased to be a normal human being long ago. It hit his nose and a second later his brain. Instantly, every nerve in his body was on fire, screaming. He closed his eyes and clenched his hands into fists to keep himself from spinning around and dashing for the goblet.

"Well?" Asche said.

Vindt turned to find the Singer standing right in front of him. He had not heard him approach and involuntarily took a step back.

"Don't want it?" Asche said in fake astonishment, raising an elegantly arched eyebrow. He let the goblet dangle from his fingertips.

Vindt snatched it. Before he could drink, however, Asche covered it with his palm. "I know you're dying for it, Thyd, but this is my blood, not Silhorveen's. Drink it slowly. Heed my words, lest you regret it." He placed his cool hand on Vindt's and casually controlled the motion with which Vindt raised the goblet to his lips.

With the smell of blood entering Vindt's nose, his mind went blank. A red film clouded his vision; the beating of his racing heart was all he could hear. As soon as the blood touched his tongue, he gulped it down greedily, despite Asche's warning. After another gulp, Asche forced the goblet away. It wasn't necessary.

Vindt jerked his eyes open and gasped. He had the same symptoms as before, his racing heart, the roaring in his ears, his burning body, only now they didn't come from something being amiss but from an overdose of this very substance. This was not the way it was supposed to be. It felt like a demon raging inside him, devouring his organs, boiling his blood. And at the same time, it filled him with a strange... rapture.

He dropped to his knees and shot Asche a desperate glance.

The Singer returned it with indifference. "I told you."

Asche crouched in front of him, goblet in hand. "It will get better in a moment. Breathe."

Vindt did, in, out, in, out. Slowly, the blaze inside him shrank to a glow. Again, Asche held out the goblet. Instantly, the greed was back, as fierce as before. Blood, the taste of it. Vindt didn't know if the Singers' blood tasted any different from human blood. Perhaps his senses had adapted, had forcibly relabeled something that had become vital to him from disgusting to the sweetest thing he had tasted in his life.

Asche watched him drink with detached interest. After only two more sips, the goblet was empty. Vindt resisted the urge to use his finger to wipe up the thin layer of blood still clinging to the goblet's walls. "That's all?"

"Enough to spare you the withdrawal symptoms. More would be a waste." Asche took the chalice from Vindt's hand and put it back on the table next to the now bloodied knife.

Vindt stayed where he was. He felt heady, light and heavy at the same time. The sensation resembled drinking

Silhorveen's blood, yet couldn't be any more different. Now that the demon inside him had quieted, it no longer felt wrong. On the contrary. He tried to remember what it had been like back at The Haven with Shahen's blood, whether he had noticed such a difference when switching to Silhorveen's. But he couldn't.

Part of the yearning lingered; Asche had only given him so much of his blood. It didn't matter. Compared to the agony tormenting him minutes ago, it was nothing.

Vindt closed his eyes and permitted himself a small sigh. He was even about to say thank you when he came to.

We cannot afford to lose Thyds.

No, there was nothing to be grateful for. Nothing at all.

CHAPTER 7

The convoy of wagons rumbled along, enveloped in dust and the sounds of squealing wheels and trotting hooves. The sun assailed Vindt as if it held a personal grudge, but he was glad to leave Silhorveen's tent in bright daylight, to be on the move, with no shackles around his ankles. In the morning, he had feared Asche would force him to travel inside the wagon to keep him out of sight. But the Singer didn't seem to care what people thought. Perhaps he was even looking forward to the rumors about himself having raised Vindt from the dead, laughing a little more about human fatuity.

It would take a few days before they caught up with the Sylian army. Until then, Asche had ordered him to stay with his own wagon and retinue. To keep Vindt under control, supposedly. Ehlan and the others were traveling at the very end of the platoon's long line. Vindt was not sad about the wall of wagons and men separating him from the groaning body.

Asche himself had gone ahead with most of his servants

and their horses, either to join Plotliw and the other Guzzar mounted soldiers, to go hunting or just for a ride; Vindt didn't care. He expected not to see them again before the end of the day, when they set up camp for the night. For the first time in ten years, he didn't have a Singer near him. For the first time in ten years, he could breathe.

He didn't even mind the barren landscape they traveled through. Dusty earth, some rocks. A plant the Guzzar called cacti dominated the sparse vegetation. They differed in size and shape, but some of them looked suspiciously like humans, stretching their round, flat limbs into the air in a gesture of threat or entreaty. Vindt wondered if they *had* been humans, punished for their sins by an unforgiving god, or cursed by demons.

He maneuvered his horse close to one of the distorted figures and cautiously picked a fruit from among the many thorns. Cursed or not, the fruits were tasty.

A lanky boy barely of age steered Asche's wagon with its bright blue cover sporting the Singers' sinuous patterns. Two mounted servants guarded it. One was the male half of the peculiar couple who had stood guard before Asche's tent yesterday. The other was a grumpy-looking man who, with his copper skin and dark hair, blended in with the Guzzar soldiers surrounding them.

Vindt was sure that apart from watching the wagon, they also kept an eye on him. During the morning, he had casually moved his horse to different positions, once even dropped behind a few feet. Each time, the blond man had steered his own horse to keep him in his field of vision. Now and then their eyes met, but the man's face with its unusual green eyes stayed expressionless. Neither he nor the other two attempted to speak to him. Sometimes they talked in voices too low for him to understand, casting him more or less covert glances. They didn't make the anti-demon sign; still, the prospect of the evening among Asche's servants did nothing to lift Vindt's spirits.

The servants. And Asche himself.

As expected, they only caught up with the riders when they settled in for camp.

By that time, Vindt sported a sunburn. Guzzar's scorching sun had bleached his already blond hair even more and darkened his otherwise fair skin. Though he was thus more tanned than ever before in his life, four weeks inside a tent had taken their toll on his coloring.

His neck was the worst. He could have protected it by undoing his braid, but he would never do that. In Pel, open hair was a sign of bawdiness. Only whores wore their hair down in public. Just another reason for his disdain for Singers. Their unraveled hair aggravated the air of frivolity their ambiguous gender and languid movements held anyway.

Besides, it was a special braid.

In Pel, some braids were worn repeatedly, at celebrations, in times of mourning, on holidays or during hunts. Others, people donned only once in a lifetime, a boy on his initiation day, bride and groom at their wedding and the dead to go to the afterlife.

The braid Vindt wore now, which he had worn ever since Pel's fall, was made for war. Or a personal vendetta.

Vindt knew that no one around him understood, which maybe was a good thing. *He* did.

The two men who had watched over him during the day now tended to the horses. Trying to ignore his itching skin, he made a point of grooming his own gelding, double-checking hooves and shoes and even fiddling twigs out of the horse's matted mane. He hoped the men would leave without him and grant him some time to himself, but as soon as they finished, the blond man with the green eyes signaled him to follow.

It was dark when they reached the others. Night fell early and fast in Guzzar, something Vindt would never get used to. Both blue tents, Asche's big one and the servants' smaller one, were pitched; the usual moat of suspicion separated them from the surrounding tents. His palms were damp. He felt transported back to when he first had to present himself to the Leruvian court, where his father had sent him for education, under the scrutinizing eyes of the king and queen and several dozen courtiers.

He stopped in the shadows and counted the people. Five. The young man who had steered the wagon earlier was chopping vegetables. A broad man with dark brown skin beside him was skinning some animal. The cauldron, suspended over the fire, exhaled a steady swirl of mist into the air. Vindt's stomach gave an audible growl.

As soon as he stepped into the firelight, conversations fell silent, and all eyes turned to him. Before he could react, however, the man skinning the animal wiped his hands on his trousers, got up and put his muscular arm around Vindt's shoulders.

"Vindt, right? Listen, I'm sorry you have to put up with us for the next couple of days, but since you survived Thrithid, there's at least a chance you'll survive us as well."

A collective groan rose into the air, and a few voices hissed, "Risi."

"What?" The muscular man, apparently named Risi, let

go of Vindt's shoulder and made a defiant gesture. "Did I ask him how he got out? No, I did *not*."

Sighs and shaking heads met the remark. The lanky young man cutting vegetables picked up the half-skinned animal and held it out to Risi. "Could you just sit back down and finish the hare?"

Risi did as told, not without muttering something unintelligible into his enormous black beard.

"Sorry if he offended you," the female version of the man who had been watching over Vindt during the day said in heavily accented Lyskú. "He's just—"

"Offended—what?" Risi turned to Vindt. "Did I offend you?"

"Uh... no." It was the truth. Vindt was rather... lost. The scene was a bit bizarre.

Risi gave the woman a triumphant look.

Vindt lowered himself to the ground, a little away from the others. The male twin sat down next to his sister and talked to her in a foreign language. Vindt was sure by now they weren't slaves. They wore their blond hair in a braid and the sides of their heads shaved, which exposed their ears. In contrast to Asche's other servants, they didn't have earrings.

Mercenaries? Did Asche pay them for their service? That Asche couldn't afford as many slaves as he wished was unlikely.

Another curiosity was the twins' weapons. Vindt had believed the scabbards dangling from their waists held swords. During today's journey, however, he had watched the man more closely and noticed the curved form of his scabbard. The hilt also looked peculiar. The woman's weapon was the same. Scimitars.

Neither in Pel nor in any country Vindt had visited in his former life did people use sabers. Even in the past decade of traveling with Silhorveen, he had never encountered anyone with a similar weapon.

"Wanna have a look?" the woman asked.

Vindt blushed. He had not realized he was staring. "If I may..."

Instead of unsheathing the weapon, the woman opened the belt that fastened it around her waist and handed him the entire scabbard. "I'm Narrapemet, by the way. You can call me Narr. And the talkative guy over here is Kishoon, my brother, as you might have guessed."

Kishoon snorted, but gave Vindt a nod.

"Vindt." He smiled wryly

"Yeah, we know."

As Vindt unsheathed the scimitar, he thought he heard a jarring noise, similar to the squeaking of rusty hinges. He looked around in confusion, straining his ears, but only the usual camp sounds shrouded him.

He hefted the blade. It was wielded with only one hand and thus notably lighter than his own sword—an awkward sensation. He made a few slashes at the air. The sabers he had seen drawings of were different; the blade widened toward the tip before tapering again. This one was thinner, but of even width. But far stranger was the metal. In the flickering light of the fire, it was difficult to see, but the steel had a peculiar color. It looked white.

"What kind of steel is this?"

Narr's eyes swept over the others, who followed the conversation with evident interest. "Have you never seen this before?"

Vindt shook his head.

"Well, it's…" Again, her gaze wandered.

When it met the eyes of Asche's seneschal, the old man moved his head in a subtle, almost invisible "No."

"I can't really tell you," Narrapemet said. "It's a special steel. The Kvahad-thed had it made for us."

She looked back to the seneschal, who returned her gaze, face impassive.

Interesting. Vindt handed the scimitar back to Narrapemet and sat down again. "Where are you two from?"

"Liut."

"That's a country?"

Narrapemet nodded.

Vindt tried to figure out whether he heard the name before or read it on a map. If so, he had forgotten about it. "Where's that?"

"Somewhere… west."

It must be many miles west, given the stark contrast between the twins' appearance and the dark-haired, copper-skinned people who populated this corner of the world.

"And how did you end up—" Vindt was about to say "here" when he realized it was the wrong question—"in Asche's service?"

"Because that's what we wanted."

"To work for a Singer?" It struck Vindt as the most ridiculous thing he had heard in a long time.

"For Asche." It was the first time her brother had contributed anything to the conversation, and not the only reason Vindt looked at him in astonishment.

"A friend of our father was in Asche's service for most of his life," Narrapemet explained before Vindt could ask. "When he got too old, he came back to Liut and… well, he advertised the job to us."

Vindt snorted. "With what perks?"

Narr gave him a puzzled look. "Aside from having the honor of working for a Singer and seeing things few humans get to see in their lives?"

With some effort, Vindt kept himself from rolling his eyes and nodded.

"Good money." She grinned.

So his guess was correct; they were mercenaries. He wondered how much "good money" implied, but his mind lingered on the first part of Narrapemet's answer. Having the honor of working for a Singer... Gaal, even those two, though they were no indoctrinated slaves.

"You worship Singers in Liut?"

At this, they both gave Vindt a strange look. "Of course," Narrapemet said.

Yes, of course.

"Do many women in Liut become soldiers?" he asked, to change the subject but also because he was curious.

Kishoon grinned and talked to his sister in their own language.

Narrapemet shook her head, but laughed. "He told me to tell you that no, it's just me who's been like this ever since, never doing what a decent girl should do."

She said something to her brother which made Kishoon laugh.

"You must excuse him," Narrapemet said to Vindt. "He understands everything and also speaks Lyskú alright, he's just too shy to do it."

So that was the reason for her brother's silence. Vindt understood him. During his time at the Leruvian court, he'd felt like an idiot every time he opened his mouth.

Although he learned Ler at home, it took him ages to form sentences that went beyond "Hello," "I'm sorry" and "Thank you," or dare to say them aloud. With the Singers' language, it was different. Once he had drunk Shahen's blood, Vindt could understand and use it without a second thought. Even his pronunciation was flawless.

"But seriously," Vindt said, picking up the lost thread of the conversation, "what about women taking up arms in Liut?"

"Whether you take up arms isn't a question of gender, but of caste. Our family has belonged to the warrior caste for generations. I could've chosen a different path in life, but it would've been rather awkward. Poor Dad." She laughed. "He would've been heartbroken. I know this seems weird to most of you."

It did. Vindt knew legends of female soldiers who had won fame and glory defending their countries against invaders, even in Pel. Depictions of Gaal commonly featured her wielding a sword, but the weapon's purpose was fighting demons. And that was it.

"Ah, here you are." A soft voice from behind pulled him out of his thoughts.

He turned to face Asche's smiling Thyd. Reisen was his name, he suddenly recalled. He'd just come out of Asche's tent. Vaan emerged with him, but she only cast a brief glance at the people around the fire before she walked on, probably back to Ehlan and the others, with whom she had stayed during the day.

Vindt hurried to get to his feet.

"No, no, please, sit." Reisen placed a hand on Vindt's shoulder. "I was just wondering how you're doing."

Vindt tried to figure out if the Thyd was making fun of

him. Aside from Ehlan the other day, no one had wondered how he was doing in the past ten years. But since Reisen continued to smile, Vindt took the question seriously. "Good." He forced his mouth into a smile.

Reisen studied him as if searching for signs of a lie, fatigue or demonic essence. "I'm glad."

He looked as if he wanted to add something, but after a glance at the others and the steaming pot, he merely said, "Dinner will be ready soon."

With another smile, he disappeared into the darkness.

CHAPTER 8

Indeed, dinner was ready soon. Someone handed Vindt a bowl of steaming stew. He itched to take the food and go somewhere else, but that would probably not be very polite. And not allowed. So he ate in silence and listened to the conversations.

Halfway through the meal, Risi pointed his spoon in his direction. "So, Vindt, did you also grow up at the famous Haven?"

Only a moment of hesitation passed before he answered. "Yes." He put emphasis on blowing on the contents of his spoon. Vindt hated lying, but he had no intention of sharing the truth with these people, to talk about an ordinary, happy life as a lord's son and how it had reached an abrupt end on the day of Pel's final battle.

Risi sighed. "So another I have to envy."

Vindt coughed, almost choking on a bit of meat in his stew. "Envy?"

Risi cast a side-glance toward the lanky young man who had cut the vegetables earlier. His name was Jun or Joon or something. With his copper skin and short dark hair, he resembled the grumpy one who had watched over Vindt during the day.

"From what I've heard, it's paradise," Risi continued. "Wine streaming from lustrous fountains, naked women lolling on sun-baked rocks amid refreshing ponds in front of sparkling waterfalls—"

"You're such an idiot." Jun glowered at Risi. "I've never said anything like that."

"Fountains, ponds, waterfalls."

"Fine. But the rest's a product of your lewd fantasies."

Risi grinned. "Then Vindt, won't you tell me what it's really like? I never tire of hearing stories of the paradisiacal Haven."

Vindt quelled a mirthless laugh. *Paradisiacal...*

Risi was even right. If you looked at the surface. Its awe-inspiring beauty only made it worse. Like the Singers' looks, it was a trap, a sugar coat around a poisonous pill, irony.

While Vindt pondered how to phrase his words without choking in earnest, Narr sighed. "Oh please, not The Haven again. I'm sure it's fantastic, but, really, I can't hear it anymore." She cast Jun a sour look.

"What? I said nothing. Risi—"

"That's enough." A crisp voice cut him short. It was the first time Calveen, Asche's seneschal, had spoken. "The Haven isn't a place to rave about like children watching a jester show." His scowl turned from Jun to Risi. "And nor is it a place to project one's wanton fantasies upon. It's sacred. Should you decide to speak of it again, do so with the utmost respect." His sinister look landed on Vindt.

Sacred—Gaal. Gods lived in sacred places, not demons. Vindt had wondered sometimes if The Haven had been a temple compound once, thus the name, and the Singers occupied it, killed the priests and eradicated all signs of whatever gods they had worshipped.

Jun looked mortified. Risi did too, but moved his hand in imitation of a croaking mouth where Vindt could see it but it was hidden from Calveen's eyes.

Vindt stifled his laughter. He was starting to warm to Risi.

It was a pleasant evening, like all of Guzzar's evenings, the only advantage of the country's torrid climate. The buzzing of an unseen army of insects filled the air. Cicadas, the Guzzar called them. Vindt had come to cherish their monotonous nocturnal concerts.

Though the battle was only a few days ahead, the air was free of tension. Cheerful voices, even laughter, drifted to them from other parts of the camp. Maybe Plotliw's men were confident the Singer would win this war for them, or the prospect of fame and glory which war held for so many men put them in a boisterous mood rather than letting fear paralyze them. Then again, it could simply be the relief of being able to act, the hope for a decision, whatever it might be, after the uncertainty and inaction of the past weeks.

The fire cast its flickering light on faces and bodies, bringing life to otherwise lifeless matter. Where it hit the walls of the tent, the intricate lines moved like the tendrils of some demoniac creature. As if the tent itself were a living organism. Vindt knew it was not solely the effect of the firelight. It happened during the day too, sometimes, not when he looked at it directly but when he watched the tent out of the corner of his eye, movement which was gone as soon as he focused his gaze. Silhorveen's tent had been the same.

Asche's presence reached him even through the fabric, teasing fingers that nudged his consciousness, and reminded him of his dependency.

As if in response, his right wrist itched. Surreptitiously, he scratched the bare, pale skin, trying not to draw attention to the missing bracelet. Perhaps its absence was a sign. Perhaps his entire resurrection was. If the Singers were clueless about his return from Thrithid, someone or something else might have rescued him. For a reason.

"So, has Asche fought any Singers before?"

The question snapped him out of his thoughts. Jun had asked it, not directed at him but at Reisen. Vindt himself had been dying to ask the same, but hadn't dared. Once again, he wondered how much time Reisen had spent at Asche's side. After observing the Thyd more closely, he had lowered his age estimation. The gray streaks in his short hair and trimmed beard were deceiving; his face looked younger. Mid-thirties rather than forties. Whatever difference this meant in actual years.

Reisen shook his head.

"No?" Jun said in amazement.

"They don't fight each other," Calveen snapped, but then realized his mistake and added, "Usually."

"Don't they now?" Risi scratched his enormous beard. "Some kind of law, or what?"

"A tacit agreement," Reisen said.

"That is, when a Singer learns that the others already have one, he retreats?" Jun asked.

"It never gets that far. They know who's called for a Singer and who hasn't."

"It *usually* never gets that far," Narr pointed out.

Reisen smiled wryly. "Yeah, well…"

Everyone looked at him and Calveen, the same apparent question on their faces.

"So why—?" Jun started, but Calveen cut him short.

"They have their reasons."

"You know the other Singer?" Vindt asked.

"He's from the High Council as well," Calveen said curtly, repeating what Vindt already knew.

He thought of their brief conversation in Plotliw's tent the other day. It had made little sense to him then, but he recalled a name. "Not Ru," he said tentatively.

At this, both Reisen and the seneschal looked at him in astonishment.

"How'd you…?" Reisen started, but then realized and smiled. "No, not Ru."

"Ru? Who's that?" Risi asked.

"None of your concern," Calveen barked. "And as for the other Singer—"

"His name is Tuait," Reisen said.

The remark earned him a scowl from Calveen. Reisen returned the sinister glance calmly.

Tuait. The name didn't ring a bell. Again, Vindt wondered what the reasons for the Singers' unusual engagement in battle might be. Animosity? Hatred?

Vindt remembered what Ehlan told him about Asche being known for making up his own laws, for snubbing other Singers. Maybe this was about settling old scores. And if they were already eviscerating the law, then perhaps what Asche had said to Plotliw at the end of their conversation was also prone to exceptions. Perhaps they *would* fight to the death.

Before Vindt could dwell on it, he became distracted by

a song wafting over from another part of the camp. A normal, human song. The singing men were too far away for him to distinguish the words, but it was a cheerful tune, seemingly popular; more and more voices joined in. After the first came another. The sound of a lute mingled in. It had been a long time since he had last heard music. He smiled despite himself. "You know these songs?"

No answer came. Vindt was about to repeat his question when he realized no one was humming along or smiling. Even Risi, whose smirk seemed to be chiseled into his face, stared gloomily into the fire.

"Someone has to—" Calveen began, but the grumpy-looking, copper-skinned man who had watched over Vindt interrupted him.

"Not me."

"But you speak the language best," Narr said at once.

"Risi does just as well. I went last time."

"Oh no, come on, let's not have this discussion again," Jun said. "Someone should go now, before—"

At that moment, a new song drifted over from where the unseen player sat. This time it was a ballad, and only one voice sang, a full, round voice that, though male, soared to surprising heights. Vindt was no music expert, but it sounded beautiful.

Risi closed his eyes. "Fuck."

"See now, I knew it." Jun's boyish voice held a hint of panic.

He was not the only one casting anxious glances toward the huge blue tent.

Narr rose. The torrent of words she spat out in her own language ended with "idiots" in Lyskú. She grabbed the man beside her by the elbow and, ignoring his protests, dragged him along in the voice's direction. After a moment, Risi and Asche's Thyd followed, Risi not without spitting another heartfelt "Fuck" into the air. Both men righted their sword belts, as Narr and her companion had done earlier.

"What's the matter?" Vindt asked the remaining men.

"He... well..." Jun glanced toward Asche's tent again. "He doesn't really—"

"It hurts his ears," the seneschal said firmly, looking Vindt in the eye.

Now it was Vindt's turn to focus on the massive tent with its moving pattern. "It hurts Asche's ears when people play music?" He pronounced each word with care, wanting to make sure he understood correctly.

Jun nodded eagerly. Calveen continued to stare at him.

The distant voices grew louder, or perhaps their number increased. After a moment, the lute sounded again, accompanied by the voice, the latter wavering.

"And the others went to—"

"Cut off that insult to my ears," a familiar, chill voice finished. "Apparently to no avail."

At once, everyone was on their feet, people's rising followed by bows and muttered "Kvahad-theds."

Asche's habit of appearing without sign or sound was as impressive as it was unnerving. The fire threw flickering shadows on his face, causing the lines on his robes to shift and twist, as it had earlier on the walls of the tent. The light reflecting in the black eyes made them look as if they held their own burning flame. At this moment, the Singer truly looked like a creature from the underworld.

Without another word, Asche went in the direction the others had gone. Calveen rushed to follow him. A part of Vindt didn't want to see what was going to happen.

Another was deadly curious. He had halfway risen when Kishoon reached for his arm and shook his head.

Reluctantly, Vindt lowered himself back to the ground. What would the Singer do? Kill everyone without bothering to say a word? At least the lute player? Sever his fingers, tear out his tongue and burn the lute to cinders? Or would he limit himself to torturing everyone who happened to be around until they begged for mercy and promised to never play or sing another tune in their lives?

Abruptly, the song and the angry voices died. A taut silence fell. The hum of the cicadas and voices from other parts of the camp still reached Vindt's ears, but the sudden disappearance of the other noises left a gaping hole in the sound tapestry which had previously hovered over the camp.

After another moment, Asche returned, the rest of the group in tow. Whatever he had done, the Singer's face didn't give it away. He went straight into his tent. The others stood around, lost, avoiding each other's eyes. Vindt swallowed the "What happened?" burning on the tip of his tongue.

Calveen said, "Let's pack up for the night."

And so they did. The music didn't resume.

CHAPTER 9

After three more days on the road, they caught up with the Sylian army.

The last night before the battle was a short one; they rose way before dawn. Everywhere in the darkness, people were getting dressed and strapping on weapons. Apart from occasional bellowed orders, voices were reduced to whispers and murmurs, as if the men were afraid of stirring the enemy, who was preparing for battle just like themselves.

Vindt had not expected Calveen to order him to be a part of Asche's guard. The others wouldn't need him. Perhaps they didn't want to leave him in the camp, unguarded. From the seneschal's tone, Vindt concluded the old man wasn't particularly thrilled. But Asche's word was law.

The onset of dawn revealed something almost as unsettling as the impending battle: an overcast sky.

For weeks, every morning had greeted them with a firmament of dazzling blue. Now, a thick gray blanket hovered above them, pressing down on land and people as if it had a weight of its own. No wind blew, not the smallest gust. The air was stagnant, suffused with a heavy, sweet stench Vindt attributed to the tiny pink flowers of the few bushes dotting the landscape.

Asche rode his horse over to talk to Plotliw. Even from where Vindt stood with his own gelding, he could see the commander's furrowed brows. He wondered what the two men were talking about. Surely not last-minute changes in tactics. When a Singer was involved, tactics were of no importance. Silhorveen, at least, had never cared for whatever battle strategies his employer settled on, nor had he paid attention to the opponent's expected maneuvers. For the Singers' "work" it didn't matter where on the field people were, whether on horseback or foot, moving or merely standing around, what weapon or armor they were using.

Their song killed them just the same.

Silhorveen had been adamant about sticking to three principles, though. He would not start singing right away, but let the battle play out for some time before intervening. Neither would he kill all the soldiers he could, but only as many as it took to guarantee his principal's victory. And finally, he would stop singing at the point from which the battle's outcome was determined, leaving the rest to the men on the field.

When a commander first hired a Singer, he usually met those rules with incomprehension and protest, which rarely subsided even after hearing the reasons. Men's concern was not the outcome of the war itself, not even the victory, Silhorveen would say. It was about them *gaining* it. Soldiers needed to experience the frenzy of battle, the movements of their muscles, the strain, the fatigue, to hear the sound of steel on steel, feel the fury and the fear, smell sweat and blood, sense the pain of their own wounds, the uncertainty.

In a way, they even needed to die, or at least look death in the eye, the possibility of failing. If the victory were solely owed to an androgynous demon, disappointment would follow, frustration, even rage—resentful energy which would find its way into other forms of discharge.

Every time Vindt listened to the Singer's "explanations," a surge of anger overcame him. Those reasons—even *if* they bore a beacon of truth—were condescending to the point of humiliation, another proof of the mundane ways of the human mind, its inferiority. He was sure that exactly that, the humiliation and nothing else, was the rules' underlying reason. When had anybody heard of a Singer giving a damn about human sentiments?

Asche's and Plotliw's talk was as brief as expected. Soon, the Singer turned his horse, and he and Reisen joined the group of servants and the unfortunate Guzzar soldiers designated by Plotliw to form Asche's personal guard.

To Vindt's surprise, Jun was with them too. The young man had been in charge of cooking and steering Asche's wagon every day, which had led Vindt to assume he was only responsible for "domestic" duties. He didn't carry a sword, but a bow, like most of the other men in the group, including Vindt, alongside their swords. Vindt doubted they would need them. Plotliw had probably designed half of his battle plan to back up his investment of fifty thousand crowns.

Vindt looked out over the plain, which was soon to become the battlefield. The dry ground was the color of rust, strewn with stones and rocks. A few crooked trees and spindly bushes braved the arid climate. They increased where the terrain sloped down to the far right, hinting at a hidden creek. Small hills rose from the earth, each as tall as a man. It looked as if a gigantic mole had left its mark. Or as if the ground had a skin disease.

"A burial site," Risi said in a low voice. He had moved his horse to Vindt's side and was looking out over the plain, one hand shielding his eyes from a nonexistent sun.

Vindt nodded. He had assumed as much.

In Pel they had once heaped mounds on people's graves as well, at least on those with a high social status such as chieftains, warriors and priests. The custom had vanished. Nowadays, they simply buried the dead. The Guzzar didn't even bury their deceased anymore, but burned them, a fact which had filled Vindt with horror when he learned about it. How were people supposed to go on to the afterlife without their bodies?

"And Plotliw doesn't care about spilling blood right on his ancestors' heads?" In Pel, no one would ever have allowed a battle to take place on a gravesite.

Risi shrugged. "Suppose the man cares about winning this war. Soon. On whatever grounds."

From where they stood, it was hard to guess the Sylians' true numbers, but it looked as if they had replaced the men Silhorveen had taken down a month ago. They outnumbered Plotliw's army again, which dysentery had further diminished until Asche, as promised, had gotten rid of the disease.

A Singer in one's ranks meant the opponent's number of men was of little or no importance. But this time, the other side had a Singer as well.

Now it was Vindt's turn to shade his eyes. He sifted the gray-brown rows of the Sylian soldiers for a patch of blue.

Calveen had confirmed that blue was indeed the color reserved for members of the High Council.

He finally spotted the Singer on one of the mounds. He had fair hair, that much Vindt could discern; for details, let alone the features of his face, the figure stood too far away. A pity. Curiosity gnawed at him. Another member of the famous High Council, one who didn't mind breaking the Singers' laws. Well, *tacit agreement*, whatever. Tuait. Vindt remembered the name well.

The clouds had not moved an inch. They didn't seem like individual clouds at all, but formed a leaden lid, pressed down onto the scenery by the hand of an unseen giant. They also swallowed the colors, leaving the landscape steeped in shades of gray and brown. Even the sounds had changed, become muffled, as if they were underwater.

Despite the hundreds of men and horses on the battlefield, it was strangely quiet. The stillness of the moment before battle, an intake of breath, a skipping of heartbeats, unheard curses, inaudible prayers, a blankness of minds. The sudden immediacy of mortality. Vindt knew it all too well. The Kallejdi had not been the first trying to overthrow his homeland. Only the first to succeed.

The sweet scent of flowers had reached him too on that fateful day a decade ago, a sudden whiff of innocence and life amid the reek of horse, sweat, blood and death. Before he knew it, he stood on Pel's battlefield again, panting, sweating, bleeding from several cuts and an unfortunate spear wound in his shoulder. The sharp twangs of his sword as it clashed with the blade of an enemy filled his ears.

And then, out of nowhere: song. And not song. A disembodied draft, rising and falling, beautiful, horrid. Vindt froze, his sword stalling in mid-movement, overwhelmed with an indomitable urge to stop and listen. His opponent stalled too, an expression not of enthrallment but disgust on his face, which, at that moment, Vindt attributed to himself. Only years later, when he saw this expression repeated on the faces of the soldiers they were fighting for, did he realize it didn't target him.

The song was all around. Everything else faded to insignificance: the enemy, the battle, his friends, the reason for this war, his past and future. His existence. The song was everything, was the end, his death. And yet, he wanted to succumb to it, to die.

Before he could, it withdrew, casting Vindt back into the hell of reality. He stood gaping, uncomprehending, as the song drifted across the battlefield, seizing people's bodies, creeping into their minds. Vindt watched the expressions of his companions change, not into terror but something softer, surprise, resignation. Before they fell down dead. Friends, family. He couldn't see his brothers at that moment, but they were out there, somewhere. Dying.

The soldier he had been fighting, though unaffected by the song, stood as immobile as Vindt, panting, squinting at him. He could have overwhelmed Vindt with ease in his state of torpidity.

The soldier adjusted the grip on his sword. "Fight." He waited another second before he launched.

"Time to get ready." Risi's voice from somewhere close and a world away.

It took Vindt a moment to realize the battlefield he was standing on wasn't in Pel; the armies facing one another were none of his concern, and nor was the outcome of this war. Risi turned his horse to take his position. A part of the memory stubbornly lingered, a soft buzz in Vindt's ears.

Like the other Singer, Asche had climbed a mound. He stood perfectly still, hands dangling at his sides, black hair flowing down over his shoulders. In the colorless landscape, the blue of his robes shone strangely bright, as if lit from within.

Vindt's hands trembled almost imperceptibly. His eyes wandered up the Singer's back. Left side, a horizontal line from the spine, a vertical from the shoulder, meeting. He could almost see the heart through fabric and skin and flesh, feel it beating. He felt his own heartbeat too, slow and hard, like an echo. The skin on his right wrist screamed the absence of the bracelet into his awareness, a gaping void in his reality. It swallowed all thoughts but one: *Gone. I can kill again.*

The bow slid into his hand of its own accord. An arrow from the quiver on his back followed. Steady moves, practiced hundreds of times. He didn't check if anyone was watching. He had forgotten about his surroundings, about the battle. Only the sweet smell of flowers made it into his consciousness, indiscriminate between present and past. He had not planned this. He was not even here. It was not him holding the bow but a ghost from his memories. A ghost who had come for revenge.

The buzzing in his head grew until it eclipsed all sounds but the heartbeat, his and Asche's, aligned. His fingers quivered, but it didn't matter. He wouldn't miss.

His eyes narrowed as he cocked the arrow. The bow's sinew almost touched his cheek. No one and nothing around him moved. A frozen world. Waiting. For the strike. For deliverance.

The heart—so fragile, so vulnerable.

A heart like his.

Shoot.

But somehow his fingers wouldn't obey. They already cramped from tightening the sinew.

A heart like any human's.

No! Not human. Demon! They killed your friends, your brothers. They kill all the time. They will kill now. He *will. But you can prevent it.*

The bow in his hands sank down before Vindt knew it. Something inside him sighed, exasperated, weary.

A roar rose into the air from the ranks of Plotliw's soldiers. The clang of spears and swords on shields followed, and then the racket of a multitude of feet and hooves charging forward. On the far side, the Sylians charged as well. Two giant, multi-limbed insects which a moment later rammed their stingers into each other's flesh.

Vindt hardly noticed. He felt dizzy, as if he were waking up from another dream. The buzzing still echoed in his head, fainter now.

Fool, a voice inside him hissed.

Vindt sat immobile in the saddle for what seemed like an eternity, his mind blank but for the voice that kept insulting him.

Only after the buzzing in his head ceased did he become aware of the stillness that must have already manifested a while ago. It was not the gut-wrenching, universal silence a Verdur imposed; the din of the distant battle still reached his ears. It also *felt* different. The stillness came from nowhere in particular and was everywhere at the same time. His skin tingled.

Vindt's horse sensed it too. It stood unusually still, head raised. Its ears twitched in all directions, scanning the air for... whatever, danger, a signal. The entire landscape seemed to wait, not for his strike this time.

Ground and air vibrated.

Asche didn't sing yet; at least, Vindt couldn't hear anything. But suddenly he knew, and it was one of those strange understandings that sometimes came to him out of nowhere since becoming a Thyd, that Asche *had* begun to sing.

The vibrations intensified, slowly at first, faster with every passing second. Now Vindt *could* hear something, at the limits of his perception, a steady, high-pitched noise, like a distant scream. And then, from one second to the next, the scream was there, surrounding him, hammering against his eardrums with cruel, strident might.

Chaos broke out. Faces contorted. Hands went to ears to block out the screeching sound. Horses went berserk. Vindt dropped bow and arrow, needing both hands to prevent his own gelding from dashing away.

The scream spiraled into the air, drawing other sounds to it, sounds which hadn't existed before, sounds of air and earth, of rocks and plants, of the clouds. They swelled and collided with one another.

Vindt could no longer hold his horse. He jumped off and let it run. Out of the corners of his eyes, he saw that on the battlefield, not one soldier was standing anymore, neither Guzzar nor Sylian. Horses were running off in all directions.

The impact of the two clashing voices washed over them, falling and rising, entwined like lovers, striving to throttle each other with merciless tenaciousness, oblivious or indifferent to their devastating effects on their surroundings. The air pulsed in an unsteady rhythm.

How long could humans endure this before their minds

and bodies collapsed?

Like an answer to his thoughts, the scream rose to a mind-twisting, body-bending crescendo.

And then something snapped.

The silence that fell was absolute, a world drained of sounds. After some time a breeze rose, blowing softly over the sprawled bodies on the battlefield, brushing the branches of the crooked trees and spindly bushes, stirring up heaps of dust.

Darkness surrounded them, as if night had already fallen. When Vindt looked up, he found the stagnant gray blanket of clouds above them had turned into a moving black mass. The sound of thunder made him wince. A second rumble followed, and a moment later, it started to rain. Not the erratic drops of the other day but a downpour of the kind he had rarely experienced, even in his homeland. Within seconds, it drenched him to the skin. The dry earth couldn't absorb the mass of water. Puddles formed, turned into streams which wound their way down the sloping ground toward the trickle, carrying soil and stones and broken branches with them.

Not all the soldiers on the battlefield came back to life. Vindt squinted out onto the plain, but a considerable number of men remained on the ground. From the distance and through the curtain of drops, it was difficult to tell friend from foe, yet he knew those who remained motionless were not Plotliw's men.

He killed them.

Asche stood as before, motionless, palms facing upward. The Singer's eyes were closed, his features relaxed, almost soft. He was smiling.

Asche's hands dropped; his eyes opened. For a long moment, he stood gazing out over the plain, his face back to its familiar impassivity.

Sounds of clashing weapons, of screams and curses, drifted over to them again, muffled by the rain. Vindt knew it would only be a matter of minutes before the Guzzar defeated the remnants of the Sylian army. As it always was. As it had been in Pel a decade ago.

Why didn't I shoot?

Around him, the others moved. Vindt hardly noticed his drenched clothes, nor the water dripping from his face. He still wasn't fully there, his mind in some parallel dimension where the arrow would have loosened. And struck.

The Singer descended from the hill. His mare had run away with the other horses, but came trotting back now, Reisen's gelding in tow. She eyed her master with reproach. Asche said something to her that Vindt couldn't hear and scratched the horse behind the ears. For a moment it seemed the mare would pull her head back in a huff, but then she lowered it, enduring the caress, looking somewhat defeated.

Asche mounted, and Reisen followed suit.

"Get the horses and head for camp." Despite being low, Asche's voice rang clearly through the torrential rain. "I've got business to do. I don't know when I'll be back. Don't wait for me."

As he turned his horse, his gaze met Vindt's. In the depth of the black eyes flickered a lightless glow. The corners of his lips didn't lift, yet Vindt knew the Singer was smiling at him. The hairs on the back of his neck rose.

With no visible sign from his rider, Asche's horse leaped into a gallop, and he and Reisen disappeared into the rain.

CHAPTER 10

Were it not for the noise they made, they could be stealing away in the middle of the night like thieves. It was dark, dawn still several hours away. No one came to witness their departure, and not a sound was to be heard from the surrounding tents. Still, Vindt was sure everyone was lying awake, listening with relief to their preparations.

Five chests filled with silver crowns supplemented their usual equipment. As much as Risi and the grumpy-looking man—who was called Layyad, as Vindt had learned—tried to do it cautiously, each chest hit the bottom of the wagon with a thud that carried all the way to the end of the camp. Surely Asche could have done something about the noise, but he just stood beside the wagon, looking like he was enjoying each echoing thud. A parting salute.

By the time dawn broke, they had put a fair distance between themselves and the camp. The sky was as clear as ever, not a single speck of white staining the vast blue canvas stretching above them. On the dry ground, not a puddle or even a patch of darkened earth remained. As if yesterday's rain had never occurred.

But it had. And everything else, too.

Already, his killing attempt felt surreal, more like a dream than something he had actually lived. The easiness with which he had lost control creeped him out. As did the idea of the consequences. Yet, poking through the relief of not having loosened the arrow was... regret.

Asche was riding at the front next to his Thyd. Vindt's gaze turned to him, as it had done a hundred times already since their departure. The Singer wasn't wearing his robes, but the same plain tunic and leather breeches as on the day they had met. A strange sight. As strange as Reisen, Risi and the others, who had also donned simple tunics instead of the blue ones they had been wearing the last few days. Even the dyed cloth usually covering the wooden walls of the wagons was gone.

Vindt cast Narrapemet, who was riding next to him, a surreptitious glance. He could simply ask her what this was all about. Only, he felt... *shy* wasn't the right word. They had talked a little, occasional words, always friendly. Perhaps that was the problem. It had been a long time since he had been around a woman for more than a quick conversation about prices at a vendor's stall. That his thoughts went in a certain direction was only normal.

Half a head shorter than Vindt, Narr was as sturdy in build as her brother; her features were rather coarse. Even though her unusually curved green eyes were fascinating, she was not his type. Then again, he never really had a "type," and in the last ten years, he had become notably less picky. And that Narr was a soldier intrigued him. He could see her well-trained body, even through her clothes. Over the last few days, he had caught himself a few times wondering how it looked naked, what it would feel like to sense firm muscles instead of soft, yielding flesh under his hands.

His last time having sex was ages ago. Well, a year. It was true what Ehlan had said: Vindt had tried to get the innkeeper's daughter into bed in Neir Darin. His "trying" had turned successful after only a couple of prolonged eye contacts, a few smiles and a handful of compliments. Sex with the girl was nothing he would dream about for years to come. *But it had been sex.*

Being forced to stay with Silhorveen seven days a week, twenty-four hours a day, had brought his chances for a fuck close to zero, paid or not. In the case of the inn girl, he not only had to *ask* the Singer for permission, he had to stay within the reach of his voice at all times. It was humiliating. But the alternative had been bleaker.

Hoping his face wouldn't give his thoughts away, Vindt maneuvered his horse closer to Narr. "Can I ask you something?" He gave her what he hoped was an innocent smile.

"Sure. Shoot."

"Why aren't you wearing your servant tunics?"

"I fear you'll have to ask Asche that question."

"Do you always travel like that?"

"Mostly."

"But why?"

Narr laughed. "Asche doesn't very often provide explanations with his orders. I think... he might not like the attention."

That Vindt found hard to believe. But what other reason could there be?

Silence ensued. Narr smiled. Vindt smiled back, racking

his brain for something to say to keep the conversation going. "So, um, actually, you know, I was wondering about what you said the other day. The thing with the castes in your homeland."

Narr's eyes lit up. "Oh, you want to know about Liut?"

Vindt nodded, relieved and excited to have asked the right question.

Narr began talking.

* * *

To Vindt's surprise, the servants' tent they pitched that evening, though made of the familiar silky water-repellent material, was not blue, but a sun-bleached beige, no patterns. Asche's tent was beige as well, and, more strikingly, less than half the size of the pavilion they had set up for him earlier.

If Asche's plan was to hide his identity as a Singer, the bright red tent with its unmistakable writhing shapes which Ehlan, Fora and Silhorveen's other servants had erected for themselves thwarted it.

Vaan had come to Asche's tent every evening during the past few days, but it was the first time Vindt had seen Fora and the rest of his old companions since the Singer ordered him to travel with his entourage. He realized he had not missed them. When he asked Calveen whether he was supposed to spend the night in their tent now that the two parties were no longer separated, the answer he got was, "Didn't the Kvahad-thed tell you to stay with his host? So you will."

Vindt went to do what he had promised Risi this morning: help with the horses. It was mixing business with pleasure. Vindt loved horses; he had sat on one before he could walk. Besides, Asche's horses were... special. Silhorveen's mounts, although of high quality, well trained and thus ridiculously expensive, had been bought whenever the need for a horse arose. Asche's horses were all so similar, they had to be of the same breed. Their coats came in only two different colors, either dark brown or, as with Asche's own mare, a dark, dappled gray. Their low and muscular build curiously didn't make them look stocky, but gave them an air of nobility. All the horses were beautiful, but Asche's was the most beautiful in the herd. Of course. Vindt was sure the Singer had chosen the mare because of her looks, well aware of the mesmerizing image the two of them gave off.

Fora and another of Silhorveen's servants arrived with their horses first at the small creek, so Vindt and Risi had to queue. While they waited, Asche's mare brought her head close to him and blew her warm breath into the crook of his neck. Vindt had made sure to be the one taking care of her. A whim. Curiosity. Besides, he was pretty sure Asche wouldn't like him handling his horse.

The mare nibbled at his shirt, then proceeded down to his pants.

"She's looking for treats." Risi grinned.

"You feed the horses treats?" Vindt was surprised.

"Dear goodness, no. The Kvahad-thed would kill us." Risi looked in all directions, then leaned closer to Vindt and said in a low voice, "But *he* does."

"Asche? He feeds the horses treats?" Vindt tried to picture the scene, but failed.

Risi put his index finger to his lips. But he grinned again. "Just her." He pointed his chin toward the mare, which continued to nibble at Vindt's clothes.

Risi stroked her nose. The touch made her abandon Vindt and search the big man's body for treats instead. "Spoiled little diva," he said with tenderness.

"She seems quite... uh... friendly." Vindt found that remarkable, considering who her master was.

Risi laughed. "Gentlest horse I've ever met. Toward people. The other horses she bosses around. Knows very well who she's carrying on her back."

As if she had understood the words, the mare flattened her ears, turned her head and bit the horse to her right, which had sneaked up on the group unnoticed. The gelding gave an anguished squeal and retreated a few steps.

Risi raised his dark eyebrows at Vindt as if to say, "See?"

"Did Asche buy them all at once? They're the same breed, aren't they?"

"Oh no, he breeds them."

"*Breeds?*" Vindt had a hard time imagining any Singer, much less Asche, wasting his precious time on something as trivial as horse breeding. Besides, for doing so he would need a *place*, a, well, home. Singers had no homes; at least, that was what Vindt had always believed. With Silhorveen, they had been on the road since the day Vindt was bound to him. They rarely stayed in the same place for more than a couple of days. If Silhorveen had a "home," Vindt had never been there, and the Singer never mentioned it. Neither had they ever visited another Singer at his homestead.

"What's her name?" Vindt's hand wandered to the tender spot between the mare's nostrils.

"Schiida."

Vindt frowned. Schiida, where had he heard that?

Then he remembered. His involuntary laugh caused the mare to take a step back and snort in irritation.

"What's so funny about that?"

"The legend of Sikandem, don't you know?"

Risi seemed to sift his brain for memories. "Never heard of it."

"Never mind. It's... a tale. Did Asche give her that name?"

"Sure. Who else?"

Schiida. Either Asche possessed an unexpected streak of self-irony, or he was indeed a megalomaniac.

Schiida in "The Legend of Sikandem" was a demon horse with red, gleaming eyes, flames instead of mane and tail, horns sprouting from its head and claws instead of hooves. The horse before him, one hind leg bent, her lower lip drooping, couldn't be further away from her namesake. What had made Vindt laugh, however, was that the Schiida of the legend carried Tehered, the ferocious demon king, who, apart from sporting two legs instead of four, looked quite similar to his horse. In the tale, Tehered spent his time hunting human souls, torturing them in the cruelest of ways. In the end, the tale's human hero, Sikandem, defeated him.

With ease, Vindt replaced Tehered's fiery-red hair with black in his imagination and the gleaming red eyes with gleaming black ones.

A demon king. How fitting.

When they were done with the horses, it was still some time until dinner. Vindt decided to get rid of the layer of sweat and dust covering his body. He gathered his things and made his way through the darkness back to the stream.

"Going for a wash, too?" Reisen appeared beside him, the usual wry smile on his lips.

Vindt forced himself to return it. So far, Asche's Thyd had had nothing but friendly words for him. Still, something about the man discomfited him. Perhaps it was the smile he cast him whenever their eyes met. Or that Asche's blood also flowed through Reisen's veins, an idea that felt unjustly intimate. Or simply because he was a Thyd, a walking mirror to something Vindt preferred to ignore. Every time Reisen and Asche were together, on horseback or foot, standing or sitting, Reisen disappeared; he became a shadow. It was what *Thyd* meant. Vindt had often thought how apt the term was, describing precisely how *he* felt, what *he* had been the past ten years, not someone but some*thing*, tied to another, condemned to follow him wherever he went, disembodied, hollow, something that died together with its originator, something with no *raison d'être* of its own.

They washed in silence. Vindt seized the opportunity to soap his sweat-drenched shirt.

"Don't mind him," Reisen suddenly said. "Calveen, I mean. It's nothing personal. He treats me the same way. Or would if he dared. He doesn't... He's not very fond of Thyds."

"Not fond... You mean—"

"Jealous."

Vindt continued to rinse his shirt. "Idiot."

"Why does that make him an idiot?"

"Because..." *It's a damn curse*, Vindt wanted to say, but after a look at Reisen's serene figure in the dark, he kept quiet.

"I see," Reisen said, smiling again. "I heard you... You're not very happy about being a Thyd. How old were you when they found you?"

"Twenty-five."

"A pity."

That they found me—yes.

That he had had the chance to live the life of a normal human being, a happy life, totally Singer-free, was not.

Reisen returned to his initial topic. "You know, Calveen, he's old. His days by Asche's side are numbered. He's already stayed longer than servants usually do."

"Why doesn't Asche send him back?"

"Suppose Calveen begged him to stay."

"And Asche agreed? Why would he?" Vindt wrung water from his shirt. "Don't tell me he's attached to the man."

"Why does that seem so absurd?"

Vindt stopped wringing and looked at Reisen.

Because he's a Singer.

He didn't say it. Instead, he stepped out of the creek and put on his clothes, including the wet shirt. The air was still hot, and he relished the damp linen against his skin.

"I understand him," Reisen continued. "He's still fit for his age, but things are going downhill. His eyesight isn't the best anymore; he has a constant pain in his hip, although he's quite good at hiding it. He lives with the daily fear of being replaced. And then there's us, the Thyds, eternal youth, able to stay by a Singer's side, maybe not forever but if we're lucky, for centuries."

If we're lucky...

Vindt tried to evoke some kind of sympathy for Asche's seneschal, but failed. Why should he? The man and his feelings were none of his concern. He thought of Ehlan. The other seneschal had surely been devoted to Silhorveen as well, to his job. But Vindt was sure he wouldn't have minded being sent back to The Haven to enjoy his twilight years.

He wondered why Reisen was telling him all this. "Well, I think I'm going back. I'll see you la—"

"Vindt." The Thyd paused and looked toward their tents, as if to make sure no one was within earshot. "Can I ask you something?"

Here we go.

"Well, I was..." Reisen's voice was so low, Vindt had to strain his ears to understand the words. "I just... Asche said you don't, but maybe he... well, I mean..." He interrupted himself and with a sudden determination said, "How was it?"

"How was what?" Vindt had no clue what the other man was getting at.

"Thrithid."

In the darkness, Reisen's face was only a vague outline, his expression difficult to make out. More than seeing it, Vindt could feel the fear. It took him aback. Reisen had seemed so calm, unflappable, at peace with himself and the world.

Vindt knew the others were curious to ask him about Thrithid. Their eyes, whenever they looked at him, gave them away. From what Risi let slip the other day, there seemed to be a silent agreement—or an order—stifling their nosiness. Still, Vindt had expected someone to ask, eventually. Of all people, he had not expected that person to be Reisen.

A wave of pity invaded him. Absurd, he might as well pity himself. He thought of the tiny crack in his mind that opened at unforeseen intervals, not sufficiently wide to make out what was behind it but enough to breathe an icy draft into his chest. He hoped that in the darkness, Reisen couldn't see him shudder.

"It's true; I can't remember anything. I'm sorry."

"Yes, well, I thought so. It's... I think it's better that way." Reisen sighed. "Sorry, I know this is awkward..."

"No, no," Vindt hurried to say. *Awkward* wasn't the word. "I... um... I'm going back."

Reisen opened his mouth, closed it again, and just smiled.

The forlorn hooting of an owl accompanied Vindt on his way back to the tents.

CHAPTER 11

The next day, Vindt made sure to ride beside Narrapemet again. He tried to convince himself it was solely because he enjoyed their conversation. However, in the afternoon, after they had stopped for a quick lunch and mounted again, it was Kishoon who brought his horse close to Vindt's. He smirked at him without saying a word until Vindt became unnerved. "What?"

"Not look too much better at sister mine," Kishoon finally condescended to say in his broken Lyskú. "Or Layyad puts knife here." He pointed between his legs.

It took Vindt a moment to understand what he was hinting at.

"What? I haven't..." He could feel his face changing color, and from the way Kishoon's smirk widened, Narr's brother had noticed it too. "You mean Narr and Layyad. The two are..." He didn't know how to put it; he had no idea of Liut's customs. A couple? Together? Engaged? Married?

"Fucking," Kishoon finished the sentence, nodding

happily, apparently proud to know this word.

Not for the first time, Vindt thought humans had probably introduced the term to the Singers' language. Swear words in general. "We were just *talking*."

"Talk now, fuck later." Kishoon was still grinning.

Narr and Layyad—could that be? Vindt had never seen the two... well, in a situation suggesting that. Besides, Layyad wore a permanent scowl and, most important, he was a slave, whereas Narr was a free woman. But whatever the case, he couldn't deny a stab of... disappointment? Envy?

"Well, thanks for the—"

Vindt *said* "information," only he couldn't hear the word anymore. His voice had vanished, swallowed by a sudden antagonistic scream along with the rhythmic squeal of the wagons, the trotting hooves, the words of the heated conversation Risi had been having with Layyad behind them. Instead, silence entered his ears as if someone was ramming their fingers into them all the way through to his brain.

He let out an inaudible noise as fear whipped down his back. While his gaze still sought the Verdur, his body, trained over a decade, had already reacted. His mouth opened along with his mind, ready to be controlled by a Singer's voice. However, all he felt was a faint echo of the familiar pull. Asche's voice *had* risen into the air, but it was a mere brush instead of the iron grip he knew from Silhorveen, which was *necessary*.

Fear cresting, Vindt *forced* his body to react, to engage in the fight. When it eventually did, and a feeble tune rose from his throat, he realized he was an idiot. He didn't need to fight; he was no one's Thyd anymore. Reisen's voice had long since joined Asche's, challenging the aural mire.

Only then did he also see the Verdur. The abrupt movements of the creature's semi-translucent body and its constant shape-shifting were as sickening as ever. Occasionally, it solidified into a distinguishable form, an animal or an arbitrary mix of several, sometimes even into something looking disturbingly human but distorted, flesh bulging, skin creasing, growing limbs where it shouldn't. Its insubstantial eyes conveyed ire, hatred, menace.

The Verdur was not after him, he knew; his targets were Asche and Reisen. However, one of them dragging Vindt down into Thrithid had flayed his fear down to its raw, primal core. It was no longer merely about dying.

That was when he realized that the voices of Singer and Thyd were not the only sounds resisting the aural nothingness. A different song mingled in, cruder, barer. With it came the tart, metallic smell Vindt had grown so accustomed to over the past few weeks in Silhorveen's tent. But the half-dead Singer was too far away. Which left only one other potential source for the stench:

Demons. Real ones.

They were invisible, but Vindt didn't need to see them. Their smell, the din they emitted, and a gut feeling alone were enough to mark their presence. As a final proof, the demon-repellent amulet dangling from a cord around Vindt's neck grew warm and burst into angry vibrations.

As if Asche had noticed the amulet's reaction, he yanked his head in Vindt's direction, gaze fixed on his shirt. Their eyes met for a split second before the Singer returned his attention to the surrounding chaos.

A new kind of terror pushed Vindt's heart into another race. He had always believed demons to be afraid of Singers.

While traveling with Silhorveen, they had hardly ever encountered any, and when they did, the Singer had chased them away with a lazy rise of his voice. The shapeless, translucent creatures attacking them now were either of a different kind or very brazen. Not only were they attacking despite the presence of a Singer; the longer Vindt watched, the more convinced he became they had it in not for humans but for Asche, like the Verdur.

He was at a loss as to what to do. The constant up and down and in and out of sounds scourged his nerves. The demon stench scraped his throat as if he had swallowed a jar of eroded metal shards. Clear thinking became difficult even without his horse snorting, rolling its eyes and spitting foam. The amulet would protect him; at least, it had in the past. The others...

... jumped off their mounts and drew their swords. Vindt watched with a mixture of disbelief and desperation. Steel was useless against demons—any human-made weapon was. Still, it looked like the others were fighting something that had no limbs to sever, no organs to wound, no heart to pierce. Demons were invisible. Risi, Narr and the rest slashed at thin air. Jun rose from the seat of the wagon and let arrows fly from his bow, his brows furrowed in concentration.

Vindt followed an arrow with his eyes, horrified to realize it was flying straight at Reisen. A cry of warning escaped his lips. In the commotion, it went unnoticed.

Before reaching the Thyd, the arrow stopped in midair. A sharp, hissing sound emerged, followed by a non-human scream full of anguish and fury. The arrow burst into white flames. Something translucent and liquid-like plummeted to the ground, where the dry earth absorbed it, leaving no stain.

Captivated by the demons, Vindt had forgotten all about the Verdur. He was reminded when its shape-shifting figure was upon him out of nowhere, wrapping him into a multi-limbed embrace. For a moment, he felt nothing. Then panic crashed down.

No, please.

It was all he could think, the words repeating over and over in his head. The rest of his mind had turned into a black pool of terror. *Struggle*, a feeble voice somewhere inside him ordered, but the Verdur's violent silence paralyzed his body.

To Vindt, this seemed to go on for ages, though it was probably only a few seconds before two combined voices, powerful and determined, swept the creature away like a hand swiping a cup off a table.

Dazzled, Vindt remained on the ground. He didn't even remember falling off his horse. When he sat up and looked around, the agonizing rise and fall of noises had stopped. The silence engulfing them had become normal again, punctuated by ordinary sounds, trotting hooves, heavy breathing. The demons' metallic smell still hung in the air, like a warning. But they were gone, and so was the Verdur.

One by one, the others lowered their weapons. Asche and Reisen, the only ones who had not dismounted, now did. The Singer released his mare and hurried over to Layyad, who was kneeling on the ground. The man clutched his chest, face ashen, eyes widened in terror as his body lost its contours. Vindt had seen people touched by demons before and wasn't keen on witnessing it again. Still, his eyes remained on the gut-wrenching metamorphosis, pulled by this inescapable fascination the horrible sometimes held.

Asche sang. Layyad's blurred body swayed, his mouth opened. It looked like he was about to scream, but no sound came out. His eyes bulged from his face. A shout rose into the air. It seemed to come from the man's mouth, yet it was not human, a crooked noise which made Vindt's stomach churn.

Layyad's body solidified again.

Asche got up. "Has anyone else been touched?"

Everyone shook their heads.

"Well done." Asche looked at each of his servants.

Only then did the others sheathe their weapons. Narrapemet strode over to Layyad. She dropped to her knees and placed a hand on his shoulder. Her expression oscillated between concern and anger. It was the first time Vindt saw the man smile, and the first time he saw him and Narr in a situation suggesting they might be more to each other than simple companions.

Shakily, Vindt got up. Demons...

His hand went to his chest, feeling for the metal of the amulet beneath the shirt. It had stopped vibrating but was still warm. An echo of their sounds hung in Vindt's ears. *Demons' song,* they called it back home. It only underpinned Vindt's theory about Singers. Their song might be different, one ugly, one beautiful, but they were the same in essence.

He scanned his surroundings for the alterations demons left in the landscape. At first, he couldn't see any, but then he noticed the bushes nearest to them were gone, as was the sparse grass beneath their feet. The earth was also different from before, lighter and coarser-grained. Tiny changes compared to what Vindt had seen in his life: trees turned into rocks, creeks becoming ponds, a meadow changing into a bog, a plain becoming a landscape of rolling hills. Or things or animals disappearing. Horses vanished from their pasture, a bird's nest found empty.

Though that was disturbing, it was far more unsettling when things or animals *appeared* out of nowhere. The latter didn't happen to people, at least as far as Vindt knew. But people vanished, whole families along with their homes, an entire village. The last two things Vindt had never witnessed himself, and from what he knew of Gaal's priests, it hadn't happened on Kärö, his home island, for hundreds of years. Gaal protected them. As the lord, Vindt's father had instigated regular offerings at the island's various temples and had the priests perform their sacred rites to shield his people from the demons' greed for human souls.

"And you." A crisp voice startled Vindt out of his thoughts. "Next time we're attacked by a Verdur, I'd appreciate you not waving your arms and shouting, 'Hey, I'm a Thyd too, come and get me.' I am busy enough defending myself and my own Thyd; I don't have time to babysit another." Asche looked like the epitome of Lord Tehered, about to eat Vindt's soul.

Vindt clenched his fist. "I'm sorry, Kvahad-thed, but I don't know what you're talking about. I did nothing."

"Then tell me, how did the Verdur recognize you as a Thyd?"

"They just do, don't they?" Vindt was acutely aware of the others' eyes on him.

"You responded to my call. My blood's running in your veins, not much, but enough for us to have an unfortunate connection. When it calls, of course, it will also call you. But there is no need to respond. No, there's not only no need, it's idiotic, reckless, suicidal. Don't do it again. Do I make myself clear?"

Vindt remembered the feeble pull, how he had tried to force his body to react, for fear, because he thought it was the right thing to do. That was what Asche was now blaming him for? Vindt almost choked with the injustice of it.

"Very clear, Lord Teher..." His blood stopped moving. "Kvahad-thed," he murmured hastily.

But it was too late. Asche, who had already turned toward his mare, came ambling back over until he stood right in front of Vindt. Vindt tried to take a step back, only to find the way blocked by his horse.

Asche's expression was as unreadable as ever, but the familiar spark in the depths of his black eyes heralded nothing good. "I see," he said, so low only Vindt could hear. "The Legend of Tehered. I'm surprised. It's unknown on this side of the First Sea. But then, you're from Pel."

"The Legend of Sikandem," Vindt corrected before he could avoid it. He held his breath. Gaal, what was wrong with him?

"Is that what you call it? Interesting. Let me guess. You played Sikandem as a child, swinging your wooden sword at the poor kid who had to take on the role of the vicious demon king."

This was true. But only in part. Mostly, *Vindt* had ended up as Tehered. Against his two elder brothers, he had never stood a chance when they distributed the roles. Those games were not the happiest memories of his life. Not only was he denied the hero's glory, but Tehered was regularly beaten up by Sikandem and his invented knight. Only when playing with the servants' kids living at the holding did Vindt embody the role which was his due as a lord's son, and show Tehered what it meant to ignite his wrath by tampering with innocent human souls.

"See, that's the difference between us," Asche continued placidly. "I've always pretended to be Tehered. In my game, I defeated Sikandem. Oh, no, no, I didn't kill him. I slowly eviscerated his chained, twitching body with my claws and ate his blood-dripping organs one by one, liver, kidneys, lungs, heart, reveling in his screams." Asche took another step forward, which brought them so close their bodies almost touched. "And the soul for dessert."

Involuntarily, Vindt's gaze went to the Singer's mouth. He imagined, almost saw, Sikandem's blood dripping from it. As if in response, Asche languidly licked his lips. The sight had an immediate effect on unexpected regions of Vindt's body.

"But regardless of our shared childhood memories." Asche took a step back; his voice returned to the placid tone from before. "I prefer to be addressed by my proper title."

"Of course, I'm sorry, Kvahad-thed." Vindt put emphasis on the last word.

He spent the rest of the journey cursing in silence.

CHAPTER 12

By the time they set up camp in the evening, Vindt had mostly overcome his sulking and was more keen on finding out what the hell had happened today. A Verdur *and* demons. Ask Ehlan? He was almost certain he wouldn't get an answer, at least not one he liked. Since no one was talking about it, Vindt didn't dare to raise the subject in front of the others either. He needed one of them alone, Narr preferably, risking a knife between his legs. Or Risi.

The moment presented itself earlier than expected.

When Calveen assigned Risi to the first night watch, in a moment of presence of mind, Vindt volunteered to keep him company. The seneschal's face crumpled into a scowl, but before he had the chance to say anything, Risi's hand landed on Vindt's shoulder in a bone-crushing slap.

"Fantastic," he exclaimed, grinning from ear to ear and exposing two rows of crooked teeth.

Calveen continued to glower at Vindt, but there was not much he could say.

Vindt had never minded night watches. He had always gotten by on very little sleep. As a kid, he had habitually roamed the castle's nocturnal halls and corridors, out of insomnia but also because he chose to. He liked the silence, its special quality, or perhaps rather the change of sounds. In the darkness, awareness differed from daytime, senses became altered, refined; it was like transforming into another being. Among the many nicknames Vindt bore as a child, his nocturnal ventures had earned him the sobriquet of wraith.

There it was, another memory of home.

Vindt groaned. After Silhorveen had bound him, he had put a lot of willpower into burying the memories of his former life deep in his mind. For whatever reason, his miraculous resurrection had cracked the carefully cultivated layer of clay on top. Ever since, fragments of the past came slithering into his awareness at the most inopportune moments, called forth by the smell of horse dung, by the angle the light fell through the foliage of one of the scarce trees, by the noise of plates scraping stone. Or, like now, attracted by the sounds and smells of the night.

Vindt tried to push them back. Risi had gone to pee, but would be back any minute, and he had a job to do.

But the memories persisted. Perhaps it was the night; perhaps he was weary. Faces and voices appeared at random, only to be almost immediately replaced by others. Kelden, the son of their stable master who was born on the same day as Vindt and who he had grown up with, more brotherly than his two real brothers, notably older than himself.

He remembered Forrowar, the stallion he had trained himself from when he was a foal and who had nearly killed him once, the heated argument he had with his father to not sell the destrier, which would have brought in a notable sum. He thought of the lazy turn of windmill wings, of the sensation of his hands plunged into a sack of rye flour, of the rich smell of broken earth and the feel of a bow against his shoulder while scouring the woods for wild boar or deer in autumn.

Revdt came to his mind, his second-eldest brother, telling him the story of their grandmother, who was the first —and last—woman to lead the Great Hunt after the death of her husband.

It all entailed not a feeling of loss, but of profound regret.

In contrast to Revdt, Vindt had never had the urge to see the world, let alone live elsewhere than on the island he grew up on. He *had* traveled. Age fifteen, he spent two years as a squire at the Pel court, and later, another year in Leruv. He had gone raiding across the sea with his brothers or on trade missions with his father. Still, it would never have crossed his mind to leave Kärö like Revdt had when he turned nineteen. It didn't bother him that he would never rule. In fact, he had always shirked away from the weight of responsibility and the boredom of politics. He would have been happy to work for Keronn, his oldest brother, once he became lord, oversee trade and tributes and otherwise spend his time on the back of one of his horses or at sea, and someday, perhaps, teach his kids to ride, sail and hold a sword.

Only now that he had lost it did he realize how he had taken all that for granted: the people, the windmills, the rain, the sea, the tranquil prospect of his life.

"Thanks for the company, man," Risi's voice pulled Vindt out of his reminiscences. "Appreciate it." Risi lowered himself onto one of the logs they had dragged over to the fire earlier.

"My pleasure." Vindt tried to give his voice a cheerful tone as he forced the memories back into the dark corner they belonged in.

Risi's eyeballs and white shirt stood out from the surrounding darkness, moving as if detached from an actual body. At that moment, the clouds parted and a ray of moonlight reflected off the many rings in the man's ear. Vindt's gaze fastened on the one which marked the loss of his freedom. Not for the first time, he wondered how Risi had ended up in slavery. Given his features and skin tone, it was apparent he came from Sro-Hak, the Forgotten Isles or one of the surrounding lands. He could still have been born at The Haven. Singers bought new slaves on their journeys all the time. Sometimes they ended up there, married and had children. Risi's mother or father could have been one of them.

But, as had become clear on the day they met, Risi had never been to The Haven. Also, he spoke Lyskú fluently, but with an accent, and sometimes he made mistakes. The many earrings and the grayish tattoos on his broad arms were further signs that the man had once belonged to a different culture.

"You're from Sro-Hak?" Vindt deemed that an innocuous question to start a conversation, at least compared to those about today's attack that he was aiming at.

"Sali Sa."

"That's—"

"One of the Forgotten Isles. Not a paradise with wine fountains and naked women in abundance, but still quite nice." He winked.

Vindt felt a stab of guilt for having lied about growing up at The Haven. It was too late to correct that now, and besides, he still didn't want to talk about his past. Shortly, they would arrive at The Haven, and then they would part anyway.

"How'd you get into Asche's service?" he asked, hastily adding, "If I may ask."

"Sure. Ain't got no secrets. The guy who owned me before had me working as a penny fighter. The Kvahad-thed saw me fight and bought me on the spot. And glad he did." Pride suffused his voice.

Penny fighter. Vindt had never heard the term, but he knew what Risi meant. Dueling for money. In Pel, they had called men like him by a dozen different names, blade mongrels, bleeders—the name referring to the loss of money rather than of blood—duelers or spring knights. Their official name was probably prizefighters. His father had called them whores.

"How long ago was this?" Vindt asked.

"Can't remember. Over ten sun turns."

"And before? I mean, how'd you get into slavery?"

"Parents sold me."

"*What?*"

A movement in front of Vindt suggested Risi shrugged. "Happens all the time. Don't blame them. Surely had their reasons. Might've had it a lot worse, had they not."

That might be the healthiest way to look at it; still, parents selling their children into slavery was something Vindt found hard to fathom. They fell silent.

With their departure from the camp, they had also left the cicadas' soothing buzz behind. The unnerving sounds of the messenger birds had replaced it. Usually, the animals sat quietly in their cages, but the presence of their relatives in the other wagon seemed to provoke them into lively conversations, preferably at night.

However, the birds' intermittent cackling was less disturbing than Silhorveen's groans.

Another of the Singer's wails made them both twitch. Even the messenger birds interrupted their annoying cackling for a moment, frightened or listening for a hidden message. An excellent opportunity perhaps to change the subject. Vindt wondered how to phrase his next question, so it didn't seem like he had no clue what had happened today, but couldn't think of anything and decided to simply get to the point.

"What happened today?"

"What d'you mean?"

"We were attacked by a Verdur *and* demons."

"Uh, that..." Risi averted his eyes. "Well, we bested them."

"You've been attacked by a Verdur and demons before?"

"Well, hmm, yes. Been a while."

"Why?"

"It's in their nature, ain't it?"

"But why together?"

Risi chuckled nervously. "Vindt, man, you ask strange questions. Don't know. Need to ask the Kvahad-thed."

"And your weapons... You drew your swords, and Jun, he... I think he killed a demon with his bow."

"Oh. Haven't noticed that. Good boy." Risi nodded. "Excellent archer."

"You cannot fight demons with steel." It sounded a little more aggressive than Vindt had intended. "Not with any weapon."

Risi watched him for a moment before saying, "Ain't no normal steel." He unsheathed his sword.

Vindt heard the same squeaking sound of rusty hinges as when he'd pulled Narrapemet's scimitar from its scabbard. This time, he was sure it was not a product of his imagination.

Risi held out the blade to him. It was made of the same white metal as Narr's scimitar. The color was visible even in the darkness, as if bathed in its own light. It didn't illuminate its surroundings.

"What is it?" Vindt asked.

"No idea. The Kvahad-thed had it made for us. But whatever, it fights demons. Verdurs, too. You don't have one?"

"Verdurs?"

"Well, in a way. It's not like what it does to demons, and it's nothing compared to the Kvahad-thed's song, but, well... kind of damage it does. Enough to defend us, I reckon, although, well, they've never attacked us so far."

The blade was not entirely white, or it was, but not evenly. The change of color formed a pattern, another variation of the sinuous shapes the Singers decorated their world with. Only in this case, they were white instead of black. The longer Vindt looked, the clearer the lines became. They also seemed to turn three-dimensional, suggesting an impossible depth to the blade.

"May I touch it?"

"But don't do it too long. It'll give you a... well, just don't."

Vindt wondered what that meant, but his curiosity won over his trepidation. He ran his fingers over the strange material. It felt warm, and there was a slight, almost imperceptible vibration—no, rhythmic concussions, like... a heartbeat.

Hastily, Vindt withdrew his fingers. They had gone numb, the entire hand. He moved his fingers in alarm.

"Don't worry. It'll go away in a minute." Risi sheathed the sword again.

"You all have these swords?"

Risi's eyes nodded.

Vindt was more confused than before. If these swords and scimitars and arrows could fight Verdurs, at least to some extent, why had Silhorveen not possessed them? Unless...

"Do all members of the High Council have these weapons?"

Risi gave a quiet chuckle. "Sorry, but I'll have to pass again. Asche's the only Singer I know. Does it matter? We've got them. But from your questions and the look on your face, I take it you don't have a sword like that?"

Vindt shook his head.

"Ask the Kvahad-thed for one."

Yes. When the sun rose in the west. Vindt was not even sure he wanted a sword like that.

One with a heartbeat.

CHAPTER 13

Asche had not bothered to tell him where the Door was, but they were heading due north. After a week of travel, bushes and trees grew in greater numbers; sometimes they even afforded the luxury of shade. Traffic was sparse. The few riders overtaking them or traveling parties approaching from the opposite direction eyed them with unconcealed curiosity. Vindt was not surprised. Even without flagging their identity as a Singer's host, their sheer number, two wagons and more than a dozen well-armed men, was no common sight. They were a peculiar travel party besides.

Most of Silhorveen's retinue, as well as Jun and Layyad, blended in more or less with the copper-skinned, dark-haired people that populated this part of the world. Everyone else sported at least one feature or a combination of a few that let them stand out among the locals like poppies in a wheat field. Risi, with his enormous muscular body and his dark skin, and Vindt himself, with his blond hair and at that moment not so fair skin, were probably only topped by Kishoon and his sister, with their strange clothing and armor, their exotic features and the fact that Narrapemet was a woman-at-arms.

Vindt was used to people staring. Far more curious was that Asche himself drew fewer looks than Vindt would have expected, fewer even than Silhorveen. His aura of power seemed to have vanished, too. Perhaps Vindt had gotten used to it in the meantime, but he didn't think so. Asche could control his aura, raising or lowering it at will. Now, watching the eyes of the passersby slide off him like water off a duck's back, he wondered if Asche could even *invert* it, and make himself as inconspicuous as one of the passing peasants on their scrawny mules.

At midday, they sometimes sat down at an inn to eat, but to Vindt's dismay, never stayed overnight. Vindt wouldn't have minded sleeping in a proper bed for a change. Asche never joined them to eat at the inns, but went with Reisen to see to whatever business. Or to keep his precious Singer body from being crammed in with a bunch of vulgar, sweating, eating, chatting humans...

Fortunately, Asche showed as little interest in talking to Vindt as Vindt did in talking to Asche.

His streak of luck ended one afternoon when they were making camp, and Calveen stepped up to him. "The Kvahad-thed wants to see you."

Vindt groaned inwardly. "Asche? Why?"

"It's Kvahad-thed to you, and you'll find out when you go. Which is *now*."

Vindt opened his mouth to tell Calveen to fuck off, but managed to shut it before the words were out.

It was dark by the time Vindt entered Asche's tent. An oil lamp and several candles lit the interior; still, it felt like stepping into a dark lair. He expected to be met with a predator's sharp smell, but the only aromas reaching his nose were those of earth and burning wax and a whiff of something that reminded him of the ocean.

Someone had removed the fabric separating Asche's section from his Thyd's so that the tent's interior extended into one big room. In the shadows, Vindt glimpsed the Singer's bed. He wouldn't have been surprised had Asche donned his robes for the "audience," like on the day Vindt had first come to his tent. But he was still in the travel clothes he had been wearing ever since leaving Plotliw's camp. He was contemplating a board with wooden figurines which looked faintly like a chess game. If so, Asche was playing against himself. Vindt hoped he would lose.

"Kvahad-thed." He tried not to let his apprehension show, but a lump had lodged in his throat, flattening the words. He never felt comfortable in a Singer's presence, but something about Asche frayed his nerves in a different way.

The Singer languidly turned to him by turning the entire chair around. The candles illuminated one half of his face now, the other lying in darkness.

Lord Tehered, the demon king, Vindt couldn't help but think again. He stifled the nervous laugh the idea threatened to pull from his throat, but failed to keep the corners of his mouth from twitching.

"I'm happy to see my presence always cheers you up," Asche said promptly. "A scarce phenomenon. Normal humans are gripped by irrational fear as soon as they lay eyes on me."

Normal humans—what was that supposed to mean? And their fear wasn't irrational. It was most healthy. Unable to miss the gleam that had ignited in Asche's eyes, Vindt couldn't shake the notion he had again carelessly spoiled the meeting before it even began.

"You wished to see me?" he said, in an attempt to guide Asche's attention back to whatever whims had prompted him to summon him.

Asche's reaction was silence and his perpetual stare. Vindt forced himself to return it. It wasn't mere defiance, but a prey's primal instinct not to let the predator out of sight. Silhorveen had never looked at him for longer than a few seconds. In fact, he had made a point of pretending he didn't exist. It had riled Vindt up often enough. Now, he realized he preferred Silhorveen's ignorance over Asche's piercing attention.

After what seemed an eternity, Asche rose with the same gracious movement as he had the day he gave Vindt his blood. And with the same languid prowl, he sauntered toward him. Vindt tried to read from his face what might be coming, but the Singer's features were schooled into the usual impervious mask.

As soon as he reached him, Asche held out his hand. "May I?"

"May you... what?"

"See the pendant." His gaze dropped to Vindt's chest.

The amulet. A memory flashed through Vindt's mind, the Singer's eyes turning to him during the demon attack the moment the amulet started to vibrate, activated by the demons' presence. He had forgotten about it.

His resistance was almost physical. He'd carried the amulet since he was born. His father had had it made for him by the priests, like the ones made for Vindt's two elder brothers upon their birth. Even though the priests received no little money for it, the amulet was a favor, a gift from Gaal, nothing one could simply buy, a symbolic part of her shield. The protection charm embedded into it was sacred, centuries-old magic solely known to Gaal's priests. It worked, Vindt knew. The few times demons had attacked him, they had never touched him. He had felt the amulet's power and how the demons shied away from it.

Did Asche plan to take it away from him? Because he wouldn't tolerate any magic besides his own, magic like this, pure and holy, from the gods? Vindt didn't even want the Singer to look at it, or worse, desecrate it with his touch.

But what did it matter what he wanted?

Gritting his teeth, he pulled the amulet from beneath his shirt and held it up. Asche didn't bother to ask what it was for, but took it between his fingers and sang quietly. The rune engraved on its surface glowed. Though Vindt knew the amulet was useless against Singers, he nourished the irrational hope that Asche would at least suffer a blow.

He didn't.

The corner of Asche's lips slowly lifted as the gleam from before ignited in his eyes. Then, without warning, he threw his head back and laughed.

The sparkling sound caught Vindt as profoundly off guard as it had the first time he heard it, weeks ago. He soon snapped out of it. Ire took over. Mocking a gift from Gaal meant mocking the goddess herself. He jerked the pendant from the Singer's grip and stuffed it back under his shirt.

Asche's laughter stopped as abruptly as it had started. "Do you know what this is?" Amusement imbued his voice.

"A token from my goddess," Vindt spat.

"Your goddess... Gaal, no?"

Her name coming from Asche's mouth sounded just as blasphemous as his laughter.

Vindt was hardly surprised the Singer knew about Gaal. Ehlan had surely told him where he came from, and Singers had an eerie knowledge about the world and its cultures.

"This is *not* a trinket. It works. It has protected me many times." He didn't know why he was even bothering to try and convince Asche of the amulet's nature, its value.

"Oh, I don't doubt that."

To Vindt's irritation, the Singer began to circle him. The movement brought back his initial trepidation, momentarily pushed to the background by the surge of fury. He clamped down on the urge to rotate to keep the Singer in front of him. Only his head tilted. "Does that mean I can keep it?"

"Oh, of course," Asche said behind his back. "Did you fear I would take it from you? No, no. I'm glad you're wearing it."

The words didn't hold any apparent mockery, but what else should they be?

Fine. Are we done then?

The Singer continued to circle him.

Since Vindt had drunk his blood, Asche's aura of power didn't feel as menacing and oppressive as before, rather tentative, reaching out for him with soft fingers, a being of its own, which sensed Asche's blood in his veins and longed to reunite with its severed part. Vindt throbbed with the craving to get away from it, yet something inside him sought the touch. He hated that something.

With every circle, his apprehension grew. The amulet had apparently only been an opening act. This was about something else.

Eventually, the Singer stopped his prowl in front of him and cocked his head. "So?"

"So?" Vindt repeated, his voice strained by equal parts trepidation and annoyance.

"Why didn't you loose the arrow?"

For a moment, Vindt had no clue what Asche was referring to. Then the ground opened up, a gaping hole sucking the blood from his body and refilling his veins with an icy draft from its depths.

Impossible. He cannot know. This is it. I'm dead. Erratic thoughts popped into his head, vanishing and reappearing. He rummaged through his mind for something to say, anything to get his neck out of the noose, but apart from the repeating words, his brain was barren.

The Singer's gaze was a constant, dark weight, his expression inscrutable. The lack of hints about what was going on in his mind drove Vindt mad. Silhorveen's rage after Vindt's arrow struck him had screamed from every inch of his face, from the way he held his body, his every gesture. Admittedly, Asche didn't have an arrow stuck in his back, but Vindt was certain Silhorveen's reaction had been no different than had he caught him merely trying to kill him. The worst of all crimes, and worse committed by a Thyd.

Through the panic's suffocating grip, regret at not having loosed the arrow worked its way into Vindt's veins again. Even if he had failed, he could at least have tried, done something, *acted*. Sometimes he wondered if his true motivation for having tried to kill Silhorveen ten years ago was not his hatred but the desire to, for one moment, escape the cage of impotence they had locked him in.

"I didn't... shoot," he eventually croaked.

"I'm aware of that. But again: Why?" There was a hint of thoughtfulness to Asche's voice, as if he were genuinely interested in the answer. "It was so convenient. I had my back to you. No one was paying you any attention. Afraid to fail again and be punished?"

Again? Did he know about Silhorveen?

"Please. I didn't mean to kill you. I just…" Vindt didn't know what to say. What did it matter why he didn't carry through with his plan? He had raised a bow at a Singer's back with murderous intent—enough to earn him whatever punishment Asche deemed appropriate. Aside from chaining him with another bracelet.

His hand went to his bare wrist. The Singer's gaze followed the movement. Before Vindt could react, Asche reached out and pushed up the sleeve, exposing the wrist. The skin, sheltered for a decade from the sun, looked as smooth and vulnerable as a baby's. Casually, Asche rested a thumb on the conspicuous vein. Vindt felt his pulse race against the finger, like some tiny creature trying to escape its prison. The need to yank his hand back was overpowering.

Asche's cool eyes rose to meet Vindt's. "Did you know that after you tried to shoot Silhorveen, he sought permission from the High Council to kill you and get himself a new Thyd?"

Vindt paled. His pulse hammered desperately against the Singer's thumb.

"We rejected it, of course," Asche continued, stroking the thin layer of Vindt's skin as if he wasn't aware of what he was doing. "Did you know?"

Not sure his voice would obey, Vindt shook his head. No, he had not known. Would it have mattered? He had expected to be killed back then, even longed for it. The bracelet was worse. Or so he had thought, oblivious of Thrithid at the time.

Fear pulled at his nerves, but from deep down, something else bubbled up. Silhorveen had reported the incident to the High Council. That meant Asche had *known* about Vindt's attempt to kill him, and thus about the bracelet keeping him from trying again, all this time. And to judge from the lack of surprise at the sight of Vindt's bare wrist, he was aware too that the cuff had vanished. And like this, *knowing*, he had handed Vindt his weapons and ordered him into his guard during the battle.

He yanked his hand free and shook it as if he could shake off the touch. "So you knew," he spat. "All this time. Even so, you handed me my weapons and put me behind your back. What was that? A test? A game? Did you hope for me to shoot? Are you disappointed I didn't?"

His words weren't merely childish bravery. A part of him longed for punishment, for physical pain, for anything that meant escaping the feeling of being a toy in a cat's playful grip. What else was this but a game? A Singer from the High Council. Or merely Asche. Silhorveen had been cruel sometimes, but straight, predictable. He didn't play. That gleam in Asche's eyes. A bored, overfed cat looking for entertainment.

Asche's only reaction to Vindt's outburst was his continuous dark stare. The void in it fueled Vindt's fury further. His hands itched with the need to crack that mask. "Come on, let's get it over with," he hissed. "I tried to kill you. Punish me. It's what you ca—"

"Stop." Asche's voice was quiet, almost soft, but it silenced Vindt as if someone had gagged him. "If it was a test, it was a test. If it was a game, it was a game. If I decide to punish you, I will do it when I want to. I asked you a question. Why didn't you shoot?"

Vindt glared at the Singer. "Because I'm a coward."

"Don't." The same quiet voice, sharp and slicing in its softness.

"Don't what?"

"Lie. I'll ask you one last time, why didn't you shoot?"

Vindt averted his eyes from Asche's piercing stare. He opened his mouth and shut it again. What should he say? The truth was, he didn't know. Why didn't he shoot?

The heart...

"I don't know." Vindt studied the flattened patch of grass under his feet. There was no need to look up to feel the unwavering weight of Asche's gaze. He expected him to insist, to continue pressing for "the truth." But the taut silence merely stretched on. Vindt stroked his wrist in another vain attempt to get rid of the imprint of Asche's thumb on his exposed veins.

"You're... strange," Asche said at length, his voice as devoid of emotion as his face.

Vindt almost laughed. The question of which of them was stranger was debatable. "Are you going to request my death from the High Council now too?" he asked scathingly. He didn't know what drove him.

"I *am* the High Council—did you forget?"

You're a fucking part of it, you arrogant bastard.

"Then what's the verdict?"

"Being you seems to be a punishment in its own right." Asche strolled back to his chair and sat. "I pity the Singer who will have to put up with you in the future."

What?

Vindt's hands twitched, eager to draw his dagger and throw himself upon the Singer in an actual attempt to kill him. Or at least crack that mask.

He closed his eyes and concentrated on his breath. The dark gaze resting upon him incessantly, watching, feeding, did not shorten the time it took him to calm down. He waited for Asche's next move, the strike. Nothing came.

Asche's last sentence made it back into his awareness. "So I'm going to be assigned to another Singer? When?"

"I told you the Council has yet to decide your fate. And... investigate your resurrection."

"What does that mean? You know I have no memories."

"Which complicates the matter. But someone or something got you out, and some of us are keen to find out what or who."

"What's your theory?"

The corners of Asche's lips lifted almost imperceptibly. "Perhaps your goddess rescued you, so you could take revenge."

Vindt paled. It was what he had been thinking.

He can't read minds like that.

Asche's voice took on the bored tone of before. "Or it's one of those million strange things which just *happen*. A question of statistics. In a thousand of years, why wouldn't a Thyd resurrect?" He made a lazy gesture with his hand. "You're dismissed."

What? That was it? No punishment, no bracelet, nothing? Asche had only summoned him to demonstrate his universal knowledge, make a show of his sky-high superiority. To play with his fear and helplessness.

Burn in hell, Vindt thought, realizing at the same moment that Asche would do exactly that. Only, unfortunately, not now. It would be a lie to say he wasn't afraid of what the High Council would decide to do with him, but it could hardly be worse than Asche's presence.

"When will we reach the Door?"

Asche's lips curled into a knowing smile. "Soon enough."

Right. Vindt turned to go, but Asche called him back. "One more thing. I think I would feel a little more... comfortable not having to suspect an arrow pointing at my back all the time. How can we ensure this?"

Don't worry. The next arrow, I'll shove directly up your ass.

"I could, of course, put another bracelet around your wrist. But that would be a little... boring, wouldn't it?" The glitter in the depths of his eyes flared. "Why don't you swear by your goddess?"

An inarticulate sound escaped Vindt's throat, somewhere between a laugh and a choke. Gaal—the man was sick.

"To me, that means nothing, of course," Asche continued placidly. "But to you, it would mean a great deal, would it not? An invisible bracelet."

The urge to pull out his dagger and ram it between the Singer's gleaming eyes almost kept Vindt from breathing.

"So?"

Vindt closed his eyes. No choice. As usual.

Gaal, forgive me.

"I swear by Gaal I won't... I won't point an arrow at your back again," he hissed through clenched teeth, the words barely understandable.

Asche smiled. "I'll take the pointing arrow as a symbol, encompassing any threat to my life."

"Fine," Vindt snapped. "Can I go now?"

"In a minute." Again that glittering spark in the depths of Asche's dark eyes. "How about, as a sign of meeting

actions to intentions and, say, as a seal to our contract, you...
changed your braid?"

Vindt paled. Gaal, he knew even that. Was there no end
to this?

His braid. A reminder of another life, his past, his
beliefs. The embodiment of his vengeance. A flag for the
ones who had fallen. A goal. What would he be without it?
The slave they always wanted him to be.

*Damn, Vindt, get a hold of yourself. It's nothing, just
hair. Changing your appearance won't change a thing about
how you feel. About what you are. Play along. It doesn't
matter.*

Vindt's knuckles cracked. His nod was barely a
movement at all.

Asche leaned back in his chair. The flickering light of the
candles danced on one half of his newly unreadable face.
"Good night, Thyd."

Before Vindt could say or do something he would regret,
he stormed out of the tent.

CHAPTER 14

"Your hair's different." Narr smiled at him.

So much for Vindt's hopes no one would notice the changed braid.

He was the last for breakfast. The question of which braid he should weave his hair into had kept him inside the tent for quite a while. Eventually, he had put it into the simplest that occurred to him, one without meaning, the way Kishoon and Narr wore it. But then he had changed his mind again and made the one worn by people in mourning. If Asche knew about the meaning of the braids in Pel, he would recognize it. The Singer could hardly say anything about him displaying his grief over people he'd lost. It wasn't vengeance. But still a statement.

"I liked the other one," Narr said. "It looked complicated. I always thought it must take you ages to braid it. But it was also very pretty." She smiled again.

Women. They could wrap themselves in armor and let a dozen scimitars dangle from their waists, and still they would notice someone changing their *hairdo*. Vindt couldn't refrain from casting a surreptitious look toward Layyad, who was following their conversation with narrowed eyes.

"I've always wondered if it had a special meaning," Narr went on.

"No." *Gaal, could she drop the subject already?* "It's just... You're right. This one's more practical." Which would have been true, had braiding the other one not become such a routine in the past decade, he could do it asleep. It had almost taken him longer to make this one. A sudden idea quickened his pulse. He aimed for a casual tone as he said, "Do you want me to braid your hair the way I had it before?"

Layyad perked up.

"Oh." Narr's face brightened. "Would you do that?"

"Of course." Vindt hid his excitement behind a smile. Narr wore her hair shaved at the sides. It wouldn't be the exact same braid as Vindt's, but... close.

Narr was already eagerly pulling the leather ribbon from her braid.

Vindt cast a look at Asche's tent. He had not seen the Singer yet, so he was probably still inside. But he might come out at any moment.

"Inside?" Vindt asked, pointing his chin toward the servant tent.

Layyad gave a grunt. Narr merely glowered at him and got up.

Vindt followed her. On his way, he glanced again at Asche's tent, his lips curling.

You can play? Fine. I can, too.

* * *

They entered the foothills of a mountain range and the terrain became steeper, the road bumpier. Vindt would have cherished the rocky walls rising on either side of the road for their shade—if they had not formed the perfect places for an ambush.

In the past decade, attacks on their small band had been frequent. Singers didn't conceal their wealth. It was apparent in the quality of their horses, their equipment, their garments, their weapons. Splendor called for greed. And recklessness. None of the attackers had survived the endeavor, so Vindt didn't get to ask questions and confirm his theory. But he assumed the attackers were oblivious to the existence of Singers, didn't recognize Silhorveen as one, were foolish idiots or very desperate. Since no one in Asche's retinue had donned the usual colorful, pattern-laced clothes which heralded a Singer's host, they formed an even more vulnerable target.

Vindt wasn't the only one eyeing the ridges with a frown. At one point, Layyad took the wagon's reins from Jun, who stayed beside him on the coach box, bow in one hand, an arrow at the ready in the other. The others too kept one hand on their bows, gazes fixed on the looming mass of rocks. Vindt was about to get his own bow from the wagon when he hesitated.

I think I would feel a little more comfortable not having to suspect an arrow pointing at my back all the time.

Right. And since I swore by Gaal...

Vindt left the weapon where it was.

Narr couldn't braid her hair herself, so Vindt took care of it for her every time it came undone. He did it in the open now, to reassure Layyad that Narr's only body part he touched was her hair, and that nothing but discomfort motivated the occasional grunts she made during the procedure.

When Asche had emerged from his tent that morning, he had skimmed Vindt's new braid with a smile only visible to Vindt, a dagger of glee gliding softly into his guts. The hatred it triggered became suffused a moment later with his own dark mirth as Narr's braid caught the Singer's eyes. Asche hesitated almost inconceivably; his forehead creased into the shadow of a frown. When his glance turned back, it was with the gleam Vindt had spotted many times now, a sign of demonic life in the desert of his features. For a second, Vindt even believed he saw the corners of his lips twitch. Then the Singer turned and walked up to his demon mare, who was waiting saddled and bridled beside Risi.

Vindt didn't bother to quell his own smile.

* * *

Early-morning sun filtered through the leaves of the trees surrounding their campsite. Vindt took a bite of his flatbread. Jun had baked it yesterday on the hot stones after the fire had burned down to embers. He still found it strange that someone cooked for him. He, Fora and the others, even Ehlan, had taken turns preparing meals. Of course, some did it more often than others, but still.

When Vindt asked Jun if Asche had taken him on to be his chef, however, Jun shook his head. "Nah. Just like it. And I prefer my meals to be edible." At this, he cast a meaningful look at the others.

After breakfast, Vindt helped to take down the tents and stow them in the wagon, along with the rest of their gear. It surprised him how fast Asche's servants had integrated him into their daily chores. Ehlan, Fora and the others were still with them, but Vindt hardly talked to them. It felt as if he'd left them long ago.

"Vindt, man." Risi. Vindt recognized the broad man by his voice and the crushing weight of his paw, which landed on Vindt's shoulder almost every time he addressed him. "Could you fetch the beasts from—"

He didn't get any further.

From the corners of his eyes Vindt perceived movement. A faint rustle sounded. A second later, an arrow struck Risi's upper arm while another pierced Vindt's shoulder. Vindt gasped. Risi swore and, with another curse, ripped the arrow from his flesh.

Vindt's gaze darted around only to find half a dozen men emerging from the trees. More were moving beneath the canopy's shadows.

Good Gaal, they were being attacked *again*, this time not by creatures from the underworld but by people, humans.

Vindt's hand instinctively reached for his sword, but Asche's voice was already rising into the air. For once, Vindt was glad for its lethal effect, though the rage in Asche's song made the hairs on his arms stand on end. It was... more than rage, the need for punishment, for... revenge?

Song or not, standing in the middle of the clearing made Vindt a prime target. A little belatedly, he followed Risi's example and dropped to the ground. A second later, another arrow struck the ground just inches from his face.

What the fuck is taking him so long?

Only a few days ago, Vindt had witnessed Asche taking down a fucking *army* within minutes. Surely, he could handle a few bandits?

Vindt turned just in time to see another arrow hurtling toward him. Before he could react it burst into flames. Following its trajectory, Vindt spotted the shooter. The man reached for another arrow. Before he could let it lose, Asche's song struck him. He erupted into flames, much like his arrow before him. He wasn't the only one—several attackers were now ablaze, filling the clearing with the stench of charred flesh and agonized screams.

Vindt rose to his feet and eventually drew his sword, though apart from the writhing flames of the man-shaped torches nothing seemed to be moving anymore. The screams had ceased too. Vindt spun around, but found no attackers left alive.

Great.

But... what about their own men?

Alarmed, Vindt scanned the area again. Risi was rising beside him, cursing again. The others were gathered near Asche's tent. Narr stood wide-eyed with her scimitar drawn, seemingly unharmed. Jun and Kishoon were clutching parts of their bodies, faces contorted in pain. Vindt heaved a sigh of relief. Wounds didn't matter. Asche would heal them in no time.

He was about to relax when his eyes fell on a motionless body sprawled on the ground at the edge of the clearing. He stared at the arrow protruding from the chest, waiting for the body to stir.

It didn't.

Slowly, Vindt drew closer. Unlike the arrow which had struck him, the one stuck in Reisen's body had hit home: chest, left side, between the third and fourth ribs. No chance. Terror sprouted from Vindt's own unharmed heart and conquered him like ice crystals covering a windowpane.

He crouched and reached out to the exposed throat, seeking proof of something he knew there would be no proof of.

Before he could touch the vein, someone yanked his hand back.

"Don't touch him," Asche hissed. "All of you, step back. Don't get close to him."

By now, the others had drawn nearer too, faces white, eyes wide, forming a ring around the man on the ground. Puzzlement found its way into their expressions at Asche's order, but they obeyed, a well-trained reflex to the Singer's demanding voice.

Reisen. A Thyd. Dead. Or not.

Vindt heard his own blood roaring in his ears. He didn't know exactly what he would see now, *how* it would happen. Only the ultimate state was familiar, Silhorveen's skull-like face that still haunted him in his dreams. He was sure he didn't *want* to witness it. The desire to turn and run, to hide, was overwhelming. Yet he remained standing, transfixed, staring.

The ground vibrated almost imperceptibly. Noises drifted in, a multitude of voices, whispering to each other in no language known to humans. The grass around the body withered, turning brown, then black, as if consumed by an unknown disease. Mist crept out of the blackened earth. The outline of the body blurred. The whispers grew louder, excited, joyful, triumphant.

Vindt recognized those voices, not consciously, but something inside him knew. Though he couldn't discern the words, he understood what they were saying, the glee, the teasing, their claim to this soul and the promise of what they would do to it in the hours, days, years, maybe centuries to come.

How was it? Reisen's voice in his head from only a few days ago.

At this point, Vindt reached the limits of what he could bear. He spun around and strode away, paying no attention to where he was going. He reached a wagon and pressed his hand against the rough wood for support, bending over, waiting, *wishing* for his stomach to get rid of its contents. But it didn't. He retched and retched some more, but his body refused to surrender to his mind's craving.

How was it?

Vindt lowered himself to the ground, leaned his back against the wheel and hid his face in his hands.

He didn't know how long he had been sitting like that when someone crouching down in front of him made him look up. Asche's face was as pale as bone, the lips pressed together into two bloodless lines. The dark, burning glow in the black eyes would have made Vindt recoil, had it not been for the wheel at his back.

"You're wounded." Asche sounded as if he wanted to strangle him.

Vindt had forgotten about the arrow hitting his shoulder. It was gone, so he must have pulled it out at some point. A red circle framed the hole in his shirt. Now that he focused on it, the wound's pulsing pain reached his consciousness.

Silhorveen had healed him a dozen times from all kinds of wounds, knife cuts, a broken leg, a rusty nail stuck in his foot. In the beginning, it had disgusted him, but eventually he gave up his resistance. Not only was it pointless, he had learned to find the service rather practical.

However, the idea of *Asche* healing him filled him with dread.

"It's nothing." He pulled the shoulder back.

"Take off your shirt." The Singer's voice brooked no disobedience, and Vindt did as he was told.

Asche's gaze grazed over his chest before it fastened on the wound. It was only a second, but enough for Vindt to become overly aware of his honey-colored skin, the curly blond hair, the scar on his right breast, his nipples, whose light brown seemed to have darkened as well under Guzzar's blazing sun. It took him a lot of effort not to put the shirt back on.

Asche placed his cool fingers next to the wound and sang. The familiar tug spread beneath Vindt's skin, the warmth. He turned his face in the direction he'd come from. The body was gone. An elliptic patch of blackened grass marked the spot where it had lain. He wondered where they had put him. In the wagon next to Silhorveen, probably. Singer and Shadow, side by side, as it should be. Except those two didn't belong together. It was he, Vindt, who was supposed to be lying there.

How was it?

An inarticulate whimper escaped his lips.

Asche stopped singing. "Am I hurting you?" It sounded like, "I want to hurt you."

Vindt shook his head, lips pressed together. He thought about crying. It was what people did when someone died. He had not cried in ages. He wouldn't now. He hardly knew Reisen. And yet, his death had shaken him to an extent he wouldn't have believed.

Vindt studied Asche's white face, the set jaw, the burning eyes. What was he feeling? Were Singers capable of feeling anything? Irateness, yes; it poured from Asche in suffocating waves. But anything else? Grief?

Vindt remembered Ehlan's words about Asche being *old*. He and Reisen could have been together for centuries, never far apart, day and night, every day of the year. He had always believed Singers wouldn't get attached to anyone, least of all humans. But if what Reisen had told him about Calveen was true, it might also hold true for Reisen himself, even more so.

The image of the burning archers came to his mind. The smell of charred flesh still filled the air. Asche had certainly already known by this time that Reisen was dead. Was this his way of expressing grief?

"I'm sorry," he heard himself say before he thought about it, as soon as Asche stopped singing.

The Singer's burning gaze bored into his. Impossible to know what he was thinking. "You don't need to rest your arm. It's fully functional."

He got up and walked away.

CHAPTER 15

Vindt relished the weight of the shovel, the texture of the smooth wooden handle, the sensation of his muscles contracting and relaxing. The metal made a scraping sound when he drove it into the earth. A thud followed when the soil landed on the existing pile. The sounds were good, pleasant, normal, distracting him from others. At some point, the hole became so deep he had to jump in to continue. Veins of sand and stones riddled the dark earth. Roots protruded from the walls.

His arms and back ached; blisters covered his hands. But he was unwilling to stop, glad to have something to do, something physical to keep his mind from wandering, his attention from turning to the groans. Silhorveen and Reisen lay in the wagon at the other side of the clearing. Their noises carried.

This was the last hole. Hole, or...

Vindt was not sure if he would call them graves. If they were even allowed to call them that. The Guzzar didn't bury their dead; they burned them. No matter what Vindt thought about that custom, it would have been the right thing to do, if only out of respect.

They had tried. But the burnt bodies, or rather the heaps of melted, charred flesh left of their attackers, would not burn again, as if everything the fire could consume was gone.

When Vindt asked Asche what they should do with the corpses, the Singer just spat, "Leave them, eat them, hang them from the trees as a warning. I don't care."

It was Vindt's idea to burn them and, when that didn't work, to dig the "graves." Friend or foe, it was a sin to leave the dead or their remnants to whatever roamed these mountains—animals, ghosts, demons.

"Finished?"

Kishoon was looking down on him from the edge of the hole. Sweat ran over his broad bare chest. An impressive scar stretched from his left nipple to his right hip. Someday, Vindt would ask Kishoon how he got it. Not today.

Vindt looked around. The hole was wide and deep enough to fit a few of the heaps of flesh. Thirteen, a lot. It was futile to ponder what had brought the men to attack. It was always the same anyway, their money, their horses, their possessions. Still, he wondered if they would have refrained from it had it been more obvious they were the host of a Singer.

Vindt climbed out of the hole and used the tip of the shovel to push the last remaining heap of attackers into it. Together, they filled the hole with earth. Vindt murmured a quick prayer, as he had for all the bodies. He was not sure whether he was doing this because he thought everyone deserved good wishes for their afterlife, regardless of their deeds in this life, or if those unknown souls were not even the subject of his prayers but a placeholder for the man Vindt wished to say them for.

No prayers would reach the place where *he* dwelled now.

They walked over to the creek. Vindt took his time to wash, submerging his body, cherishing the water's cool caress.

"Must go back," Kishoon said.

Vindt nodded. Kishoon had to return for the same reasons Calveen had only permitted one of them to help Vindt with the corpses. The death of his Thyd had left Asche helpless should it come to a Verdur attack. The strange white swords, scimitars and arrowheads were his only remaining means of defense now. Of course, anyone who owned one was not allowed to leave the Singer's side for long. Nor would they, even without Calveen ordering them to. Besides the grief, worry darkened their faces.

Vindt was worried about himself.

From the idea of Asche's sudden vulnerability to the next was only a tiny step, which—given the shock of Reisen's death—had taken him perhaps a little longer than it would have under different circumstances. But he had gotten there.

What did a Singer do when his Thyd got killed?

Travel to The Haven to get a new one.

If there was none available at the time?

Still go to The Haven and wait until they found another or until a youngster came of age. Verdurs didn't attack The Haven.

But The Haven, or rather the Door leading them to it, was still a two-week journey away. While Asche had a Thyd, free, alive, of age, right by his side.

That they would assign him to another Singer he had

known all along. The prospect had never cheered him up. But the idea of Asche becoming his new master made his skin crawl. The Singer disconcerted Vindt in a way he couldn't describe.

A chance remained it wouldn't happen. Asche was certainly as happy about making Vindt his Thyd as Vindt himself. *I pity the Singer who has to put up with you in the future*—he remembered the words well. If Asche had the opportunity to bind another Thyd, he would take it.

Besides, before Vindt could be bound to anyone, Silhorveen's blood had to leave his body, meaning he had to go through withdrawal. Asche had given him his blood only a few days ago. It would take at least six weeks for his body to clean it. Still, somehow, Vindt couldn't shake his trepidation.

His skin began to shrivel in the rushing water. Reluctantly, he sat up. He had to return.

How was it?

Vindt winced. He wondered if he would ever be able to banish the question from his head.

Or the face of the man who had asked it.

* * *

Night came, inevitably. The sounds of the day dying, silence crept in, not promising and soothing as before but menacing, paving the way for the noises mercifully shoved to the background by others in the past hours. Even the messenger birds didn't pick up their conversation, as if the presence of something different, disturbing, demanded their attention. Apart from the occasional forlorn call of a night bird, the groans and wails drifting into the night from inside Silhorveen's wagon became the only sounds on the stage.

Vindt had not even attempted to crawl into the tent and sleep. Instead, he sat close to the fire, immobile, listening. Every time a moment of silence reigned, he waited for the next groan, stiff, tense, as if expecting the next lash of a whip. And just like the imaginary comparison, his body twitched each time.

Although Silhorveen's erratic groans and wails had never ceased to affect him, in a way Vindt had grown accustomed to them, like one might get used to the itching of a never-healing wound. He had believed—or hoped—he would be prepared.

He wasn't.

Worst of all, he could distinguish between the two voices.

Whether it was a trick of his mind or not, the agony resonating in the sounds Reisen made, the despair, the fear, exceeded anything he ever believed to have perceived in Silhorveen's voice. It wasn't fair. Reisen was just *human*. Singers ending up in Thrithid was cruel, but it was part of their world, it *belonged* to them. Perhaps it was even punishment for using their dark skills, the price of their powers.

Humans, however, had nothing to do with it. The Gift, this strange physical condition, was nothing a Thyd chose; his service for a Singer was forced upon him.

But who cared?

Though Calveen had divided the others into two groups to take turns sleeping and keeping watch, no one went to bed. Those not patrolling Asche's tent sat with Vindt by the fire, staring into the flames, pale, wide-eyed, clutching parts of their bodies, or, like Narr, chopping away bark and wood from a twig. As soon as she had reduced one to the size of a finger, she dropped it and started over with another.

For the first time since he'd come to this country, Vindt felt cold.

"I can't stand it." Jun was the first to say out loud what everyone was thinking. "Please, someone make that stop, please. I can't, really, I can't." He curled up into a ball like a hedgehog, his upper arms pressed against his ears, his knees against his arms, rocking back and forth, whimpering.

"Jun," Narr started, but then lost the thread of what she had wanted to say, and only increased the force with which she attacked the piece of wood in her hand.

From the corner of his eye, Vindt saw movement. When he turned, it was the first time he actually watched Asche approach, rather than having him appear at their side out of nowhere.

Everyone rose. The pain in the others' eyes deepened as soon as they looked at the Singer.

"I'm sorry, Kvahad-thed," Jun mumbled. "I just... I just can't—"

"Bring me my ginsha." Asche's voice was so cold it made Vindt shiver.

Jun blinked at him for a moment before spinning around, hurrying toward the wagons. The others woke up from their daze as well; the veil which clouded their eyes cleared.

"May I... call the others?" Narrapemet asked.

Asche gave a curt nod.

After a moment, Narr returned with Risi, Layyad and Kishoon, who had been guarding the tent, and also Vaan, Fora and the rest of Silhorveen's retinue. Everyone took a seat around the fire, cautiously, as if attending a sacred ceremony. Their eyes were filled with pain, but also with something else, despair... hope?

Vindt had no idea what was going to happen. He had not understood what Asche had told Jun to fetch.

The Singer lowered himself onto the log Narr had been sitting on before. He sat motionless, staring into the flames, his face the familiar mask. There was a sudden frailty to his figure which Vindt had never seen before.

Jun returned, carrying a triangular wooden case that looked too heavy for him. Cautiously, he placed it at the Singer's feet. Asche opened it and took out... a harp. Gently, almost lovingly, he let his long pale fingers glide over the strings while he turned the pins in the frame to adjust the tuning. After a last run, he silenced the quivering strings with his palms.

The others' palpable anticipation had infected Vindt. His body was as tense as the chords beneath Asche's fingers.

But just as Asche moved his hands to play, a wail, louder and more painful than the previous ones, cut through the night. It warped the faces around the fire and rippled through people's bodies like waves breaking a lake's still surface after a stone's throw. Asche's hands stopped in mid-motion. His already pale face went a shade whiter. Before the sound faded, with sudden determination, he began to play and a moment later to sing.

Vindt's heart stopped, and with it the world.

Forgotten was the wailing, the body it came from, the fire, the others, the night, time, space, past, present and future.

It was not the Singer's cruel dark magic, it was song as Vindt had known it all his life, melody, music. Only, he had never heard music like this before. The tunes of the harp entwined with Asche's voice, engulfing his body, filling his soul. He was held, lifted and carried away. His flesh dissolved, his bones melted. He didn't care. The voice was everything left, all that mattered. Deliverance. Salvation.

He surrendered to it without resistance.

It took him a long moment to realize the music had stopped and Asche's voice no longer filled the air. The echo of it lingered, gently strumming his nerves, as the Singer's fingers had strummed the strings of his instrument a moment ago.

Vindt tried to recall what Asche had played—not the melody, he knew he would not be able to recall that, only whether it had been a sad or a joyful tune, fast or slow. But he couldn't. He had no idea what he had just witnessed. He felt like he was waking up from a dream whose story he'd forgotten but whose sensations lingered on, unconnected, forlorn. In the flickering firelight, the faces of the others looked absent, drugged; their cheeks were flushed.

They sat in absolute silence, no wind in the trees, no nocturnal animals scurrying through the underbrush, no bird calls. Even the gurgling of the creek and the crackling of the fire had fallen silent. And no groans.

Vindt had just thought it when another sound full of agony jolted everyone out of their reverie. Bodies tensed; pain returned to faces.

Asche straightened his back. His hands caressed the harp's strings once more, and a moment later his voice rose into the air again, soft and seductive, determined and demanding.

This time, when the song ended, before they had time to return to reality, before another groan could rip their illusory shelter apart, Asche sang again.

And again. And again.
He sang the entire night.

CHAPTER 16

Dawn must have come a while ago, but Vindt only noticed after the last note of Asche's last song had died away. Though he could no longer hear it, the melody prevailed, resonating in his body, his heart, his soul. His cheeks were wet. He knew he had been crying, noticed it in the process, not caring, not feeling embarrassed, just letting the tears run. Everyone else's eyes were red and swollen too.

Vindt longed for Asche to caress the harp's strings again, to continue singing. His entire being yearned to stay in that bubble the Singer's voice had created, let the melody envelop him, let the notes carry him away. Vindt realized a Singer could kill this way, holding his victims captive, making them forget to eat and drink, forget themselves, lost in rapture until their bodies gave out.

A beautiful way to die.

But it was over; Vindt knew Asche would not sing again. The Singer looked tired. He stared into the embers of the fire, eyes out of focus or focused on something Vindt couldn't see.

His first night together with Asche's retinue in Plotliw's camp came to Vindt's mind, when Asche had gone to silence the singing soldiers and the lute player.

It hurts his ears.

Of course it did.

Asche put the harp back into its case and rose, signaling to Calveen. The seneschal got up immediately. The two men walked a few steps away. Asche said something to the old man which Vindt couldn't hear, but at the words Calveen turned and glowered at Vindt.

Uneasiness spread beneath Vindt's skin, writhing and squirming like a living being.

Calveen walked toward Asche's tent, while the Singer came strolling back to the remnants of the fire. Their eyes met.

No, it's not possible. Reisen has just fallen. And I have to go into withdrawal first. It doesn't make sense.

"Layyad," Asche said, not taking his eyes off Vindt. "Your sword."

Without hesitation, Layyad unfastened the belt holding his sword and handed it to Asche.

"Take it," the Singer said to Vindt.

Vindt reached for the weapon without looking.

"Put it on. If we get attacked by anybody or anything, human or not, draw it. We are going for a walk."

At this, everyone rose.

"Just the two of us," Asche said.

The others shifted, their eyes darting back and forth between Asche and Vindt.

"But Kvahad-thed," Narrapemet began, "you can't... I mean, it's not wise—"

"I don't think we will be attacked. We're not going far."

Asche's eyes: deep, dark, pulling. "Come."

Asche turned and walked toward the edge of the clearing, the side opposite the one they had come from the day before yesterday. Vindt thought he couldn't move; he didn't *want* to move. However, his feet inched forward despite himself.

He had believed the path leading here from the main road would end at the clearing. Now, reaching the trees, he saw that it continued. It was much narrower here and so overgrown it was hardly recognizable. The rocky ground sloped steeply upward. After a few yards, it gave up its disguise as a path altogether and turned into stone steps, which, though cracked and bent, were a little too even to have formed naturally.

Asche set one foot before the other with certainty, never losing his balance on the uneven ground. Not once did he look back to check if Vindt was following.

Vindt gazed up the mountain to see where they were heading, but trees and bushes blocked the view. He concentrated on walking, one step at a time, on his labored breathing and the sweat trickling down his back.

It's not that. It can't be. He wants to show you something, tease you, whatever. Relax. Walk.

Watching the Singer's hands dangling by his sides, Vindt noticed with irritation that the fingertips were bleeding. Asche had been playing all night, plucking at the harp's metal strings with his delicate fingers; it was probably normal. But why didn't he heal them?

The steps ended, opening up into a plateau. To their left and on the opposite side, the mountain continued to rise. To their right, the ground dropped, offering a spectacular view of the foothills and a row of jagged mountains in the distance, but it was the pyramidal building in the plateau's center that caught Vindt's attention. It was so high he had to tilt his head back to see the top. Its walls climbed in terraces, each step the size of a man. Although Vindt had never seen such a building, it was obviously a temple.

Whatever deity people had venerated here, their worshippers had abandoned the place long ago. The stones were cracked and crumbling. Sections of the wall had come down in small avalanches. Bushes and trees grew everywhere. In the middle of the side facing the cliff, the giant steps split into smaller ones, forming a stairway more apt for human legs. It led up to a ledge and a half-buried hole in the wall, which seemed to have been the entrance portal.

"A Xixit temple," Asche explained before Vindt could ask. "There are more of them up the mountain." He pointed his chin toward the towering cliffs in the background.

"Xixit—that's the people or the god?" Vindt wasn't really interested, but as long as they talked history, nothing else would happen.

"The people. Their culture vanished over a thousand years ago."

For more than a thousand years of abandonment, the building was in amazing shape.

"They were excellent builders," Asche said, as if he'd read Vindt's thoughts.

"You've seen the temple when it was still intact?"

Asche's lips curled into a faint smile. "Nice try."

Vindt shrugged. It *had* been an attempt to get at Asche's age.

"What god did they worship?"

"The sun. The moon. A pity you didn't live back then. You would surely have been elected as high priest."

Vindt frowned, unable to grasp the meaning of the last sentence.

Asche didn't elaborate, but looked him in the eye. Despite his unease, Vindt returned the gaze stubbornly, only to realize Asche was not looking *into* his eyes, but *at* them.

Could it be...? No, that was impossible. Asche had known him for less than a month; Vindt's eyes had not even made a full turn. It took people years to notice the color changing. Most never did. From gray to deep green and back in a moon's cycle.

"Moon child," Asche said.

He knew.

In Pel, they called people like Vindt *växling*, changeling, or, depending on the character of the person talking, *svika*, deceiver. He'd heard the term *moon child* before, but not very often. It was the most beautiful name.

"You're lucky you didn't end up in Gaal's holy fire," Asche said.

"My eyes are not white."

"Ah, of course. 'Demon eyes,' you call those, don't you?"

"Because those people—"

"Are possessed."

"I was born with these eyes. Demon eyes you get—"

"When you hit puberty. A whim of nature, just like *your* eyes. No demons involved. Innocent people burned, I'm afraid."

Asche returned his glare with perfect calm. "But whatever the case," he continued, "I didn't bring you up here to discuss humans' random ways of interpreting the world. Or your certainly intriguing eyes. I thought a place brimming with the vestiges of the past would be a good place to talk about... the future. Yours. Mine." Asche's eyes held the same look as when he had ordered Vindt to follow him, its depth, its weight, increasing with every second.

"Ours."

Vindt's heart stopped, then started to race, along with his thoughts, which tumbled over one another in their attempt to flee or get his attention.

"But I've got to go into withdrawal," he blurted out. "It doesn't make sense for you... I mean it's... And Reisen, he's —"

"Dead."

No, not dead.

Vindt bit his lip. He had not wanted to say what he had so blatantly said, to make it so obvious that he didn't—

"You don't have to go through withdrawal." Asche's voice sliced through his thoughts. "Or you do, but there's a shortcut."

Vindt opened his mouth to ask what that meant, but Asche silenced him with a gesture. "Let's put all our cards on the table, *Vindt*." It was the first time Asche called him by his name instead of merely addressing him as *Thyd*. "If I had the chance to choose from ten Thyds, nine of them found as children and raised at The Haven, docile, obedient, convinced that serving a Singer was the greatest honor possibly to be bestowed on a human being, and one pointing an arrow at my back, guess who I would *not* choose. But unfortunately, I don't have that choice. The journey to The Haven will still take two weeks. Without a Thyd I won't get there alive, that is as certain as nightfall.

And you, I'm afraid, don't have a choice either."

As certain as nightfall—bullshit. There was a *possibility* of a Verdur attack, sure, but with Silhorveen they had not been attacked *that* frequently. Vindt remembered months with no attacks at all.

"But you could," he said, making another desperate attempt, "make me your Thyd now, and then replace me at The Haven with someone more... appropriate."

"Have you ever listened to the oath Silhorveen recited to you hundreds of times? The Bond's sacred, meant to last a lifetime, to be broken by death alone. It goes far beyond your body's physical dependency on the blood. Withdrawal or not, the only way you can be bound to another Singer now is through Silhorveen's fall."

Asche paused for a moment, and when he continued, his voice changed. "I know you think your fate is entirely in the hands of others, of us, the Singers. And that's true. But it is up to you what you make of it. Here's some advice. Your resurrection from Thrithid is something no Singer or Thyd has ever achieved before. Take your return from the demon world as an opportunity, a chance for a new life, the possibility of leaving the old Vindt behind and starting from scratch. It will make both of our lives easier."

Gaal, not this again. Except for the part about his resurrection from Thrithid, he had heard this a dozen times before. Vaan had said something similar; Ehlan had, Silhorveen, even Fora.

His choice—rubbish. He might have returned from hell, but he had done so with his memories intact, his ideas, his beliefs. He had returned as the same person he was before. It was impossible to change into someone else just like that. More importantly, he didn't want to. An obedient slave, that was what they wanted him to be. But he wouldn't. They could take his freedom. They would never take his will, no matter how many talks they held, how often they punished him, how many bracelets they put around his wrists.

"What about this shortcut?" He changed the subject to buy time. "If there's a way to spare Thyds the withdrawal, why are you even letting them enter it?"

Let them suffer for no reason.

"Because taking this shortcut is... not pleasant."

"For me or for you?"

"Definitely more for me. In fact, the entire procedure is so unpleasant, no Singer would choose that route unless he was insane. Or very desperate."

As if Asche had ever felt desperation in his entire fucking centuries-old life. Still, Vindt's discomfort grew. "So how...?"

Instead of answering, Asche pulled back his upper lip to reveal... canines.

Vindt looked at them blankly. He had never noticed that a Singer had them, not Asche nor Silhorveen nor anyone. Perhaps they could *make* them grow. But what for? His own incisors grew when he was about to drink a Singer's blood. So... did Asche want to drink *his* blood?

He imagined the knife of the Binding cutting his own veins instead of the Singer's, his blood dripping into the goblet, Asche lifting it to his lips. Surely the Singer would find drinking human blood disgusting. But what sense would it make?

"Wrong place," Asche said.

Vindt followed the Singer's gaze to find he was stroking the inside of his left wrist, the bare one. Asche took his hand

and guided it to a spot on Vindt's neck.

Realization came upon him like a bucket of cold water emptied over his head. He took a step back. His hand, which he had lowered, rose again to feel the vein, the rapid pulsing of his blood beneath the thin layer of skin. So vulnerable, so easy to pierce with... two sharp teeth.

Asche returned his terrorized gaze calmly. "As I said, the procedure is far more unpleasant for me than for you."

"But how...? Can you...?"

"Suck the remnants of Silhorveen's blood from your body—yes."

Asche turned his head. Calveen stood near the stone steps they had climbed to reach the plateau. He carried a towel and—the goblet and knife of the Binding.

Vindt's eyes jerked back to Asche.

"I cannot afford to waste time." The Singer's gaze was adamant.

Wait! Vindt wanted to shout, but what was there to wait for?

Asche held out his hand and the seneschal came over and gave him a small flask. "I said this is a shortcut to withdrawal. The state you usually reach in two months, you will now reach within minutes. You still have my blood in your veins. It will most likely alleviate the symptoms, maybe even offset them. To be honest, I don't know. This situation is as new to me as it is to you."

Asche pushed the flask into Vindt's unresisting hand. "It's the drug they gave you at The Haven when you were to be bound to Silhorveen. It will ease the pain. Take it if you want. It won't make a difference for... the process."

The process... Withdrawal symptoms. Pain. Within minutes. Vindt had an abstract notion of what that meant, *might possibly mean*, but his brain would not quite process it. Did he want to take the drug?

"Just keep it in your hand if you're not sure," Asche said. "You can take it anytime." His eyes sought Vindt's, and for a moment a faint smile broke the surface of his impassive features. He nodded. Then he stepped around him.

Vindt's heart was beating so hard it was about to burst from his chest. Though Asche contained his aura of power and was careful not to let his body touch Vindt's, his presence at Vindt's back pulled at him, an acute, dark gravitation.

"I am afraid you will have to bend your knees. You are taller than me."

Vindt turned. The Singer always seemed to tower over him, but now, looking closely, it was true: Vindt was the taller of them, only a few inches, but still...

His legs trembled as he did as he was told. The Singer's hand came to rest on the opposite side of Vindt's neck, as if to keep him from moving.

"Tilt your head." Asche's voice was very close.

Reluctantly, Vindt obeyed. Although it was only two sharp teeth about to pierce his neck, the sensation was no different from waiting for a sword to strike. Strands of Asche's hair brushed the nape of his neck; the Singer's warm breath grazed his skin as he leaned forward. Goosebumps erupted at the spot, trilling down Vindt's back. He closed his eyes and clutched the small flask in his hand.

The grip around his shoulders tightened. And then Asche sank his teeth in.

A groan wrenched itself free from Vindt's throat; he couldn't prevent it. He tried to concentrate on his breath to wrestle down the panic threatening to close his throat. The pull in his neck soon extended into his entire body, insubstantial tendrils growing from Asche's canines into the veins, down to the tips of his fingers and toes. His body struggled, refusing to give up the blood which had been a part of him for ten years, to let it be stolen in an instant by some vile intruder. His heart beat against the suction, resisting, defending.

Vindt had been unaware of Silhorveen's blood in his veins, but now he sensed it leaving him. For every drop that went came pain, scraping and burning. Pain and dizziness. The flask in his hand crossed his mind, but he only clutched it tighter. He wanted to... feel.

White and red patches filled the space behind his closed eyelids. The ground beneath his feet swayed, as if along with Silhorveen's blood, Asche was sucking all the strength from his body. Pink mist engulfed his mind. If this continued for much longer, he would faint. Was Asche aware of this?

A moment later, his knees gave way. He fell.

And was caught.

Asche lowered Vindt's body to the ground, crouching down with him, teeth still buried in Vindt's neck. The Singer's breathing was as labored as his own, and the sucking had become less controlled. Blood trickled down Vindt's neck.

Eventually, the Singer yanked his head back and gasped for breath.

Vindt longed to turn and see Asche's red-stained canines, see the blood dripping from his mouth as he had imagined it the other day. But he was too weak to move.

"It's done." Asche's voice was strained.

The right side of Vindt's neck felt strangely cold and exposed after the damp heat of Asche's mouth. Abandoned.

Asche lifted Vindt's right hand and opened the fingers clutching the flask.

"You didn't take it."

No.

Vindt breathed. It was all his limp body could still do, and even that was difficult. The familiar burning agony of withdrawal filled his body, but muffled, as though the man who sensed it were another, sitting an inch beside him. His body leaned heavily against the Singer's chest.

A breeze carried the smell of salt and seaweed to him, of bleached wood and shells drying on the beach. The smell was familiar, comforting, and Vindt let it envelop him. He could almost hear the waves crashing against the rocks, feel the salty spray on his face. What a strange illusion. The sea was miles away.

Footsteps drew closer. Calveen. The Binding. Now. Vindt's heart gave a jolt.

"Watch," Asche whispered into his ear.

Vindt's eyelids seemed to be filled with lead, and he only managed to lift them halfway. Yet, he obeyed. He *wanted* to watch.

Calveen knelt in front of them. He held goblet and knife, looking as stern as ever. Asche stretched out his left wrist. He had already removed the bracelet.

Vindt stared at the exposed skin. There was no scar, even though the Singer cut it every month. There never was. The skin at the spot was thin, the blue veins underneath clearly visible. Their pulse was powerful, alluring. His incisors grew at the sight, as craving roiled through him, so fierce he couldn't stifle a moan. His vision narrowed down to the small patch of human flesh within the reach of his hand, the source of his drug. He wanted, he *needed* to sink his teeth into it, pierce the skin and the veins' delicate walls and drink.

Before he knew it, he had grabbed Asche's wrist with both hands and pulled it toward his mouth.

Asche foiled the movement effortlessly. He didn't wrench his arm from the grip but pulled steadily against Vindt's ongoing attempts to bring the wrist within reach of his teeth. Part of Vindt's brain knew he was making a fool of himself, but it stood no chance against his body's aching desire.

"Shhh," Asche whispered into his ear, so low Vindt was sure Calveen couldn't hear. "Not now, not today." Gently but firmly, he opened Vindt's fingers and pushed his arms down.

Helplessly, Vindt watched as the seneschal took the knife and cut Asche's veins with a slow, practiced movement. The sight of the blood spilling from the wound elicited another moan in his throat. He wriggled in the Singer's grip. The liquid's heavy, rich smell assailed his nose, filled his head, set his nerves on fire.

Asche took the goblet from Calveen and brought it to Vindt's lips. Vindt's next moan drowned in the liquid entering his mouth. He swallowed greedily.

While he did, Asche spoke:

"With my blood, I bind you. I bind your body and your soul. My blood will fulfill your destiny. You will be my shield and my sword. You will be my voice. You will depend on me as I will depend on you. You will defend my life with yours, and I will do the same for you. This Bond is sacred. It shall only be broken by death."

Vindt had heard these words a thousand times; Silhorveen had recited them to him at each and every

Binding. Perhaps the very first time the Singer had said them in a special voice, with intonation, doing the occasion justice. If so, Vindt couldn't remember. Back then, he was at the peak of withdrawal, his mind pumped to the brim with drugs; he hardly noticed the ceremony at all. In the Bindings to come, Silhorveen had more or less rattled off the oath, and Vindt had not paid attention. Hollow words.

This was different.

Perhaps because he had not taken the drug, or because of the strange situation, his helpless body in Asche's embrace, the Singer's face so close to his own his lips almost touched Vindt's ear. Or because Asche's voice *was* different, not only from Silhorveen's but also from his usual tone of cool detachment. Each word became a nail the Singer drove into Vindt's mind, a hook he pushed into his soul, a ribbon that bound him.

The Binding. For the first time Vindt understood what it meant, its impact, its finality. The Singer's heart beat against Vindt's back, strong and fast, like his own. Heat emanated from his body.

Again, Vindt believed himself on the shores of the sea. Then he realized that, though no waves were crashing against rocks, no drops of water fell on his skin, the smell of salt and seaweed was not a product of his imagination.

Asche smelled this way.

The Singer brought the goblet to his lips again. It was almost empty. Vindt swallowed the last drops as eagerly. He sighed. The full dose of Asche's blood had sent him into a state beyond reasoning, beyond caring for anything but the sensations in his body.

His gaze fell on Asche's right hand. The fingers were still bleeding. It no longer seemed strange to him, but natural, logical. Made for him.

With the image of lifting the hand to his mouth and sucking the blood from the fingertips, Vindt closed his eyes and gave himself up to inebriation.

PART II
FALL

CHAPTER 17

Ten years had passed, and nothing had changed.

They had emerged through the Door on the higher part of the mountain; most of the terraces lay spread out beneath them. Streams pooled into ponds covered with water lilies and cascaded in waterfalls down the levels. An abundance of flowers and trees grew in a way that looked feral and meticulously arranged at the same time. Wooden buildings in their light, temple-like architecture were scattered about, seemingly at random, breathing coherence. Beauty, wanton and pure.

The Haven.

Vindt waited, for something, dread perhaps, vestiges of what he had felt a decade ago. However, apart from the apprehensive tension coiling in his stomach at the prospect of the Council meeting tomorrow, he felt nothing.

The passage through the Door had been swift, a strange tug at his chest, a moment of disorientation, and then The Haven. Asche and he had not gone alone. They had taken the horses, Vaan. And the two groaning bodies.

Vindt turned in time to see the servants take them away. He shuddered. Where did they put them? In a vault, kept clean of dust and spiderwebs by the Singers' dark magic? Eternally.

Vindt shuddered again, this time triggered by the memory of their passage. They'd had to cradle the moaning, twitching bodies before them on the horses. Vindt had been supposed to carry Reisen, but his entire body had revolted. Mercifully, Asche let him take Silhorveen instead. The brief ride was still a nightmare, but slightly less horrific, enough to prevent him from fainting. The switched order of the bodies had caused quite the stirrup among the servants who welcomed them. Which Asche seemed to have enjoyed.

On cue, the Singer stepped up beside him and looked down the terraces.

"Happy to return to your beloved coven?" Vindt quipped before he could stop himself.

"Coven? This is the demons' capital, my dear Vindt. And here their king has arrived to reclaim his throne." Asche proceeded down the wide stone steps.

Vindt couldn't help the laugh that surged, but turned it into a cough. Gaal. One day, Asche's ego would simply crush him. He followed, along with the servants who had come to their greeting.

They descended stairs, crossed bridges and plains, climbed other stairs, until Asche stopped. "This is where we part. Someone will collect you tomorrow morning and bring you to my quarters."

A wave of unease trickled through Vindt. The Singer had told him yesterday that—for unknown reasons—the first night, they would sleep in separate places. At the time, Vindt had welcomed the idea. Now, he felt a strange reluctance to be left alone.

"In the meantime, be a good Thyd and behave. For a change." Asche flashed Vindt a smile before he crossed toward a stairway at the far end of the plateau, leaving Vindt to glower after him.

A sturdy servant politely waited for him to follow. Again, they walked along winding paths, up rocky stairs, down again, over arching bridges, along merrily gurgling streams and sparkling waterfalls. Vindt thought of Risi. For days, the man had lamented about Vindt's luck to visit the famous Haven again, while he and the others had to stay behind.

You *would love this.*

A smile lifted the corners of his mouth.

Every servant who crossed their path stopped to bow to Vindt as soon as they laid eyes on his blue tunic. *Reisen's* blue tunic. One of an entire bunch of unwanted legacies. Vindt hated it, the legacies, as well as the looks of reverence. *The Gift*, which they ironically called the strange predisposition that turned ordinary humans into potential Thyds.

It's a fucking curse.

Once, a flock of children ran past, blissfully ignoring Vindt's status. Despite being the demons' capital, the people who called this place home were ninety-nine percent human, born and bred here or bought on the Singers' vast journeys.

His guide stopped at an assembly of small huts. Tiled, peaked roofs, dark wood, the Singers' sinuous lines carved into each pillar and beam. Blossoming trees cast their red petals on the ground and into a small pond. Spring. Fall had been approaching in the country Asche and Vindt had left.

The servant bowed. "Everything has been prepared for your comfort. Food will be brought to you at dusk. If you need something, please strike the gong." He pointed at the object hanging from a hook at the door.

This was neither the house Vindt had lived in a decade ago nor the quarters of the other Thyds of the Council members. Asche had told him that before, too. He was glad. The presence of other Thyds discomfited him. It was not so much the reminder of his own fate. He couldn't stand the way they accepted it.

The one room inside was big but sparsely furnished. Flowers in a vase in a corner permeated the air with a discrete scent. A bowl of fruits waited on the table. The table was so low, Vindt would have to sit on the floor to eat. Consequently, chairs were missing. Odd, but no surprise. He had never figured out whether The Haven's interior design was based on the Singers' preferences or a concession to the culture of the country it resided in. What ties Singers had to this human culture in particular that made them choose it as their center of power.

He plopped down onto the equally low bed, stretched his limbs and let out a sigh. Gaal, he was exhausted. Being Asche's Thyd was more draining than anything he had experienced since his fate took a turn for the worse a decade ago. Asche did nothing in particular. In fact, apart from giving him curt orders, he hardly talked to him. But his proximity sufficed. And close they were. Vindt's new position meant sleeping in the same tent, riding side by side, not to mention attending to the Singer's every fucking need. Becoming Asche's Thyd had also turned him into his personal servant.

Though Vindt hated it, this wasn't any different from

how it had been with Silhorveen. Back then, Vindt had largely switched off and ignored the Singer, who had made a point of ignoring him in turn. Somehow, with Asche, Vindt couldn't. His senses were on constant alert, waiting for... something, an attack, another game. That so far none had come didn't mollify his instincts.

He let out another sigh. Alone, eventually. Which also meant he could take off the damn cloth around his neck. He hated the sensation of the fabric against his skin, the heat accumulating under it. But without it, everyone would see the marks. Two—perfectly round. The marks Asche's teeth had left. Even after two weeks, they were clearly visible. They pulsated, as if they had grown their own tiny hearts.

Risi and the others had shown the decency not to ask questions. Asche had not healed them. As if he wanted to mark him, conspicuous for everyone, his most recent acquisition. Scars instead of an earring. As much as his pride protested, eventually, Vindt had *asked* him to make them vanish. The Singer had only looked at him with his indifferent, dark gaze and said, "I can't."

A lie? Another mystery?

Vindt rolled his stiff shoulders. His entire body was taut. He craved a hot bath. With a jolt of anticipation, he realized he would get one. The Haven sported pools, magically heated by the Singers' preternatural skills. The place's only perk.

He flicked a glance toward the towels and the soap laid out for him on a stool. Everything prepared for his comfort. Indeed.

By the time he returned from the baths, night had fallen. He had stayed in the water longer than intended, even dozed off a little, taking advantage of the unexpected opportunity of having the pools to himself.

Someone had replaced the basket of fruits with a variety of steaming bowls. The smell made his mouth water. Local dishes. A plate with bread, roasted meat and cheese complemented the arrangement. Just in case. Concerns he wouldn't like the local food were baseless, however. In his year here, he had come to, well, "cherish" the food. As much as his situation let him cherish anything.

Vindt dipped a piece of fried fish into some reddish gravy. He was about to shove the steaming, dripping thing into his mouth when movement from the window made him turn.

"I'd be careful with that. It's *very* spicy." A freckled, youthful face grinned at him. Its owner sat casually on the sill, one leg drawn up, the other dangling outside.

Vindt's eyebrows went up, only to narrow as he took in the pattern on the front of the blue tunic. A Thyd.

He deliberately swallowed the fish. It *was* spicy, but he liked it. "Got lost?" he said, chewing. It came out as unfriendly as he intended it to be.

The youth shook his head so that his brown ponytail shook. "Came to satisfy my curiosity."

Vindt was not sure if he should laugh about the bluntness or get angry. Before he could decide, the other Thyd jumped from the ledge and walked over, all smiles. "Issa."

Vindt wiped his fingers on a towel and took the outstretched hand, reluctantly. "I don't have any memories of Thrithid," he said before Issa could ask. What else would "curiosity" refer to but his resurrection?

Issa dropped into a cross-legged position on the opposite

side of the table with practiced ease. "So they say. But your reputation isn't just about Thrithid, but… hmm, how to put it? Your unconventional attitude?"

Again, Vindt was not sure what to feel at Issa's words. "You better leave, then. Perhaps it's contagious." He continued eating his fish.

"No worries. I'm immune. Devoted through to the very core of my soul. I'd die for my Singer." He paused. "Well, I will." He laughed again.

Vindt wondered if the Thyd was slightly insane. And then if he should offer Issa some food. He decided against it. The sooner the other left, the better. "How old are you?" he asked, chewing. With the ponytail and freckles, Issa looked barely of age.

"Somewhere in my sixties. What?" he added when he saw Vindt's face. "You know the blood keeps us from aging."

"It slows the process."

"As good as stops it."

Again, Vindt wondered how old Reisen had been, how long he had been with Asche. "You knew Reisen?"

The perpetual smile vanished from Issa's face. He lowered his eyes. "He was very… He was a nice guy."

"Doesn't your destiny creep you out? Eternal torture." Vindt knew it was a cruel thing to say. Besides, it wasn't *your*, but *our*. But something propelled him to discomfit the other.

"Like everyone else, I try not to think about it."

The pained look on Issa's face made Vindt regret his question. He took a breath. "I'm sorry."

Issa's smile returned. "The price for my curiosity. The others tried to talk me out of visiting you."

"The other Thyds?"

Issa nodded.

"You all know each other?"

"Inevitably. Well, apart from Fernando. His Singer is new to the Council."

"Your Singer has been in the Council for a long time?"

"Yes."

Vindt finished the fish and put some rice into a bowl of broth with chewy green leaves and cubes of some non-descriptive white substance which looked like cheese but wasn't. "Does he treat you... well?"

Issa looked puzzled. "Sure. I'm his Thyd. Does Asche not treat you well?"

Vindt was not sure how Asche was treating him. *Well* wasn't the word. But he hadn't asked with Asche in mind.

"It's funny you two ended up together." Issa chuckled. "Asche has a reputation too, you know."

So he had heard.

"Is it true that your sword can fight Verdurs?"

Vindt's eyes flicked to the scabbard he had carelessly tossed in a corner when he came in. Issa followed the gaze.

"You don't have one?" Vindt asked.

"No one does. Just you. I mean, you and Asche's other servants. May I have a look?" Before Vindt had time to answer, the other Thyd got up and walked over.

Vindt leaned forward and caught his wrist. "If you ask permission for something, wait for it to be granted."

"Just wanted to have a peek. May I?"

"No."

Issa's frown made him look like a boy whose parents had denied him a treat. Vindt was not sure why he had declined the request. Asche had not forbidden him to show off his sword. Apparently, their existence was common knowledge.

"You know how he made them?" Issa asked. It didn't sound like a question, but like, "You don't know, but I do." And indeed, when Vindt didn't answer, Issa narrowed his eyes and said in an artificially grave voice, "He killed his Thyd and used his heart."

Vindt should have laughed, but instead he went pale. Reisen's sword was yet another of his unwanted inheritances. His former blade had been forged for him here at The Haven, tailored to the dimensions of his body, made of expensive Ist'ivan steel. It was perfectly balanced. He had used it for ten years; it had felt like another limb. But Asche wouldn't hear his arguments. Steel which could fight demons and Verdurs—of course the Singer wanted Vindt to carry one. Just another reason Vindt did not. Though he hated it, he often touched the blade, strangely drawn to the repulsive sensation it triggered, the faint pulse under his fingers, the... heartbeat.

"Well, that's what the rumors say. Is it true?"

"I have no idea how he made them," Vindt said emphatically. "And I don't want to know." He had finished the soup and now eyed the remaining bowls.

"No?" Issa's eyebrows rose. "You're weird." He cast another longing glance toward the sword, but lowered himself back down again.

"What else do the rumors say about Asche?" Vindt said it mainly to change the subject, but he also *was* curious. He settled for a bowl with undefinable vegetables in a red sauce.

Issa leaned back on his palms. "They say he lets you drink his blood directly from his wrist."

Vindt spat the contents of his mouth onto the table. Gaal, why had he asked? With a napkin, he tried to clean up the mess. "And why would he do that?"

"*Does* he?" The curiosity in Issa's eyes differed from what it had been when he asked about the sword. There was something else in it: greed.

"No," Vindt exclaimed, a little more forcefully than intended.

"It's against the law, you know."

"Fine. Asche doesn't do it." And more important: he, Vindt, didn't do it. And never would. Sinking his teeth into Asche's vein...

Issa tilted his head. "You know why it's forbidden?"

"No. And I don't—"

"It transfers a part of the Singer's power to the Thyd."

"Wow," Vindt said with no enthusiasm. "Glad no one does it then."

"It's the way they did it before, in the beginning. Have you never asked yourself why your incisors grow when you're about to drink the blood? You know why they changed it?"

"I have a feeling I will in a second."

Issa smiled. "Because the Thyds rose up against their Singers. The Thyd rebellion, they call it."

"So you came to talk me into joining a secret Thyds-to-power movement, grab Asche's wrist in the next Binding before he seals his veins again, and sink my teeth into them?"

Issa giggled. "I thought it would interest you."

"No." Not only that, Vindt had had enough. He wanted to eat the rest of his food in peace. He was about to cast Issa out, but then thought of something. "You know what they're doing tonight?"

"You're changing the subject."

"Smart boy."

Issa sighed. Then his mouth quirked into a grin. "They're having sex." He raised one palm in a placating gesture in response to the annoyance that had probably manifested on Vindt's face. "No one knows for sure. But it's what everyone believes. Have you never heard them?"

"I've never been to a meeting of the High Council."

"Not just the members of the High Council. Every Singer, every time they meet. Have they not cast you out of the tent or the room for hours? Have you not seen their necks afterward? The bite marks on one of them."

With Silhorveen, they had rarely encountered other Singers, two or three times; one had been Asche. But, yes, they had sent him out, and now that he thought about it, at least on one occasion he had heard noises that might have sounded like moans. He had dismissed the thought of sex immediately. For some reason, he found the idea revolting, perhaps because they were both men.

Silhorveen *did* have wounds on his necks afterward, though, half hidden under his long brown hair. Whatever brief thought Vindt had spent on their origin, bite marks had not figured among them. Before Asche sank his teeth into his neck, he had not even known Singers had canines.

Though it had seemed exaggerated, now Vindt was glad he had put back the cloth around his neck when leaving the baths and forgotten to take it off again.

"You mean they bite each other?" Disgust and incredulity vied for dominance in his voice.

"Only one bites, the more powerful one. It's a hierarchy thing. The Weighing, they call it."

"And you know this, or it's something your lewd minds came up with to have something to talk about?"

Issa shrugged. "It's nothing they've officially taught us, if that's what you mean. But it's pretty obvious. Next time, just listen closely. Besides, you'll see them all tomorrow. Look at their necks."

"You mean they'll throw an orgy tonight?" It didn't come out as sarcastic as intended.

"No, they do it consecutively. They visit one another at their houses. That's why we cannot sleep there."

"You mean *everyone* visits *everyone*?"

"They lead solitary lives. At some point, all the pent-up..." Issa cleared his throat. "*Energy* has to find an outlet." He broke into laughter. "Uh, uh, you should see your face. You really didn't know, huh?"

Whatever. Let them fuck one another. It was none of his business. He should have followed his initial impulse and cast the not-so-young man out immediately. "Look, Issa, it was nice meeting you, but it was a tiring journey. I'd very much like to finish my meal and have an early night." It wasn't even a lie.

"I see." If Issa was offended, he didn't show it. He unfolded his legs and rose. "Bye-bye, then. If you change your mind and fancy some company, we'll be at the baths later. It'll be fun. There aren't so many occasions where we can be without our Singers." A grin accompanied the wave of his hand as he exited the same way he had come: through the window.

CHAPTER 18

Vindt was still asleep when a servant came to fetch him late the next morning. It was a long walk again, up and down The Haven's stairs and winding paths. The house they eventually reached looked like a bigger and more luxurious version of Vindt's accommodation. Here too trees in blossom cast their petals on the roof and ground, white this time.

Asche was nowhere to be seen, though Vindt felt his presence. The servant indicated the first of two doors leading from the spacious room they had stepped into. "Your room." Then he pointed at a low table in a corner. "Breakfast has been arranged for you. The meeting will start in an hour."

Vindt nodded, and the woman left.

Vindt sat down beside the table. Food was the last thing he craved now, yet he grabbed a still warm bun. From behind the closed door at the other end of the room, Asche's aura drifted out to him, accompanied by occasional undefined noises. An hour, then he would meet *them*. His stomach gave a nervous flutter. The seven oldest Singers. The night before going through the Door, Asche had warned him they would want to read his mind again.

"And then?" Vindt had asked.

"Nothing. You have no memories."

"What if they want to kill me?"

"Then we should try to talk them out of it."

Vindt didn't find it funny.

Listlessly, he nibbled at the bun. Whatever Asche was doing behind that door, it took time. Minutes passed, half an hour, more. Somewhere distant, a gong sounded, deep and hollow, sending a shiver down his back.

Vindt should have been expecting the Singer to appear before him without sign or sound. He hadn't. And, frankly, he couldn't have been prepared for *this*. Vindt jumped, his gaze only briefly skimming over Asche's dark blue robes. They differed from his usual formal attire; the fabric was stiffer, the cut, the embroidery of the same silver as the underlying tunic, which showed at the hems of the wide arms, the robe's bottom, the neckline. Then his eyes fastened on Asche's face.

He was made up, heavily. Silvery dust made his cheeks glitter above reddened lips. Dark mascara weighed down the long lashes. Silvery-black lines under his eyes grew into an intricate pattern running up the temples, meeting at the center of his forehead. He had braided his hair, though "braiding" didn't come close to the complex formations he had brought the black mass into. It piled on top and fell down to his shoulders, the strands interwoven with silver threads. Long filigree silver pendants dangled from his ears.

Any human man would have looked ridiculous, artificial, overdone. To Asche, the makeup and hairdo did something Vindt couldn't describe. As if he was seeing the real Asche for the first time. The awe he had felt at their first encounter crashed down on him with imminent might. His soul cowered, small and humble, human, nothing.

"Let me know when you're done staring," Asche said dryly. "I'd prefer you did it now than have to deal with it throughout the entire meeting."

"I..." Vindt started, but his voice cracked. His gaze fastened on the elongated line of Asche's neck. Usually covered by the mass of dark hair, he had never seen it. *Like this.* Exposed, naked. Perfect smooth skin. Except for the two red marks on one side.

It's true then.

A dull buzz ignited at the back of his scalp and rushed down the length of his body into his fingertips, his groin. The sharp points of his incisors pressed against the insides of his lower lip. The urge to grab the neck and sink his teeth into the untainted skin on the other side made him sway. Claim what was his. Leave his mark like Asche had left his.

His mind recoiled from his own thoughts as if burned. What was he thinking?

He jerked his gaze away from the exposed neck, back to Asche's robes, then to his own clothes. He was wearing the formal blue of a Singer's servant, but, compared to Asche, he was utterly underdressed. "Shall I..." He cleared his throat, once, twice. "Change?"

Asche's made-up lashes lowered and rose as his gaze traveled the length of Vindt's body. "They won't look at you anyway."

"I thought the meeting was about me."

"About you as a principle. Not you as a person."

"Then I can stay here, no?" He meant it only half as a

joke.

"And miss the show?" Asche reached out and touched the fabric around Vindt's neck. "This has to go, though."

"Won't they... I mean, what if they get the wrong idea?"

A moment of silence passed. "And which idea would that be?"

Vindt felt his cheeks redden.

"Take it off." With that, Asche turned and left.

* * *

It was raining when they made their way up the mountain. Asche, whom Vindt had never seen protecting himself against any kind of downpour before, sang to keep them dry.

"I spent hours getting myself to look like this. I won't have it destroyed in a few minutes by *weather*."

Vindt's gaze darted around, to avoid staring at Asche but also because he was on the nervous lookout for the other Singers.

"They're already there," Asche said.

"How'd you know?"

"Because we're late."

"Oh."

The corners of Asche's lips curled. "The important guests always arrive late to the party."

They reached another of the mountain's many plateaus. Asche led them to a building at the center, which looked no different from any other building at The Haven; it was only bigger. Half a dozen servants stood in a line in front of it, bowing deeply at their approach. All were clad in blue robes, which looked like a stripped-down, humble version of what Asche was wearing.

Asche gave the smallest nod of recognition, before he strode inside, his weary Thyd in tow.

Vindt could feel the other Singers before he saw them. Unlike Asche's aura, which would reach out for him in a flow of possessive curiosity, the others' felt like dogs pacing the boundaries of their kennels, the hair on their backs raised, growling. They paid Vindt no mind.

They crossed an antechamber toward the two open wings of the opposite door. Asche strode through without hesitation. "Lovely to see everyone," he chirped. "Am I late? My apologies. Couldn't find my favorite eyeliner."

The attention of the entire room swung to them like the wind turning. Asche walked up to the round, hip-high table that dominated the heptagonal room. The table and the chairs surrounding it were made of shiny dark brown wood, carved excessively with the Singers' beloved writhing lines. Water jars, mugs and baskets with fruit stood on top. Four Singers had already taken their seats; two were still standing.

Asche stopped next to one of the occupied chairs. Silver and blue threads adorned the blond braids of the Singer sitting in it. They mirrored the blue on his eyelids and in the intricate pattern painted on his forehead. The look in his equally blue eyes would have made Vindt recoil had it targeted him. Asche smiled.

Seconds passed, in which the face of the fair Singer darkened by the second. No one spoke; no one moved. When eventually the latter rose, the room seemed to let out a breath. For a split second, Vindt was convinced the Singer would spit in Asche's face. However, he turned wordlessly and took the farthest empty seat.

"Thank you, Tuait. It's my favorite seat, you know." Asche lowered himself gracefully into the now vacant chair, arranging his robes with dedicated care.

Tuait? The Singer Asche had battled. And bested.

Turning the knife in the wound.

The seven oldest Singers. Asche was right; it was quite the show. Very different in terms of hair, skin color and features, they all wore the same stiff blue robes. With all the makeup and blank expressions, their faces looked more like painted masks than the faces of living creatures. Besides the earrings and the obligatory wide bracelets covering their wrists, most sported additional jewelry, smaller bracelets, rings. Their appearance set them in a limbo between genders, between the realms of gods and demons. A place, as Vindt was acutely aware, he had no right to be in. Their auras tugged at the edges of his awareness like the drone of angry hornets.

And Issa had been right. All their necks sported bite marks in varying numbers. Worst off was a white-blond Singer whose near-translucent skin looked like it had been ravaged by some wild animal.

Several animals.

The Singer, noticing his attention, looked up with pale blue eyes. And *smiled*.

Vindt was so baffled he returned the gaze for a few seconds before he came to and hastily averted his eyes.

Only when the two standing Singers took their seats did he realize he knew one of them. Shahen. With the silver-blue robes instead of his former red and the paint on his face, he looked very different from the man Vindt had known a decade ago. The golden lines on his forehead contrasted well with his umber skin, as did the threads of the same color woven into his many black braids, which were draped as artfully around his head as everybody else's.

Shahen. The Singer who by forcing a cup of blood down Vindt's throat had sealed his fate. The Singer who had locked him up in a cabin and nearly let him die of withdrawal after his escape attempt.

Shahen gave no sign of recognition. He sported more than one pair of bite marks, on *both* sides of his neck. Vindt wondered if they wore braids so that everyone could get a good look. Meant to make a point.

There were no more empty chairs. Asche seemed to have forgotten about Vindt's existence, like everyone else. Lost, Vindt positioned himself diagonally behind him, like the shadow he was. On impulse, he rested a hand on the chair's carved wooden back.

"Fine." A Singer with a blood-red flower tucked behind his ear put his palms on the tabletop. It formed a strident contrast to his glossy black hair. "Now that we are all here, including the reason for this meeting, I assume, we can start. I think we're all clear why we came together. To find out how this..." He flicked a glance in Vindt's direction and stalled. The black brows furrowed as he looked at Vindt properly for the first time. No, not at him, at his neck.

Automatically, Vindt's hand rose as if to cover the bite marks.

The Singer's glance went from Vindt to Asche. "You cleaned him?" Barely concealed disgust underpinned the words.

At this, a murmur went through the group and five additional pairs of eyes fastened on Vindt's neck.

Asche smiled. "It's not as bad as everyone thinks, you know? You should try it. You might come to like it." He looked entirely unperturbed, his posture relaxed.

The flower-adorned Singer cast Vindt's marks a last look,

then cleared his throat. "Right. So we came together to discuss the Thyd's return from Thrithid, and then decide what to do with him."

"Only one way to find out," the Singer to his right said. He had the same black hair and willow-leaf-shaped eyes as the flowery one, his skin a fawn brown.

"Yes, let's read his mind." Tuait stared at Asche while he said this, as he had the entire time, his animosity so palpable, Vindt imagined a sheet of paper bursting into flames when held in his line of vision.

"Let's first hear what Asche can tell us, as he was the first to see him after his resurrection," the apparent leader of this meeting said.

"Indeed he was," murmured the Singer sitting to Vindt's left. With his copper skin and black hair, he reminded Vindt of Jun and Layyad. A moment of strange silence ensued as all gazes fastened on Asche.

"Not much to tell," Asche said lightly. "We received the war call from the Guzzar commander, and then the note from Silhorveen's seneschal about the Thyd's miraculous awakening. Since I happened to be in the area, I decided to mix business with pleasure and—"

A chuckle from the other side of the table interrupted him. It came from the Singer sitting next to Tuait. His skin was a rich sepia; his dark brown hair had the same reddish touch. Like Shahen, he wore his hair woven into many tiny box braids adorned with golden threads. His back rested casually against the back of the chair, the ankle of one foot on the other thigh. His left hand toyed with a ring on the tabletop. Vindt looked at his neck, then looked again. No bite marks.

Asche cocked his head. "Will you let us in on the joke,

Ru?"

Ru? Wasn't that the name Reisen had mentioned ages ago in Asche's tent?

The ring rolled over the table. "Nothing. Just, you, well, *happened* to be in the area. I mean, it's great that someone *happened* to be in the area."

Asche leaned back in his chair too.

"And I assume by 'business,'" Ru continued, "you refer to the war call. *Petty* business. At least, that's what you called it the last time we talked about war calls."

Asche watched Ru with the air of indulgent patience parents sometimes adopted when confronted with their child's tantrum.

"No answer?" Ru asked.

"Oh, I would love to give you one. If there was a question. Perhaps, do I think that engaging in human wars is beneath me? I wasn't aware that my views on the world are of interest to the matter at hand. Depending, of course, on what the matter at hand is."

"You took the war call *before* the note about the Thyd's resurrection arrived."

"That is correctly calculated."

"And shortly after, the Thyd of the Singer you replace resurrects from Thrithid."

The gazes of the other Singers wandered between Asche and Ru with tense anticipation.

"And a few days later," Ru drawled on, "another of your Thyds falls victim to an *accident* and the resurrected Thyd becomes yours. That's, well, how to put it? A *remarkable* chain of coincidences."

Another Thyd?

Asche didn't seem surprised, let alone upset, by the

strange direction the conversation had taken. No one seemed to be surprised. He leaned forward, put both elbows on the tabletop, rested his chin in his palms and looked at Ru with big eyes. "Are you jealous, Ru? Would you like to have a resurrected Thyd too? If you asked *nicely*, I might lend him to you for a few days."

The face of the white-blond Singer twitched as if he was about to laugh, but returned to impassivity a second later.

Ru was completely unfazed. He didn't even look exasperated. Vindt got the strong feeling this was not the first conversation of this kind.

Asche leaned back in his chair again, resting his hands on its arms. "Why don't you make all our lives easier by just saying what you want."

Ru stopped playing with the ring. He put it back on and folded his long fingers on the tabletop. The metal of the many additional bracelets he wore beside the two wide ones clicked softly against the wood. "You brought him back."

The entire room held its breath. With sudden clarity, Vindt realized this sentence was what everyone had been waiting for. The soft gushing of the rain coming in through the open windows seemed abnormally loud.

A ghost smile played about Asche's lips. "You're the second person who believes me capable of raising the dead. I'm flattered. I assume you have proof? After all, your flattery implies a death sentence. Let's see," he went on when Ru merely continued to look at him. "I was the first to arrive at the scene, answering a war call, which, as we have just learned, I haven't done for a century. My Thyd was killed shortly afterward, enabling me to bind the resurrected one. Not to forget that, a decade ago, I argued for this very Thyd's life when Silhorveen and everyone else requested his death. Then again, a Verdur killed Silhorveen. You're welcome to check for yourself, as I brought his corpse with me. Of course, I could be in league with Verdurs, but then, I was a two-week journey away from Silhorveen and his retinue when the Thyd woke up, so... I turned into a bird and flew the distance back and forth at night?"

The pale Singer looked as if he was about to laugh again.

The Singer on Asche's other side cleared his throat. "I think we should read his mind."

"Oh." The Singer with the near-translucent skin spoke up. "Didn't Asche already do that and—" He stalled as five pairs of hostile eyes came to land on him. "Uh, well, I thought..." He blushed.

The sight absorbed Vindt's attention for half a minute. He had never seen a Singer *blush*.

"We *will* read his mind," Ru said. "Although we'll be wasting our time."

Asche nodded thoughtfully. "Because I erased his memories."

"Because you erased his memories," Ru echoed.

"Will you remind me again *why* I brought him back and made him my Thyd? *Apart* from my notorious penchant for brute, blond-haired humans who try to kill their Singers."

"Let's just—" Ru began.

"Oh, right," Asche interrupted him, beaming. "He has moon eyes."

At this, Ru's expression faltered. For the first time since the meeting had started, he *looked* at Vindt, at his eyes. It was no friendly gaze.

"If we're already on the matter, shall we discuss my swords again?" Asche asked lightly. "Or that I battled another Singer on the way to binding the resurrected Thyd?"

"You did what?" the Singer with the flower asked into the murmur that had erupted at this last piece of information.

"Oh." Asche raised his eyebrows. He was good at this. "Did Ru not tell you?"

The Singer's gaze darted between Asche and Ru. "You two didn't—"

"Ren Zian." Asche looked startled. "Not *Ru*, obviously. He would never break the rules, would he? As opposed to the others..." He cast Tuait a look of flaunted innocence. "I won."

This time, the Singer with the near-white hair failed to stifle his amusement. He chuckled into his fist, and made an apologetic gesture when Tuait turned to him, eyes shooting daggers.

"And why did you do this, if I may ask?" The flower-adorned Singer, who was apparently called Ren Zian, turned to Asche.

"I fear you need to ask Tuait. *I* had the assignment first."

Ren Zian opened his mouth to say something, but when Asche merely continued to look at him with wide, innocent eyes, he shut it again and turned to Tuait. "Is that true?"

Tuait crossed his arms over his chest. A muscle in his jaw twitched.

"Why in the name of the First—" Ren Zian began, but Ru placed his palms on the table and got up. "Enough of this charade. Let's get it done with." He rounded the table.

Vindt's mouth went dry. Reading his mind—they were going to do it now.

Ru was about to pass behind Asche's chair when he

found his way blocked. Asche had tilted the chair on its hind legs at an angle that clearly defied gravity. Or not. Asche kept the balance by clinging to the edge of the table with the toes of one foot. Vindt was not the only one staring. Had Asche been barefoot the whole time?

"Not you," Asche said softly, smiling up at Ru.

"Why not, if I may ask?"

"Personal reasons. Wonder why you bother at all. I erased his memories, no?"

Vindt had no idea what desperate whim propelled him, but he cleared his throat. "Can I choose?"

Six pairs of incredulous eyes fastened on him. Seven, as Asche's was among them. They looked as if a dog had started talking. The ensuing silence cracked under Asche's sparkling laughter. He laughed so hard he held his abdomen as tears smeared his precious makeup.

"This is—" Ru started.

Asche made a placating gesture as he tried with visible effort to calm down and to dry his eyes with his sleeve without smearing the makeup. "I have nothing to do with this, I swear." He chuckled some more. "But why not? Why not let him choose?"

"Yes, why not let him choose?" the white-blond Singer seconded to everyone's apparent dismay. He recoiled as five sets of eyes threatened to flay him.

"Ren Zian." Ru's voice was quiet, but it had the same effect Vindt had so often witnessed when Asche talked. No one spoke up.

A mix of disappointment and trepidation rushed through Vindt. He didn't know why, but he would have chosen the pale Singer. The idea of him reading his mind was not as intimidating as that of everyone else. Somehow, he preferred Ren Zian over Ru, though.

The white-blond Singer gave Vindt what was probably supposed to be a reassuring smile, but Vindt had different concerns at that moment. Focused on Ren Zian's approach, he almost jumped as a hand squeezed his shoulder and a familiar cool voice next to his ear whispered, "It will be over in a minute." When he turned, Asche's gaze was one of mild interest; his hands rested casually on the arms of his chair.

Ren Zian stepped behind him. Vindt exerted all his willpower to remain still as cool fingers came to rest on his temples. His right hand clawed the back of Asche's chair; sweat broke from his every pore. He had barely closed his eyes when a searing pain exploded in his head. He heard himself scream. His body twitched as insubstantial tendrils pushed through his brain. His knees threatened to give way, but something held him upright. *Stop it*, he wanted to shout, but all that came out of his mouth were continuous, inarticulate screams.

He had no clue how long this went on before Asche said, "That's enough." His voice was as quiet as Ru's had been before, but Ren Zian stopped singing, and with it, the pain ceased.

Vindt clutched the back of the chair. Sweat trickled down his skin; his mouth was filled with blood. He must have bitten his tongue. He clamped down on the impulse to spit it out onto the beautiful mosaic floor.

"Here." A glass of water appeared before his face.

Vindt drank, washing down the blood. There was no sympathy in Asche's eyes, but something about the cool, examining gaze was strangely comforting.

"You can only do that so often, you know?" Asche said lightly as he leaned back in his chair. He looked at Ren Zian, who had taken his seat too. "Happy?"

"He's got vivid memories of Thrithid and the Verdur attack before. Then only after waking up again. In between: nothing."

"And the Verdur attack," Shahen said, "*was* a Verdur attack?"

Ren Zian nodded.

"No doubt?"

Ren Zian shuddered. "No doubt."

"Anything else that's... well, strange?" the Singer to Vindt's left asked.

"I didn't have time to find out more." Ren Zian cast Asche a glance.

"Then we should do it again to make sure," Tuait said.

Asche sighed. "As I just pointed out: you can only do it so many times without causing permanent damage."

"We will kill him anyway," Ru said.

"What?" Vindt exclaimed.

Asche leaned forward and rested his lower arms on the table. "And why would you do that, Ruhadar ben Istre?"

Ru played with his ring again. He didn't roll it over the tabletop this time, but twisted it between his long, manicured fingers. "Tell me why we should *not* do it."

"For the same reason we didn't do it ten years ago."

"Which... uh, was?" the Singer with the light-blue eyes asked cautiously.

Vindt wondered if he had forgotten or if he simply had not been present a decade ago. Perhaps he was new to the Council. Issa had said there was a new Thyd. It would explain some things.

"Because we don't have enough of them," the one to Asche's right hissed, shooting him an impatient glance.

"He tried to kill his Singer," Ru said.

"Yes. And we settled that ten years ago." Asche's voice held the faintest hint of impatience now. "Or are you worried about me? That's sweet, Ru. But I'm not Silhorveen. I can handle him."

"Okay." The impatience in Ren Zian's voice was more than a hint. "We can discard the possibility that he escaped on his own, right?" He looked around the table. Reluctant nods and murmurs of agreement. "That he got out with the help of one of us is—"

"Unlikely."

"Impossible."

"A very probable possibility."

Three Singers spoke at the same time. The last sentence came from Tuait.

Ren Zian closed his eyes for a moment. "I think we—"

This time, a gesture from Asche interrupted him. "It *is* impossible that a Singer got the Thyd out of Thrithid." His voice differed totally from before, holding a strange intensity that caused a tingle beneath Vindt's skin. "It is impossible because the Law cannot be broken. This we all know deep down in our souls and bones. And even if, in the very unlikely case that a Singer *did* the impossible, a Singer with powers no one has ever seen or believes possible, would the First not have struck him down immediately and killed the Thyd?"

Ru hardly moved, but Vindt could feel his rising annoyance. His voice was pressed as he said, "You know very well why they didn't intervene."

"Ah, right, because of *the oath*." Asche leaned back in his chair, the familiar glint in the depths of his eyes, a ghost smile on his lips.

The atmosphere in the room had tilted into something Vindt couldn't name. The eerie silence had fallen again, a thick coat of stillness covering a seething liquid. Vindt had no idea what anything that had been said meant.

Ru briefly closed his eyes, opened them again and said, "The Thyd will—"

"The Thyd will not be killed." Asche's words cut through the room like the blade of child-Vindt's dagger had cut through insects, all the flaunted lightness in his voice gone. The auras of the other Singers recoiled as if beaten.

They fear him, Vindt realized with a start.

"You know"—Asche flashed a smile—"I have grown fond of him."

The clinking of jewelry filled the room as the Singers shifted in their seats. All glances flicked to Ru. His face was still impenetrable, but the anger underneath charged the air. "Very well." He raised an eyebrow the way Asche did so often. "The next meeting is in nine months. Let's see how things are then."

Ren Zian reached up to check on his flower, which had not moved an inch, and ostensibly cleared his throat. "Is there anything else we need to discuss today that can't wait until the next meeting?"

No one spoke. Vindt had the impression everyone wanted to end this as soon as possible.

"Great," Asche said, rising elegantly from his chair. "It was a pleasure talking to you all again. I'll see you later."

Without waiting for a reaction, he took Vindt by the elbow and dragged him out of the room.

CHAPTER 19

"What the hell was that all about?" Vindt asked when they were out of earshot.

Asche didn't answer, but pulled Vindt along to the stairs at the other end of the plateau and climbed. The Haven was a damn maze, but Vindt was sure this was not the way back to their quarters. "Where are we going?"

Before reaching the stairway's top, Asche veered left onto what could hardly be called a path and eventually let go of Vindt's arm. They wriggled through underbrush and climbed rocks, the Singer with his usual silent grace, Vindt panting and sliding and getting caught in thorny twigs, until they finally emerged onto another of the mountain's many plateaus. It was small, partly overgrown, strewn with rocks.

Asche strode to the other side, which, Vindt noticed with unease, was the edge of a precipice. The vivid image of the Singer throwing him down the mountain, conveniently disposing of his body, flashed through his mind. Which wouldn't make sense after he had just defended Vindt's life against his brethren. But you never knew...

However, the Singer merely gazed at the horizon, seemingly oblivious to Vindt's existence. The view was admittedly spectacular. A vast expanse of smaller peaks and valleys extended before their eyes until they hit a stretch of dark blue in the distance. The ocean. Vindt took a surprised breath. He had not known The Haven was so close to the sea. The last time he had seen the ocean must have been years ago, on a ship with Silhorveen, on their way to some war. Though it was too far away for it, Vindt believed he could feel its breeze on his face, the smell of seaweed and salt in his nose.

Beside him, Asche let out a sound between a sigh and a moan. "This is the only place on this wretched mountain where I can *breathe*." He walked a few steps and pulled himself onto a ledge of rock. His makeup still showed smears from his laughing tears; a few black strands had escaped the impeccable braid; twigs had caught in his robes. Vindt eyed the naked feet dangling before his eyes, and the memory of the toes curling around the tabletop returned to his mind. An affront. A calculated provocation. One of many.

"So what now? Did *you* bring me back from Thrithid?"

It took a while before the heavy-lidded eyes turned to him. "I'm not sure what exactly it is that happened in that room that makes you think you can talk to me in that manner, *Thyd*."

Vindt didn't need to hear Asche switching back from his name to *Thyd* to grasp the underlying threat and realize he had overstepped. He took a breath. "Forgive me," he said, and belatedly added, "Kvahad-thed. It's just... I didn't understand. My moon eyes—"

"Are a mere whim of nature."

"Then why—"

"Forget about what you heard. It has very little to do with you. Ru has some severe... issues. I admit the idea of me rescuing you from Thrithid is very romantic. But even you must be able to see that if I or any Singer had that power, between you and Silhorveen, I would hardly have rescued you."

That seemed logical. But if his brothers believed it...

"Okay, me set aside," Vindt said, trying a different tactic, "*are* there differences between Thyds in the strength of their Gift?"

Asche smiled. "Wanting to be special—such a strange human trait. But you already are special, dear Vindt. Your insolent temper is unprecedented. And, of course, moon eyes are very rare."

His eyes *again*. Were they a sign of something after all? Hidden powers? It had startled Ru to learn about them.

"The others fear you," he said, just because he wanted to know how Asche reacted.

"They fear all and everyone. When it comes to me, their prevalent emotion is a different one."

Hatred. "Tuait—"

"Is an idiot. He knew what the outcome of that battle would be. No idea why he engaged in it at all."

"The others didn't even know about it. You mentioned it to humiliate him."

"Did I?" Asche smiled.

"And Ru, why does he hate you?"

"You think Tuait hates me because of that battle?" Asche chuckled. "And Ru doesn't hate me. Quite the opposite. He simply has an unusual way of showing his affection."

Vindt thought of everything else Ru had hinted at. His memories of Thrithid might have vanished—or been eradicated—but he remembered his own "death," the erratic shape-shifting twitches of the creature that took him and Silhorveen down, its suffocating silence. A Verdur, no doubt. Ren Zian had confirmed it. And Reisen... had been killed by bandits; this he had witnessed with his own eyes. He might not have seen the arrow striking, but he had seen Asche's wrath afterward, the way he killed the archers, his distress.

Yet...

Vindt looked at Asche, this slightly disheveled demon king on the rock's ledge, confident, at ease. Was he capable of hiring people to make Reisen's death seem like an assault and then killing them in cold blood to erase any evidence?

Yes.

The answer came without hesitation, without doubt. He shuddered.

But why?

Asche jumped from the ledge and landed soundlessly on his bare feet. Eyeing Vindt's braid with a frown, he touched his own hair. "I don't understand how you wear that every day. Don't you get a headache?" He strode to the gap in the underbrush through which they had entered the plateau, obviously expecting Vindt to follow.

Talk over. Of course.

"Can I stay here?" Vindt hastened to ask. "Just a moment."

"To do what?"

"Have some time to myself. Digest. That was... a lot. Please." It was true. Every cell in his body craved a moment alone, Singer-free. This was a place where he too could breathe—with Asche gone.

"Fine," Asche condescended. "No more than an hour. And be careful. Wild animals roam these mountains."

He vanished into the bushes as soundlessly as he had emerged.

As soon as Asche was out of sight, Vindt hauled himself onto the ledge he had vacated and slumped back against the rock. It was raining again, a soft drizzle. Gray clouds prowled the sky. Vindt didn't care. He closed his eyes and felt for the rock under his hands, for the raindrops' caressing touch on his face, for the smell of wet earth and eucalyptus trees. Sensations, simple and undemanding.

Gaal, what had he gotten into?

He tried to replay the meeting in his mind, recall what had been said, but it was difficult to bring his memories into a coherent order. The dull ache behind his forehead, a vestige of the mind-reading, didn't help. He was massaging his temples when a feeling in his guts told him he was being watched.

Oh, fuck all the demons, you said an hour, he groaned inwardly before he opened his eyes.

It wasn't Asche.

Vindt's heartbeat sped up as his gaze darted around. The rock at his back, the gaping abyss to the side. No escape route.

"Relax," Ru said flatly. "I didn't come to kill you."

"To admire the view?" Vindt's voice was strained.

Ru's eyebrows narrowed. "Your insolence might amuse Asche; it doesn't amuse me. Get down."

"For w—"

"Get. Down."

Heart hammering, Vindt let himself slip off the ledge. Standing before him, Vindt noticed with dismay that Ru was an inch taller. As if it would make a difference. Physical strength wasn't what mediated the odds here.

"I want to talk to you," Ru said coolly.

"You mean read my mind?"

"Why would I? You have no memories."

"Because Asche erased them?"

Ru's eyebrows narrowed again. It suited him. "Asche killed his Thyd, as he did the one before. He will kill you. It's a mere question of time."

Vindt didn't know what to say to this. Ru had already made those insinuations in the meeting.

"Asche wants power," Ru continued. "And he will do anything to gain it. He will kill you and everyone in his way, Singer or human. It won't be the first time. He's mad."

Vindt swallowed. "Why are you telling me this? I'm his Thyd, bound to him by blood."

"I want you to help me stop him."

"*What?*"

"I assume Asche hasn't let you drink from his wrist yet."

Gaal, that again. Vindt had a sudden epiphany. "Your Thyd doesn't happen to be called Issa?"

Ru didn't answer. As with Asche, the Singer's formal attire emphasized his gender ambiguity. Yet, somehow, even with all the jewelry and makeup, he looked much more masculine than Asche. Unusual compared to the dark-skinned people Vindt had met so far, his eyes were a light gray.

"The answer to your question is no," Vindt said. "I already told your Thyd that."

"Sometime soon he will. When that happens, I want you

to send me a message." He took Vindt's hand and pushed an elongated metal object the size of a nail into it.

"This is...?"

"A whistle. It doesn't make a sound when you blow it, at least none you can hear. But it will call one of my messenger birds to you."

"Okay. Look, I'm sorry, Kvahad-thed, but whatever schemes you Singers are up to, it's none of my business. I have no idea what you're talking about, or Asche, or any of you during that meeting, for that matter. And, frankly, I don't want to know. Here." He held out the whistle.

Ru made no move to take it. "Don't you want to know what I will give you in return?"

"There's nothing that—"

"Freedom."

Vindt's mouth was still open, the remaining words of his cut-off sentence on the tip of his tongue. His mouth fell shut; the words evaporated. "What?"

"You tell me when Asche makes you drink from his wrist, and in return I will grant you freedom. That's what you want, no?"

A melee of thoughts accompanied the chaos of warring emotions in Vindt's chest. "You can't give me freedom. The Bond can only be broken by—"

"Death. And the High Council."

Vindt's pulse switched to an odd rhythm. *He's lying*, his brain claimed. But in his treacherous heart, something emerged through the whirlwind of his emotions like a sprouting flower. Something he had not felt in years. "I depend on the blood."

"There's an antidote."

You fucking wretched bastards.

Vindt felt like drawing his dagger and ramming it straight through the Singer's vile heart, but he pushed his anger down. "You'll never give me my freedom," he said carefully. "Even if I do as you ask. As soon as you have your information, you'll forget about me, about our deal. At best. More likely, you'll do what you long to do now: kill me."

"I thought you would say that." Ru took off the wide bracelet on his left wrist, the one used in the Binding. And a dagger. Before Vindt had time to react, he cut his veins. Ru sang quietly, and a pattern of the Singers' sinuous dark lines appeared on the rocky ground between them. He held his bleeding wrist over it. As soon as the first drop hit the center, a non-human scream rose into the air from nowhere and everywhere at the same time. The lines erupted into black flames.

"I swear by my blood, if you do what I ask of you, I will erase your dependency on the blood and give you your freedom."

More blood fell onto the pattern, greedily consumed by the black flames. Then Ru sang again, and the bleeding stopped. The lines disappeared, leaving no trace.

"This is the most powerful vow a Singer can make. The blood is our source of power, our soul. Breaking this vow means my death." Ru reached out and closed Vindt's limp fingers around the whistle. He was about to say something else, but suddenly he perked up. "Put it away. Now."

Vindt's hand moved without his doing. The item vanished into the pocket of his trousers. A second later, Asche appeared in the gap in the underbrush. His face showed no signs of surprise. He strolled over, casually, as if they had all agreed on meeting here and he was just a little late.

"Funny. I warned my Thyd about roaming predators." He flicked Vindt a glance. "He read your mind?"

Vindt's heart was beating all the way up into his mouth. Fearing his voice would fail, he shook his head.

"I arrived in time then," Asche said pleasantly. He leaned back against the rock next to Vindt.

"Leave us." Ru didn't look at Vindt, but the order was obviously directed at him.

Vindt didn't need to be told twice. The auras of the two Singers strained against their leashes like combat dogs, drooling, eager to rip each other to pieces. He didn't want to be anywhere near when that happened.

Asche didn't react or even looked at him. Vindt took that as acquiescence. He had barely moved, however, when pale fingers closed around his bicep.

"My Thyd takes his orders from me." Asche smiled.

"I want to talk to you." Ru's voice was strained.

"Surely you won't say anything my Thyd can't hear?"

Vindt shot Asche a pleading look, which the Singer pretended not to notice. If anything, the pressure on his arm increased.

Ru's face showed no emotions, but Vindt saw the muscles in his jaw clench. "Asche, please—"

"Don't beg, Ru. It's disgusting."

Endless seconds passed before Ru said in a voice that made Vindt's skin crawl, "I will take you down, Asche. If it is the last thing I do."

Asche let go of Vindt's arm and planted himself right in front of Ru. Being notably smaller than the other Singer, he had to gaze up. Somehow, he made it look as if it was the other way around. "You look horrible, Ruhadar, you know that? Not sleeping well? Is something bothering you? Take me down, you say? But you know what? You don't have the time. You'll be dead first."

The hairs on the back of Vindt's neck rose.

Asche retreated a step; his fingers closed around Vindt's arm again. "I assume that was the gist of what you wanted to say?" The smile he flashed Ru was so cold, Vindt wouldn't have been surprised had their breath condensed in front of their mouths.

Something rippled across Ru's face, an emotion Vindt couldn't place. He didn't speak.

Asche shrugged. "Fine. Goodbye. Oh, and don't sneak up on my Thyd again, will you? I don't... like it." With his free hand, he blew Ru a kiss; with the other, he dragged Vindt back the way they had come.

Vindt only woke up from his trance-like state when they arrived at their quarters. Asche didn't let go of his arm but dragged him through the common area into his own room. It was far more ample than Vindt's.

Only after passing the threshold did Asche eventually release his arm and walk over to a small table. A flat bowl stood in front of a huge mirror, next to several neatly folded pieces of cloths. Asche lowered himself onto the chair and took off his earrings.

Vindt shifted. "Okay, can I—"

"So." Watching his reflection, Asche picked up a piece of cloth and rid his face of the makeup. The strange intimacy of the situation did nothing for Vindt's already frayed nerves.

"What did Ru promise you? Freedom?"

Something dark entered Vindt's body through his pores,

pooling in his stomach. Silence trickled between them for several seconds before Asche turned around. Vindt's gaze fastened on the cloth he was holding, the black streaks tainting the white.

"You believed him?" The Singer's voice was even, light. "Just like that, or did he make some show with his blood?"

Vindt couldn't tear his eyes away from the black-stained cloth. "I didn't…" His voice broke before he could finish the sentence.

"I'm not blaming you, if that's your concern. I am positive you didn't seek Ru out and ask to become part of his schemes. Seems like you did believe him, though. What? That he can undo the Bond? Or that the Council can?" Asche chuckled softly. "Poor Vindt. I wish I could have spared you this. I assume he asked you to spy. In general, or something specific?" Asche followed Vindt's gaze. When he saw what it rested on, he folded the cloth and put it on the table. "Look at me." His voice was soft.

Reluctantly, Vindt turned his gaze. The Singer's eyes were still ringed with a thin black line. Only now did Vindt realize how much Ru's words and the small metal object in his pocket had filled his heart with hope. Asche's unyielding black gaze peeled the skin from the desperately twitching emotion, cut away its flesh and shattered its bones.

"He wanted me to let him know when…" Vindt's vocal cords moved, his tongue. Not him. "When you make me drink from your wrist." His eyes went to the wide bracelets around Asche's wrists, the only jewelry he had not taken off. Which he never took off but for the Binding. Vindt thought about Issa's visit and what he had told him about the Thyd rebellion, Asche oblivious of both.

"Anything else? About me?"

"That you're mad, and..." Vindt paused. "That you will kill."

"Mad..." Asche repeated. His eyes went out of focus as he gazed at the air in front of him. Eventually, he nodded and stretched out his hand.

Vindt stared at the waiting palm. The dark something which had crawled into his body earlier writhed and squirmed. "What..." He knew perfectly well what.

"The whistle," Asche said softly.

Vindt trembled as he reluctantly fumbled the object from his trousers. Asche's long pale fingers closed around it. The eviscerated heap of hope inside him let out a last moan. And died. "How long were you watching us?"

"I wasn't watching you." Asche toyed with the whistle. "Ru is merely predictable. I shouldn't have left you alone."

"Is anything he said true?"

"About me being mad and wanting to kill people? You already think I'm mad. If my intention is to kill people, you will find out eventually."

"Did you kill Reisen?"

For a second, he had the impression a shadow skittered over Asche's face. Then it was gone. "Don't get me wrong, Vindt. I said I know it was Ru who approached you. But I do take this personally." He held up the whistle. "Whatever Ru told you, it's a lie. Forget about freedom." Asche bored his black eyes into Vindt's; his voice lost what little warmth it had held before. "And don't ever think of betraying me again."

The hollowness in Vindt's guts turned a fraction colder. He was about to protest, say that Ru pushed the whistle into his hands, that he didn't even have time to agree or refuse before Asche arrived. But of course he had thought about it. And now Asche had taken the choice from him before he could make it. Rage flared, dulled by desperation.

Asche put the whistle into a pocket of his embroidered robes. "Until we depart, you will only leave this house in my company. Ru will be at the Pledge with me tonight, and I will make sure there won't be any other unexpected visitors." His voice turned soft again. "It was a tough day. Get some sleep."

Vindt wondered briefly what the Pledge was, but decided it didn't matter. Instead, he went into his room as told and collapsed onto the bed, where he curled up into a ball. He stared at nothing until sleep took him.

CHAPTER 20

Darkness had fallen when he woke up. For a blissful second, he lay in the thought-free limbo between sleep and waking, innocent, weightless, then the recent events came down on him like one of the waterfalls outside. He turned onto his stomach and buried his face into the pillow. Then he pulled the pillow over his head. The memories stayed.

Damn Ru. Damn himself. Vindt trusted Ru no more than Asche, or any of them. However, for the first time in a decade, he had allowed his mind to contemplate freedom as an actual possibility. He had no clue what this wrist Binding thing was all about, and he couldn't care less. But it was a door. Had been.

Damn Asche for his preternatural intuition. Or knowledge. Or spying skills. Damn him in general. Damn them all. Their schemes didn't matter to him. What mattered was whether Ru had been sincere with his "reward." If bringing Asche down was really the last thing he planned to do in his life, a Thyd's freedom might not be such a big price to pay, no?

It meant betrayal.

So what? Vindt might have felt a beacon of solidarity with Asche during the meeting, but that surely was a side effect of the Bond. Or that, in that moment, the Singer had stood between him and a pack of demons wanting him dead.

He had to meet with Ru again, no matter how. Tonight, given they would leave tomorrow morning. Asche had claimed both of them would be at the Pledge. Another of their sick rituals.

If Asche found out, he would kill him.

No, he wouldn't.

The realization struck. Punish, yes, but not kill. That Asche had gotten him out of Thrithid still seemed ludicrous. Yet, he seemed to want Vindt alive. He had saved him in the meeting, and, if Asche was to be believed, ten years ago when Silhorveen wanted him dead. Whatever his motives.

Punishment. Vindt almost laughed. Oh, he *did* fear it. But the fear was nothing compared to what risking it might yield.

Asche had left the house already. Vindt felt the absence of his aura. When he closed his eyes and concentrated, he could sense its location, sense *him*, at some distance up the mountain. With Silhorveen, he had never felt anything remotely similar. It was uncanny, but right now, he was glad. He didn't have a plan on how to approach Ru. He would come up with one once he had an overview of the situation.

For now, the plan was simple: follow Asche.

Clouds hid the moon, but the fluorescent flowers

planted along the paths plunged the night into navigable twilight. Vindt's brief concerns about Asche having put up some magical barrier to keep him inside turned out to be baseless. He followed the aura's thread up the mountain to the building where this morning's meeting had been held, then crossed the plateau to the same stairs Asche had led him up afterward.

The top of the stairway was still a dozen steps ahead when suddenly his amulet grew warm and began to vibrate, and a familiar acidic, metallic smell made its way into his nose. Vindt froze. Demons? Here, at The Haven?

Then he heard the song. Not one voice but several, in harmony, entwined. Praising?

Beckoning.

His instincts told him to run, but his mind overruled them. This was his only chance. He continued. With each step, the stench grew worse; the heat of his amulet increased, as did his heartbeat. The singing became louder too, more urgent, a squirming choir that made earth, air and his blood vibrate.

The moment Vindt took the last wary step over the plateau's edge, the song and the demons' stench assailed him like a pack of wolves. The heat of his amulet exploded, the metal burning painfully into his skin. Stifling a scream, Vindt jerked the cord from his neck and cast the entire thing into the darkness. He dropped to his knees; his body curled up as he pressed his palms to his ears in a vain attempt to shield himself against the onslaught on his senses.

Bluish light illuminated the plain before him. Distributed in a wide circle in its center, still or again clad in their flamboyant attire, the seven Singers of the Council were... Wait—what? *Kneeling?*

Vindt's eyes went wide. Bowed heads, eyes closed, their palms facing upward in a gesture of offering. Their song, as beautiful as ever, sounded demure, reverent.

Vindt would have wallowed in that image were not indeed demons filling the air, so many, so strong, that the entire clearing blurred and writhed. Their smell scraped Vindt's nostrils and throat and made his eyes water. He pulled the hem of his shirt over his nose. To negligible avail. The demons didn't attack him, but their presence drained the life out of him as if they held him in their embrace. His instincts took over then, pushing him into survival mode, silencing his protesting mind.

On his hands and knees, he retreated, crawling down the stairs he had just climbed. Only when he had almost reached the bottom did the hold of song and stench loosen enough to let him stop and take a deep breath. He cast an anxious glance behind him. Nothing was following. Still, the stench clogged his nostrils and mouth. Spitting on the floor didn't help.

"What are you doing here?" a sharp female voice snapped. "This area is reserved for the High Council." The woman glowering at him from the stairs' bottom wore the formal attire of the servants that had welcomed them to the meeting this morning.

"I..." Vindt shot a glance up the mountain. "I just..."

The woman's eyes narrowed. Two more servants, both men, stepped up beside her. "This is a forbidden area for you. We're going to accompany you back to your quarters."

A mixture of panic and desperation washed over Vindt. No, that couldn't happen. He needed to meet Ru. Tonight was his only chance. He gave the two men a once-over. They were slightly smaller than him. Whether they were experienced fighters was hard to tell. He might be able to overthrow them.

And then?

His mind raced, but came up with nothing.

One man gestured toward the stairs leading down. Vindt let out an inaudible scream before he walked in the indicated direction.

It probably didn't take long for Asche to return, but Vindt felt each second like a rock heaped upon his chest. The two men had not left after delivering him to the house, but stood guard outside. If the woman had not already told Asche about his Thyd's nighttime endeavor, they would.

He felt Asche's approach long before he heard the two guards' low "Kvahad-thed." Even their bow was audible.

"We need to tell you—" one started.

"You can leave."

"But—"

Apparently, Asche didn't need words to cut the servant off a second time.

"Of course. May you rest well, Kvahad-thed."

Vindt listened to the receding footsteps with growing trepidation. None approached; as usual, Asche simply appeared in the open door to his room. He must have renewed his makeup before leaving for the ritual. The intricate lines on his forehead were back, the lidded lashes, the silvery powder on his cheeks, the red lips. The braid, the earrings, the formal robes. "Why did you leave early?" he said without preamble. "You missed the best part."

Vindt tried to steady his racing pulse. "How do you..."

"You have a habit of screaming your presence into everyone's face."

Vindt caught the object Asche tossed him in reflex before it hit his face. His amulet. He clenched it as Asche stepped into the room. In the pale glow of the phosphorescent plants coming in through the windows, the Singer's features were hard to distinguish, but under the makeup he looked... tired.

"Enjoy the show?" Asche continued placidly. "Did it make you happy? The almighty Singers on their knees."

"I don't know what... I was shit-scared."

"Were you now? I only wished you were shit-scared of disobeying my orders."

"I thought... I only wanted—"

"To meet Ru."

Vindt closed his eyes and braced himself for the punishment.

None came. Instead, Asche said, "I'll tell you again, Ru is a liar. There is no way of undoing the Bond. You've seen how keenly he wants you dead. And I'll tell you something else I've already told you: freedom is a flexible cage whose boundaries are yours to define. You have choices, Vindt. Make use of them. Wisely."

With that, Asche turned to go. At the door, he paused. "It's funny. You're the first Thyd who tried to kill his Singer, the first Thyd returning from Thrithid, the first Thyd to attend a meeting of the High Council. And now you're the first Thyd who has ever witnessed the Pledge." The glint in his eyes ignited. "Seems like you're special after all."

* * *

Timid rays of sunlight peeked through the clouds the next morning as Vindt trailed behind Asche along The

Haven's sloping paths once more. They would leave soon, but first, the Singer had to see to some final "business." Or so he had told Vindt, and also that this business was none of Vindt's concern; he would have very much preferred to go alone. But roaming predators.

The long building that seemed to be their destination was flanked by smaller houses at each end. A porch ran its length. It seemed vaguely familiar. They were approaching the stairs leading up to the main entrance when a sudden, gut-wrenching wail made Vindt stall. The sound was so full of agony, Vindt's innards contracted in sympathy and with the immediate desire to make it stop.

This wasn't the place where they kept the shriveled, moaning corpses of their fallen, was it? "Where are we?"

Asche proceeded up the stairs. The wail climbed into a crescendo. It didn't sound like the sounds Reisen and Silhorveen had made, however. It sounded like—

A woman emerged from a door, carrying a bundle of crimson cloths decorated with the Singers' sinuous lines. The source of the screams.

A baby?

Her face lit up when she saw Asche. She bowed as much as the bundle in her arms allowed. "Kvahad-thed. We're so glad you could make it. And just in time." She looked at the wailing child, her smile turning into a pained expression.

Asche took the baby from her and his expression *transformed*. He smiled, a smile not full of mockery or disdain but genuine, tender warmth. His entire face lit up, a gentle glow whose heat Vindt thought he could feel even from this distance. Having seemingly forgotten about Vindt's existence, Asche lowered himself and the baby onto a rocking chair.

And sang.

It was the second time Vindt had heard Asche sing like this, but nothing could have prepared him for its effect. The unearthly voice enveloped his brain, suffused his blood and rippled through his body with strident urgency. Beautiful. Inescapable. Vindt barely registered that the baby's wailing stopped. He stood entranced, a hand on the porch's railing for support.

After what could have been seconds or ages, Asche's voice abated. The song's echo hung back, a quiver in the planks beneath Vindt's feet, in the air, a mournful longing in his body and soul, the almost painful desire for the song to continue. After another moment, only emptiness prevailed, a hole carved into the world's core.

The baby's lips were curled into a stunned "O" as it looked up at Asche with huge brown eyes. His tiny brows furrowed. A sequence of guttural noises escaped his mouth which, after a moment, bore a distinct note of frustration. His brows narrowed further as he intensified his attempts.

"He's trying to imitate you." Vindt realized he was smiling and quickly forced the corners of his lips down.

The signs of frustration on the baby's face gave way to fully fledged anger. He looked like he was on the verge of crying again. Asche's smile deepened. He brushed the baby's cheek with the back of his fingers. "It will take some time until he can."

With a last grumpy sound, the baby gave up on his attempts to imitate Asche's song. He turned his head and glowered at Vindt, as if to blame him for his failure. The boy couldn't be more than a few weeks old, but the gaze in his brown eyes was strangely intense. From one second to the next, the features lit into a beam, and the baby stretched out his tiny hands toward Vindt, making happy, gurgling baby noises.

Asche's eyebrows rose. The smile as he turned to Vindt lost some of its warmth, but didn't vanish entirely, nor did the glow on his face. Vindt's heart skipped a beat.

"Want to hold him?"

"What?" Vindt said, alarmed.

Asche peeled the baby out of the blanket. In a smooth motion, he rose from the chair and pressed the boy into Vindt's startled grip. With a mixture of terror and self-consciousness, Vindt stared as the tiny hands closed around the cord dangling from his neck and pulled the amulet out. A triumphant gurgle escaped the baby's throat as he shoved it into its mouth.

"Inexplicable as it is, he seems to like you," Asche said dryly.

Vindt stood frozen, having no clue what to do. He wasn't fond of babies. And this wasn't even a baby, which it hadn't taken much to realize. It was a damn fucking baby *Singer*.

He remembered the building now. The nursery. They had shown it to him back when he lived here. What they didn't explain was how the babies came into existence. Singers were all male. Unless... Vindt had never seen a Singer naked. They looked androgynous enough. Perhaps they were hermaphrodites.

He cleared his throat. "Where does it come from?"

"Some place in the world."

"With trees growing Singers?"

Asche's lips curled into a smile. A fraction of the glow the Singer's face had held a moment ago came back to life. So strange. "That would be nice. Unfortunately, it's much worse. We're born to humans."

"*You're what?*" Vindt almost dropped the gurgling bundle in his arms.

"In case you haven't noticed, we are all male and thus lack certain prerequisites to carry out the task of pregnancy."

So much for his theory. "You mean you fu... you sleep with human women?"

Asche looked at him blankly. "No Singer would ever stoop so low as to touch a human."

A moment of awkward silence passed. Vindt held the black gaze, the back of his neck prickling.

Wouldn't you?

Asche was the first to look away.

Vindt cleared his throat. "But how...?"

"We know when one of us is born and where. Then we go and..." Asche's smile deepened. "Steal it right from the cradle. It's what demons are supposed to do, isn't it?"

It was indeed. All the tales Vindt's mother had told him... "Is that a joke?"

"Yes, but not in the way you think."

Before Vindt had time to ponder what that meant, a sudden stench made his nose wrinkle. He looked at the baby with renewed terror. "Uh. I think he shat." He tried to hand him back to Asche, but the boy clung to the amulet with unexpected strength. The tiny face looked at him defiantly.

"It's a baby," Asche said. "They do these things."

Somehow, Vindt had expected Singer babies to not do "these things."

Eventually, Asche had mercy and took the boy back from him. The baby let the amulet go with a dejected expression, but as soon as Asche smiled at him, his face lit up again. He reached out and grabbed strands of the Singer's hair instead, pulling and gurgling merrily. Asche offered him a finger, which the baby eyed warily, then stuffed into his mouth.

Vindt stared.

"He'll need to eat," the woman eventually said. Vindt had forgotten about her.

Asche seemed as reluctant to hand her the baby as the baby seemed to leave his arms. When the woman pulled out her breast, however, its resistance changed into eagerness.

Cry. Shit. Drink milk from a human breast. Born to humans... It all only raised more questions.

"Hethel's in class," the woman said while the baby suckled peacefully at her breast. "He was crestfallen when he heard you would come while he was away."

"Give him this." Asche pulled something from his pocket and handed it to the woman.

"He will be overjoyed."

Asche's face went back to the usual impervious mask. The change was remarkable. Vindt felt as if he had seen something forbidden. Perhaps he had. The Singer wouldn't have brought him along had it not been for "roaming predators."

"Let's go." Asche strode back the way they'd come.

Nodding goodbye to the woman, Vindt fell in beside him. "Hethel's a child Singer?"

Asche didn't answer. They walked in silence for a while, until the Singer suddenly asked, "Do you have children?"

Vindt squirmed under the strangely intense gaze. This was the most personal question a Singer had ever asked him, perhaps the first personal question ever. He was not sure if he liked it. Or if he wanted to give a truthful answer. He didn't even know what the truth was. Liz had been pregnant when he left for the war, but she had lost a child before. Even if she had given birth to this one, Vindt had no idea what had become of her, of them, of his family. They could be dead or enslaved, or perhaps—this was an option too—his father had just sworn his allegiance to the usurpers' regent.

As to an offspring…

Had the outcome of the war been different, and Liz had carried the child to term, he would have married her. His father didn't approve, regardless of the fact that Liz wasn't of noble birth. In Pel, no man would marry a woman who had not yet proven her fertility. Having lost a child was even worse.

Back then, Vindt didn't care. What did it matter if he had children or not? He might be the son of a lord, but the third son. Unless both his elder brothers died, he wouldn't rule. What would he need an heir for, or a daughter to arrange a strategic marriage?

"No," Vindt eventually said, "I don't have children."

"Would you like to?"

"And you'll babysit?"

"Why not? I like children." The Singer resumed his steps.

Vindt waited, but nothing else came.

Eventually, they reached the plateau where they had entered The Haven two days ago. It felt like much more time had passed. A happy whinny welcomed them. The demon mare pranced on the spot, tugging at the reins in the hands of a servant. Asche patted her neck and stroked her nose. A moment later, Vindt saw her munching.

He's really feeding her treats.

He pulled himself into the saddle of his own horse. *Reisen's* horse. Keke. Another unwanted inheritance. Vindt had liked his old gelding.

He shifted around but couldn't find a comfortable position. Something poked into a body part he definitely didn't want something to poke into. He stood in the stirrups and felt the saddle with his hand. There. Some object where no object should be. It seemed to be covered by a patch of rough leather. What the hell?

Annoyed, he tugged at the leather's edges until it came loose. Something slid down from under it toward his thigh. Vindt caught the object before it fell to the ground. Metal?

He sank back into the saddle and opened his palm to inspect it, only to close it at almost the same second. His heart started pounding so hard the entire Haven must hear it.

"Ready?" Asche's voice seemed to come from far away. The Singer had mounted too.

Vindt's hand trembled; he needed several tries to make the object vanish into the pockets of his pants. Then he hastened to maneuver his horse close to Schiida, trying to keep his expression neutral.

Asche cast him a searching look. "Becoming nostalgic about leaving?"

Vindt managed to fake a snort. "Yes."

The dark gaze rested on him a moment longer, then the horses moved. Asche sang. The Door. Vindt didn't pay attention. His entire awareness was on the shape in his pocket.

The shape of another whistle.

CHAPTER 21

The number of birds was impossible to quantify. The water of the lake vanished under the blue mass of heads, bodies and legs. They plowed the shallow water with their long curved beaks, their spindly legs clicking like twigs breaking; their chatter filled the air. Now and then, for no apparent reason, the birds took flight, all of them together, as if one had given an unheard signal, a giant, multi-limbed creature, twisting and turning in the sky, forming loops and circles, rising and falling.

Vindt had no idea what made them concert their moves like this, or what prevented them from colliding. It was magic. They had been standing here for at least half an hour, but he was nowhere near growing tired. Even the horses seemed spellbound, watching the spectacle with pricked ears.

"This life does hold some perks compared to your former." Asche had managed to sneak up on him even though he was riding his horse.

Vindt made a point of keeping his eyes on the birds.

Sure, in the decade he had spent traveling with Silhorveen he *had* seen things that filled him with wonder and awe, sandstones sculpted into the most bizarre of forms by the wind in some desert, black-sand beaches and white lakes, the caves of Sphi with their forests of stalactites and stalagmites that glowed in their own phosphorescent light, countless animals he had heard of only in tales or never at all.

"There's a difference between watching this as a free man," he said quietly, so the others couldn't hear, "or as a slave."

"Slave…" Asche sighed and turned Schiida to continue down the road.

With a last glance at the birds, Vindt and Keke followed.

They were still within sight of the lake when they set up camp in the afternoon.

Broad smiles and enthusiastic "welcome backs" had greeted Vindt upon their return from The Haven. Narr had squeezed his shoulder, while Risi broke some of his bones by taking him into a one-armed hug. Jun prepared a special welcome-back dish. Even Layyad awarded him one of his rare smiles. Vindt was moved. Though he had only known the others for a few weeks and had been away for a mere two days, he had missed them.

Ehlan, Fora and the rest of Silhorveen's retinue had already moved on, having to travel to The Haven "the human way," by land and sea. It would take them months. They had said a brief goodbye before Vindt left, but the prospect of carrying Reisen had taken up Vindt's mind so much he had hardly paid attention.

A sliver of regret nudged his chest now, for the failed goodbye but also because, for the first time, he wondered if he could have actually been *friends* with the people of his former retinue. If he had tried. There had been quite the change in servants, like Ehlan, who had only replaced Silhorveen's former seneschal two years ago. But Fora had been a constant companion throughout those past ten years, and treated Vindt as amicably as his taciturn, grumpy nature let him.

Whatever, it was too late now.

A week's journey lay ahead of them to the port town where they would board a ship to Asche's home. Vindt still found the idea of the Singer owning something so mundane bizarre.

"It's a harsh place, but full of beauty," Narr explained upon Vindt's inquiry as they set up Asche's tent together. "On the coast. Actually, it's more or less *in* the ocean. And that's how it feels inside. As if you were underwater."

A blurred image of waves crashing into cliffs formed in Vindt's mind, tied to a faint longing. The strange effects of Asche's blood.

"And he breeds horses there?"

Narr laughed. "Who told you that?"

"Risi."

"I don't think he literally breeds them. But yes, there are a lot of horses. Most of them live half wild in the hills. They come when he calls them. It's quite a sight."

Narr fastened cords to the pegs while Vindt steadied the pole. His mind tried to create the image of Asche calling horses. Others came: Asche playing games with him, Asche scaring the shit out of the mightiest living Singers, Asche with naked feet and painted lips, Asche singing to a baby. Asche, the enigma.

Keeping his hand from tracing the whistle in the pocket

of his trousers took some effort. Why would the Singer let him drink from his wrist? That he was keen on transferring a part of his powers into him, as Issa had claimed the process would achieve, seemed ludicrous. Even more so if what Ru had said was true, that Asche *craved* power. He was already one of the mightiest Singers. But who knew? Everyone—apart from himself—seemed to hunger for power.

Since the meeting, his mind kept returning to the events of his "death" and the weeks after his resurrection, trying to remember the in between, the spot which—according to Ru—Asche had eradicated. To no avail, obviously.

He replayed Reisen's death, too. Killing his Thyd to bind *him*. No matter how much Asche denied it, the seed of doubt was sprouting. Vindt wouldn't put *anything* past the Singer. He also remembered something Asche had *not* mentioned in the meeting: him and Silhorveen having met a year ago. By chance? The strange dream he had that night, involving Asche—what if it had not been a dream, if the Singer had been there, in his room? To do what?

Besides, Ru would hardly accuse Asche of being responsible for his resurrection on a whim. If Asche had told the truth during the meeting, it was a crime to their laws, even implying a death sentence. Another oddity. Should they not be glad someone had that power? Use it "appropriately" in the future by not wasting it on a trite Thyd but to resurrect their precious own?

Which brought him to the "First." Asche and Ru had both mentioned them. Asche claimed that they would have struck him down for his "crime," but apparently they hadn't. And Ren Zian had once said, *In the name of the First*, a phrase in which Vindt, in his place, would have put his goddess. He had always wondered if Singers bowed to any gods. People always venerated *something*, no matter where in the world they lived. Then again, Singers were no people. It wouldn't have surprised him if they simply worshipped themselves.

But now, the First. Vindt had the strong feeling he had seen them the night he followed Asche up the mountain to their weird ritual. The Pledge. It made sense. Bowing not to gods but to demons. Asche was right; the idea that something more powerful than Singers existed lifted Vindt's spirits. On the one hand. On the other, it was unsettling.

Asche wasn't happy bowing. This, too, Vindt was sure about. Though the Singer hardly gave away anything while talking, he didn't bother to—or couldn't—hide some of his emotions. Apart from the sarcasm, Vindt remembered well the bitterness when Asche had alluded to Vindt having seen them knee—

An inverted scream not ten feet from him tore him from his musings. For a split second, his mind hovered between knowledge and denial. Then fear exploded in his chest as he dropped the pole.

In all the years with Silhorveen, he had dreaded each new Verdur attack, how the Singer penetrated him with his voice, invaded his very being, manipulated him, used him. With Asche, the dread had become threaded with something rawer, primal. Heart racing, Vindt tried to brace himself for the violation.

Which never came.

His voice rose before he even heard Asche sing, eager to meet the other in a choreographed, smooth twirl. Reunion. More. It felt as if he himself was becoming part of something else, of *someone*, assimilation, return. Power—to destroy, to kill—flooded his veins and sent his heart thrumming.

Singing. His nature. Him.

His panic dissolved. Instead, anticipation, grim and confident, made his nerves quiver. His ears and vision sharpened. There it was. The Verdur. The enemy. Its writhing translucent shape whirled around them, reforming, dog, woman, doe, bird, as if it wanted to mock the existence of creatures of flesh and blood. From the corners of his eyes, he saw Narr retreating and drawing her sword.

Vindt focused on the Verdur, its antagonistic voice, its gravity, the threat, the promise to kill. The hatred in its shape-shifting eyes was burning, new and yet familiar, while it circled him with its choppy movements, seeking the hole in their defense.

There was none. His and Asche's voices pierced through the inverted screams, ripped them to pieces, elegantly, effortlessly, even though the Singer stood on the other side of their campsite. His lips had curled into a wolfish smile.

Vindt wanted to hear the Verdur's not-sound again, the surprise in it, the fear, the agony.

And he did. One. Two. Three times.

That was when the angry vibrations of his amulet and an acidic, metallic smell strangled his euphoria. Arbitrary noises pierced staccato-like through the Verdur-imposed silence. Demons. Again.

His fear rekindled.

Asche's voice *split*. One part stayed with Vindt, softly guiding; the other lashed out at the new attackers. Narr and the rest of their group launched into their theatrical sword dance. Jun shot arrows at nothing. Which reminded Vindt he now had a sword like theirs too. His hand had just touched the hilt when Asche's voice in his head stopped him.

Leave it.

Through the haze of the demons' shapeless figures, Vindt watched the Verdur retreat into the trees, the succession of its changing forms fast, erratic. Wounded. A pang of disappointment clanged through him. He wanted real victory. Death.

He heard the thundering hooves a second before he was pulled onto the running horse like a child. No way Asche could have done that with physical strength alone. Schiida was unsaddled and unbridled, but Asche sat secure and steady. Vindt had ridden bareback before, but a long time ago, in the rider's position, where the ups and downs were gentlest, not where he sat now, almost on the rump. He had no choice but to hold on to the Singer's waist to keep from falling off.

A beacon of concern for the fate of the others, left behind with the demons, crystallized in his mind, but the headwind whisked it away. The mare dashed through the underbrush, pushed forward by her master's determination and the unabating force of their song. Twigs and leaves lashed at Vindt's arms and face. Before them, the fleeing Verdur tumbled, fluttered, careened.

Get it.

The mare leaped over a fallen tree. Vindt's hands tightened around the Singer's waist in reflex as he almost lost his balance. Strands of Asche's hair brushed his cheeks. A voice inside him whispered, *That's wrong*, but the thundering of his heart and Schiida's hooves drowned it out. His head was light, dizzy. He *felt* the Verdur, its distress. His own excitement. Asche was playing; the pursuit was a game. The rush of the chase. Voice and voice, bow and arrow. Loosened. Hitting its target.

He had never heard anything like the sound that followed, an inverted scream that shook the ground, tore the leaves from the trees, bent trunks, broke branches and ripped bark. He felt the Verdur's struggle, its desperation, its wrath, surging, culminating—

Broken.

Gone.

Schiida came to an abrupt halt. Vindt felt her chest expand and contract in rapid succession between his legs. He was panting himself, as if he had been running alongside the mare. He felt dizzy. His blood still pulsed through his veins in a rhythm that was not his. Heat came from everywhere, the mare's body, Asche's, his own, pushing sweat through his pores. Their joined breathing was the only sound to be heard. No birds, no animals, no wind. The landscape holding its breath.

Now that the chase was over, the places their bodies touched crawled to the forefront of his awareness, chest, groin, thighs. Asche's flanks under his hands. So strange. Not a demon's squirming nothingness but an actual body, bones, flesh. Touchable. The buzz at the back of his scalp returned. This close, Asche's scent of waves and tides was overwhelming. How could someone smell of the ocean?

A sudden tremor rose under his touch, crawling upward, increasing, heralding the avalanche. Then Asche tossed his head back and laughed.

The sound was deep and hoarse, nothing like the light, sparkling noise Vindt had heard from him before. It echoed among the silent trees, cast back, hollow and warped. A flock of birds took off to the sky, chirping in anguish. Asche laughed so hard, his delicate body under Vindt's hands shook.

Let go.

But only when Asche turned to face him did Vindt let his hands sink down, slowly, avoiding calling attention to the place they had rested the entire time.

Asche's cheeks were flushed. He was... grinning. His canines showed, pointed and gleaming, a predator on the prowl, prey fallen. His eyes burned, roaring black flames, sending out sparks, devouring everything in their wake. Vindt had seen this look before, seen those eyes, heard this laughter, not in Asche, not in any Singer, but in humans.

Ru's right. He's mad.

Asche's hungry, triumphant gaze almost pushed Vindt off the horse. Vindt held on and returned it, the old defiance.

"That was... fun." Asche rolled the last word around in his mouth like a piece of candy.

Vindt was not sure. He was... shaken. Chasing after a Verdur, killing it. He hadn't even known that was possible. Everything Silhorveen and he had ever done was defend themselves, their lives. At some point, the Verdurs had given up and disappeared.

Asche's smile vanished. He looked at Vindt as if he were noticing him for the first time. "Off."

Vindt glared at him. *You pulled me up here.*

He was no acrobat to pull one leg the entire way over Asche's upper body to dismount, nor could he swing it back without leaning into the Singer. He had no choice but to unceremoniously slide down Schiida's butt. The mare turned her head and looked at him indignantly.

He tried to glimpse the place the Verdur had hovered

last, but Asche moved the horse so that it blocked his view. A familiar smell hit his nose, tart, metallic. At the same time, he heard… whispers?

But that—

"Move." Asche pointed his chin in the direction they'd come from.

With Schiida blocking his view, Vindt couldn't see the ground, only the circle of ravaged trees, as if a giant beast had pivoted on the spot as it lashed out with its claws. The smell intensified. The whispers grew louder. As they had when Reisen—

"Now."

Schiida took a step forward, forcing Vindt to either sidestep or turn and start walking. He opted for the latter. The demon mare stayed close on his heels, propelling him forward. He looked back in irritation. "Would you mind keeping a little distance? I can walk by myself."

Asche's black gaze hit him, and a second later, Schiida's torso. So much for where the mare's loyalties lay.

Vindt stumbled forward and caught himself at the last moment.

Bastard. If it wasn't for me, you wouldn't have bested the Verdur the way you did.

He didn't know if that was true, though, if anything in all this was *his* doing, *his* power. Was he special after all? His Gift stronger?

"The others," he said, guilty conscience hitting. "We should hurry. We left them al—"

"They are fine. The demons are not after *them*."

Which was proven true a second later when they came down on them out of nowhere, their cacophonous song full of anticipatory triumph. Asche grinned. And sang. The determination in his voice had changed into an unflappable, almost gleeful confidence. He didn't even bother to dismount. The demons were gone in a heartbeat, dissolving or fleeing, hissing and howling, leaving them in a landscape which looked nothing like before.

"Let's go." Asche pointed his chin toward their camp.

Vindt cast a last look back, but there was nothing to see apart from trees, and no sounds to be heard but a soft rustle in their branches.

CHAPTER 22

After three days at sea, relief filled Vindt's body, like a tension accumulating for years had dissolved into the churning waves. Having spent half his life on boats, living inland for so long had carved a perpetual gnawing ache of longing into his chest.

Today's sky was as gray as it had been ever since they left port; a cool wind blew a constant, fine drizzle into their faces. The others sat hunched in their water-repellent cloaks, looking miserable. Vindt felt great. He relished the sensation of the spray on his skin, the damp, rich air that filled his lungs. It smelled of fish and tar, of rotting seaweed and wet cloths. When he licked his lips, he tasted salt.

Gaal, how he had missed the sea.

The dice were going round, accompanied by taunts and laughter, groans of loss and exclamations of victory, but Vindt was only halfheartedly paying attention. Asche stood at the prow, watching the ocean. He always stood there, immobile as the wooden figurine below him, day and night.

They had killed a Verdur, *easily*. From the others, Vindt

knew Asche had never done it before.

There's nothing special about you.

You miserable liar.

Calveen emerged from the cabins. The seneschal had joined them in their games on one or two occasions, but mostly kept to himself. Or to Asche, the slimy prick.

Vindt watched them exchange a few words, then disappear together into the ship's innards. To treat Calveen's headache, presumably. On their first day at sea, Vindt had "caught" them, Asche touching the old man's temples, singing softly. In contrast to the mind-reading, to judge from the relaxed, almost rapt look on Calveen's face, the procedure must be rather pleasant.

Bet the pervert's addicted to it.

For whatever reason, Asche didn't heal Calveen's hip. The ailment wasn't very conspicuous, but since Reisen had mentioned the seneschal's ailments to Vindt, he had become observant. Of the dwindling eyesight, he had detected no sign, but Reisen had surely been right about that, too. The moment when Calveen would be more a burden than help was on the horizon. Months? Years? Not long, in any case. Vindt felt a warm surge of glee.

"Your turn." The leather cup with the dice appeared in his line of vision.

Vindt dutifully shook the cup. When he peeked under it, he realized he had missed which number Layyad had said. "Uh. What did you say?"

Layyad grinned. "Double five."

"Hey, that was not—" Jun started, but Layyad elbowed him. "His fault if he doesn't pay attention."

"Euh... Pair of sixes, then." Vindt passed the cup to Risi, completely failing to feign a poker face.

Risi smirked. "Up, up."

Vindt sighed and threw another crown of the allowance Calveen handed him every month into the pot.

Risi toyed with the cup without shaking it. "You know, Reisen was good at this. Remember how he would fidget and smile, making everyone believe he was lying? And then he was right." He chuckled. "I mean, we knew he did that every time. And still fell for it."

The others laughed too. However, after a few seconds, they fell silent. Backs straightened, faces took on a conscious expression.

Reisen. It was the first time anyone had mentioned him.

Risi cleared his throat. "Sorry. It's just... my brain keeps expecting him to put his hand on my shoulder and startle me to death. You know, how he always did that, sneaking up on you just like Asche and looking all innocent when you jumped with a near heart attack."

Eyes went out of focus. Vindt could almost see the memories replaying in their minds. It made him uncomfortably aware of how he had taken the man's place. A place he would never be able to fill. He rose. "I think I'm going to—"

"Oh, don't go." Narr reached for his wrist as she dabbed at her eyes with the sleeve of her other arm. "Perhaps that's actually a good clue..." Encouraging nods met her searching gaze. "Look, Reisen's death was hard for us, but... we really want to welcome you to the group. I mean, officially."

Vindt lowered himself back onto the heap of coiled rope he had been sitting on. "Uh... thank you, that's—"

"And we have a gift for you," Jun interrupted him. "A welcome gift." He nudged Narr with the tip of his foot.

Narr produced something from the pocket of her

trousers and handed it over. It was a pendant attached to a thin leather cord, round and translucent, made of what looked like glass. A small leaf was embedded in it, the color of rust, in the inconspicuous oval form most leaves had. Vindt still recognized it. It was common in Pel. It had surprised him when he had first spotted the plant, which grew in close proximity to rivers and creeks on this side of the First Sea. Its prevalence, however, was only one reason he was so familiar with it.

"It looks a bit boring," Jun rushed to add, "but it's great. It changes color with the cycle of the moon, from green to red and back. Really. Moonturner, the plant's called."

No, *mandyrka*—moon worshipper.

Vindt looked from Jun's beaming face to the others, waiting for the inevitable words: *We chose it because it matches your eyes.*

Nobody said it. No one was even looking at his eyes. Had Asche not told them? Then why did they pick this of all plants? His color-changing eyes were no secret. He only hated the attention that usually came with it. The suspicion, sometimes. The stares. That no one but Asche had detected his changing eye colors yet didn't come as a surprise. People hardly ever did.

"I don't know what to say. It's... Thank you." He tried to sound pleased, moved—which he was—but his puzzlement dampened the enthusiasm. It made him feel bad. A welcome gift. No one had gifted him anything ever since the Singers forced him into their service.

"But that's not all." Jun's eager voice cut through Vindt's thoughts. "You know what that is?"

"Uh... you said yourself, a moonturn—"

"No, no, not the leaf, the stuff around it."

"Glass?"

"How'd you get a leaf into glass?" Risi snorted. "Ever watched how glass is made? Stuff's glowing hot when liquid. Everything it touches would just burn up."

It was true; the pendant didn't feel like glass. It felt... strange, not cool but warm, soft and hard at the same time.

"A bloodstone," Jun said, apparently happy to reveal the secret. "Our blood. We all gave a drop, and then Asche turned it into that. Well, I think he also used something else, soil or something, but whatever, our blood's in there too."

Vindt's gaze inadvertently went back to the prow, but Asche had not returned. "Asche made this?"

The others nodded.

"Hey," Layyad said, the usual frown on his face. "We won't be heartbroken if you don't want to wear it around your neck all the time, by the way."

The others groaned.

"He claims the cord scrapes his neck," Narr explained. "That's why he's not wearing his."

"So what? I still carry it." Layyad took a small translucent ball from one of his pockets. "See?"

"You've all got one of these?" Vindt asked, surprised.

They nodded and pulled their pendants from beneath their shirts.

"But all different," Kishoon pointed out. "Look." He held his stone out to Vindt. It contained a blue flower he didn't recognize.

"Flower is Tsjuka," Kishoon explained. "It's not many blue. Normally white. Blue one gives luck."

Embedded into Narr's was a pale violet crystal. When she held it over the planks, it amplified the dull daylight, painting a bright circle on the ground.

"At night, when the moon is out, you can even use it like a little lamp," she said. "Cool, no?"

"Yours?" Vindt asked Risi.

Risi passed it over to him. Vindt gave a laugh. "Isn't that —"

"A khesim," Risi interrupted, voice defiant. "They are sacred. They represent Pethal, the morning form of Ak, the sun god."

... *a dung beetle*, was what Vindt had wanted to say. Because that was what the tiny black creature inside the stone was. How a bug rolling shit over the ground could end up as a representation for a god was beyond his imagination, but he nodded appreciatively.

"They bring luck," Risi added. "And... uh... well, you know."

"Potency," Layyad said, resolving Vindt's puzzlement.

With Risi's skin tone, it was difficult to see if he blushed, but Vindt had the strong feeling he did. "Well, yeah. But— hey—the khesim was a gift from the others."

"Seems like they thought you needed it," Layyad said.

What Jun's pendant held, Vindt couldn't discern. It looked like a heap of fine reddish threads.

"Hair from the first deer I shot," Jun said proudly. "It brings me luck, lets me aim more precisely."

"You shot that deer after you joined Asche's retinue?"

"*What?* Are you joking?" Jun snapped. "I was eight when I shot it. I carried the hair in a little pouch before."

"Sorry, didn't mean to offend you. So the others asked you what you wanted in your pendant?"

Jun glanced at Layyad. "He stole it from me."

"What? Without you knowing?" Vindt shot Layyad a doubtful look. Even if using the hairs for the pendant was admittedly a good idea, stealing it was quite an intrusion into someone's privacy. "What if Jun hadn't liked it?"

The tall man shrugged. "Knew he would."

"Sure I did," Jun said, grinning and clutching his talisman. "It's so much better this way. The pouch always got wet, and I could never look at the hair."

Layyad's pendant was the largest. It held a black claw, which Layyad explained came from a night eagle. It was meant to give strength and luck while hunting.

Vindt turned his gaze to the stairs leading below deck. "Calveen's got one too?"

The others exchanged glances. Layyad shrugged.

"'Suppose so," Risi said.

"He got cord around neck," Kishoon said.

"You've never seen it?" Vindt asked.

"Nope," Risi said.

Interesting.

"But seriously, eh?" Risi said. "Don't have to wear it if you don't want to. No one's gonna be offended. It's not a sect thing, just a tradition."

Vindt tied the cord around his neck. The pendant came to rest on top of his amulet.

"What's the other necklace?" Jun, who had followed his movement, promptly asked.

Vindt took out his amulet without thinking. "A gift from the priests. It protects me against—"

That was when he realized his mistake. The priests. *His* priests. Back in Plotliw's camp, he had told the others he had grown up at The Haven. Rectify the lie? This meant he would need to tell them the rest of the truth too, about his past, his hatred.

"Against?" Jun prompted, at the same time as Risi asked,

"Which priests?"

"Against demons," Vindt said hurriedly, answering Jun's question.

"Seriously?" Jun's eyes widened. "And it works? Why don't we all have an amulet like this? Which priests gave it to you?"

"It's not like the swords," Vindt quickly explained. "I mean, its effect is far less. And the priests... Uh, actually, I don't know. We... uh... met them on the road. A long time ago. No idea which god they served. But they gave me this, and I... I thought it looked nice. To be honest, I didn't believe it worked at first, but, well, yes, it does a little."

"Can I have a look?" Jun's eyes shone.

After a moment's hesitation, Vindt handed the necklace over. "There's a rune engraved into it. It glows when demons are close."

"That's so cool," Jun said. "I want one too." He handed the amulet over to Layyad, who studied it with furrowed brows.

"I think you're fine with your arrows," Risi pointed out.

"But for how long? The attacks are increas—"

"No, they're not." Risi glowered at Jun.

But they were. Of course, Vindt didn't know how it had been before he joined Asche's retinue, but they had been attacked *twice* after Asche and he killed the Verdur. The last time on their way to the port, in the middle of town. It had been utter chaos, people screaming, parts of the cobblestoned street and entire houses exploding. Jun couldn't use his bow for fear of hitting something more substantial than a demon.

It wasn't the first time Vindt was afraid, but somehow his fear took on a different connotation. Perhaps he'd picked up something from Asche besides the usual wrath: concern. Doubt.

They bested them, in the end, but not without cost. Jun and Narr were both touched by a demon; Narr's leg had turned into a lump of clay, roots poking out. It took Asche a while to fix them up. He looked visibly drained afterward. He still did.

"Why is he attacked so often?" Vindt asked what he had been wanting to ask for a while. "My former Singer was never attacked by demons."

They exchanged glances.

"You don't know, or you don't want to tell me?"

"We don't know," Narr said. "Calveen, probably. We asked him, but he said it was none of our business."

It was about their lives. How could that not be their business?

Vindt had his own theory, though. It involved someone saying, "I'll take you down, even if it's the last thing I do."

Somehow, he didn't want to discuss it with the others. Of all the things he had *not* told them about what happened at The Haven, Ru, the promise of freedom and the venomous conversation the Singer had with Asche thereafter were the last on the list.

His amulet arrived back with him. At least the talk about the attacks had distracted everyone from his made-up story about the priests. He was about to put the cord back around his neck, but then untied the bloodstone and put both pendants on one cord.

"Thanks again. For the bloodstone, I mean. I appreciate it. A lot." He smiled.

It was true. The pendant felt warm and soft against his chest. It radiated another kind of heat, one that pierced his skin through to his heart.

CHAPTER 23

They entered his body. Eyes, ears, his anus, even the pores were good. Sometimes they drilled their own holes through his skin, into the tissue and deeper, avoiding vital organs for the time being. They ate him from the inside. He heard them chewing.

Scream!

He obeyed.

They tied one of his feet to a hook on the ceiling, let him dangle, sway, gently. Occasionally an unseen hand pushed.

Laughter.

They sang while they burned patterns into his skin. Children's songs, counting rhymes.

One, two
we came just for you
three, four
the masters of gore
five, six
the mind plays its tricks

seven, eight
your soul on the plate
nine, ten
got trapped in our den

At first, he didn't realize there was a different voice, music, melody. Song. It was distant, the faint glow of a wavering candle, approaching. It pierced the darkness, challenged the other voices. So sweet. It sang a word, soft and beckoning.

Vindt. His name.

A hand reached out to him, cool fingers on his burning forehead. He moaned.

The song surrounded him, shrouded him, took him into its embrace. It lifted him, faster and faster, into the light, into—

Vindt jolted into a sitting position and blinked. Familiar surroundings took shape before his eyes, shades of gray, arbitrary forms turning into the nocturnal sight of their cabin. Pale moonlight streamed in through the multipaned windows, turning the black silhouette of the Singer crouching beside his cot into a shadow among others, a demon who had come to get him in the dark of night, like his mother had told him.

"What are you doing here?" Vindt hissed.

"You had a nightmare." In a fluid motion, Asche rose.

Vindt tried to recall what he had dreamed, but apart from a strange sensation in his body, he couldn't remember. Sweat drenched his clothes.

"And you... Why...?" Vindt's hand reached for his forehead. Cool fingers had touched him there. In his dream? He could still feel them, as if his skin was made of clay and the fingers had left an imprint.

"I can't sleep when you scream."

Sleep? Asche never slept. "I *screamed*?"

"Your consciousness might not remember; your subconsciousness does."

"Remember what?"

"Thrithid."

An icy fist clenched around Vindt's chest. Since Silhorveen and Reisen had gone and with them their nocturnal lament, Vindt had pushed the idea of his fate away into a deep dark corner of his mind. He knew he had nightmares, and he suspected they might have to do with his round trip to hell. He had not known he screamed.

"I thought you erased my memories."

A smile ghosted over Asche's lips. "Just the part where I rescued you." He turned. "You will sleep dreamlessly now."

"Wait." The imprint of his fingers on Vindt's forehead was pulsing, burning. "What did you do?" *Have you done it before?*

Asche walked out of the cabin and closed the door behind him.

Vindt sank back onto the cot. The bed was makeshift, brought in for him. In the corner of the spacious room, Asche's actual bed was closed off with curtains. The captain's quarters. The wiry man had basically forced them onto the Singer. He had even cast other guests off the ship to make room for them. A stroke of luck. Terlikastra was a small port; the *Naughty Seagull* was the only ship going in their direction large enough to take their wagon and the horses. After the incident with the demons, the chief of the city guard had made it clear they were not welcome, never mind Guzzar's usual reverence for Singers.

Vindt closed his eyes again, listening to the groans and creaks as the vessel plowed through the night. However, sleep wouldn't come. He tossed and turned for half an hour before he caved and got up.

Cool, salty air hit him as he stepped onto the deck. The night was cloudless, starless too, for the moon stole their light. Only a small crew manned the deck, but the sails were hoisted. The men acknowledged his presence with a silent nod.

Asche stood at his usual spot, staring out over the ocean. Vindt wondered if Singers ever felt lonesome. Issa had been right: they led solitary lives. Traveling alone, surrounded only by servants, humans. The few encounters Silhorveen had had with his kind were brief. Perhaps others were more social. Vindt doubted it. As the Council meeting had made plain, they even went for each other's throats like feral street dogs—literally—when they met in greater numbers.

His intention had been to walk to the other end of the deck, but his feet had a mind of their own.

Asche didn't give any sign of recognition upon his approach. Vindt waited. When nothing came, he followed the Singer's gaze. Black waves, rising and falling. The ocean's nocturnal melody was soft, more a purr than a growl. Suddenly, he had the odd sensation of being on a ghost ship, steered by a black-haired demon on their way to the ghost realm. Somehow, it wasn't a scary idea.

"I'm surprised you're wearing it." Asche's voice was as velvety soft as the sea.

For a split second, Vindt had the strange impression of still looking at the ocean, as if the Singer's body was made up of the same moonlit waves. He blinked, and the illusion faded.

"The bloodstone," Asche explained. "They told you I made it, no? Not afraid of the dark magic it might contain?"

Vindt's hand rose to the bulge the two pendants formed beneath his shirt. "Does it?"

"No more than your amulet, at least."

Vindt didn't need the glitter in the depths of Asche's eyes to know he was being made fun of. "The leaf... the moonturner was your idea, wasn't it?"

Asche stayed silent.

"But you didn't tell the others about my eyes. Why?"

"Did you tell them?"

"No, but—"

"So?"

"Why did you mention them at the Council meeting?"

"Wasn't that apparent?" Again, that ghost smile on Asche's lips. "To annoy someone."

Ru had not been so much annoyed as startled. Moon eyes. Aside from setting him apart—alternately in a positive or negative way—Vindt had never seen them as a sign of anything.

A sign of fucking what?

It was only then that he realized Asche's hair was wet, *dripping wet*. It clung in strands to his face; dark traces on his shirt showed where droplets had run down. "You didn't go for a swim, did y—"

"Do you play chess?"

"Huh?"

"The game with the checkered board humans use to act out their penchant for killing each other when there is no actual war at hand."

Vindt gave an involuntary, mirthless laugh. Gaal. He never knew whether Asche said these things to—

successfully—rile him up, or if he really believed them. "I used to. Back when I still had a life. Why?"

"You any good?"

"No."

In contrast to his father and his two elder brothers, Vindt had never been an avid chess player. During the summer, no one had ever gotten him to sit down in front of a board to move figures around when there was so much to do outside, things which let him move his body. Because of his limited practice and even lower interest, he always remained a mediocre player—to the dismay of his father, who, for whatever reason, believed it befitted a lord's son to excel in chess.

"Want to play?" Asche asked. "We have the pieces somewhere."

"Are you serious? I'm *human*. I would lose against you if I were a champion player."

"Don't you like being defeated?"

What kind of question was that? "Definitely not. I like to win."

"Losing is an acquired taste, you know. Once you've done it a few times, you'll start to... well." Asche bored his glinting eyes into Vindt's. "Get addicted to it."

Vindt's skin prickled. He wasn't sure whether the Singer was still talking about chess. It was true what he had said— he liked winning—and even more true what he had not said: he abhorred losing. This was totally—

"Of course, if you want to go back to sleep," Asche said, interrupting his thoughts, "I understand humans need a lot of rest to restore their limited—"

"Fine. Let's play."

The corners of Asche's mouth lifted ever so slightly. He indicated the direction Vindt had come from with a gesture that was almost a bow. "After you."

The chess board already sat on the table, the squares populated with the figurines of Asche's peculiar other game. Though the Singer set it up almost every night, Vindt had never seen him move a figure. Some pieces resembled the ones in chess, others not; all were exceptional pieces of handicraft. Dominating the board were two tall men on each side, one beautiful and slender with long hair, the other crude-looking with a sword. Singer and Thyd. Whether Asche played against himself or there was an opponent somewhere with whom he exchanged moves, Vindt had still not figured out. The Singer sent and received so many messenger birds, Vindt wouldn't be surprised if he used at least some of them for his entertainment.

Asche stored each figure away in their satin-lined case with dedicated care, almost tenderness.

"Did you make them?"

Asche didn't look up. Vindt was convinced he wouldn't get an answer when the Singer said, "They were a gift."

A gift from a friend. The idea seemed strange, like the idea of friendship between Singers in general.

Asche tossed the pouch he had plucked from one of their trunks over without warning. It hit Vindt's chest before he caught it reflexively.

"Still know how to set them up?"

Vindt's hands were sweaty. After positioning a few pieces, he stopped. No queens. The tallest four figures were all men, Singer and Thyd, like the figures Asche had just packed away.

"Which one's supposed to be the king?"

"Guess."

"Should my king not be the Thyd?"

"And the Singer doing all the work for you?"

"The queen's the most powerful piece."

"And the king is the most valuable."

"But useless."

"Want to play or debate?"

Vindt stifled a sigh and put the remaining pieces in their not very logical positions. He placed the light-colored figures on Asche's side, so that the first move would be his.

The Singer turned the board around. "I grant you a head start. Ready?"

A part of Vindt had remained convinced Asche would taunt him and send him away, or whatever, but not play *chess* with him.

Gaal, why did I agree to this?

The candles on each side of the table cast flickering lights on the board, adding additional nuances of light and dark to the existing ones, twisting the otherwise immobile pieces into life. Vindt's fingers trembled slightly as he shoved one of his center pawns forward. Asche's long fingers reached out without hesitation to make his countermove. He then rested his arm on the back of the bench and took a sip from his goblet.

"Is that wine?"

"Want some?"

"Seriously?" Silhorveen had never touched alcohol; neither had he permitted his servants to drink except for very special occasions. "Doesn't it have consequences? Like, when a Verdur attacks."

"I could raise your voice if you were in a coma, flayed

and dissected. Besides, I don't think we will be attacked at sea."

"Because Verdurs can't travel across water?"

"Because it would be too easy for me to escape. So?"

Too easy to escape. Vindt thought of the demons again. Perhaps he could make the best of the situation and pry information out of Asche. Perhaps the wine would loosen his tongue. "Okay."

He rose to take one of the mugs from their hooks on the wall, but Asche pushed the goblet over. "We can share this."

Vindt eyed it warily. It suddenly seemed to hold much more than wine. Sharing a cup with a Singer…

… meant nothing.

The taste was almost shocking, the dense aroma of earth, and grapes, and sun, full and sensual. A familiar and yet alien heat spread through his stomach and into his head. He took another sip. When he lifted the goblet a third time, Asche covered the top with his palm. "Enough for now. I hope the wine will give your chess skills a boost, golden boy."

Vindt's hand, about to put the goblet down, stalled in mid-movement. "What did you just call me?"

"Isn't that what your name means? Though 'golden' is a poor translation of 'vin' into Lyskú. No other language has so many words for colors as Pel. 'Vin,' the color of rye."

"I didn't know you spoke Pel."

"How strange. You know me inside out, and yet this detail has escaped your attention. 'Vin'—the color of your hair. Did your mother call you that when you were a child, my sweet golden boy?" Asche's teeth showed through his smile. They were very white.

"You're not my mother," Vindt hissed.

"Adorable. Do you want to make your next move, *golden boy*?"

Vindt groaned inwardly, but did as told.

They fell into silence, shrouded in the rain's monotony as it pattered against the tiled windows, gusts of wind, the flicker of the candles. Vindt supposed Asche had cast some magic on the figures, since they stood unaffected by the ship's rolling movements.

Asche was right about the wine. After a decade's abstinence, two gulps of the rich liquid were enough to cast him into a pleasant lightheadedness. Though the game's outcome was clear, Vindt found himself thinking in earnest about his moves.

"Did you play chess with Reisen too?"

"Occasionally. He wasn't fun to play with. He didn't mind losing." Asche's smile didn't conceal the signs of fatigue in his face. They had grown worse since they'd been at sea. Vindt even caught whiffs of the acidic, metallic note imbuing the Singer's ocean scent. The idea of a weakened Asche was... strange.

"I like the gray better," the Singer said into his thoughts. "I think it's their true color. Rock—pure, hard, honest. The green is like moss covering it, deceiving."

Vindt frowned, confused. Then it hit him: his eyes. *Again.* He felt his wine-colored cheeks turn a few shades darker. "Look, I... Can I ask you a question?"

"You just did."

"I was wondering..." This wasn't exactly subtle, but... "The attacks, the demons... is Ru sending them?"

Asche chuckled. "An understandable conclusion from your point of view."

"That means no?" Vindt asked, surprised. "Why are they

after you then? Silhorveen was never attacked by demons." And by a Verdur only every few months.

"So many questions…" The insinuation of a smile curled the corners of Asche's mouth. "I'm curious too, you know? If I hadn't taken the whistle from you and I *did* make you drink from my wrist, would you betray me to Ru?"

Vindt's heartbeat sped up. Again, he needed to exert a lot of willpower to keep his hand from tracing the object in his trousers. "You *have* taken the whistle, and you haven't made me drink from your wrist."

"Not yet, in any case. What if I lied to you and Ru's blood vow was real?"

"You like playing games, don't you? But I don't like being played with."

"Then why are you here?"

The rekindling buzz at the back of Vindt's scalp intervened with his attempt to think of a scathing retort.

"But to answer your question: yes, golden boy, I like games." The soft purr in Asche's voice was in exact rhythm with the buzz in Vindt's head. "So, how about I answer your question regarding the attacks, truthfully, and in exchange, you answer mine, just as truthfully? You have my word it won't have any consequences. Either way."

That was absurd. Asche knew—must know—the answer. Vindt had nothing to lose by saying it aloud, did he? "You go first."

Asche smiled. "No, Ru doesn't send the demons. In fact, he is a victim of the same attacks. As are Ren Zian and Shahen and Tuait and all the rest of them. Being a member of the High Council is such an honor, it comes with a death sentence." Again, bitterness underpinned the heavy sarcasm in his words. "Sounds like a joke? Well, it is, but not in the way you think. Actually, it has nothing to do with the Council, but with age. Five hundred years, more or less, then we... *expire*. Since Singers do not die of old age, it is only fair that something helps to keep the balance, no? You know what 'Verdur' means."

Guardian. It had never made sense to Vindt. It still didn't. The bitterness of the words reflected in Asche's eyes, which made him think... "You believe it isn't fair."

"So. I answered your question." Asche took a sip from his goblet. "Your turn."

Asche had said it wouldn't have consequences. Still, Vindt couldn't shake the feeling of stepping into a trap. He tried to give his voice a steadiness he didn't feel. "If it meant my freedom, of course I would betray you to Ru."

Nothing in Asche's face moved. "Interesting. You know the procedure is outlawed, don't you? Caught red-handed, it would mean my death. Or did Ru forget to tell you that?"

Vindt paled.

"Knowing that, would you still do it?"

A wave sloshed against the windows. Like an unobserved child concocting mischief, the sea had become rough over the last few minutes. The buzz in Vindt's head extended into his fingertips. "I won't answer that. It's absurd. I've already answered your question."

"I think you would, golden boy. But why don't we take a step toward proof?" With a slow, practiced movement, Asche removed the bracelet from his left wrist.

"What...?" The room collapsed with a swishing sound; reality condensed into a few inches of exposed skin. Desire flooded Vindt, burning, demanding, quickening his breathing, turning his incisors into canines. "This is a joke," he hissed through clenched teeth.

"No one is laughing." Asche moved his wrist ever so slightly.

Vindt clasped the tabletop with both hands to keep himself from darting forward and sinking his teeth into the clearly visible vein. "Where's Calveen?" He could barely hear his voice over his thumping heart. He yanked his eyes away.

However, Asche's face was at least as unsettling as his naked wrist. The glint in his eyes had flared into a hungry fire. "Do it."

This was insane. Vindt fought, but his self-control crumbled second by second. A force greater than himself pulled him from the bench and pushed him to his knees a moment later. His hands reached out, grabbing the arm. Smooth skin under his hands, delicate bones.

One day I'll break them.

"Do it," Asche hissed again, voice urgent. His cheeks were flushed.

And Vindt obeyed.

Teeth.

Skin.

Blood.

Someone groaned, Asche or himself, indistinguishable. Vindt didn't wonder for a second how or where to bite. All he felt was certainty and confidence and this overwhelming, all-consuming desire. He had the right to do this. The blood was there for him, was his, and this was the way he was meant to get it. He drilled deeper, lacerating skin and flesh, riving the veins, sucking, swallowing.

Hurt.

The buzzing in his head drowned out all other sounds, sending tremors down his body. Asche's heart beat against his mouth, racing, as if it were trying to fight him. As the arm squirmed in his grip, Vindt kept it in place; he wouldn't let go until he was done, until he had sated this fathomless greed inside him.

Eventually, he withdrew with a gasp. Asche's blood roared through his veins, mingling with his, combining into something else, a filter removed, something unleashed.

He wiped his mouth with the back of his hand. It came away red. His drugged mind let him perceive a red halo around the Singer's body. Lord Tehered, the demon king—returned.

Asche was absentmindedly stroking his bleeding wrist. The glow in his eyes had dulled, as if hiding behind a veil. He seemed dazed. Through his parted lips, Vindt glimpsed his canines. At the sight, his own receding incisors grew again; heat pooled in his groin.

Bite. Again. Take what was *his*.

In a quick motion, Asche sealed his veins and put the bracelet back on. He shook himself like a dog coming out of the water. "Well."

Bracing himself on the bench, Vindt shakily rose. Asche reached for the board with the same arm Vindt's teeth had just penetrated and, languidly, moved his rook. "I hate to give you another blow, golden boy, but…" He smiled up at him.

"Checkmate."

CHAPTER 24

Vindt was awoken by his own moan. For a moment he lay trapped in the limbo between the remnants of his dream and the room's edges and angles as they peeled from the twilight. The dream's images dissolved almost instantly; its sensations prevailed. The feeling of smooth skin under the points of his teeth, its resistance, giving way. His incisors slicing through flesh, blood gushing from the wounds into his mouth in a sweet stream. The pressure. The heat. The taste.

Vindt swallowed. No blood. A second of confusion, then disappointment. Then embarrassment.

Gaal...

Vindt groaned into his pillow. So he had dreamed of it *again*.

The remnants of the headiness Asche's blood had created didn't help his efforts to claw out of the sleep's cocoon. Even after three days, it had not fully subsided. Neither had his fury.

Letting him drink from the wrist—precisely as Ru had predicted—and two minutes after asking him what he would do if he still had the whistle. A death sentence! A joke, another lie—in any case: part of the game.

And Vindt the pawn.

Gaal, how Vindt hated him. He was utterly tempted to blow that fucking whistle and be done with it. Only, by doing so, he might be treating the plague for cholera. Ru's damn blood vow. If only he could work out if it was a thing or not. But how? The only people who knew—Asche certainly, Calveen probably—were the last ones who would be willing to tell him. He had tried surreptitiously with the seneschal and received a venomous rebuke.

Motivated by some hitherto unknown streak of masochism, he had asked the Singer why he had made him drink from his wrist, confronting him with what Issa had told him about the Thyd rebellion and the transfer of power.

"Did Ru tell you that?" Asche had asked, chuckling. "It's a tale, golden boy. Or do you feel any powers?"

No, Vindt didn't. He didn't feel different at all. Apart from the skin under his bracelet having started to itch. Which was annoying, but quite possibly unrelated.

A gray sky and a messenger bird taking flight into it greeted him when he eventually made it onto the deck.

Though their plumage was rust-colored, the birds always reminded Vindt of a smaller, leaner version of ravens. A weirder version. They could retain a few phrases of Lyskú and repeat them at their destination. Singers could also record longer messages into a tiny ring fastened to the bird's leg.

The only destination humans could send them to was The Haven. Singers could send them anywhere. Somehow, the birds were able to pass through Doors.

Watching Jun standing at the rail and following the bird's flight with a guilty expression, Vindt couldn't help but grin. Silhorveen had allowed no one but himself and his seneschal to send messages. The birds were precious. It was the same here, except for Jun.

Initially, Vindt had believed the young man was sending his messages to a lover at The Haven, until Risi told him the addressee was his mother. He wondered what whim had prompted Asche to let him.

Vindt took deliberate breaths of fresh sea air while stretching his muscles in an attempt to clear the haziness from his mind. Asche was talking to the captain. By now, Vindt had an idea why the weathered man had been so keen on taking them onboard. According to the maps and the rather mediocre wind, they should have reached Kelfo, the small island for their stopover, after a week. The journey had taken them three days.

Risi, who spoke enough of the sailors' language to hold basic conversations, had told Vindt that storms were the norm in these waters at this time of year. The agitated sea from the other night was the roughest weather they had experienced.

Could be coincidence. Or Asche bewitching the ocean.

"Come to the prow." Calveen's harsh voice pulled him from his thoughts. "The Kvahad-thed has something to tell us."

"Good morning to you, too," Vindt chirped at the seneschal's back, as the man was already moving on to Layyad and Narr.

He made a point of finishing his stretching before he joined the group.

Asche bothered with no more niceties than his seneschal. "Tomorrow we will reach port," he said without preamble. "We will not take the inland road, but the coastal road." A murmur rose. "It's longer, yes, but less populated. It's safer, too, for other reasons."

"You think we'll be attacked?" Risi said.

"No," Asche said. "I know."

More murmurs rose.

The Singer turned to Vindt. "In case it is demons *and* Verdurs, forget about the latter. I will handle your voice. Concentrate on your sword. That's not an option, but an order."

"How long will it take us?" Anxiety only partly motivated Vindt's question. He couldn't deny a nagging curiosity to see Asche's homestead.

"If everything goes well, a little more than a week." Asche nodded. "That is all."

The group dispersed, to pack, presumably. Vindt went back into their cabin too. Not that much packing was required, but he had nothing else to do. He was pondering what "safer for other reasons" meant when Asche startled him into a heart attack with another example of his stunt of appearing without sign or sound. "How are you feeling?"

Vindt halted in his movement. "Are you sure that is the question you want to ask? It kind of implies you care how I feel."

"Don't worry. It's not in a sense of well-being, just scientific interest."

"Are you waiting for my powers to manifest?"

"What an asset you would be during the coming attacks."

"Why are you so sure we're going to be attacked?"

"Do you listen when I tell you something?"

The Singers' "expiry date." Yes. The thing was, Asche was tired. Not that Vindt was worried about the Singer, of course. But Asche's doom meant his own.

"But, whatever the case," the Singer continued, "I want you to accompany me tonight."

"*Accompany you? To*night. On a swim?" Though he had never seen Asche jump into the sea or climb back onto the ship, Vindt was sure by now he went for a swim every night. No wonder he was tired.

"I'm glad you are not opposed to the idea."

Vindt very much was. "To go where and do what? And I'm *human*. I can swim, but—"

"I'll wake you when we're leaving."

* * *

Vindt couldn't believe it. Not when Asche's hand on his shoulder shook him out of a dream about yet another bloody wrist, and less now, standing at the ship's stern. It was pitch black, water and air merging into one dark mass.

"The ocean has Doors too," Asche had condescended to inform him earlier, and also that Vindt didn't need to be afraid of drowning.

Sure. Even *if* Vindt's mind believed him, thousands of years of survival ingrained into his species had each cell of his body screaming with trepidation. Where exactly they were heading or why Vindt's presence was required, Asche wouldn't say.

The Singer took Vindt's hand, fingers entwining. Vindt

twitched automatically, though the firm, cool touch was reassuring.

"Trust me." With unexpected strength, Asche pushed them both over the railing.

The impact of hitting the icy water drove all the air from Vindt's lungs. Instincts made him paddle frantically, trying to stay above the surface. With the same strength with which Asche had pushed him over the railing, he now pulled him under.

Don't panic. I told you, you are safe. You can breathe the water. Relax. Asche's voice sounded directly in his head.

The hell he would. Opening his mouth would fill his lungs with water, which meant fucking death. A sudden warm current, transmitting from the Singer's hand, dampened his panic. He bubbled a sigh out of his mouth and...

He couldn't really *breathe*, but somehow, the water entering his lungs didn't kill him either.

It didn't take long before they broke the surface again.

Wherever they had emerged, it wasn't night. Not far away, waves crashed against a coastline of low rocks. Asche pulled Vindt toward it. The Singer didn't seem so much to swim but to glide through the water like a fish. In a little bay, where the current was gentler, he let go and climbed onto a rock, lending Vindt a hand to help him do the same. He sang to dry them.

"Where are we?" Vindt's gaze darted around.

Weather-worn rocks surrounded them, shades of gray as far as he could see. No trees, no plants, not even earth. The crashing waves underpinned a strange, anticipatory stillness. A cool wind blew, pulling blond strands from his braid. He looked up at the sky. Or the place the sky should be. Dusk-like twilight hovered above them, no sun, no clouds.

A whisper sounded behind him. Vindt spun around. Nothing. The sound came again, from a different direction. He tried to listen, but as soon as he focused, it was gone. Goosebumps erupted on his skin. "Where are we?" he repeated, warier than before.

"You wouldn't like the answer." Asche started walking inland.

By the time Vindt caught up, Asche was climbing an overhanging boulder with the grace of a lizard. Vindt scrambled after him. "How long do we have to walk?"

"We've arrived." The Singer stood a few feet away on the rocky, wind-swept plain. There was nothing special in the landscape apart from…

Two prone bodies.

From where he stood, Vindt couldn't see their faces. However, a sense of foreboding made his skin tingle. When he joined Asche, he took a sharp breath.

The shriveled faces and colorless eyes had left the men unrecognizable. Vindt still knew. One's long dark hair and the other's short and gray-speckled.

"Where the fuck are we?" Vindt asked for a third time.

"In Thrithid," Asche said, and added, when he saw Vindt's face losing all color, "Of course, Thrithid doesn't exist as such. Let's just say, if Thrithid had a physical representation, it would be this. But don't worry, you are safe with me."

"Why are they here?" Vindt had automatically lowered his voice to a whisper. *And why are we?*

"Because this is where we bring them."

Vindt looked around, bracing himself for the sight of other withered, groaning bodies. Only rocks met his view.

He thought about the giant vault full of moaning bodies he had imagined. "And you let them just... lie around?"

"It makes no difference." Asche crouched down beside Reisen's body. A dagger appeared in his hand, the blade as colorless as the sky.

"What are you doing?"

"Committing a crime. Fulfilling a promise." The Singer laid his free palm on Reisen's chest. Then he closed his eyes and sang. A second later, he rammed the dagger between his eyes, up to the hilt.

A scream rose into the air, but not from the corpse, not from anywhere. The body twitched and changed. The sinuous, silvery dark lines in the face receded; color returned to the skin, and flesh to the face. The eyes, gray again now, stared at Asche. For a split second, Vindt believed he saw a glimpse of recognition—a... smile?—before they went dead for good. The body crumbled to ash; the flakes stirred, and the wind carried them away. A pile of clothes was all that remained.

The whisper was back, many whispers, in fact, angry, without apparent source. Vindt looked around anxiously, but Asche paid them no mind.

From the folds of Reisen's clothes, Asche retrieved a pendant and put it in his pocket. A bloodstone. The Singer used the clothes to wipe gore from the blade, then rose. He looked down at Silhorveen for a long moment before crouching again. His fingertips brushed the shriveled forehead, lightly, as he had back in Silhorveen's tent. His face was the usual mask, but Vindt had the impression he was holding an internal debate. With sudden determination, Asche repeated what he had done to Reisen.

Vindt's body jerked at the sound of another cracking

skull.

Asche sighed. The fatigue on his pale features had become even more prominent. When he rose, he stumbled. Vindt reflexively reached out to steady him, but pulled back his hand when the Singer cast him a piercing look.

He killed them.

The realization was only slowly sinking in. A prayer rose, words he had wanted to say for Reisen weeks ago. He mumbled them now, waiting for a mocking comment from Asche. But the Singer only stared out over the ocean, seemingly lost in its eternal ebb and swell, the wind tussling his long black hair.

He waited until Vindt was done, then walked back the way they'd come from. His gait was heavy.

"What about the clothes?" Vindt asked.

"It makes no difference." Asche disappeared down over the boulder's edge.

After a last glance at the hollow heap of fabric, Vindt followed him back into the sea.

CHAPTER 25

It was their second day on the coastal road to Asche's home.

In Pel, the cliffs were made of gray granite or frozen lava, black as the Singers' souls. Here, the rocks dropping into the churning waves to their left were a dirty white. Other than that, the landscape was ridiculously similar: the ocean, free and feral, crashing against the cliffs with righteous anger, the wind clawing at hair and horses' manes. Seabirds circled above, pushing their cries through the water's perpetual roar into the damp and earthy air. Before them and to their right: endless hills, lush, rolling. Occasional shrubs huddled together under the gray sky, their leaves beginning to turn brown in the approaching fall. Rare trees stood like forgotten outposts, gnarled and wind-beaten.

The wagon rumbled and creaked on the poorly maintained road. As Asche had predicted, apart from forlorn farms, they encountered no settlements.

Vindt knew he should be alert for potential attacks, yet his mind kept wandering back to the murder of Reisen and

Silhorveen. Or their rescue. The sound of a breaking skull, the recognition in Reisen's eyes, the... smile? Asche crouching over the vanished bodies, blood-stained blade in hand.

What had that been? An act of guilt, of redemption? Or something serving a greater purpose? Part of whatever weird plan the Singer was up to.

"Don't you tire of staring at me?" The black eyes rested on him with their usual uncanny weight.

Blood rushed to Vindt's cheeks as he averted his eyes.

"Is there perhaps a question tormenting you?"

Vindt huffed out a laugh. *One.* "If it's possible to spare your brothers their torment in Thrithid, why don't you simply kill them all?"

"Because it is not possible. At least as 'not possible' as getting a Thyd out of Thrithid."

"I see. So I was dreaming the other day. Why did you even bring me along?"

"I thought you would enjoy a little excursion."

Vindt stifled a groan. It was futile. "So that's your job, making trips to Thrithid and delivering your brethren?"

"I'd like that. A little draining, perhaps..."

Vindt could see that. The signs of fatigue in Asche's face had not vanished. "That's why you don't do it?"

"Or because we have no way of finding them. I only found Reisen because he has my blood in him. And then we probably don't even try because killing them comes with a death sentence."

Gaal. The wrist Binding entailed death, too—if Asche had told the truth—just like resurrecting a Thyd. Vindt had never thought that Singers abided by any laws. And here they were. "Did you make these laws or—"

Vindt's amulet grew hot and erupted into angry vibrations a split second before the ground exploded.

Keke gave a squeal as he was knocked off his legs. With reflexes Vindt didn't know he possessed, he jumped off the falling horse a second before it buried him. He had barely hit the ground when his voice rose into the air, joining Asche's. Then the Verdurs were on them.

Ignoring the sharp pain in his shoulder, Vindt rolled away from the frantically kicking legs. Earth and stones struck him, while noises faded in and out. Once again, the demons' cacophony pierced the tangible, sticky silence. Three Verdurs. More? The demons' stench poisoned the air.

Vindt's guts were reeling in sync with the ground. Rocks flew in every direction, hitting his head, shoulders, chest, legs. He covered his face with his arms. Though he heard and felt Asche's voice, he couldn't see him. Instead, he spotted Schiida dashing off—riderless. Cold fingers touched his heart.

A second later, the Singer appeared by his side. The rain of objects stopped so abruptly, Vindt swayed. They stood in a bubble, an eye of stillness amid the storm, a shelter created by the Singer's voice. Asche grabbed his arm and pulled him closer. Fatigue dulled the wrath emanating from him. And also: the fear. The idea would have struck Vindt for its ridiculousness had it not been so disconcerting.

The earth trembled and lurched like a bucking horse. Only Asche's grip kept Vindt from being knocked off his feet. He tried to spot the others, but couldn't through the rain of flying objects.

Your sword—draw it. Asche's voice in his head.

Vindt's hand obeyed before his mind could. He'd barely touched the hilt when the sword sprang into his hands, the blade bright white. It vibrated, rhythmic concussions, the drum of a beating heart. He let the blade move of its own accord, slashing at whatever threw itself against the boundaries of their bubble. The Verdurs' screams nearly drowned out the demons' din. Their shapes were no less erratic than what Vindt was used to, but more... human. Wings and claws, superfluous limbs, additional eyes, arranged around a semi-translucent human body. Or perhaps, sheltered in Asche's bubble, Vindt saw them clearly for the first time.

The demons' power and determination slammed into him from all sides. It felt as if earth and air were turning against them. His amulet vibrated angrily. It could not really fight them, but at least its magic seemed to distract them.

Vindt squinted into the whirling haze, again seeking the others, but couldn't see further than arm's length. Their bubble shook, then dwindled. Then ripped.

A triumphant not-cry nearly tore Vindt's eardrums apart. Before he even had time to panic, the shape-shifting figure of a Verdur was upon him. The grip of Asche's hand on his arm slipped, and he was thrown through the air again. The creature followed, reaching for him with tentacles instead of arms. Its inverted screams pulled Vindt under. The last time a Verdur had come so close as to touch him was the day he and Silhorveen were defeated. The surrounding air vanished; a clammy cold pressed onto his skin. Vindt's voice broke.

Silence, the harbinger of death.

No.

Panic howled through him, primal and deep. Blackness crept into his vision like ink.

The sword in his hands came up. Another inaudible scream rose as the embrace slackened and the blackness receded. Sounds returned, the demons' cacophony so loud he winced.

He jumped to his feet and set himself back into a fighting stance. Why didn't Asche sing?

The Verdur had recovered from its blow. It hovered a few feet away, a spindly woman with a snake's head, blurring into something wolfish. Vindt felt its strange, insubstantial gravitation, its translucent eyes on him, the hatred in them.

Something has to keep the balance.

Stones and twigs struck him; dust blew into his already burning eyes. The air was full of an odd, menacing energy. Made of demon-fighting steel or not, he would not be able to defend himself against a Verdur with just a sword.

The thing attacked again. Vindt's sword buzzed in response, the light of the blade bright, almost blinding. He waited for the impact, but a sudden roar soared into the air, followed by what sounded like an explosion. Again, Vindt was thrown off his feet and catapulted through the air. When he hit the ground, his voice rose, entwined with Asche's. Relief flooded his veins as they swept the Verdur away in the middle of its new attack.

Asche appeared at his side. One look at his face, however, made Vindt nearly drop the sword. It wasn't the ashen color, nor the scratches and streaks of dirt, which tainted the perfection of the Singer's features. Sinuous lines between black and silver had sprouted on his throat and chin the same way they once had on the not-dead

Silhorveen.

An army of contradictory feelings sprang up in Vindt's chest.

Whatever happens, hold on to my arm. The echo of Asche's voice reverberated in his head. *Don't let go. You hear me?*

Vindt had no time to answer. Darkness descended, then the ocean came down on them, pulling them along, toward the cliff.

His grip on Asche's arm tightened a second before they fell into nothing. Vindt screamed. The water fell with them, down and down. The impact with which they hit the ocean's surface drove the last of the air from his lungs. His mouth opened in panicked reflex. Water filled his lungs as terror stiffened his limbs.

Don't. Let. Go.

Vindt's slackening grip tightened again. Eventually, his body remembered it could breathe underwater. They swam, fast, Asche dragging Vindt along, following a nonexistent current. Vindt's limbs went numb in the icy water; his mind followed. He lost track of time. After what could have been minutes or hours, his chest was brusquely lifted out of the water.

He pulled himself onto the ragged rocks and coughed. It took some time for his senses to readjust. They had come to rest on what seemed to be an outcrop of the white cliffs, too tiny to even be called a bay. Around them, the rocks rose.

"Where..."

He blinked, and then again, but what he saw didn't change. Asche was lying face down on the rocks beside him, bone-white fingers clutching the stones. His body still hung halfway into the water, hair fanned around him like black seaweed.

Vindt waited, but he didn't move.

"Kvahad-thed?" The ocean's roar was so loud, he could hardly hear his voice. "Kvahad-thed. Hey." He reached out, but withdrew at the last moment. He waited some more. Eventually, he gingerly touched the prone body. All his senses expected Asche to jolt into life and strike him down. When he didn't, Vindt closed his slightly trembling fingers around the shoulder and shook.

When again nothing happened, he shook a little more firmly. With the same result.

"What's the matter? You're not..." No, not *dead*, otherwise Vindt would be too. But... unconscious? Vindt had never heard of an unconscious Singer.

His momentarily calmed pulse sped up again. The white cliffs enclosed them; only a small opening connected the bay to the ocean. It felt like a cave, a cave without an exit. A sense of dread threaded through the absurdity of the situation.

"Okay, Kvahad-thed. I'll pull you out of the water now, okay?"

Vindt adjusted his weight on the slippery stones. Heart hammering its anxious protest against his chest, he grabbed the limp body under the armpits and heaved it onto the small ledge. He had to steady Asche with one hand to keep him from falling over. The mass of black seaweed hair still covered his face. Gingerly, Vindt reached out to pull it back.

And took a hissing breath.

The lines. Not only were they still there, they had grown, extending over the chin and mouth, reaching halfway up the cheeks. The lips were almost as pale as the surrounding skin. And they were moving.

Vindt brought his ear closer. All that reached him, however, was Asche's shallow breath. It sent a shiver down the back of his neck. Vindt nearly jumped as something burning hot closed around his wrist. Looking down, he found the Singer's fingers wrapped around it, thumb resting on his veins. A current of power, and then a strange, dream-like feeling came over him. The sound of the ocean dimmed; his vision narrowed, and expanded again a moment later.

Before him was the mouth of a cave, white cliffs reaching up on either side. He walked in, advancing into the darkness with sure steps. Daylight faded. He could still see. A tunnel. At the end was—

The image tore apart with an ear-splitting scream. Pain exploded. The skin was ripped from his body, burning irons driven into his flesh. Blood clouded his vision. He screamed.

The pain ended as abruptly as it had begun. Vindt panted. The pale fingers which had wrapped around his wrist once again lay limp on the wet rock.

Asche's mind. That was where he had been. The cave was a memory. And the pain was...?

Vindt looked up the white walls behind him. If there was a hole in the cliffs, he couldn't see it. Would it lead to Asche's house? Vindt had no clue how far they had traveled in the ocean.

Five hundred years and then we expire.

Again, Vindt eyed the unconscious body. Impossible. Wrong. As if the world had cracked through the middle. He stared a long time until it occurred to him to scan the surroundings for their attackers. Nothing. Well, obviously. If demons and Verdurs had followed them here, they would have been dead by now. The amulet around his neck was cold, and as still as the strange sense inside him which sometimes alerted him to Verdurs. Relief remained absent. It was a mere question of time until the fiends picked up their trail. With nothing but his sword, it would be over in seconds.

Asche's head had tilted back and was now resting against the rocks. He looked almost relaxed, as if he was taking a nap. Vindt followed the lines down his neck and into his shirt, clearly visible through the wet white fabric. They grew from the heart. The lines were hideous, in a way. In another, they suited him, not so different from the pattern he himself had painted on his face for the Council meeting. What did they mean? The excruciating pain Vindt had felt in his head. Was Asche in Thrithid? But then, why was he still alive?

Vindt had never before seen Asche with his eyes closed. The dark stare hidden behind the lids, he looked soft, vulnerable, still not human but... The high cheekbones, the elegantly curved eyebrows—beauty without menace.

At his mercy.

The idea chased a flock of contradictory emotions into the hazy skies of his mind. Glee was among them, as was the faint echo of the once familiar alloy of anger, hatred and the need for revenge. But another sensation Vindt couldn't name overshadowed them, synchronized with the faint buzz in his head.

Vulnerable. At his mercy...

A shiver ran through his body, accompanied by his chattering teeth. He needed to do *something*. Move. Or sit here and wait for Asche to wake up. Or die. He needed help. But from whom? If they waited, perhaps the others would find them.

The others... Vindt had not spared them a thought until

now. Asche's powers had not sufficed to protect himself and Vindt. What were the odds they had survived? Metallic anxiety coated his tongue.

But no, the demons and Verdurs were not after them, as Asche himself had pointed out the other day. Still, sitting around idly, waiting for them to find them down here, wasn't an endearing idea either.

For a start, Vindt took off his drenched clothes and wrung them out. The improvement against the cold was negligible. He looked up at the cliff again. The cave entrance Asche had shown him could be here or anywhere. It had better be here, or they were doomed. They were also doomed if the entrance was a lot further up, because even if he made the climb, how would he get Asche there?

One step at a time.

For once, luck was on their side. Vindt had barely pulled himself over the ledge overshadowing their resting place when he stood before the gaping hole from Asche's memories; only the rock's slope had hidden it from view. Vindt stared into the darkness. He could probably haul Asche up here, but then what? *Carry* him? Vindt shook himself. Better to explore the tunnel alone, see where it led, and hopefully come back with help.

The walls were curved, but the tunnel's middle section was high enough for him to walk upright. Moving quickly on the upward-sloping ground brought some pleasant heat back into his freezing body. However, the further he advanced, the more he felt like he was dragging a rock behind him, its weight increasing with every step. He stopped.

He couldn't just walk away like this, *abandon* Asche.

Gaal. He wasn't abandoning anybody. Getting help was

the most rational thing to do.

He set off again, only to stop a moment later. The feeling of committing a fatal error stung at his nerves. What if the Verdurs and demons returned?

Then Asche would die in exactly the same way as if Vindt was beside him.

But Vindt had the sword.

Which would help them as much as a toothpick against a pack of hungry wolves.

And yet. The idea of Asche dying out there alone was...

Vindt's exasperated groan echoed eerily between the tunnel's walls.

Oh, fuck the Bond.

He cursed all the way back.

CHAPTER 26

"Okay, listen."

Asche sat the way he'd left him.

"I need to get you up there. If I could sing elegantly to do it, I would. Unfortunately, I only have my crude human muscles."

If touching the Singer to shake him had been an act of overcoming, it was nothing compared to the prospect of what he was about to do now. Again, it wasn't revulsion, only this profound sensation of not being entitled, of committing sacrilege.

"Kill me if you must. *Afterward.*"

His hands trembled as he hauled the Singer up, overly aware of the places their bodies touched. It took him several attempts, during which Asche's body hit the rocks at different angles and with varying force. But he managed. One sleeve of Asche's shirt ripped in the process; the scratch beneath bled slightly. An injured Singer—another crack in reality.

The wound wasn't deep. Still, Vindt tore a sleeve from

his own shirt, ripped it into strips and wrapped them around the wound. After the ordeal of getting him up onto the ledge, loading the limp body onto his shoulders was a ridiculously simple task. It felt no less wrong for it.

Clamping down on all thoughts and emotions, Vindt walked once again into the darkness.

Without the sun, it was impossible to tell how long he had been walking. Hours, for sure. It was dusk when he had set off. It must be night by now.

Though every muscle ached, Vindt was glad he had taken Asche with him. The tunnel turned out to be longer than he had hoped. Perhaps it would end in a few feet. With night having fallen outside, he wouldn't be able to tell. Strangely enough, just like in the momentary glimpse of Asche's memory, he could see in the dark. He had no mental capacities to question it. He was just glad. Walking while carrying a limp body was hard enough without the additional impediment of blindly stumbling over jutting rocks or hitting his head.

He had taken several breaks on the way, but he feared this one was the last for today. He was at the end of his rope. The idea of spending the night in this clammy shithole wasn't conducive to lifting his spirits, but what were the alternatives? At least they were not short of water. Small rivulets had run down the tunnel's walls along the whole way. He spotted one here, too. Vindt's stomach was a grumbling pit, but he had gone more days without food during his life.

As carefully as possible, he put Asche down and examined his own ankle. He must have twisted it while hauling the Singer up onto the ledge. The initial stinging pain had given way to numbness. The skin was hot. He ripped the second sleeve from his shirt, soaked the strips in the trickle of water and wrapped them around the joint. The relief was transient.

Asche's head tilted to the side; a groan escaped his lips. Vindt flinched. He had tried to wake the Singer at every break; he didn't bother now. It was futile. Asche had a fever. Or whatever Singers got that resembled the corresponding human condition. Their skin touching in various places while carrying him, Vindt had not been able to miss the burning. Humans with a fever needed liquid. Singers perhaps didn't. Then again, Asche had this peculiar relationship with water.

Vindt propped him up against the wall next to the rivulet and let some water run into his cupped palm. An inch away from Asche's mouth, he hesitated, overcome with the same profound reluctance to touch him.

Oh, fuck it.

His fear that he would have to force the water into Asche was baseless. The Singer's lips parted the moment he brought his hand to them; his Adam's apple bobbed. Vindt's heartbeat sped up. Perhaps... "Hey, Kvahad-thed, are you awake again?"

No answer. Vindt waited. When nothing happened, he gathered more water, trying to focus on anything but the soft touch to his fingers. Asche drank but didn't wake up.

A shiver shook Vindt's body. Now that he'd stopped moving, the cold crept in again. His clothes had almost dried from his body heat, only to get soaked again by his sweat. It wasn't going to be a pleasant night. If only they had something to cover them with. Well, they didn't. At least Asche's clothes were dry from all the heat the Singer emitted.

Vindt arranged his limp body into a position that was as comfortable as the ground and circumstances allowed. Keeping watch was meaningless. If Verdurs and demons found them, he wouldn't be able to do a thing. Vindt doubted he could sleep, shivering on the hard stones.

Exhaustion dragged him under in no time.

* * *

He was under water. Currents whirled about him, gently, warm, holding, guiding. Sunlight sent its dancing rays through the surface above, but the world beyond was of no concern to him. He could breathe. Water was eternity, a part of him, a stroke on his skin, a soothing rush in his ears. Water was music, was sound.

Unfortunately, the floating water soon morphed into the cold, hard ground of the tunnel. Vindt ignored that fact for a moment, and simply continued to lie where he was, eyes closed, relishing the sensation of the warm body in his embrace.

He screamed, first as his head hit the curved ceiling, and then again as his weight came to rest on his right foot. His leg buckled. If he had not reached for the wall on reflex, he would have dropped to the ground. That fucking ankle.

Pale-faced, he stared down at Asche. He hadn't been *cuddling* him, had he?

Survival instincts, his body moving in his sleep to the only source of heat available.

Gaal...

Vindt hobbled over to the rivulet and splashed his face and neck with cold water. It cleared his dizzy head somewhat; his accelerated heartbeat took longer to calm.

He didn't know how long he had slept. His body was sore; his muscles ached. But he felt awake, refreshed. Enough at least to continue.

He scowled at his ankle. The joint had swollen overnight; the flesh pressed painfully into the fabric of the makeshift bandage. Injured. For a decade, a Singer had conveniently healed every wound as soon as he got it. A strange, almost forgotten sensation. One of the few of his former life he was *not* keen on returning to.

He unwrapped the bandages, soaked them and put them on again. Yet, when he put his weight on the foot, he let out a sharp hiss of pain. Walking wouldn't be pleasant. Carrying Asche...

Well, it couldn't be helped.

He eyed the bandage around Asche's arm for a few indecisive seconds before he cautiously unwrapped them. It really was only a scratch, already halfway scabbed. Still, Vindt put the bandage back in place. The arm, so thin. He could break it with ease. His thumb traced the smooth inside until it touched the wide golden bracelet with its sinuous lines. It had always seemed like jewelry to him, decoration, a sign of the Singers' superiority, the way kings wore their crowns. But, in a way, they also resembled shackles.

Vindt's mind went back to The Haven, to Asche's scathing comment—"Did it make you happy? The almighty Singers on their knees"—to the bitterness in his voice when he was talking about their "expiry date," to things said during the meeting, Asche's "conversation" with Ru.

Power—was that what Asche wanted? Or was it... something else?

The Singer's breathing was shallow. The winding lines

had grown overnight; the fever, too, had risen. They might be safe from demons and Verdurs at Asche's home, but what the Singer needed for *this* was the help of his brothers. Vindt doubted one would be waiting at the end of the tunnel.

Through the fabric of his trousers, Vindt felt for the whistle. He had the means to call a Singer.

No, that was silly. Ru was the last person on earth to *help* Asche. But between sure death and at least a chance of survival...?

Vindt reached for his amulet instead. He had not prayed in a long time. He wasn't sure if he could now. Pray for one of the very demons Gaal fought, for the enemy. And himself. Asche's death would mean his own. That was the truth. He closed his eyes.

Mother. Warrior. Forgive me. I know I haven't turned to you a lot lately, but look, if it was you who rescued me from Thrithid, perhaps you can help me again, just one more time —I mean, help... us. I know he's a demon, but he's not... He's...

Vindt stopped. He didn't know what Asche was or wasn't. Suddenly self-conscious, he let go of the amulet. The echoes of their nocturnal embrace lingered just beneath the surface of his awareness, the imprint of a burning body in his arms, lungs pumping, heart beating.

Expunging his wayward emotions with a varnish of brusque resolve, he said, "Time to move on, demon king."

And so they did.

* * *

To Vindt's relief, it didn't take long before the end of the tunnel came into view. He dropped Asche a few feet before reaching the mouth and peeked out. An overcast sky greeted him. Contrasting with the darkness he'd just left, the dim light was enough to hurt his eyes. He squinted. To his left, the ocean was untiring in its attempts to vanquish the cliffs. Before him, green, rolling hills stretched, until they too hit the inward-curving cliffs. A road cut through them, lined by paddocks with grazing sheep, horses, perhaps cattle. In the distance, where the cliff turned, the road led to a cluster of houses, a farmstead, apparently. Hardly likely to be Asche's home, or…?

Vindt took a few cautious steps into the open. His amulet was still, the ocean's roar uninterrupted, but he remained wary. Walk alone to the farmstead and come back with a horse or even a wagon to transport Asche? He discarded the idea for the same reasons he had not been able to leave the Singer behind yesterday. What difference did those few yards make?

He loaded the Singer back onto his shoulders and limped toward the road. He had only taken a few steps, however, when his amulet exploded into furious vibrations. A dark pit opened in his stomach, threatening to swallow him whole.

No.

He dropped the body and positioned himself over it, sword drawn, facing their doom.

Demons soaked the air around and above them, oozing their acidic, metallic smell. Verdurs hovered at a distance, three at least. They had not begun their perverse, soundless shouting yet—the peaceful growl of the waves still reached Vindt. Instead, they were watching, waiting. Vindt gripped the hilt of his sword tighter. "What are you waiting for?" he shouted. "Get it over with, you fucking cowards."

The demons writhed around them, making Vindt turn on the spot. He felt their confidence, their gleeful anticipation, almost as if they were laughing. And then he understood. This wasn't an attack.

It was an execution.

If someone gave a command, Vindt didn't hear it. They all moved at the same time, demons, Verdurs, stench, sounds and their inversion, crashing down on them in a wave of inescapable horror. Vindt lost his sword as he fell, covering Asche beneath him. His arms closed around his body, face diving into the mass of black hair, seeking the ocean smell.

The last sensation he would have.

CHAPTER 27

They didn't die.

A voice, angry and powerful, drove into the onslaught's midst from out of nowhere, like an iron wedged into a log. The deadly weight vanished, exploding into cries of outrage and furious hisses. Shapes and sounds, dissonant, screeching, mingled into seething chaos. Vindt looked up, convinced he *was* dead, because, at a short distance, blinding white on a dark horse: a Singer, his Thyd next to him, both singing.

Vindt scrambled to his feet and picked up his fallen sword. As he set himself in a fighting stance again, more horses appeared. Their riders jumped off, drawing shining white blades. Risi, Kishoon, Layyad. Even Calveen. The relief washing over Vindt was so strong, he staggered.

The Verdurs and demons had recovered from their initial blow and were attacking again. The Singer's voice differed greatly from Asche's, a tingle of bells, a sweet, lethal melody. Its power didn't match Asche's, but it lacked the tiredness Vindt had perceived in the latter's song lately. And he was determined. As were the others, as was Vindt. He hadn't carried the Singer on his back for two days to let him be fucking murdered now.

The Singer and his Thyd appeared by Vindt's side. Vindt registered their blue tunics, but busy with hitting at everything in his vicinity, he didn't have time for an inspection. It didn't matter who the Singer was; he had come to their rescue.

Sounds floated in and out in the usual aural ordeal. Occasional shouts and curses from the others, cut off and warped. The earth vibrated in an angry hum, but didn't buckle as it had the last time. The forces seemed to be less, in numbers or power. They'd believed it would be a walk-over, certainly.

From the corner of his eyes, Vindt watched Risi go down under a swiveling, translucent mass. He let out a cry of fear as he slashed at the shape-shifting figure of a Verdur in front of him. When it retreated a few feet, Vindt made a run for the struggling man. At least he tried to, but a hand on his shoulder held him back.

He made an attempt to wiggle free. "Let me—"

"No." The Singer's hand was unyielding. He tore something from a cord around his neck and tossed it at Risi and the demon cluster with uncanny precision. For a second, nothing happened, then an explosion of light followed by a wave of familiar pressure kicked the legs from under Vindt.

He scrambled to his feet again. Risi was down on his hands and knees, but alive, cursing. The demons were gone. Vindt frowned at Asche's prone body; the pressure wave had felt exactly like his aura. But the Singer lay as before, limp, unconscious. Odd.

Vindt braced himself for the next onslaught, only to find that the din of noises and not-sounds had abated. The remaining demons were dissolving into air and earth. In the distance, two Verdurs fluttered away, bird-like and strangely human. The wind's harsh blow and the ocean's angry roar were back, caressing Vindt's ears.

"In the name of the First," a sparkling voice behind him said, "that was close."

Vindt turned to face its owner. Androgynous features, pale skin and milky-blue eyes framed by white-blond hair. Vindt's eyes went wide. "You."

"I take that as an expression of joy." The Singer smiled, the same smile he had cast Vindt across the table during the Council meeting. "A pleasure to meet you again, little Thyd. We haven't been properly introduced. My name is Dina."

"Uh, Vindt," Vindt said, and hid his hand which was about to reach out for a shake in his pocket.

Dina crouched down beside Asche, a frown replacing his smile. He brushed strands of hair from Asche's face and sighed.

Vindt shifted his feet impatiently. "Are you not going to heal him?"

"I'm afraid this is beyond the ambit of my powers."

"What?" Vindt went from stupefaction to the onset of panic in a second. "But then... what do we do?"

Dina rose. "Humans pray in these circumstances."

That was a joke. "But what's wrong with him? He seems... I think he's dy—"

"Shhh, little Thyd." Dina laid his palm on Vindt's mouth. "Help is on its way. Hopefully. There's nothing we can do for now but get him home. At least we will be safe from Verdurs and demons there." He smiled again. "You are hurt. Please, let me heal you."

"No, wait, we first need to—"

Dina's pale hand came to rest on Vindt's chest. A familiar heat spread through his body, searchingly at first, assessing, then mending and soothing. Like Dina's song, this, too, felt very different from Silhorveen's and the one time Asche had healed his shoulder, more cautious, almost... tender? He immediately relaxed into it.

"That's it. How's the ankle now?"

Cautiously, Vindt put his weight on it. "Perfect." He found himself smiling. "Thank y—"

"I'm gonna break your fucking bones, you bastard." Risi's arms closed around him with every intention of meeting action to words. "We were dead worried." He let go, only to slap him so hard in the chest, Vindt stumbled a few steps back. The anger in his eyes was real.

"Easy." Kishoon laid a hand on Risi's arm and pulled Vindt into a more human hug.

Layyad clasped his hands around Vindt's. "You gave as a helluva shock, man." His frown looked as friendly as Vindt had ever seen it.

Calveen didn't come to greet him. He was down on his knees; one hand clutched the hilt of the sword he had rammed into the earth for support. Vindt hadn't even known the seneschal owned one. Vindt expected Dina to walk over to heal him too, but the Singer only glowered at the crouching figure. After a long moment of hesitation, he eventually moved.

"It's okay, I'm good," Calveen hissed through clenched teeth.

"Are you touched?" Dina inquired, voice cool.

Calveen shook his head.

Dina rolled his eyes and made an exasperated gesture toward the sky.

"He didn't want him to come," Layyad whispered beside Vindt. "Because he's old and stuff. Calveen insisted."

Risi walked over and helped the man to his feet and then over to them. As soon as Calveen laid eyes on Asche, he made a noise between a gasp and a cry. He hobbled the last steps alone and dropped to his knees. His hand reached out.

"Don't—" *touch him*. Vindt stopped the words in time, realizing he had neither a reason nor the right to say that.

Calveen's hand hovered over the Singer's face, then fell down again. Tears streamed down his cheeks.

Vindt averted his eyes. The others, too, shifted in obvious discomfort.

"What's the matter with him?" Risi asked, voice heavy with concern, obviously referring to Asche and not his crying seneschal.

"I don't know. We fell into the ocean, and when we came out, he was unconscious."

"How did you get here, then?"

"Tunnel." Vindt pointed to the gaping mouth in the rocks behind them.

"You carried him?" Risi's eyebrows rose.

"What about the others?" Vindt hastened to ask. "Narr and Jun."

Layyad's face hardened. Risi cast Kishoon a look; he clenched his jaw. "Jun's fine," Risi said slowly.

Buds of fear blossomed in Vindt's heart. "And Narr?"

"Fine," Kishoon snapped with ferocity. His eyes were strangely veiled. "Alive."

"Alive, but...?"

"Demons' touches are a fickle thing," Dina answered in Kishoon's stead with his quiet, sparkling voice. "Even Singers cannot always heal them. She lost an arm. The right one."

The blood left Vindt's face.

"Is just arm," Kishoon huffed, face grim. "Life is important."

Yes, it was, but... "I'm sorry." Vindt touched Kishoon's shoulder in a helpless gesture. He also turned to Layyad, but the man crossed his arms before his chest and avoided Vindt's eyes.

"Where are they?" Vindt looked around. Two more men in blue tunics and their horses were standing a little apart, but there was no sign of the rest of Asche's or Dina's retinues, nor of the wagons.

"We rode here full speed. Others are far behind," Kishoon said.

"So, where are we?" Vindt eyed the landscape of horses in their paddocks and grazing sheep. Behind the farmstead in the distance, an eroding formation of white rocks that Vindt hadn't noticed before jutted out into the sea.

"Uh, well, Asche's home." Dina signaled for one of his servants. "We'll have to hoist him into the saddle. Best you ride with him, Vindt."

"No, I will." Calveen limped up to them.

Dina's face darkened. "Is there something wrong with my voice or with your ears?"

The menace in the words seemed to be lost on the seneschal. He pointed at Vindt. "He will—"

Dina let out a sound of frustration. "One more word and I'll turn you into a groundhog. Now get out of my sight."

Calveen glowered at Dina and Vindt, but then hobbled toward his horse. One of Dina's servants must have caught the mounts, which had scattered during the attack.

Risi leaned in to Vindt and murmured, "Groundhog? Can he actually do that?"

Vindt shrugged.

Dina's Thyd approached, a shy smile on his face. Umber skin and hair, black curls closely cropped to his scalp. With his lithe frame, high cheekbones and long lashes, he looked almost as androgynous as a Singer. "Fernando. Nice meeting you."

They shook hands.

Vindt would have expected Dina to sing to get Asche onto the servant's horse in a more dignified manner. But after Vindt had mounted, Risi and Layyad hoisted the Singer up as awkwardly as Vindt had to get him into the tunnel. Vindt didn't need to feel his body's heat to know Asche's condition had worsened again. His relief about their rescue gave way to the niggling concern from before.

His death means mine.

About a dozen people had gathered in front of the farm's gate and watched their approach with apparent excitement. Asche's home—a farmstead. Vindt didn't know what he had expected, but not this. It was quite large, the main building with its two stories almost a mansion. Still.

Dina didn't ride through the gate, however, but stopped to talk to a tall, elderly woman. Then he turned his horse onto a minor road leading around the building and toward the cliff.

"Where are we going?" Vindt asked, turning in the saddle to look at the receding farmstead.

"Well, to Asche's... uh... house." The Singer blushed. "Oh, you thought it was the farm? No, no, it's... uh... this." He looked ahead, face wrinkled as if he had a toothache.

But ahead of them was nothing but the precipice and the heap of eroding rocks.

Eroding rocks with windows. Vindt's jaw dropped.

Resting on a small isle, connected to the mainland only by a narrow bridge, sat the ugliest... well, "building" Vindt had ever seen. Made of the same dirt-white stone as its foundation, an assembly of angles, cuboids and spires crouched with no visible concept, let alone aesthetics. It looked like it had been thrown together by an infant having a tantrum.

"*This* is Asche's home?"

Dina's blush deepened. "It's very nice on the inside."

The moment Vindt entered the "building," he remembered what Narr had told him about Asche's house: "It feels like being underwater." It did. The sound of the waves crashing against the cliffs echoed through the hallways as if they were inside. When Vindt put his fingers to the white rock, he felt the sea's vibration, its *heart*. It was a pleasant feeling.

The house's interior looked like what Vindt would have expected of the mansion of some minor lord, wooden floors softened with plush rugs, oaken doors. The furniture was sparse, resembling the hodgepodge of the building's exterior. Bare of paintings or tapestries, the white walls were carved all over with underwater scenes, swirling currents, schools of fish between forests of corals and seaweed, an octopus looking up indignantly at a starfish sitting atop its head.

Vindt gave a small laugh. "Did Asche do that?"

Dina eyed the octopus and nodded, sighing. He led them upstairs to what must be Asche's quarters, a living area and a smaller bedroom. Cautiously, Vindt put the limp body into the creaking four-poster. Asche twitched, and another groan escaped his lips. Dina and Vindt both flinched; the crease in Dina's forehead deepened. He sat down on the bed and gently traced the dark silvery lines on Asche's face. It was a very intimate gesture, and suddenly Vindt wondered what Dina was to Asche. An ally, a friend. Or...?

"The help you mentioned," he said to cover his sudden awkwardness, "is another Singer, right?"

Dina shook his head.

"No? Then who... what..."

Dina didn't answer, but continued to softly stroke Asche's face.

Vindt wished he would stop. "Okay, whoever. When will they be here?"

"I hope soon."

"And if not?"

Dina raised his gaze to one of the windows. Beyond, the sea coiled and rolled under an indifferent sky of gray clouds. "Well..."

"You must be able to do *something*. You can't just let him..." *Go to hell. And me with him.*

Dina rose. "I need to get some rest. Please, one of you, watch over him."

"One of you" referred to either Vindt or Calveen. The seneschal had followed them together with Fernando, Dina's Thyd, and two servants.

Vindt nodded while Calveen said, "Of course."

They glowered at each other.

"I will stay," Calveen said firmly, eyes shooting daggers at Vindt.

I'm his Thyd. I brought him here. His death will be mine; I should at least be there when it happens.

But Vindt shut his already opened mouth before the words were out, irritated by the odd urge to fight for something he shouldn't have any urge to fight for.

"Fine." He shrugged.

Dina smiled at him. "We'll get you a hot bath and food. How does that sound? And then you should rest too."

It was true. He was dirty, tired and hungry. And yet... He looked back at Asche.

Dina's hand came to rest on Vindt's shoulder and steered him gently toward the door. "Don't worry, Calveen will take good care of him."

Yes, probably. But that wasn't the point.

CHAPTER 28

It was pitch black when Vindt awoke. The hot bath and the ocean's soothing lullaby had dragged him under as soon as his head hit the pillow. His room was next to Asche's. When he had gone to bed, he had left the door open. It was closed now. Calveen, the prick. Aiming for privacy with his beloved and apparently still alive master. For how much longer?

Vindt pondered going back to sleep. Instead, he listened to the churning waves, feeling for their soft vibrations in his veins. Asche and the ocean—so strange. Eventually, he rose and tiptoed to the door. It was made of solid wood, yet Vindt could clearly hear a man's breath through it, slow and heavy in his sleep. Not Asche. Cautiously, he pressed the handle and opened the door a crack.

A sole candle was burning on the nightstand next to the bed, chasing shadows over the unconscious Singer and the figure in the chair beside it. Calveen's slumped posture confirmed what his breaths had suggested. Vindt approached the bed as soundlessly as he could, but a few steps into the room, a board under his feet creaked. The seneschal's body jerked up. He blinked, then his gaze hardened. "I thought you were sleeping."

"I was." Vindt took the last steps toward the bed. "Like you."

"I didn't sleep. I was just—"

"Dosing?"

The seneschal's expression darkened some more, but when he opened his mouth, Vindt continued, "Nothing wrong with that. You're..." *old*, he had wanted to say, but then settled for, "tired. The last few days have been exhausting for all of us. I've rested. I can take over."

"Over my dead body will I leave him alone with you."

"You think I'll do what? Draw my dagger and kill him?"

The long, taut silence was answer enough. It was also enough for Vindt's patience. "Oh, fucking hell, Calveen. Why would I kill him?"

"You hate him."

"What? I—"

"He's been searching for so long," Calveen ranted on, sparing Vindt the decision whether to confirm or deny it. "And then he... got *you*." The last word he spat, voice quivering. "You have no idea—"

"Searching for what?"

Calveen's chest heaved under his agitated breaths. He rose from his chair and took a step in Vindt's direction. However, as soon as his weight came to rest on his right foot, his leg buckled. He let out a cry between surprise and pain. Vindt caught the falling man on reflex.

"Get your filthy hands off me."

That was the knife to Vindt's last thread of patience. He basically threw Calveen back into the chair and planted both his hands on the arms. Calveen recoiled, but had nowhere to go.

"Now listen to me, you fucking son of a bitch," Vindt hissed. "I'm done with your jealousy. I didn't choose to be a Thyd—you know that very well. I'd give my right hand to trade places with you or anyone. I hate my fate, yes, from the bottom of my heart. But I don't..."—*hate him*—"kill people, in cold blood, in their sleep. If I wanted to do that, I had a million opportunities the last two days while I was fucking *carrying him*."

Calveen's eyes were full of the hatred he claimed Vindt felt for Asche. But at least Vindt had silenced him.

"Fine. Now." Vindt righted himself. "Go and get some fu—some rest while I keep watch."

He had to endure some more hateful staring until Calveen eventually got up again. Vindt could virtually see the words the old man wanted to spit at him. Thankfully, he kept them to himself. His limp was so pronounced he almost hobbled. Vindt refrained from coming to his aid. He didn't sympathize, but... "Why didn't you let Dina help you with that?"

Calveen awarded him another spiteful glare. "Do you know anything about Singers? Healing drains them. Severely. I told Dina not to bother and save his powers for... more important things."

No, Vindt knew nothing about Singers. *Healing drains them.* He thought of Asche curing an entire army of dysentery, and turning Narr's leg from a lump of earth and roots back to a normal human limb.

"Heroic," he said dryly.

"Of course, you will never understand." With that, Calveen made his not very graceful exit.

Heaving a sigh of relief, Vindt lowered himself into the now vacant chair. In this room too the soft limestone was carved with scenes of ocean life. The octopus again—Asche seemed to like him; he appeared almost everywhere. This time he was clinging to the tail fin of a dolphin and letting himself be dragged along. Vindt failed to imagine Asche creating all this.

The lines on the Singer's face had grown over the past several hours. Vindt should've expected it. Yet, it fed the niggling feeling which had budded some time ago in some place in his body. Asche's breathing was shallow; heat emanated from him in a steady flow. The sour, metallic smell had intensified too.

Vindt didn't understand why Dina couldn't do anything. Or wouldn't. Who could this ominous help that wasn't a Singer be? Well, whoever it was, the odds that they would arrive within the next few hours, *in time*, were...

With a sudden, strange certainty, he knew Asche wouldn't survive the night. The thought was... as strange as the feeling inside his chest. His hand reached out without his doing.

A sudden flapping sound from the window made him stall. He turned, but apart from the wavering reflection of the candlelight, there was nothing to see outside. The sound came again. As if someone was throwing pebbles at the pane. Now, he did see something... fluttering?

A wayward seagull. Or...

Vindt hurried to rise.

Please, Gaal, let it be a messenger bird.

He opened the window to an angry croak and a whirl of feathers. The bird flew into the room and landed on the back of the chair Vindt had just left, shaking its rust-colored feathers. It was indeed a messenger bird. Except that its outline wavered and blurred as if it was about to dissolve. The black eyes stared at Vindt with discomfiting intensity. "Leave," it croaked.

"Huh?" Messenger birds could retain a few sentences of Lyskú and repeat them at their destination. They didn't give orders. Vindt should wake Dina. The bird had probably been instructed to only deliver its message to a Singer. He headed for the door.

"No need for the other Singer."

Vindt stopped, as did his heart. The words at his back had not been spoken by a croaking bird but by a human voice. A female one.

Slowly, Vindt turned. And indeed, the bird was gone. Before him stood—

"Gaal." Now it was him croaking.

He didn't know how he knew. It was just a woman. Besides, back in his homeland, his goddess had been depicted with blond hair and blue eyes, reflecting the looks of the country's population. The hair of the woman in front of him was fiery red, her eyes green. However, the demeanor, the serene look on her face, her unearthly beauty... and something else, something he couldn't pinpoint, something he had felt every time he went to the temple, a presence of divinity—a faint draft by then, now a storm. Her eyes seemed to see right through to his soul.

He dropped to his knees. "Gaal, Mother... I..." He paused. "Did you come to heal *him*?"

"This. Isn't. About. Healing." Her voice was an odd staccato, as if she had to force each word out.

"But?"

"Guiding his. Soul back from. The. Place you call Thrithid."

Vindt flinched. He should feel relief, and he did. On the one hand. On the other, he was... lost. After all these years, his goddess had come, only not in answer to his prayers, to free *him*, but to save one of their worst enemies. *She* was the help Dina had been waiting for?

"You know what he is, don't you? He's—"

"A demon." The glint in her eyes resembled Asche's.

"But then..."

"Don't. You want me to. Save him?"

"No, yes, I do." *But can you free me, too?*

She sauntered toward him. Now, in motion, her outline flickered again as it had when she was still a bird. It reminded Vindt of something, but the thought slipped away before he could grasp it.

Her aura of power wasn't unlike Asche's either, coiling around him assertively. A shiver cascaded down his spine as she reached out. He had expected her to touch him, but she pulled the cord with the two pendants from under his shirt. Ignoring the bloodstone, she twisted the amulet between her fingers, a frown on her face. She brushed the embedded rune with her thumb. "I made. This," she eventually said, slowly, as if she needed to tell it to herself. Her face took on a strange expression, wistful almost.

Vindt's breath caught. "I know," he whispered. "It has protected me many times."

She let go of the amulet and smiled. "Asche is a. Demon. Yes. But he regretted his. Sins. And stepped into the side of light. He serves me now. I need. Him."

Vindt stared at her in disbelief. "Need him for what?"

The woman—Gaal—smiled. "To bring justice." She

retreated toward the bed. "Now. Go."

Shakily, Vindt got up. The woman's aura flared, pushing him gently but firmly toward the door. Before he knew it, he found himself stepping outside.

"Have. Faith," she said in her staccato voice, smiling.

The door closed before Vindt's face.

For long minutes, he stood in the corridor, staring at the wood. Awe and fear mingled with the faint sensation of being mocked. Faith—okay. But faith and belief didn't always coincide. His hand rose to his amulet. *I made this.*

He woke from his stupor and hurried down the corridor to Dina's quarters. The Singer opened the door seconds after Vindt's first ferocious knock. Nightgown askew, hair disheveled, his frown conveyed alarm. "What—" he started, but Vindt grabbed him by the elbow and dragged him back the way he had come. "Someone has come, the help you called, I think. I don't know. A bird. No, a woman. Gaal."

Dina pulled him to a stop. He looked ahead in the direction of Asche's room, eyes narrowing. "Gaal?"

Vindt blushed. "My goddess."

Dina watched him with an inscrutable expression. "What does your goddess look like?"

"Well, she's blond. Normally. Only, now, here, she had, well, red hair and green eyes. She's tall, in any case. And beautiful. Is she the help you were waiting for?" His voice was urgent.

Hesitantly, Dina nodded. "I think so."

A part of the tension holding Vindt in its grip dissolved. "Okay, then let's go and—"

"Wait. I've never..." Dina bit his lip. The gesture was very un-Singer-like. Then again, Dina was un-Singer-like in many ways. Only hesitantly, he started to move. When they reached the door, instead of opening it or knocking, he laid his palm on the wood. Vindt strained his ears, but no sounds could be heard from the other side. Minutes passed.

Vindt fidgeted. "I really think we should go in."

"We wait."

"What if she's not saving him but—"

"Shhh." Dina's palm came to rest on Vindt's mouth again.

This wasn't right. They shouldn't be simply *waiting*. Vindt couldn't. He paced up and down the corridor, casting impatient glances at the door.

After what seemed like an eternity, it suddenly opened of its own accord. Dina took a step back, visibly reluctant to enter. Vindt had no such qualms. He strode in. The woman, a bird again, was sitting on the windowsill. Her contours writhed and blurred more than before.

Dina walked into the room as if he was treading on eggshells. He made an awkward bow to the bird and sang something. The bird sang back. It gave Vindt a last piercing look, black eyes gleaming with... amusement? Then it flew away.

Wait, Vindt wanted to shout. *Are you really my goddess?*

But it was gone.

Warily, Vindt approached the bed. The Singer's eyes were still closed, but he looked asleep rather than unconscious. His chest heaved with regular, deep breaths; the lines on his face were gone; the tart, metallic smell was still conspicuous, but down to a trace.

Reluctantly, he retreated a step to make room for Dina. The Singer sat down on the bed and took Asche's hand in both of his. "It will be some time until he wakes. But he's..."

His voice quivered. "He's safe." He took a deep sigh, then looked around. "What happened to Calveen?"

"I threw him out."

Dina's eyebrows rose. "Go, get some more sleep, little Thyd. I'll watch him now."

"I want to know what happened here. Why did Gaal... *Was* she Gaal?"

"It's late. We will talk tomorrow. Go to sleep now. That's an order," Dina added with authority when Vindt opened his mouth to protest. The Singer's flaring aura reminded him that Dina, as "lovely" as he appeared, was one of the most powerful living Singers.

Only not powerful enough to save Asche.

With a last glance at the sleeping figure in the bed, Vindt left the room.

CHAPTER 29

Vindt assumed Dina had ordered the servants to light a fire in Asche's chambers for his, Vindt's, sake. Singers seemed to be immune to fire's allure, the very essence of shelter and food, of life and solace. However, Dina gazed at it now, swirling the goblet in his hand, blue eyes clouded with thought. His face had gone notably paler since the woman's visit yesterday; shadows had appeared under his eyes. Vindt supposed he was trying to accelerate Asche's recovery.

Asche was still asleep, but Dina had assured Vindt he would wake up any moment.

"You cannot hear its song, can you?" the Singer suddenly murmured, eyes on the flames. "The fire's, I mean."

But Vindt could, dissonant, greedy, the soothing crackle threaded by spits and hisses. It was indeed not very pleasant. The opposite of the ocean's soothing melody. Something definitely *had* happened to his aural sense. The idea made his skin tingle. Transfer of powers. A tale, according to

Asche. But suddenly being able to see in the dark wasn't a product of his imagination, either...

The rest of Dina's retinue had arrived earlier today, together with Asche's wagon, Jun and Narr. Vindt had been glad to see Kishoon's sister alive, as she had apparently been to see him. However, her missing arm hovered between them like a ghost limb, craving attention from the living.

"I'm so sorry," Vindt had muttered, not daring to touch her.

"I'm alive. That's what counts," she had said, echoing her brother's words. True, of course, yet her voice had been threaded with bitterness.

Vindt wondered whether Dina really didn't have the ability to heal her, or if he wanted to save his powers. Admittedly, Vindt had been glad of every bit of those powers during the attack. But still...

He took a breath. "You promised to talk to me today."

"Uh, did I?" Dina made a face.

"Was the woman who rescued Asche Gaal, my goddess? And if not, who or what was she?"

Mysteries and secrets: the cornerstones of his world. Vindt was fed up with it, as he was with people using him as a pawn in their games. Even his goddess seemed to have joined the club of schemers. That Asche had "regretted his sins and stepped into the side of light" was as likely as Vindt himself waking up a Singer one sunny morning. It was something *Asche* would say to mock him. He could even imagine it, the tonality, the glint in his eyes. The same as in hers.

"If *you* don't know, how should I?" Dina said. "I've never seen the woman, only the bird, remember? And I've surely never seen your goddess."

Vindt stifled a groan. Gaal, he was like Asche. "She said she needed him to bring justice. What did that mean?"

"That was what she said?"

"Okay, let's do this differently." Despite everyone's belief about the limitations of his mental capacities, Vindt was well able to connect some of the dots. The things he had seen and heard at The Haven. The way Asche had reacted when talking about their expiry date. "I don't know if Asche told you, but..." He stopped, unsure whether Dina knew about him having witnessed the Pledge or, if he learned about it now, how he would react. He decided to take the risk. "I've witnessed the Pledge."

Dina grinned. "Wicked."

"You knew?"

"Asche told me."

"You didn't feel my presence during the ceremony?"

Dina shook his head.

That probably meant that none of the others had been aware of him either. Perhaps it didn't matter, but Vindt was a little relieved.

"What I saw, those... things—you call them the First, no? And they are your gods."

Dina chuckled. "Gods are something humans came up with." He sighed. "The First created us. If that makes them gods in your eyes..."

"They created you?" That messed with Vindt's theory. "But they are also the ones who want you dead when you get too old, the ones who attack you." The smell, the feeling, the way his amulet had reacted during the Pledge. There might be a difference in power, but otherwise, Vindt was sure they were the same.

"In a way..." Dina swirled the contents of his goblet. The wine was watered, Vindt knew.

"In what way? Dina, *please*. No one ever tells me anything. I *want* to know. I need to. I'm Asche's Thyd. I might be human, but I'm not entirely stupid. Please."

"You should ask Asche about these things."

"Asche is not here now. And you promised."

"I promised to *talk*, not what about." Dina took a breath. "Alright, little Thyd. I will try to explain the First to you, but be aware that they are hard to fathom, even for our sophisticated Singer minds. Yes, the First and what is attacking us are the same, but at the same time, they are not. The First aren't individuals, or yes, they are, sometimes, depending on the state they're in. But they tend to disintegrate, or a part of them does, and then they become what you call demons. After a time, they either reassemble or morph into something else."

It *was* convoluted. "Morph into what?"

"A rock, a tree, a finger. Anything."

"But they eat human souls. Back home, demons attacked us, even without an expired Singer around."

"No more than they *attack* animals or plants or earth. They're the essence of creation, of song, and thus of change. Everything is song; it only has different expressions."

"But the attacks on Asche and you are not random."

"No." Dina's voice carried a hint of sadness and... the familiar bitterness.

Vindt perked up. "If the First created you, why would they want you dead?"

Something in Dina's expression changed. "Because the older we get, the more powerful we become. And the First won't tolerate that, lest we become as powerful as them again."

Again. Excitement hummed in Vindt's veins. His theory, perhaps... "They punish you," he said carefully, monitoring Dina's reactions. "Not only by hunting you down when you get old but with Thrithid."

"Well now. I'm tempted to revise my opinion about the human mind."

The picture was still far from revealing itself. "But why —"

Dina raised a palm. "That's enough, little Thyd. Again, I am not the person to tell you all this. I know you think Asche will deny you the answers. But don't be so sure. He likes to rant about these things. And besides... you saved his life. He owes you."

"More likely, when he learns I *carried* him, he'll kill me."

Dina laughed. "Or that."

Vindt smiled too. It was weird; he was as relaxed with Dina as he had ever been in a Singer's presence. Perhaps the "loveliness" was an act. However, it didn't feel that way. The idea that Asche had at least one ally, or even a friend, and that it was Dina, somehow comforted him.

Unless he was more than a friend.

* * *

Early-morning mist hovered over the earth, warping shapes and sounds. Keke was all pricked ears and prancing feet. Vindt had never seen the dull gelding so agitated. He held the reins firmly. If the horse ran, he wouldn't be able to cling on for long, riding bareback, upon Asche's orders. "Unless you want to carry the saddle back."

Asche, of course, showed no discomfort at all, sitting sure and steady. He had not even put a bridle on Schiida.

The mare was gripped by anticipation too; her ears, usually turned backward to pick up each of Asche's whims, were set firmly on the approaching hills. The horses' dampened trot was the only sound in the misty landscape.

They were still in viewing distance of the farm when Asche dismounted and signaled for Vindt to do the same. "Take off his bridle."

He sang, one sharp sound, cutting through the fog. They waited. Schiida and Keke stood still as statues, eyes on the hills. Vindt's skin prickled.

He heard them before he saw them. The ground trembled, a rumble far away, approaching. And then they floated over the hill, adults and foals, a forest of whirling legs and stamping hooves, of pricked ears and gleaming eyes, a mass of gray and brown, of swishing tails and fluttering manes.

Vindt stood, mesmerized, his heart beating slow and hard. Asche was smiling, not the exact same smile he had worn while singing to the baby, but close.

The lead stallion slowed down only shortly before reaching them. Vindt would not have been surprised had he bowed to Asche in reverent greeting, but he ignored the Singer entirely, in favor of Schiida.

The mare herself had undergone a remarkable change in the last few seconds. Her eagerness had vanished, replaced by a decidedly indifferent look on her face. She walked up to the herd, seemingly oblivious of the stallion who pranced around her, tail lifted, eyes wide, nostrils flaring, snorting clouds of excitement into the misty air. The first time he came close, Schiida flattened her ears and snapped her teeth an inch short of his neck. The second time, she turned in a smooth motion and kicked him in the chest. The stallion seemed delighted.

Asche's smile deepened. "The boss is back."

"Looks like she won't miss you."

"I fear I lack certain equine aspects to merit her full love."

They watched Keke and Schiida reestablishing friendships and confirming animosities, exchanging touches, and snorts, and grunts, neighing and squeaking. Or rather, Asche watched the horses and Vindt watched Asche. The smile, the tenderness on his tired features. So strange to see him like this, alive, well, without the hideous lines on his face.

The Singer had woken up in the middle of last night. Vindt's subconsciousness had stirred him from sleep, and, before his mind fully caught up, he felt the Singer leaving. On impulse, he rose, following the trail of his aura through the house. At a small door in the basement, Vindt halted, squinting out into the darkness, at the stretch of rock, the churning waves. Asche was nowhere to be seen.

Going for a swim, of course—the first thing that came to the Singer's mind after waking up from a near-lethal slumber. Vindt considered fetching Dina. However, something made him stay, wait, hidden in the corridor's shadow. Until Asche returned.

Whatever had altered Vindt's sight let him see well enough in the darkness now. Asche was naked, his pale skin covered from head to toe in sinuous lines. The silver threaded through the black gleamed in the moonlight. This time, however, the pattern didn't inspire dread; to the contrary, the Singer looked newly born, as if the ocean had spat him out of its womb, a creature made of waves and tides, of liquid and darkness, something that would slip through Vindt's fingers as soon as he tried to grasp it.

That was when he realized he was seeing something he shouldn't. He retreated. The image of the naked, gleaming Asche, however, burned itself into his mind.

With some effort, he pulled himself out of the memory. Asche was still watching the horses.

"Shouldn't we go?" Not that Vindt wanted to leave, but whatever magic kept demons and Verdurs at bay in the house probably did not extend to the hills.

Asche sighed, and they started walking back. In the distance, the rising sun was burning away the mist on the ocean and around the house. Here, in the foothills, the disembodied gray still shifted undisturbed. It was only the second time Vindt had seen the house from the outside. Gaal, it was so ugly.

"What's so funny?" Asche asked.

Vindt had not realized he had laughed. "The house, why did you make it so..." He hesitated.

"Ugly? I suppose I don't care. I don't like houses, and less living in one. No idea how Dina bears it."

"Dina has a house too?"

"No. He lives at the Guzzar court. He's a counselor to the empress."

Vindt stopped. "*He works for humans?*"

"We work for humans all the time, in case you haven't noticed."

To kill, yes. Vindt had never wondered about Silhorveen's reasons for traveling from war to war. The way of the world, how Singers earned their living. Since Asche, he wasn't sure anymore, and not simply because the Singer had "donated" all five chests filled with the crowns he received from Plotliw to some temple along the way.

Mocking the priests, of course, who had cursed him as a demon as soon as they laid eyes on him, just to go all docile and eager when the contents of the chests had come into view.

Asche's way of having fun.

"Why?" Vindt asked.

"Why not? It's amusing."

"To kill humans?"

"Ah, you mean the battles. Isn't it humans killing each other and us helping them along?"

"There's a difference between an honest fight, man on man, and mass killing from a distance without dirtying your hands."

"Seems like the outcome is the same."

Perhaps, but—

"Killing is very difficult," Asche continued. "Even for a Singer. Hundreds of people moving, horses, friend and foe mingling. It's an art. It hones our skills. Most young Singers do it. Some take to it and continue." Asche, who had stopped when Vindt had, now continued walking.

"An art," Vindt snorted, falling into step.

"What about sword fighting? Don't you consider that an art? How many people have you killed with your sword?"

"I always had a reason, to defend my life, my country."

"The famous Pel raiders with their nimble ships, assailing countries near and far, slaughtering people, raping women and taking whatever valuables they can get their hands on. But surely you have never participated in that."

Blood rushed to Vindt's cheeks. *I've never raped.*

"Ah, but of course." Asche smiled at him. "You wielded an honest sword and not a demonic voice."

"Oh, fuck." Vindt stopped again. This was all wrong. It was the first time they were seeing each other after everything that had happened, the first words they'd exchanged. It shouldn't be like this. It should be like...

"I thought you'd die," Vindt bellowed. It wasn't what he had wanted to say, less so with such emphasis. He flinched, feeling the words hanging in the air like the mist, damp and heavy.

The black eyes assessed him. "You mean, you *hoped* I would die."

Yes. That. There was no use trying to rectify it. Better not to.

"Do you want me to thank you?" Asche raised an eyebrow.

"No, I want..." Vindt took a breath. "I want to know what happened. The woman, Gaal..."

"Ah, your goddess." The glint in the depths of Asche's eyes ignited.

To Vindt's utter surprise—and greater dismay—he found he had missed that glint. What in Gaal's name was wrong with him?

Asche glanced toward the farm. "This is not a good place to discuss this. We will end up as demon fodder—"

"You want to end it. Thrithid. The attacks." Vindt's voice was almost desperate. After the conversation with Dina, he had connected a few more dots. Or thought he had. The mission Asche was on. A quest for power, Ru had claimed, but the Singer would have said anything to get Vindt's support. Many things didn't fit into the picture yet, his own role, the wrist Binding. Still... "I just don't understand why Ru and the others... Why don't they support you?"

Asche looked at him with an expression Vindt couldn't decipher. "Because they are cowards," he eventually said, in a voice Vindt had never heard before. "Because they prefer to live their wretched little lives for the time the First condescend to grant them. Because they happily let themselves be chased around by demons and tortured in Thrithid instead of standing up and fighting, ending this farce, claiming what's ours." His eyes were burning. "You know what the Council is? An institution of self-control. It makes sure we demurely accept our fate, bow to the First with eternal gratitude for our existence and the punishment bestowed on us for our own good."

Vindt hardly dared to breathe. He felt as if he had picked up a rock and the entire mountain was crumbling down.

"Thrithid, demons." Asche threw his hands into the air in a gesture of exasperation. "Our babies didn't use to grow on trees, you know. Female Singers did exist. They killed them, jealous not only of our powers but our ability to procreate, to evolve, while they stagnated."

Vindt swallowed. "And the Verdurs?"

"Wouldn't our lives be boring without them? In case your next question is why, of all beings, humans are the key to our defense: humiliation." The last word he spat. "So, golden boy, next time you think you are the dependent one in our relationship, the slave—think again."

He bored his eyes into Vindt's before turning abruptly and walking away.

CHAPTER 30

Vindt had not realized the house had been dormant. Only now, with Asche awake, did he notice the difference. The waves' deep rumble was *everywhere*, a symbiosis of feeling and sound, quivering in his veins. Walking the corridors felt like swimming. He even dreamed of the ocean, water curling around him, carrying him, pulling him into dark depths. The dreams were utterly pleasant, the transition to reality soft and seamless.

To his surprise, he opened his eyes to darkness. Dawn was not even close, as a glance through the window told him. Something must have woken him. Voices. They came from next door, so low he would never have heard them with his usual human senses. Dina and Asche. Still not loud enough to discern the words. Vindt strained his ears to no avail.

As silently as he could, he got out of bed and tiptoed over. The limestone transmitted sounds; he had learned as much already. He pressed his ear to the wall.

"... think she was angry," Dina said.

"She's always angry." Asche.

"You don't think she's still... mad at you?"

"She came."

"Yes, but... late. I... was worried."

"If you don't trust me, Dina, we're lost."

"It's not... I'm sorry, Sansýr-thed."

"Oh, stop calling me that. You're a member of the doomed seven now too."

Dina chuckled. When he spoke again, his voice was grave, though. "Does it feel different with him, the Bond?"

There was no audible answer from Asche, but he must have made some gesture, because Dina asked, "How?"

"It doesn't matter. It will be over soon."

"Yes. I wouldn't have expected Ru to bring it up so blatantly."

"Words. He's desperate." Asche took a breath. "But whatever the case, he..." Asche's voice changed. Vindt could almost hear him smiling. "You know that he promised Vindt his freedom?"

"What?" Dina's voice was laced with genuine incredulity. "But how..."

"He lay in wait for him when I went up to the Vedsetri after the meeting. He promised to release Vindt from the Bond if he alerts him when I make him drink from my wrist. He gave him a bird-caller." Asche chuckled. "He even made an Eith to prove his sincerity."

"What did you do?" Dina didn't sound amused, rather alarmed.

"What should I have done? I took the caller and told him it was all lies and show. He doesn't know about the Eith."

"What if he finds another way of contacting Ru?"

"Him or Jun, what's the difference? You heard what I told you about Nakoto."

There was a long pause before Dina quietly said, "So, you're ready."

"I am."

For some reason, the words chased a shiver down Vindt's spine. Even the ocean stalled in its languid churning; the house held its breath.

Dina sighed. With it, the sea and the walls exhaled too. "It's getting late, Sansýr-thed."

"I told you not to call me that." Asche's voice was soft.

Dina chuckled. "I like to call you that. And it's true. Shall we?"

No answer came, but the sounds of scraping wood and rustling fabric suggested both men were rising. Vindt was about to hastily withdraw when he hesitated. The footsteps were not moving toward the door but further into the room. A moment later, he heard the same creaking noise as when he had laid Asche's unconscious body into...

... his bed.

Vindt froze. *Every Singer, every time they meet.* Issa's words.

One of the tales Thyds told themselves? Or... Asche had woken up a few days ago and neither of them had any bite marks. Then again, Asche had been weak, recovering...

Vindt pressed himself closer to the wall. For a long time, he couldn't hear anything apart from an indistinct rustle and his own shallow breaths. He was about to move away, relief tinged with a drop of disappointment, when he heard the moan.

Time seemed to come to a halt; the surrounding air grew dense.

The next moan traveled from his ears and fingertips all the way through his body, curling in his groin. Small, inarticulate noises followed. Images formed in his mind, long-fingered hands roaming over pale skin, a naked body, lithe and dripping. It was revolting, the sounds, the images, and more so him standing here, listening. And yet he stayed, riveted, his senses primed for every sound, the changes in rhythm. At some point, even without improved hearing, the noises left no doubt as to their nature. Asche and Dina didn't seem to care that someone might hear them.

Vindt's breathing came fast and shallow. The sounds pelted him like needles, driving their sharp points into his skin. A voice in his head urged him to leave, but the rush of blood in his ears drowned it out. His right hand dropped without him being able to stop it. His pants came open, lust and disgust indiscriminate. Somehow, he quelled his own moan as his fingers closed around his cock. The noises from next door forced his hand, merciless, debasing, a relentless scourging that drove him stumbling over the edge in no time, synced with the person who came on the other side.

Somehow, Vindt knew it wasn't Asche.

* * *

Vindt's breaths clouded in front of his mouth. The sun had barely risen; the terrace facing the ocean still lay in shadow. Despite the cool temperatures, sweat trickled down his bare chest and arms. His muscles ached. A welcome strain. He charged again.

Risi deflected the blow with furrowed brows. Vindt charged again immediately, strategy and skills crushed under brute force. His sword flew from his hands and landed with a clatter beside him. He bent to pick it up, but Risi put his foot on the blade. "What's the matter?"

"You standing on my sword?"

"This is not fighting, Vindt, but a child having a tantrum."

Risi did not see the push coming. As soon as he shifted his stance to keep his balance, Vindt snatched his sword from the floor and launched into another attack.

Risi was a prizefighter. He had earned his living with his sword. Vindt had surely improved during their practice sessions over the past weeks; his defeats didn't come as embarrassingly quickly as in the beginning. Still, he was no match for the other man. If Risi fought in earnest. Which he did now.

A second later, Vindt was not only missing his sword again; he found himself on his knees, one arm twisted behind his back, Risi's full weight on him.

"In the name of Faroosi and the six whistling spiders, are you not right in the head?"

"Get the fuck off me." Vindt trembled, only partly from physical exhaustion. He struggled, with the sole effect of Risi's grip tightening.

"Man, Vindt. I ask you again, what's the fucking matter?"

The fucking matter—yes, what was it? That Asche had lied to him about Ru's oath? That Vindt, after learning that, had nothing better to do than get himself off on listening to Singers having sex? Or that he had stood at a window in a room far away from Asche's chambers, putting the whistle to his lips, lowering it, raising it again, for hours, and then went to bed, completely exhausted, without having blown it, wrapped in a coat of self-disgust so thick it choked him?

"I'm sorry to interrupt, but I fear we are leaving." The

soft voice fell on Vindt's exposed back like a whiplash.

Risi's grip slackened; he stepped back. "Kvahad-thed."

Vindt rested on his haunches, counting to ten, before he found the strength to rise and turn. Dina smiled. Vindt clenched his hands into fists to keep them from closing around the Singer's neck. Around the glowing bite marks.

He made an effort to return the smile and failed.

Dina wasn't wearing his robes but a blue riding tunic, breeches, leather boots. As if he was...

Only then did the Singer's words reach Vindt's awareness. "You're leaving," he echoed.

Yes, go.

Fernando walked onto the terrace behind his master. Risi grinned at him, which, for some reason, made Fernando blush.

"We came to say goodbye." Dina reached out, apparently to lay a hand on Vindt's shoulder. Vindt stepped back. Dina's fine brows rose in surprise.

Vindt knew he shouldn't be acting like that. Dina had saved their lives and been friendlier with Vindt than any Singer before. But Vindt's jaws were locked by the effort it cost him not to stare at the bite marks.

A measured silence passed before Dina said, "Well, it was a pleasure meeting you."

"The pleasure was mine," Vindt managed to hiss, adding a belated, "Kvahad-thed."

Dina had probably wanted to say something else, but he just nodded, touched his Thyd on the shoulder and went back the way he had come from.

Fernando reached out his hand. "It was a pleasure meeting you. Hope I'll see you again soon."

Vindt took it absent-mindedly, nodding.

Hesitantly, the Thyd also held his hand out to Risi. The broad man looked at it with unconcealed amusement, then shook it exaggeratedly with both his enormous paws. "A pleasure."

"Uh, well, yes, you too," Fernando stammered, then hastened to exit after his master.

Under different circumstance, Vindt might have asked what this awkward exchange was about. Perhaps Asche and Dina had not been the only ones trading body fluids last night. Vindt had assumed Risi was only into women, but who knew?

Before the big man could remember where they had left off before Dina's arrival, Vindt picked up his sword and shirt and made for the door. "Sorry, I'm... not well. I'll see you later."

Risi's gaze on his back followed him until Vindt rounded the next corner, but he didn't ask any more questions.

Halfway up the stairs, Vindt was met by Calveen.

Fantastic.

"Where have you been?" the seneschal snapped. "The Kvahad-thed wants to see you. Now."

Even better. A talk with Asche was exactly what he needed. Vindt looked at his naked, sweat-shiny chest. "May I clean myself first?" He didn't wait for a reply, but strode past Calveen and into his room.

The house had a pipe system that brought water from the ocean to the rooms. Whether by magic or natural filtering, it came out unsalted and drinkable. Vindt soaked a towel and proceeded to wipe the sweat from his chest.

Asche lying to him—about Ru's oath, about whatever else—shouldn't have come as a surprise. Asche was a notorious liar. That the wrist Binding came with a death sentence was probably just another lie. And even if not… Asche's death—they were right, Calveen and Asche himself: it was what Vindt wanted, always had, and a little more so now. He didn't understand why he had not blown the fucking whistle.

He had just grabbed a clean shirt when the feeling of being watched made him turn.

Asche leaned on the door frame, arms folded. His eyes roamed over Vindt's still exposed chest, unhurried, from the abdomen upward. A finger's soft brush. The buzz at the back of Vindt's head, which had only diminished but never ceased since last night, flared.

The black eyes rose to meet his. With the insinuation of a smile, Asche righted himself. "Come over when you're done."

CHAPTER 31

Vindt took his time, deliberately. When he eventually entered Asche's rooms, he found the Singer cross-legged before a low table, contemplating the strange figures of his board game. Partly tucked away under his legs, his feet still showed, bare, the pale skin adorned with a reddish pattern. That was new. Vindt's mind painted the image of Dina holding one delicate foot in his hands, applying color, smiling at Asche's noises of pleasure. Whatever they sounded like. Vindt was sure the sounds he had heard through the wall last night had only come from Dina.

Not waiting for an invitation, he slumped onto the rug on the table's opposite side and pointed his chin at the board. "Did you play with Dina?" He missed the casual tone he had aimed for by a mile.

"Unfortunately, in this, Dina is no match for me."

In this and everything else. But so much for Vindt's guess that Dina was the Singer Asche had been exchanging moves with all this time. It was true, however: the board was in the same arrangement as when he had last seen it; Vindt had an excellent visual memory.

"Want to play?" Asche asked.

"This? I don't even know what game this is."

"Chess, obviously."

"You sent Calveen to call me to play chess?"

Asche reached for a pouch on a small shelf next to him. Vindt caught it with one hand and only just resisted the urge to throw it back full force into the Singer's face. "That's a joke. You don't really want to play now."

Asche stored away the figures for his other game with the same dedicated care as last time. "And why should we not? Did I miss something?"

The urge to confront Asche with what he had learned sizzled beneath Vindt's skin. Not that he had understood much. Dina asking if the Bond with him felt different was just another hint for what was already certain. And Asche being ready—for what?

What he had understood very well, though, was that Asche had lied to him about Ru's oath.

It took his shaking hands longer than usual to set the figures up.

"Shall I start?" Asche asked. "So you'll at least have an excuse for—"

"Did you fuck?" The pointed ears of the wooden horse Vindt was holding dug into his skin. The dull pounding in his head had reverted to the buzz, grating his nerves.

More than seeing it in Asche's face, Vindt felt the change of atmosphere, the tiny shift in reality, a thread pulled taut to the point of tearing.

Very slowly, Asche lowered the goblet he had been raising to his lips back onto the table. And just as slowly, enunciating each word, he said, "I don't see how this is any of your concern." His gaze never left Vindt's. "But yes, we fu-ck-ed." He turned the word into three syllables, the "ck" a click deep in his throat.

Vindt stood.

In an unhurried, flowing motion, Asche rose too. His bare feet made no sound on the rug as he came so close Vindt felt the heat of his body, a current crawling over his skin, mingling with his aura, tentatively, possessively, seeking ways inside. "I don't know what the matter with you is, golden boy." Asche's voice was very quiet, very low and very near. "But you're treading on—"

Vindt didn't hear the rest. The buzz in his head had risen to a drone, drowning out all sounds. His chest heaved as his lungs fought for air. He became aware of every body part, his thrumming heart, the dry insides of his mouth where his incisors had grown, his too-tight skin, his sizzling hands. The parts were detached, refusing to form an entity, each one disproportional, bloated or shrunk, as if he were a caricature of himself.

What do your *moans sound like?*

Vindt didn't think; he didn't plan. The space between them burned up as he dropped the horse and pushed Asche against the wall with the entire length of his body. The impact drove the air out of the Singer's lungs and cut off his surprised gasp. Vindt caught the flailing wrists and pinned them to the wall above, then he crashed his mouth to the Singer's.

His canines pierced flesh and drew blood. Asche's lips parted, in shock or an attempt to gasp for air, Vindt didn't know and didn't care. His tongue tore open at Asche's fangs. Blood gushed from the wound and pooled into the Singer's mouth, mingling with Asche's. Inevitably, their tongues met. Asche tasted of sea salt and iron, a bleeding ocean.

Vindt detached his mouth, taking heavy breaths. "Sing," he hissed.

Stop this, because I can't.

Vindt's cock strained against his pants. It was absurd. This wasn't—*couldn't* be about sex. He didn't desire Asche. He did... He wanted...

To take, possess, subdue.

Asche stared up at him with eyes as wide as the ocean, lips parted. His pupils were dilated, the black irises clouded as if shrouded by a veil. Blood dripped from his mouth and the points of his clearly visible incisors. Raw, strident lust emanated from his body in waves. With the thigh Vindt had shoved between the Singer's legs, Vindt felt Asche's hard member.

Vindt's eyes went to Asche's neck. The bite marks the Singer had received at The Haven still adorned one side. It didn't take much to guess who had left them. The other side: untainted, unclaimed. Vindt could see the pulsing vein beneath the pale skin, smell the blood. He licked his lips.

The Singer's eyes went even wider. "No."

"No?" Vindt didn't let go of Asche's wrists, but he slackened his grip so it would take a child's strength to free them. Then he waited.

Now it was Asche's turn to lick his lips. He tried to say something, but all that came out was an inarticulate noise. He *was* struggling now, ferociously—Vindt felt it—just not with his body.

"Tilt your head."

Asche's breath changed from shallow to wheezing.

Patience had never been one of Vindt's virtues, but now he watched with a strange, greedy calm, until the black eyes closed and the winner in Asche's mind pulled his head to the side. A dog's bared throat.

Now, I will leave you marked.

He sank his teeth.

His moan dissolved in the liquid gushing into his mouth. Blood—pure and unfiltered. It entered his stomach, his veins, a burning torrent. Blindly, he took one hand off the unresisting wrists and pulled the shirt from Asche's loosely fastened pants. Skin. Perfect, smooth. Flanks, abdomen, chest. His fingers moved, nerve endings hyper aware, trespassing, desecrating, leaving his human scent, his mark, traces, stains. The nipple rose pliantly under his brush. Arbitrary muscles in the pinned body spasmed.

No, this wasn't about sex.

It was about revenge.

He withdrew his teeth. Blood ran down his chin and dropped onto his shirt. Like this, from the neck, its effect was even more intoxicating than when drinking it from the wrist. A red film clouded Vindt's vision.

His hand continued its conquest, following the trail of fine hair from the navel down. A passageway the size of the universe gaped between the fabric of Asche's trousers and his skin in the depression next to the hip bone. The sudden ferocious need to plunge his hand into the body itself, bury it between the hot, pulsing organs, made Vindt shudder. He closed it around Asche's cock instead.

Asche sucked in a breath.

The Singer was hard indeed, the member as delicate as the rest of his body. It was strangely wet, not moist like Vindt's own got sometimes, almost like a woman. It made it easy to play with.

Vindt pushed down the foreskin and let his fingers glide over the swollen glans, mapping its topology, plains, rims, rifts. He had never touched another man's cock, yet it felt as if he had done it a million times. Exactly like that.

"How does it feel to be toyed with?" He could hardly hear his voice over his roaring blood and the drone in his head. "Like it? No? Just wait. It's an acquired taste, you know."

Asche's body twitched. Vindt felt the moan the Singer was struggling to contain.

Don't worry, we'll get there.

Asche didn't resist as he turned him around and pushed his body against the wall. Vindt dove his face into the mass of black hair, smooth, floating, water's fourth state of matter. The scent of the ocean was overwhelming, waves crashing down on him, dragging him under. His chest heaved. The buzz in his head expunged all thoughts and channeled all desires into one. A beacon of fear prevailed, dread even, the awareness of the abyss, the hope for something or someone to rescue them.

His lips touched a delicate ear. "Sing, in all the demons' names." His voice was a growl, barely human. "Or I'm going to take you."

The only reaction Vindt's words elicited was another burst of lust. It hit Vindt's groin with strident might. The cloth belt Asche's pants were fastened with unraveled under his fingers; the trousers fell, casualties of gravity. Vindt's eyes caught pale skin, curves, before he yanked his gaze away. He couldn't. See. This. Absurd, given what he was about to do, but seeing was too much, too intimate, too immediate.

He didn't need to see for his fingers to find their target. Still moist from Asche's cock, they slid in without resistance.

They both went completely rigid; even Vindt's heartbeat stopped.

And then Asche did moan.

It wasn't a beautiful sound as Vindt might have expected, like everything Singers produced with their vocal cords, but something ugly and primal, wrenched free from the very core of Asche's being.

Vindt's cock jerked. His last kernel of self-preservation went into non-existence with a soft plop. Hand trembling, he fumbled to undo the buttons of his pants. It almost hurt to touch his swollen cock. With the presence of a mind that had given up working, he tried to lubricate it at least some with the moisture on his fingers.

Then he took what was his.

His groan reverberated off the walls, amplified again and again, hammering back against his eardrums. He didn't move. He just stood there, eyes closed, body pressed against Asche's, breathing, feeling. The outside, the inside, becoming one. Becoming his. He must have let go of the Singer's wrists because his palms were pressed flat against the wall, cool limestone under his fingers, the relief of the carvings. Time dropped through them, forming pools on the stone floor. His mind was dazed, and yet he had never been this aware. And he wanted Asche to be aware, too. Of this. Its impossibility. The universe upended. Of the fact that he could have prevented it but had not.

Their chests rose and fell, tides orchestrated by an absent moon. The body beneath him quivered; tremors ran down Asche's inner thighs. Occasionally, the Singer's muscles spasmed violently, driving Vindt's cock further in.

The bottom of the abyss. And still room to sink.

He pulled Asche back with him, gently almost, the few inches his hand needed to close around the Singer's member again. It twitched, a panicked bird in his grasp. Vindt moved softly, fingers and body in sync, drinking in every trembling breath, every strangled noise.

He brought his lips to Asche's ear again. "I'll make you come into my hand."

The effect of his words rippled out in thick waves, the panting, the subtle change under his fingers, harder still, the final surge before collapse. Asche's breathing stuttered and his body went rigid again. Time stopped, a space of stillness. Then the world tilted. The Singer's back arched so violently his spine cracked. He didn't moan this time; he didn't make any sound as he did what Vindt made him do.

Vindt had no time to wallow in his victory. The sensation of Asche's semen spilling over his fingers yanked him back into his own sensations, reducing his perceptions to the coiling beast beneath his skin. He screamed or moaned or was as silent as Asche—he couldn't know over the roar in his head—as he sank and sank and sank.

CHAPTER 32

It took a long time until his tremors ebbed away, his heartbeat and breathing normalized. Sweat trickled down his back, each rivulet a scraping nail on his oversensitive skin. Reality pierced through his daze, cold and sharp. He felt empty, spent. Not pleasantly. The void inside him had a substance, something viscous, like liquid. It moved. Smells of blood, and sweat, and semen imbued the air. The smell was as wrong as the feeling of the body beneath him. He shuddered.

His limbs seemed to belong to someone else, but he forced them into obedience. He winced as he pulled out his softening cock and took a step back. The taste of blood filled his mouth.

Asche stood slightly bent, palms and forehead pressed against the stone, hair spilling down in rumpled tangles. He didn't move except for the spasms which still rippled through his body.

While Vindt had not been able to look at the curves of exposed skin before, the sight now stirred a cold, damp fog from the muddy depths of his mind. A nervous flutter spread in his stomach, which almost immediately turned into dull anxiety, scouring the back of his scalp. He reached out, but didn't finish the gesture. Asche's hands moved first, the fingers crawling over the stones as if looking for purchase. Vindt retreated another few steps as the Singer eventually pulled up his trousers with slow, awkward movements.

What have I done?

Asche's hand rose to the spot on his neck where Vindt had sunk his teeth in. He stared at his bloodied fingertips. The pit in Vindt's guts grew wider and deeper, his heartbeat louder.

You could have sung.

Asche turned.

With his disheveled hair, the rumpled shirt and bloody mouth, he had never looked more like Lord Tehered, the demon king. A demon king who had just received a blade in his back. The look in the black eyes brought Vindt's heart to an abrupt halt.

"Go to the wall." Asche's voice was like nothing Vindt had heard before, shards of ice cutting through his skin.

He searched for something to say, but the swirling blackness in his stomach swallowed all words before he could grasp them. He obeyed without his doing, trance-like.

"Take off your shirt."

Vindt did, his breathing shallow.

"Kneel and put your hands on the stone."

Dread filled Vindt whole now; his palms were wet. It was obvious what was to follow. So many times, Vindt had expected punishment for things he did or said, and it had never come.

He closed his eyes.

You could have sung.

He felt Asche move. Then he—

No, he didn't sing. It was only one sound, a sound that, had Vindt not known it came from the Singer, he would not have believed could originate from any living creature. Aural hatred, a vocal whiplash. It ripped the air apart, and the next moment his skin.

Vindt let out a scream. Before he had time to brace himself for the next lash, more skin split open, from his shoulders down to his lower back, a new trickle of blood adding to the previous. Another lash. And another.

Vindt gritted his teeth; his hands pressed against the rough stone. Before long, he couldn't contain his screams anymore. The skin of his back was in tatters, one open, raw wound. Vindt panted, sweat dripping from every pore. His muscles cramped. The lashes continued to fall. Flames danced before his closed eyelids.

"Stop it," Vindt eventually shouted. "That's enough."

If anything, the hatred in Asche's voice became more prominent, the impact of the lashes stronger, the intervals between them shorter. Fear sent Vindt's heart into a staggering flight. This wasn't about mere punishment anymore. If it ever had been.

He turned his head. "Stop it. Can't you see you're kill —"

The next whiplash landed on his face. It cut a bleeding gash from his eyelid down to his mouth.

And Vindt realized Asche wouldn't stop. He tried to move, to get up, but found he couldn't. His fear crested into panic. "Stop it!"

The next lash wrenched a wail from his throat. After two

more, his panic drowned in the pain. The lashes didn't only cut skin anymore but flesh, hitting bone. Pain was everywhere and everything.

Through the agony, as if to mock him, he felt Asche's semen drying on his hand.

CHAPTER 33

Vindt lay on his stomach on the earth, hands and feet spread, tied to poles. He was naked. Priests surrounded him, the abbot next to his father. Liz was there, his brothers, their eyes ablaze with disgust and hatred. The abbot held Gaal's sword. The priests sang, deep, sonorous voices, rising and falling, condemning his soul.

"Traitor," the abbot hissed as he brought the sword down and cut another gash into Vindt's bleeding back. "You betrayed your goddess, you betrayed us."

Vindt screamed.

His father looked old. "Desiring a demon—how could you?" he murmured. "Never would I have thought—"

"No, wait," Vindt shouted. "It wasn't that. It was revenge. It was—"

"Feel Gaal's wrath," the abbot spat, and cut again.

The priests' voices spiraled into a deafening crescendo.

"Wait, please, let me explain."

The images blurred, the singing voices faded. The pain in his back remained.

Voices again, talking, some distant, some near. Occasional words emerged from the murmur, floating, understandable but devoid of meaning. "Kvahad-thed, please. I can't... No human can heal... this. Please. I'm sure he deserved it, but he's of no use to you like this. You need him. We can be att—"

A sharp hiss quieted the voice. The sound let Vindt's body tremble, and inundated him with pain, before the mists rose again, swallowing all sounds.

He woke to a scream. His own, perhaps. He tried to hold on to unconsciousness, though the pain reached him even in the depths of his haze.

An old man crouched beside him, tilting his head, pouring a viscous liquid into his mouth. "Drink." The voice was as cold as the surrounding air.

Vindt tried, but he had forgotten how drinking worked. All he knew was that it was painful. Everything was.

The man clasped Vindt's mouth shut, fingers digging into the burning wound in his face. "Swallow."

And Vindt did. He felt the liquid hitting his stomach, his veins, his brain. Warm numbness spread, sealing the ends of his nerves, cushioning his mind.

For a moment.

* * *

The wistful cry of a seagull greeted Vindt's waking mind, followed by the ocean's roar.

He didn't need to open his eyes to know where he was. His room, his bed. He lay on his stomach, his upper body bare, covered by a blanket. The pain was... gone. The worst of it, at least.

Leaving his eyes closed, he reached with one hand for his

back under the blanket. As soon as he touched skin, the muscles up the length of his spine clenched. The touch itself hardly hurt, no more than touching a sunburn. No raw flesh, but skin. Intact?

No.

Vindt waited for his muscles to relax. It took some time. When they did, he made his fingers wander, trace the landscape of scarred flesh, the rifts and ridges. His hand moved with detached curiosity, like a cartographer mapping unknown terrain. Someone else's back. He waited for something to stir, hatred, regret, shame, fear. Nothing did, as if the pain had eradicated the part of his being capable of feelings.

Vindt reached for the left side of his face. Here too the edge of the pain was gone. The scar went from the eye down to the jaw, a smooth, perfect line.

Asche was near, Vindt knew, even with his eyes closed. The Singer's aura was not the usual warm current but frayed, aimless. Vindt felt his heart too, its slow, tired rhythm.

He opened his eyes to dim grayness. Asche sat a few feet away, on a stool, his back resting against the wall. His eyes were closed; his hands dangled limp at his sides.

Again, Vindt waited for feelings to stir. None did.

The long lashes rose. Asche didn't tilt his head, merely moved his eyes to meet Vindt's gaze. They burned. It wasn't the onslaught of loathing Vindt had seen in them last, but a black fire which had long ago consumed everything it could, eating itself now. It held no message.

The Singer rose and disappeared into his rooms.

Vindt closed his eyes again.

You could have sung.

* * *

The night was cloudless, moonless too. Vindt was grateful for the darkness. Surely Asche could see just as well, but Vindt doubted he was on the lookout. The night shielded him from the servants' prying eyes, foremost Calveen's. Whyever the old man had given him the pain potion, pity was hardly the reason. Ever since Vindt had woken, the seneschal had been watching him, eyes not filled with glee but wary, thoughtful. Vindt wasn't worried. Never in his wildest dreams would Calveen guess what had happened. No one would. Even Vindt's mind doubted what his memory claimed.

As if in response, the scarred flesh of his back clenched. He drew a sharp breath and pressed a hand to the wall next to him. The cramp would pass, he knew. He reached for his face, like he did a hundred times a day. The scar was a perfect line from the left eye down to his jaw.

Never forget, it said.

He wouldn't.

He had not even tried to hide it. The others' eyes had widened when they saw him, whether because of the scar or the look in his eyes.

"What happened?" Narr was the first to ask. "Why didn't Asche..."

Heal that. She had not finished the sentence, probably because she knew the answer: because he didn't want to. The Singer's ire was perpetual, even for normal humans. It oozed from the walls of the house and turned the air to resin, clogging lungs and minds.

Vindt had not bothered to answer. He had, in fact, not spoken a word since he woke up from his agonizing haze.

No one pushed him. They didn't dare. Even Risi just followed him with his eyes, brows furrowed.

And now he was here, behind the farm's stables. If anyone had seen him crossing the bridge, so be it. He waited.

He didn't have to wait long. After only a few minutes, a tall slender figure crystallized from the shadows and approached soundlessly. Without makeup or jewelry, clad in a plain riding tunic, Ru hardly looked like the Singer Vindt had gotten to know at The Haven.

"So, he did it," Ru said without greeting.

"Some time ago already." Vindt's voice was hoarse, the words flat.

"And why did you contact me only now?" Ru's eyes flicked to the scar on Vindt's face, but he made no comment.

"Does it matter?"

"We have lost precious time."

Vindt took a breath. "So, your offer still holds? You swore an oath."

"If it's true, you shall have your freedom."

"When?"

"After the trial."

Trial. Something stirred in the depths of Vindt's innards at the word, but the writhing void consumed it almost immediately. "You won't take me with you now?" Vindt had hoped for that.

"We need time to prepare. Asche has to remain oblivious as long as possible."

"Why did you come then?"

"For proof."

"Proof?" Vindt shifted uncomfortably. "I can only give

you my—" But then he knew. The void inside him opened to let something cold seep out. "You want to read my mind."

"I hope you understand it's unavoidable. I cannot bring charges upon Asche with, forgive me, the word of a human."

The cold inside him morphed into near panic. It had nothing to do with the prospect of the pain, but with what Ru would find in his mind. "No, that's not possible. I have... I don't want—"

"I'm not interested in whatever your mind hides." Ru's face was impassive. "I could not care less if you killed a child or fucked a sheep. All I care about is whether Asche let you drink from his wrist. If you think of it while I read your mind, it will be the first memory I find. I'll stop after that."

Fucked a sheep. Vindt wished he had. "Just do it quick."

Ru lifted his hands. Vindt closed his eyes and thought of the exposed wrist, the pulsing vein. With the image, the erstwhile feelings surged too, the greed, the—as Vindt now knew—lust. He didn't fight it. Let him see that. It was harmless.

Ru sang quietly. The pain was familiar, almost welcome, overlaying the pain in his back. It was over in a minute.

Something in Ru's expression had changed. "Well," was all he said.

"What do I do now?" Vindt asked.

"Nothing. Wait. Stay low. We will come in due course."

"We?"

"It will take more than me to overthrow Asche Ke'Thad."

Overthrow. The cold in his guts manifested again, forcing a shudder from him. "You think he'll... fight?"

Ru raised an eyebrow. "Of course."

Vindt steadied himself against the stable wall again. He could feel the horses inside, sleeping, dreaming. He thought of their brethren, roaming free in the mountains, Schiida among them, of Asche standing on the hill, calling—

He shook the memory away.

"I'll leave now," Ru said. "It makes no difference, but know that you did something good."

In a heartbeat, he was gone, leaving Vindt alone with the night, the ocean and the dreaming horses.

* * *

After a week had passed without anything happening, Vindt realized he should have asked Ru how long exactly it was going to take. Or perhaps it didn't matter. He was hardly aware of time, anyway. His life had become a blur. He walked the house's hallways, fingers brushing the carved walls, a wraith, hollow and soulless. All he felt was the ocean and Asche's ire. Or perhaps those were the same.

Every night, the same dream: his father, his brothers, Liz standing around his bound, tortured body. The disappointment on their faces.

Desiring a demon...

"But I made up for it," his dream-self would shout. "I betrayed him to his kind. He'll die."

Even to himself, those words didn't feel like redemption.

He only hoped Ru and the others came before he was due for another Binding. He wouldn't know how to live through it. Asche had stopped talking to him, or did so through Calveen. When their gazes crossed by accident on Vindt's lonely prowls through the house, his eyes cut him to pieces. Vindt had expected his aura of power lashing out at those encounters, devastatingly, squashing. But it seemed rather confused, reaching out questioningly, and being reigned in angrily by its owner.

Vindt wouldn't be surprised if Asche simply let him die of withdrawal, slowly and painfully. A welcome idea. It was ludicrous, but somehow, right now, Vindt longed for pain. He had to tell himself over and over again that he was on his way to freedom. However, the joy he was supposed to feel stayed absent.

* * *

They came on the tenth day.

Vindt didn't know what he had expected: shouts and curses, the rattle of chain mail, the clang of swords. But of course, they were Singers. One morning, they simply appeared on the cliff, the entire Council, dozens more. They stood in absolute silence, spread across the stretch of land between the farm and the bridge, in no apparent order, red sentinels in the gray landscape, streaked with dots of blue. Their Thyds formed another small army, close to the farm, along with their horses. The farm's denizens stood huddled together in a corner of the yard, guarded by more Singers. They watched with wide eyes.

The entire Council had come, including Dina. When the Singer felt Vindt's gaze, he lifted his head. His face was unreadable. Something twinged in Vindt's chest. *Traitor*, a voice inside him hissed.

He flinched. Yes, traitor. Him.

Perhaps they had forced him. Perhaps Dina wouldn't take part in whatever was about to happen, would even try to undermine it.

Gaal, why do I even care?

Even in their silence, the combined aura of the Singers charged the air. A beast waiting to strike. The hairs on Vindt's arms stood on end. It was this feeling which had dragged him out of the house and onto a terrace. Calveen and the others had emerged too, Risi, Narr, Jun, Layyad, Kishoon. Hands on their sword hilts, they exchanged agitated whispers as their eyes darted between the waiting army and Asche.

The Singer stood on one of the balconies, utterly still, hands on the rail, an occasional breeze ruffling his long black hair. His face was as blank as Dina's. A part of Vindt's mind was waiting for a nonchalant remark, something like, "If I had known we were going to have visitors, I would have prepared a cake." A strange, treacherous part of him was *hoping* for Asche to have anticipated this, to be prepared, laugh in everyone's faces.

Asche made no comment. And he didn't laugh.

Ru stood in front of the delegation, before the bridge, blue riding robes and dark skin, the braided hair without golden threads. "Asche Ke'Thad." His voice rang sharply through the misty morning air. "I bring formal charges on you. Letting your Thyd drink from your wrist is a crime against the Law and will be—"

A sudden murmur rippled through the crowd of Singers; a cry rose. Faces turned toward the ocean, fingers pointed. Vindt turned too.

There was no ocean. Where it had been a moment ago, bare, muddy ground stretched for miles. In the distance, Vindt still saw the water, receding at tremendous speed, soundlessly, or almost, for far away, a rumble built. He jerked his head back to Asche.

The Singer was smiling. "And will be?" He echoed Ru's

last words quietly; still, they clanged through the air for miles.

The ocean was upon them before anyone had time to react. A wave the size of a mountain came crashing down on the house, the cliffs, the assembled Singers. Vindt thought he heard a multi-voiced song rising, but it drowned in the water's roar.

It's over.

Everything Vindt felt was relief, even as the impact nearly made him lose consciousness. He let the water whirl him about, drag him down. His lungs hurt. This time, no one would help him breathe. He opened his mouth, welcoming death. But death was busy elsewhere. Water filled his lungs, but just like before, it didn't kill him. Disappointment surged, then anger. And then the water receded.

Instead of being pulled along into the ocean, something held Vindt in place, magic, song, not Asche's but still familiar. A second later, the water was gone. Vindt found himself on the firm ground of the cliff, retching. He coughed at the same time as he tried to suck in air. Someone was singing again, quietly, close to him; a hand squeezed his shoulder. The water in his lungs vanished. Vindt drew in air as if he had not breathed in years. His swimming vision solidified to a face framed by white-blond hair. His heart leaped. Won—they had won.

Dina's expression was sad. He turned his head. Vindt followed the gaze, and his racing heartbeat slowed to a halt.

A few feet away, Asche was kneeling in the mud, held down by a Singer on each side, arms twisted behind his back. He was the only one still dripping water. Ru and two other members of the Council stood in front of him; more were close. Asche's black hair clung in wet strands to his face. Vindt's eyes fastened on the thin golden hoop adorning his neck. "What..."

"A hatlù," Dina said quietly beside him. "It keeps him from singing."

Dread invaded Vindt. It didn't abate when a Singer pulled Asche's left arm to the front, holding the wrist out to Ru. Ru closed his hands around the bracelet and sang. It came off.

Murmurs and hisses emerged. Vindt knew what they were seeing: the marks of his teeth. The proof.

Ru's face was set in stone. He didn't look at Asche. And Asche didn't look at him. His head was turned in Vindt's direction. The black eyes locked with Vindt's, the glint in their depths gone. They remained on Vindt while the others pulled him to his feet and dragged him over to a waiting horse, remained during the ride past the farm, into the hills. Vindt felt his eyes long after the party had vanished from sight.

"You know how they will execute him?" Dina's voice was very low.

Vindt flinched. He had forgotten about him. The milky-blue eyes were still sad, but also... calculating, the ghost of a smile playing about his lips.

"They will call a Verdur."

CHAPTER 34

The white and pink blossoms of their last visit to The Haven were gone. Wanton splendor for a few days, then nothing but ordinary green leaves. Vindt wondered if this should tell him something, a deeper wisdom.

Yes, you idiot, the change of seasons.

In the two days since their arrival, he had hardly slept. Not that he minded. Sleep scared him. Two black eyes had replaced the dream about his father and the priests. However, the dark gaze slid into his awareness during daytime, too. He had not seen Asche since, but he knew they were keeping him somewhere close to the mountaintop. He imagined the Singer in a cabin like the one they had locked him in once, chained, with that dreadful ring around his neck. That hoop creeped Vindt out more than the imagined chains. Perhaps there were none. He had not asked Ru for details.

Ru was the only Singer talking to him. The others merely regarded him with contempt. Vindt didn't want to talk to them either, least of all Dina. Luckily, the pale-white

Singer avoided him in turn.

They will call a Verdur.

Verdur or a sword—it shouldn't make a difference; the outcome was the same. And yet...

He passed his time in the house Ru had assigned him. He would have gone to the baths, had actually once already been on his way when he remembered the scars on his back. Perhaps it was better this way. At least he wouldn't meet anyone.

On the third day, a servant came to bring him before the Council. Vindt tried his best to clamp down on his anxiety as the woman led him to the same building the last meeting had taken place in. He didn't trust Ru, oath and all. The other members might not have agreed with Ru's promise to set him free or might have overruled the oath. Perhaps he was walking toward his execution. Though his body signaled fear, his mind remained strangely unaffected.

This time, no lavishly clad servants welcomed them. Inside, the Singers had not bothered to don their festive attire either. For him, a Thyd, a human. Hostile gazes pelted him from around the table; only Dina's and Ru's remained neutral.

"Okay," Ren Zian said, but a gesture from Ru silenced him.

Ru picked up a goblet from the table and rose. "I don't think we need any formalities. I swore an Eith with my blood to release the Thyd from the Bond and his dependency in exchange for his assistance. And so it will be."

So they *had* quarreled.

Ru walked over to Vindt. "We will start with your dependency on the blood. The easy part." He held out the goblet, unsmiling.

Vindt took it, warily. The contents looked like blood; it also smelled like it. "I just drink this and... that's it?" It seemed too easy.

Ru gave a curt nod.

Vindt's hand trembled as he lifted the chalice. Freedom or death. He drank.

The taste was familiar and at the same time alien, blood indeed, mixed with something else, or altered magically. The repulsion at drinking it was so strong, it was all he could do to not retch. And it had nothing to do with the taste.

Vindt drained the cup, bracing himself for whatever was to come, the blood's metallic taste coating his gums and throat. "I don't feel anything."

"Don't worry, you will feel this now. Ready?"

"Wait." Vindt's heart beat all the way up to his mouth. For reasons eluding him, he was close to panic.

"For what? Severing the Bond—that's what you want, no?"

"I..." Of course it was.

"If you have changed your mind—no problem. You will follow Asche to Thrithid. Be sure none of us will shed a tear."

Vindt closed his eyes. "Fine. Do it."

Ru sang first, then, one by one, the others joined in. A wave of power built, reaching for Vindt, writhing and coiling. A panicked voice inside him urged him to run. He stayed, trembling, feeling how the magic took him into its grip, pushing inside. The gaze of the black eyes hit him again, as strong as if Asche was standing right next to him.

Ru spoke: "We, the High Council, installed by the First to execute their will, revoke this Bond."

The eyes vanished. Instead, a giant fist entered Vindt's body and ripped out its very core. Screaming, he went to his knees. Emptiness, all-consuming, greater than his existence, lethal nothingness. He clutched his chest as if he could hold in what was already gone.

After long minutes, the agony faded somewhat. The hollowness prevailed. His legs shook. It took him three tries to get up. Ru made no move to help him.

"That was it?" Vindt managed to croak through dry lips. "You're free."

Free. The word circled through Vindt's head. Ten long years he had been waiting for this moment, dreaming of it every single minute. He searched for the joy, but the hollowness had swallowed all emotions.

"Wait for me in your quarters," Ru said. "I'll join you after we are done here." He paused. "To see you off."

Vindt glanced at the mask-like faces around the table, failing to even summon hatred.

He nodded and left the room.

* * *

Vindt sat cross-legged on the rug, back against the wall, eyes closed. He had sat like this ever since he came in. No idea how much time had passed, minutes, hours. The emptiness filled him, his body, his mind. Cold, dead. He had tried to reach for Asche's aura, for scientific curiosity. But the thread indicating his location, that strange awareness of his presence, was gone.

Free.

Ru entered without knocking and put a pouch on the low table. To judge from the sound, it contained coins. Money. Vindt had not thought about that. Singers had held him captive for the past decade, but they had also kept him warm and fed. "For me?"

Ru didn't answer, but put a vial next to the pouch. "The potion you just drank will keep you from dying from the lack of blood. You will still go into withdrawal, though it won't be as bad. This"—he pointed at the flask—"will smooth the process. Except for your Thyd garments, you can take whatever clothes you can carry. And your dagger. The sword stays. There's food prepared for you on the porch. It will last about three days, longer if you ration it. It's about a week's journey by foot to Ling, which is the next port."

Port. Of course that was where he was heading. To board a ship to... home.

"One more thing." Ru observed him with furrowed brows. "How often did Asche let you drink from his wrist?"

"Once." Vindt's voice sounded as empty as he felt. "Why?"

"Did you... did any powers manifest in you?"

For some reason, Vindt started to laugh. Gaal, this. Well, there was his strangely altered hearing, and his new ability to see in the dark. Hardly to be called powers. "Asche told me it's a tale. And: no."

"Get up."

"For what?"

"A test."

Vindt hesitated, but what could he do? He rose. Even moving felt hollow.

Ru reached for his right, naked wrist, closed his eyes and sang quietly. It wasn't like mind-reading. No pain as the magic coursed through his body. Vindt wondered what would happen if he actually had any powers.

"I told you," Vindt said after Ru eventually let go. "Speaking of unwanted magic, can you take this off?" He held out his other arm to Ru, the one still carrying the bracelet Silhorveen had put on him.

"That's...?"

"A gift from Silhorveen. Kept me from committing suicide."

"And Asche left it on?"

"You know I can't be trusted. Now, I assume, my suicide would be most welcome."

Ru hesitated, but then reached out, closed his long-fingered hand around the band and sang again. The bracelet sprang open with a soft click.

Vindt took a sharp breath as he staggered back.

"What?" Ru's voice was only semi-concerned.

Vindt didn't know. He felt very, very odd all of a sudden. Amplified? Weightless, sensitive. Everything around him seemed sharper and clearer, the colors deeper and... more? Also, he felt the house, the steady hum of the wood of furniture and beams, the sparkling life outside, bees and birds, flowers and trees. And water, most of all he felt water, in ponds and streams and waterfalls, singing with power.

"You had this on for ten years," Ru said. "It quite possibly altered your mind. You need to adjust."

Vindt nodded as he took a few deep breaths. Something told him it wasn't that.

Ru's eyes flicked to Vindt's cheek. "You got this during Asche's capture?"

Vindt's hand went up in hasty embarrassment, as if to hide the scar. The ones on his back itched as if they were connected. "Yes."

"You want me to heal it?"

Vindt looked at him in surprise. "Thanks, but... I'll keep it. As a souvenir."

"As you wish. Good b—"

"Wait." Vindt swallowed. "When will you... Asche, I mean." He couldn't say it.

"Execute him? Tomorrow. Any other questions?" Ru didn't hide his impatience. When Vindt stayed silent, he said, "Goodbye, then. If I see you again, I will kill you."

He turned and left through the door he had not bothered closing when coming in.

* * *

Vindt lowered his bag onto the low wall lining the road, catching his breath. He was not used to descending steep, rocky mountains, carrying half a household. Drenched in sweat, muscles aching, he felt as if he had been walking for hours. Which he hadn't. Looking up, he could still glimpse The Haven's lower buildings through trees and bushes.

After a moment, he heaved the bag back onto his shoulder and continued his descent. Slowly, the feral landscape gave way to cultivated terraces. People worked in the fields, backs bent, their heads covered by huge straw heads. They smiled and waved when they saw him. It felt strange. His expectation of being greeted with hostility as soon as strangers laid eyes on his Thyd tunic was deep-rooted. Well. He wasn't wearing one anymore.

Every time he passed a house, children, dogs, chickens or a combination of them flocked to him. Vindt didn't understand a word of the children's chatter.

Around noon, the denizens of another dwelling basically forced him into a hut to have lunch. When Vindt offered money, they unleashed a torrent of angry words on him. It took them some time to realize he didn't speak the language. Eventually, he sat down with a guilty conscience. Though he couldn't discern the single words of their conversation, he somehow grasped the gist. Laughter imbued their lively chatter.

Poor people, but free, Vindt thought. *Free like me.*

Their exuberant mood reminded him of Risi's rolling laughter and Kishoon's knowing smirk.

He wouldn't see them again. Were they even still alive?

His nerves did an uncomfortable flip. What if the Council had made short work of Asche's servants? If they had not died during the attack anyway. Perhaps they had even tried to fight, to defend their master. Had he inadvertently condemned them to death, too?

No, Gaal, please.

He took his hasty leave from the peasants, bowing his gratitude.

As soon as he was out of sight, he reached for his amulet. When his fingers brushed the bloodstone, he closed them around it instead. The blood of the others. Always with him. A poor substitute. How strange that the prospect of never seeing them again stung like this. He had known them for not even two months. He had his real family, his real friends, to go back to now.

Adding his goddess' amulet to his grip, he prayed. At least he began to, but as soon as he directed his thoughts to Gaal, the redheaded bird-woman materialized before his inner eye. In the turmoil of the past few days, he had forgotten about her. If she really had been Gaal and had come to rescue Asche, what would she think of Vindt, having betrayed the Singer to his death? What if he had not done something good, redeemed himself, but on the contrary, crossed her plans?

Bring justice.

From Asche's point of view—yes. But why would Gaal be interested in helping him lift the Singers' punishment?

Well, he wouldn't find out. If he never saw the others again, so be it. He had lost many people in his life. If he had caused their deaths, he would forever bear the guilt, would be judged by Gaal herself when the time came and he stepped before her throne. There was no turning back now to undo it all.

He said a quick prayer and firmly resumed his steps.

Dusk was still some time away when his exhaustion won, and he settled in for the night. It would be cold, but it didn't look like rain. Vindt had slept in worse conditions, and he had brought a bedroll with him. The overhanging rock would protect him should the weather turn.

He managed to get a small fire going and even catch a fish in the nearby creek. The less food he had to take from his provisions, the less he would have to buy, and the more money would remain for his passage. Vindt had no idea how much the foreign coins Ru had given him amounted to. Or how much a passage home would cost. If it wasn't enough, he could offer his help on the ship. As an experienced sailor, he would be an asset to the crew. It could work.

It would take him months to get to Pel, but that was where he was heading. A surreal idea. In all these years, Vindt had never really thought about what had happened to the country and the people he had been forced to leave. He had forbidden himself to, afraid of the memories' sharp edges. Instead, his mind had reduced "home" to a blurry image of happiness, a feeling of familiarity and belonging.

Now, contemplating it with a rational mind for the first time, he wondered what remained of it. His brothers had probably fallen in the war, along with most of his friends. His father? If he had not sworn his alliance to the usurpers —which Vindt doubted—the Kallejdi would have either killed or exiled him. In any case, he wouldn't be a lord anymore. Neither would Vindt, upon his return, be a lord's son. The island's denizens would surely recognize him—he had not even aged—but what good would that do? He could hardly start a rebellion against the new regents. Or, who knew, perhaps another country had even overthrown the Kallejdi in the meantime. Ten years was a long time. The situation of his people could be any.

Then again, Vindt had never wanted to be a lord. He could just find himself some work and live a quiet, peaceful life as he had always envisioned, become a farmer, raise sheep or train horses for battle. Liz, if she and his child lived, had probably long since married another, had children with a different man. Of course, Vindt could find himself another woman, raise a family. Live. Die. As a free man.

Free. The word, always a sparkling guiding star in his mind, had still not regained its splendor. All he felt was the emptiness the Bond had left, a raw ache, screaming like an abandoned pup for its mother. However, what they had cut out had never belonged to him, an alien splinter, like a stuck arrowhead, overgrown by flesh, but festering and hurting. Lethal in the long run. Of course, removing it left a wound. A wound that would heal along with the organism.

Vindt stared into the flames. Their crackle wasn't as soothing as it used to be. He heard the fire's angry song, as he had when talking to Dina in Asche's house. Only now it was a lot louder, more precise. Vindt felt its destructiveness. It wasn't the only voice in the evening's choir. Everything sang, the rocks behind him, the air, each fucking blade of grass.

Vindt wrapped his hand around the wrist which had held the bracelet. The skin beneath was almost white and overly sensitive to the touch. He didn't know why he hadn't told Ru what had happened when he removed it. Not that he knew himself. He closed his eyes. To hear everything, feel everything—was that how Singers perceived the world? Vindt had known they possessed refined senses, but he had always thought of it as merely "better," not so different.

But it couldn't be that. The bracelet had just kept him from committing suicide. Certainly, Ru was right. He had carried it for ten years. The strange phenomenon would cease.

Along with the void. The void and the image of the eyes...

Vindt flinched. They might have vanished the moment Ru had severed the Bond, but at some point along his way down the mountain, the black, disembodied gaze had returned. It held no accusation. Which, somehow, made things worse, the emptiness: a mirror of his own feelings, an amplifier to their weight.

Without warning, his back muscles clenched. Vindt took a sharp breath, only partly because of the pain. The scars' burn pulled forth memories, smooth skin under his hands, a lithe, yielding body, the smells of blood, and sweat, and semen. A moan.

He shut his eyes. To no avail; his body responded.

Desire.

No, not that. It had been about revenge, defeat.

Desiring a demon.

No!

Raping him?

Vindt flinched again. The question had hovered in his mind ever since. But no. Nothing he had done at that moment had kept Asche from singing. Vindt had even encouraged, almost begged, him to. He was also sure about what he had felt, the emotions coming from Asche in waves so thick they almost choked him. The lust.

Gaal. Just thinking about it made him want to do it again. He had never experienced anything like it, this dark, fathomless greed, to take, to possess, transcending any physical necessities. It was... scary.

But there was want and there was want, the mind, and the body, their goals not always aligning. What if Asche's needs had overruled his iron control? It seemed improbable. And yet... What if it had been rape after all?

Had he merited the punishment? If not for rape then for witnessing something not meant for him to witness and less to take, not for any human, perhaps not even for many Singers. Worse: biting Asche's neck, making the act conspicuous for everyone. Asche would carry the scars for some time. What did the other Singers think? Could they perhaps even know who had left the marks?

Oh, fuck all demons—what did it matter? Vindt would bear his scars forever, an eternal reminder of his transgression. And in a few hours, the Singer would be dead.

Dead because of me.

Realizing he was trembling, Vindt rose and began pacing. But no, he had made the right choice, regardless even of what had happened between them. All Singers deserved to die.

Apart from the one his goddess wanted to save.

His knuckles cracked. It was too late for regrets now. What should he do? Turn? Ru had made very clear what would happen if he saw him again. Now that the Bond was broken, Vindt would not even find Asche. And even if he did, they were surely guarding the Singer heavily, had perhaps even magically chained him. With the ring around his neck, he wouldn't be able to sing. Perhaps they would take the hoop off at the moment of his execution, let him sing all he wanted, helpless against the Verdurs' inverted screams. Vindt wouldn't put that past them. Most probably they would even leave him alone to die, afraid the Verdur might take the opportunity to send a few more of them to hell.

And then what? Flee? Where to? Asche had all the Singers against him. They had overwhelmed him once; they would do it again. There was no "saving," just postponing the inevitable.

Gaal, what was he thinking?

Because, even if there was a slight chance for him to get to Asche in time, and escape with him, it all came down to one thing: to make that happen, he would need to become Asche's Thyd again.

His laughter echoed off the mountain, warped and hollow. Yes, exactly. He would turn himself back into a Thyd, renounce his freedom. To save the person who had nearly killed him, and who he had just betrayed to his death in turn.

He was clearly going mad. That was what they did to him, their last means to bind him: twist his mind.

Enough. He was tired, exhausted. He needed sleep. Tomorrow, he would be able to think clearly again.

With determination, he laid out his bedroll. Inside him, the void whimpered and rubbed salt into open flesh. Vindt stared at the dying flames. The eyes stared back. Even as he closed his.

* * *

Vindt's chest heaved with rapid breaths; sweat dripped from his bare stomach onto his pants. He had taken off his shirt some time ago and wrapped it around his waist. His bag lay further down the mountain, hidden behind some bushes. He was not sure if he would recognize the place when he came back. *If* he came back. The chances were minimal. He tried not to think about it. He tried not to think at all. Because if he did, he would spin around and run back down the way he had laboriously climbed during the past few hours.

The first of The Haven's buildings already lay beneath him. Though he couldn't feel Asche's presence as he had with the Bond intact, the remainder of the Singer's blood still drew him to the mountaintop. His only chance was the execution itself. If the universe was in their favor, and they would leave him alone and take the ring off. What were the odds...

Don't. Think.

Somewhere above, a gong sounded, once, twice, three times. The noise, deep and hollow, made the hairs on the back of Vindt's neck rise. The two servants descending the stairs in front of his hiding spot stopped their chatter and turned their faces. The feeling of running out of time made Vindt cringe. He still had a fair way to climb.

Before reaching the first of The Haven's houses, he had stayed on the road. Since then, he had fought his way through the underbrush. Tedious, time-consuming. Perhaps it wasn't even necessary. Hardly anyone at The Haven knew him. If he acted normally, everyone would take him for one of them. He put his shirt back on.

The gong sounded another time.

Vindt waited until the two servants were out of sight, then left his hideout. He walked as briskly as he dared; running would certainly call attention. He had crossed another plateau and was about to climb the next stairs when a woman carrying a basket came toward him from above. Heart hammering, he carved his lips into the resemblance of a friendly, non-committal smile. The woman—girl, rather —returned the smile as she passed. Vindt forced himself not to look back and keep a steady pace as he continued.

He passed two more servants without incident.

A few steps before reaching yet another plateau, he paused to catch his breath. His thighs burned; the muscles trembled. Another woman passed him, nodding sternly. Just as Vindt returned the nod absentmindedly, the blood left his face. He knew her. Recognition spread over the woman's features in the same instant. She stopped. Her gaze flicked back to where she'd come from, which was—as Vindt recognized now—the plateau holding the building of the Council meeting. It was the same woman who had intercepted Vindt when he had descended from the Pledge. Gaal, how much bad luck could someone have?

She opened her mouth.

Vindt's body acted before his brain caught up. Drawing his dagger, he stepped behind her, covered her mouth with his palm and pressed the blade to her throat. His hands trembled slightly, but he was determined. "I'm sorry. I wished I didn't have to do this, but..."

He looked around. No one else in sight. Not for much longer. The woman's fear throbbed at his senses. "If you do as I say, no harm will come to you. Understand?"

Short of ideas, Vindt dragged her into the underbrush until he was sure they were out of sight from the stairs. The gong sounded again.

"I'll take my hand from your mouth now. One wrong word and you're dead. Okay?"

A hesitant nod.

The woman gasped for breath.

"When's the execution?" Vindt asked.

The fear in her face was laced with something else, something harder. "You heard the gong."

Vindt's thoughts were racing. As soon as he left her, she would either scream or run to alert others to his presence. He hated the idea of gagging her and tying her up, but what options did he have? Tearing his shirt apart, he could make a makeshift gag. For her hands, he had nothing. Unless...

Vindt laughed, a mere chuckle at first, then he laughed so hard he almost cried.

Mad, I'm going mad.

The idea was ludicrous. And perfect. Unwound, the leather ribbon around his braid would be an ell's length. Enough for the woman's small wrists. It was logical, consequential even. First he had fucked a demon, now was coming to his rescue, overwhelming innocent women. This was the last missing step. From traitor to whore.

Filthy blond strands spilled over his shoulders as he released the ribbon. He almost wished the woman understood what it meant, to what depths he had sunk. He made her sit with her back to a small tree and tied her wrists behind its trunk. The sound of an approaching, multi-voiced chant made him stall. The melody was not unlike what he had heard at the Pledge. With frantic hands, he pulled his shirt over his head and ripped it into strips.

"I'm sorry." He shoved a crumpled piece of fabric into the woman's mouth and tied it with another behind her head.

What if no one found her? If she died here of thirst, and cold, and exhaustion?

No. The others would notice her disappearance and search for her. As soon as they alerted a Singer, they would find her in no time.

The chanting grew louder, drew nearer. Whoever was singing, they were moving up the very stairway in front of his hiding spot. Through the leaves, Vindt saw but shadows, a procession in blue, their advance completely silent apart from their song. Their auras writhed and squirmed, triumphantly.

Apart from one.

Gaal, he could still feel him. The sensation of Asche's battered, cowering aura was as horrible as the sight of that gold ring around his neck. Vindt wished he could alert him to his presence, let him know there was still... hope?

Song and auras grew thinner as the procession climbed. Vindt waited as long as his growing trepidation allowed before he walked to the edge of the thicket and peered out. Empty.

Vindt took a breath and climbed after them.

Only a few steps after he had left the stairs to scramble the last bit through the wilderness again, the singing stopped. And so did Vindt. He was under no illusion as to how his progress would sound to their refined ears. The mountaintop with the clearing was still a brief climb away. Though he couldn't see them, Vindt felt the Singers move about the plateau, their auras humming in anticipation.

Please, let them take off the ring and fucking leave.

"Is there anything you would like to say?" Ru's voice sounded clear through the crisp morning air. Its coldness was subtly threaded with something Vindt couldn't place.

"I hope your cock rots off while maggots eat your balls," Asche spat.

The auras of the others momentarily recoiled, but soon expanded again, hissing in indignant fury.

Again, Ru spoke. "I am—"

"One more word out of your foul mouth and I'll puke," Asche snapped. "Surely your noble conscience cannot bear to let me die with vomit all over me, you hypocrite coward. I hope they will make it last, chase you to the edge of giving up, then let you recover just to start the hunt again. You know what? I'll make sure we meet in Thrithid, and I swear to you, I will make it the hell you—"

Ru sang.

Asche laughed, shrill and cackling. The sound sent cold frissons over Vindt's skin.

Another Singer fell in with Ru, a third, then a fourth, until their voices drowned out the laughter. There was nothing beautiful in their song. It was high and dissonant, the shrieks of an agonized creature. Vindt covered his ears. Panic reared its head again. Had Dina lied? Were they executing him themselves? But no. Vindt understood their song. They were calling the Verdur.

The melody abated. The silence in its wake permeated

the air like syrup. Vindt didn't dare to peek around the rock he had taken refuge behind. He hardly dared to breathe as he felt them descending. Leaving, they were leaving! Hope spurred his heart into an unsteady gallop.

Please. Let them have taken the ring away, too. Just that. Please.

He waited until he couldn't feel them anymore, and then another few seconds. On the stairs, he would be easily spotted, but braving the underbrush would take too much time. He was still farther away from the mountaintop than he would have liked.

Vindt ran up the stairs, each thud of his feet a prayer. Please. Please. Please.

He had nearly reached the top when the sounds of his steps and his wheezing breath vanished. The rustle of the wind in the trees followed. Then the birds. A second later, the Verdurs' silence fell like Vindt had never experienced it before, crushing him with the weight of a mountain. He hit the stairs with the entire length of his body, face and palms pressed into the stones. All the air left his lungs.

He had no idea where they'd come from. All of a sudden, they were just there, many, coming for the feast laid out for them. Face flat on the stones, Vindt couldn't see more than a flurry of shapes. Their inverted cries of hunger and anticipation drilled into his guts.

"No," he wanted to scream, but he couldn't open his mouth. He couldn't move at all, bound by the absence of sound. Only his heart continued its frantic, desperate beating. As if to mock him. A high-pitched shriek rose, so full of fear and terror it even pierced through the Verdurs' acoustic void.

It was brief, yet in Vindt's ears, it went on and on and

on...

CHAPTER 35

Vindt stayed where he was, long after the Verdurs' oppressive silence was gone.

Leave.

He should. He had tried to save Asche and failed. Saving his own life was all he had left to do now.

It took him several attempts to push his upper body up, then his legs, then stand. The birds had not yet returned to tweeting. The wind remained still too. A heavy silence lay over the landscape, as if it was mourning. Five steps until the top. So close.

There was no point in going to see what he had done. However, his feet moved despite himself, slowly, each step echoing in the silence.

In full daylight, the plateau lay clearly before him for the first time, the wide, perfect circle cut into the vegetation, stones lining its perimeter. He didn't remember the two poles in the center. Asche's hands were tied to them, arms stretched out. He was on his knees. Gravity should have pulled his head down, but it was tilted backward. Sinuous, black-and-silver lines covered the skull-like face; the milky eyes looked up at the sky, unseeing, widened in terror. Asche still wore the golden ring around his neck. Vindt would have come in vain anyway.

It was no solace.

Yet again, his feet inched forward. Before the corpse, he dropped to his knees. Bile rose from his stomach, burning his throat.

This is not what I wanted.

What had he wanted? He didn't know. Revenge, a feeling born from a hurt that went deeper than the pain on his back.

Dead. No, he couldn't be. Asche had always outwitted everyone, had always been one step ahead. But the figure in front of him didn't move, the terror in its eyes a writhing, living thing, as was the tart, metallic stench it emitted. Real.

Everything in Vindt shrank, his stomach, his lungs, his heart.

No, please...

His hand trembled as he reached out.

"I'd rather you didn't," a cold voice close to him said.

Vindt's arm stalled, fingers inches from the face. His brain refused to process what his ears claimed. The voice, one that Vindt would distinguish under a thousand others.

He turned.

Asche was standing almost next to him, back resting against one of the poles, arms crossed before his chest. His delicate features were schooled into their typical neutral expression. His aura, oh so familiar, tried to reach out for Vindt, but its master rigidly reigned it in.

For what seemed hours, Vindt stared at him, at the perfect, intact skin of his face, the black of his eyes. He turned to the corpse. "I don't... What..."

"I must say I'm surprised." Asche's voice was as empty as his face. "Why did you come back? To bask in your victory? Make sure your wish was properly executed? Or did you just want to watch the show? In that case, I'm afraid that—again—you missed the best part."

"No, I..." Vindt couldn't muster the strength to rise. "I came to..." *save you*. All of a sudden, it seemed ridiculous.

"Whatever it is"—Asche's gaze roamed over Vindt's bare chest and the unraveled hair—"it seems you have to be naked for it."

Vindt had forgotten about both. He didn't care about the shirt, but the loose hair made him feel utterly exposed. His hands went to his head, then dropped again. He had nothing to fasten it with.

"Well, I'm keen to hear all about it. Later. Now, we have to leave. Some people *will* come to bask in their victory." Asche held out a hand without taking the step needed to help Vindt up.

Vindt's brain prevailed in a state of misted paralysis. The corpse. Asche alive.

The Singer perked up, listening to something only he could hear. "They are coming back. We need to leave. Now."

Vindt's legs shook as he rose. "We will never reach the Door before they catch us."

Asche cocked an irritated eyebrow at him before understanding smoothed his features. "The entire Haven is a Door. The place you and I used the last time is a mere point of convenience."

Vindt could feel the approach of the others now too. He stared at the hand, lost.

I'm a fool.

"Now." An order.

He took the hand.

* * *

One moment he was walking on the mountain's rocky ground, crisp air in his nose, the next, water filled his lungs and whirled him about. His panicked cry bubbled out of his mouth. Not again.

You should know by now you're not dying in the water. Asche's voice in his head. *Relax. Breathe.*

Vindt didn't need to heed the order for long, as his feet quickly touched the ground and his head broke the surface. He gasped and spat water. "You could've warned me."

Asche was already plowing through the shallow water toward the beach.

Vindt followed more slowly. "Where are we?"

For a split second, he expected to see the barren rocks of the place Asche had claimed to be Thrithid. Instead, pure white sand made up the beach they were heading for, stretching to the left and right as far as Vindt could see. A cluster of huts huddled at a distance before a backdrop of dense green forest. Two figures were approaching from that direction; the graceful way the taller of them walked identified him doubtlessly as a Singer.

Vindt shot Asche an alarmed glance, but the Singer continued, unperturbed. They met the two men halfway between ocean and forest. The Singer's skin was of the same dark brown as Risi's; black hair fell in tiny curls over his shoulders. He was clad in neither red nor blue, but wore a long white tunic, similar to the one worn by the young man beside him. Against his master's dark complexion, the Thyd looked pale, though his skin was notably darker than Vindt's. Both were barefoot.

The Singer beamed and stretched out his arms. "Sansýrthed."

"Fahad." Asche smiled too.

They clasped each other's elbows and leaned their foreheads together. Vindt had never seen Asche making the traditional greeting between Singers before.

Their heads parted, but Fahad seemed reluctant to let go. "Inunshi passed as planned, so I knew. Still, it's..." He sighed. "It's a relief to see you." Apart from obvious emotion, his voice held a strange but not unpleasant trill.

"Inunshi is gone?" Asche asked.

Fahad nodded. "He said you wanted..." He turned to Vindt, gaze roaming over his naked chest. "Who...?"

"I'll explain later. For now, nourishment and rest would be appreciated."

Vindt followed the Singers toward the huts, numbly, feet sinking into the soft sand. When he stumbled, the Thyd, who had fallen in beside him, held out an arm. Vindt didn't take it. He managed a murmured "Thank you," but no smile. He didn't feel like making conversation, not even to introduce himself. How would he? *Hey, I'm Vindt, Asche's ex-Thyd, the one who returned from Thrithid and then betrayed his master to his death.*

Only, the master wasn't dead.

He had barely resumed his steps when the Thyd behind him gave a small cry. Vindt turned, alarmed, only to find the man staring wide-eyed at his back. The scars—fuck.

Asche's gaze wandered between the Thyd and Vindt. "We need to get him a shirt," he said to Fahad, and walked on.

Vindt let the Thyd pass before he continued.

When they reached the huts, Fahad gave Vindt another unreadable look. His words were directed to Asche. "You want him to—"

"We will sleep in the same hut," Asche said.

The denizens of the little dwelling, humans, bowed deeply, murmuring words of reverence. They were all very small. Vindt's mind registered the women's bare breasts with the same mild surprise with which he took in the strange trees. Their slender stems went up without any side branches until they burst into a crown of huge green leaves which looked like ferns. Brown, round fruits hung from their tops like testicles.

Fahad let them into the largest hut. Its sparse furniture was made from what looked like straw and yellowish branches bent into shape. There were no beds, just some kind of woven mats.

Again, Fahad gave Vindt a side-glance, while saying, "What about eating?"

"I will eat with him. We will have plenty of time to talk later."

Fahad didn't look happy. It occurred to Vindt the Singer had probably been counting on an intimate evening with Asche. To whatever degree the intimacy went.

Still, Fahad himself brought them food and water not long after, two servants in tow. He also brought Vindt a shirt. It had a peculiar cut and was slightly too small, but Vindt was glad to have his upper body covered again. Unfortunately, Fahad had not brought him something to tie his hair with.

The food came in bowls, like at The Haven. There was no cutlery. Vindt watched Asche rip a piece from one of the round flat breads and pick up the stew-like contents with it, and wondered if he was dreaming. Between the last time they had sat together like this and now, the universe had exploded a few times and not come back together in a way he understood. It took him no effort to resuscitate the feeling of Asche's drying cum on his hands while the lashes ravaged his back, to sense the gaze of black eyes on him, the token of his betrayal; the shriveled body they had left on the mountaintop superposed itself over the eating Singer. Vindt didn't know what to feel, let alone how to act.

"How can you be eating?" he eventually muttered.

"What should I be doing instead?"

"Killing me."

"Oh, I would. In fact, I would have long ago. Unfortunately, as it happens, I need you."

Yes, that. "What for?" Vindt hated the desperation threading his voice.

Asche continued to eat in silence.

Vindt stifled a groan. *And what about me fucking you, about you whipping me to near death, me betraying you to Ru? Are we pretending none of it happened?*

But Vindt didn't say it. Perhaps this was the only way to go on, to pretend. Go on—as if there was a future. Together. "What happens now? Are we... on the run?"

"We're not running. They believe me dead. At least for some time."

Only slowly, Vindt's brain began to pick up its tasks, to think. So someone had rescued Asche before he could. Dina... Perhaps he had not betrayed Asche after all. Fahad. This Inunshi they had mentioned. Who else? "But I don't understand how... The ones who helped you forced another Singer to die in your stead?"

"He went voluntarily."

Vindt huffed out a laugh.

"What's so funny about that?"

"Why would someone do that?"

"Because he believed in the cause?"

Ending their punishment. Somehow, Vindt had thought Asche was alone on that mission. Apart from Dina. No, not "somehow"; the entire Council plus a few dozen Singers had come to overwhelm him. Where had his allies been then?

Unless…

A thought occurred to Vindt, outrageous, ludicrous. On the other hand, so very Asche. The calmness with which he was eating—as if he hadn't escaped death by a hair's width.

Perhaps he hadn't.

"Ru and the others believe you're dead now." Vindt formulated the words carefully. "That's quite… convenient. It would be ideal if demons and Verdurs believed the same."

"Life is hardly ideal, unfortunately. Verdurs will still recognize me as a Singer. And demons don't exist."

No, only the First in their "states." Vindt had enough experience with Asche's sinuous way of talking to find his way through it. "Which means dem… the First will believe you're dead too. How's that possible?"

"Let's assume our blood contains a marker, for our identity, our age. Let's further assume a Singer exists, so powerful and cunning that he has found a way to transfer that marker into another. So when this other Singer dies…" He didn't bother to finish the sentence.

"And you managed to do that in the few minutes between Ru and the others descending and the Verdurs arriving?"

Asche sighed. "It takes months to do that."

It was true then. "You planned this." Vindt didn't even formulate it as a question.

Asche's capture, his execution and, subsequently, his rescue. Only slowly did the implications sink in. The scope. Vindt went through the events of the siege. "The wave..." he muttered to himself, his voice imbued with something like admiration, "was... show."

"For once, one you didn't miss."

Vindt felt as if *he* was the ocean at that moment, something inside him receding, only to build up at a distance, the tremor, the foreboding of doom. Planning to be executed. For this to happen, Asche first had to...

Commit a crime that came with a death sentence.

Vindt almost laughed. Transferring powers, the Thyd rebellion. It didn't matter if those were tales or not; the wrist Binding had been but a means to a completely different end. And the only person to bear witness to that crime: Vindt. Which could only mean one thing.

He tried to keep his voice steady as he felt the wave building. "You were waiting for me to betray you?"

"Is that a question or a statement?"

Their conversation on the ship while playing chess, Asche asking him whether he would betray him to Ru if he had another whistle. A game within a game. The only thing which didn't fit into the picture was that Asche had taken Ru's first whistle from him. The Singer couldn't know Vindt had ano—

And that was when the last piece fell into place with a soft thud. "*You* put the whistle on my saddle."

Asche washed his hands in a bowl of water, then dried each finger meticulously on a napkin. "I'm stunned by your unexpected mental capacities. But none of this matters. What matters is that I need you to become my Thyd again. Now."

Vindt stared at him. And stared. And stared. All thoughts had left his mind, all words fled but one: *fool*. It echoed from the inside of his head, never fading: *fool, fool, fool*.

He stumbled as he rose.

"I haven't given you permission to leave."

Vindt didn't hear him, only the word in his head, as he made for the door. He felt Asche's song rising before he even heard him sing, the magic racing toward him. Without giving it a thought, he spun around and—

Sang.

It came naturally, a reflex ingrained into his being, no different from blocking a sword strike. Even the screeching sound rising into the air was similar.

Time came to a halt. Asche stared at him with the same disbelief Vindt felt himself. Vindt looked at his hands, his chest, as if those body parts would give him any clue as to what had just happened.

Asche came to first. He sang again, and again Vindt's body reacted before his mind could, and blocked the assault. Ire replaced the incredulity on Asche's face. His eyes flicked to Vindt's left wrist, the place where the bracelet Silhorveen had put on him had been.

Slowly, his face changed again. He threw his head back and laughed. "You have no clue what is happening, do you?" He chuckled some more, pointing his chin at Vindt's wrist. "Who took that off? Ru? Of course. The fool."

Vindt's naked wrist held no more clues than any other body part. "What does the bracelet have to do with... this?"

"Oh, but don't you remember what Ru told you? About the Thyd rebellion. About what happens when a Singer lets his Thyd drink from his wrist."

Dread tiptoed into Vindt's chest. "You said it was a tale."

"Oh, it is. The part about the rebellion. That it transfers powers onto the Thyd—well. Every Binding does, no matter how it transpires. Why else would Thyds stop aging? Drinking from the wrist just makes it a little more—how to put it?—immediate."

Vindt breathed, in, out. His strangely improved hearing, being able to see in the dark, the explosion of impressions when Ru removed the bracelet, as if he had grown another sense. "The bracelet kept me from committing suicide." As if saying the words would make it true.

"Until I changed its purpose."

"When?"

Seconds passed, the dark eyes weighing him down. Then, slowly, enunciating each word, Asche said, "When I brought you back from Thrithid."

And that was when something inside Vindt snapped. "You know what, Kvahad-thed?" He nodded, slowly, thoughtfully. "Fuck you."

He turned and left the hut unhindered.

CHAPTER 36

The waves lapped against the shore like an old man's sleepy breath. Vindt had never thought the ocean could be like this, so... tame. The night was cloudless, the black sky full of stars. None familiar. Fora had told him their names and constellations over endless nights. Vindt tried to remember, but found he had forgotten most, had probably never really paid attention to Fora's words, the stars, a part of a country he didn't want to be in, of a life he didn't want to live.

Of course, he had thought about running. However, he had no clue where to, no weapons other than his dagger. The forest—Fahad had called it a *jungle*—brimmed with weird plants and even weirder animals. A few of them Vindt had seen: colorful birds of all sizes, furry creatures that scampered through the trees and looked suspiciously like humans. Others he had heard. Some might be harmless, others not. He didn't even know which plants were edible.

Even his new "skills" wouldn't be of use. Being miraculously able to defend himself against Asche's song didn't seem to mean he could sing now. He had tried. However, all that came out of his mouth were the same tunes he had been able to produce all his life. They held no magic. Perhaps he needed training. Somehow, however, he was sure his voice *would* rise should Asche try once more to harm him.

At least he had braided his hair again. Initially, he had aimed for the braid he had been wearing the last few weeks, the one worn by people in mourning. But then he had undone it and just woven the simplest one that occurred to him. Not long ago, it would have brought a feeling of defeat. Now he simply felt tired.

He was surprised the natives had not taken him captive. It was what he would have ordered them to do in Asche's stead. Then again, the Singer was impossible to fathom. Perhaps he was convinced Vindt wouldn't run.

Fool, fool, fool.

Yes, he was. Giving up his freedom for nothing. Why in all the demons' names had he returned? Not that his freedom would have lasted long anyway; Asche would have come after him to make him his Thyd again. But at least his pride would have remained intact. No, not his pride. His integrity.

Foolish, humiliated and... paraded. The whistle—of everything in Asche's grand scheme, this stung the most. All that time knowing Vindt would betray him. And proving it to him. Who knew? Perhaps he had also planned the flogging.

No.

That and everything preceding it, Vindt was sure, had not figured in Asche's plan. Would Vindt have betrayed him without the flogging? He remembered well standing at that damn window after eavesdropping on him and Dina, when he had learned Ru's vow was real. He recalled the feeling of the whistle in his hand, how he had raised it to his lips a dozen times. And never blown it. What if—

A tall slender figure materialized from the darkness next to him.

Vindt's hands clenched the sand. "Fuck off."

"I want to talk." Asche dropped onto the beach.

"Good for you. I don't want to listen. I'm not going to become your Thyd again. Good night." He rose.

He had only taken a few steps along the shore when Asche blocked his way. "Why did you come back?"

"Why are you asking me that now? But if you want to know, because I'm an idiot." He began walking again.

This time, Asche stopped him by closing a hand around Vindt's wrist. Vindt had a strange flashback to the first time Asche held his wrist, ages ago, in his tent, after Vindt had not loosed the arrow on the day of the Guzzar battle. Back then, he had not been able to stand the touch for all the disgust it caused him. He couldn't stand it any more now, for different reasons.

When he pulled, the pressure of the fingers increased. Vindt felt his pulse beating against them. "Let go."

"The rupture," Asche said. "Don't you feel it?"

The gnawing emptiness, chafing Vindt's insides raw, the perpetual throb at the periphery of his awareness, no matter what he did, how busy his mind was—yes, he felt it. Having Asche near, having him touching him, made it worse. "The magic of the Bond. What do you care? You planned it. Besides, severing Bonds with your Thyds seems to be a habit of yours." He'd never had confirmation that Asche had killed Reisen, but after everything that had happened, barely any doubt remained.

He jerked his wrist free. The emptiness inside him gave a desperate cry.

Asche shook his head. "It's not just the magic of the Bond, Vindt. I know I told you there's nothing special about you or your Gift, but... of course there is. Why else would I have risked my life to get you out of Thrithid?"

The one mystery at the center of it all. Singers and their schemes—Vindt didn't care about any of it. But him, why him? "What's the truth, then?" He hated himself for asking again.

"The answer is longer. Will you hear me out? Please."

"For what your lies are worth."

Asche held out his palm to him. "May I borrow your dagger?"

"What for?"

"To prove my sincerity."

Sincerity—Vindt wondered if Asche even knew how to spell that word. Still, he warily handed him the weapon. He had an idea of what the Singer planned to do. Indeed, Asche sang, and the same pattern Ru had painted onto The Haven's rocky ground with his voice when he made his oath appeared in the sand between them. With a fast movement, Asche took off his bracelet and cut his veins. Vindt shuddered at the disembodied scream rising into the air as the blood hit the center of the lines. This time he understood: the universe confirming its presence, ready to bear witness. Black flames sprang up along the pattern.

"I swear by my blood that everything I tell you now is the truth."

Vindt felt the magic of the vow, the life-binding commitment, felt the universe watching.

Asche sealed his veins and put the bracelet back on; flames and lines vanished. Vindt took the dagger back, angrily quelling the impulse to lick the blood from the blade. For a long moment they stood staring at each other, the waves' soft lapping like fingers tapping on a tabletop. Vindt was well aware of what Asche was doing: baiting him —first into listening, ultimately into swaying him. He wouldn't succeed. But, yes, Vindt wanted to know *the truth*. "Fine."

The insinuation of a smile touched Asche's lips. A real one. "Shall we sit?"

Vindt slumped onto the still warm sand.

Asche lowered himself with his usual grace. "Just let me talk a moment, without interruption. Will you? Please."

The second *please*. It sounded wrong out of the Singer's mouth. And alluring. Vindt made a vague "Go ahead" gesture.

"To begin with: Thrithid isn't eternal. I know, Ehlan told you that, but it's not true. Our torment ends, after years, decades, sometimes centuries, however long it takes to destroy our powers and erase our minds. And then we are reborn, without identity, and no memories but the tortures we lived through. I'm no exception. But some day, centuries ago..." He took a breath. "My memories began to come back."

"It was mere fragments at first. But more returned, and with it, understanding, a process, slow and tedious, from the first doubts, to guesses, to certainties, from disbelief to a rage no one will ever comprehend, a rage that has been eating at me, and fueling me at the same time. And I began to... fight. I found ways to outwit Thrithid, to keep my memories, my powers, at least a part of it."

Something in Asche's voice chased a frisson down Vindt's arms.

"I did not only dedicate my life to this. But *lives*. Mine, and later those of others. So many times have I been on the verge of defeat, of giving up. And never have I been so close to success as now. And to finish it, I need you." Asche's cheeks were flushed. The ocean reflected in his eyes, the silver light of the moon like a mirror of his soul.

"When the First punished us, they did much more than torment us with Verdurs or Thrithid. We were told that they curtailed our powers. However, what they did was to take away a part and implant it into humans so that we had a chance to defend ourselves against the creatures they sent after us. For fun. A game."

"The Gift," Vindt murmured.

"But the Gift, your Gift, Vindt, is not just any part of the power of any Singer. It is the part of a specific Singer. The punishment happened thousands of years ago, yes. But as I just told you, we are reborn. As is the Gift."

Vindt tried to imagine it, a splinter chiseled from a Singer and implanted into a human. A specific Singer, a specific splinter.

And then it clicked.

His heart stopped, then leaped into a staggering run. The sand beneath seemed to lose its heat. "I have your part." He merely whispered it, but the words rang like war horns in his ears.

"I need it back, Vindt." The urgency in Asche's voice was almost painful. "The last missing part of my powers, the key to unlocking my erstwhile potential, to turning me back into what I really am. The key to bringing an end to this, to defeating the First. Don't you see?"

A part of Asche, inside him. It was absurd. And yet, it explained so much, the nature of their Bond, so different from what he had experienced with Silhorveen. "How did you find me?"

"There is no indication. I cannot feel or smell it. For centuries, I have roamed the world, chasing my brothers' Thyds, sneaking in on them in their sleep and tasting their blood. And humans—you die so fast! I tasted yours, one night, about a year ago, in a town called Neir Darin."

The dream. It had not been one. "Why don't you simply take it, your... part?"

"Did you never consider it strange that such a simple transgression as letting a Thyd drink from the wrist is punishable by death? The First aren't perfect. A fault, a hole in their plan, patched with another little story we were indoctrinated to believe. Thyd rebellion." He snorted. "The Gift is buried deep in your body. It takes time to, well, loosen it. And it is done by drinking my blood from the wrist over some time."

So it had had a purpose after all. "How do you get it back? I mean, when it's... loosened."

Asche drew up his upper lip in the same wolfish gesture as on the mountain, next to the Xixit temple. Vindt's hand rose to his neck in a protective reflex, though the idea wasn't nearly as revolting as it had been back then.

So that was it, the picture of the puzzle, the truth. The entire truth? Vindt had not forgotten Ru's words: *He wants power and will do anything to gain it.*

"You killed Reisen."

"I killed him *twice*."

Only then did Vindt realize, though deep inside he had known, that he had clung to the hope Asche wasn't responsible for Reisen's death after all, that it was the accident it had seemed to be.

How was it?

The question had not assailed him for some time, but now it came back, and with it the image of Reisen's face. "You think ending his torment in Thrithid redeems the act itself? Humans do not resurrect, if you remember."

Asche shook his head. "I don't know why I should tell you all this, but still: Reisen was over three hundred years old. No Thyd has reached that age for centuries, and not because they couldn't, physically. Human minds are not made for eternity. They go crazy. Reisen only became that old because I put a lot of effort into keeping him sane. No other Singer even knows how to do that. But my skills are limited, too. Reisen..."

Asche took another breath, and when he continued, his voice had changed. "You will never understand this, Vindt. You hate Singers. Reisen adored us. Me. Three hundred years living side by side. He went with me everywhere I did. He knew about my mission, not everything, but more than some of my allies. Of course, he was afraid of Thrithid. I know he asked you what it was like, the idiot; never mind that I told him you had no memories. He was afraid, yes, but even so, he wanted to die. I promised him to keep his torment as short as possible, to kill him for good as soon as I could. And I convinced him to stay until I found... my missing part."

"And Silhorveen?"

"You know how he was killed. You were there."

A Verdur, no doubt. But... "After all you've just told me, I find the coincidence hard to believe."

"I can't command Verdurs. But, yes, if it had not happened like that soon, I would have made it happen in a different way."

"What about the Singer who died in your stead?"

"I told you he went voluntarily. I will do the same to him as I did to Reisen and Silhorveen. He's not the first to sacrifice his life for this. And he won't be the last."

Vindt thought about the strange night on the ship when Asche had taken him through the ocean Door to Thrithid, or whatever that place had been, the image of him ramming the dagger into the corpses' skulls. "Why did you bring me along back then, when you killed Reisen for good?"

Asche turned his gaze to the waves. As always, when he was close to the ocean, he seemed to blend in with it, liquidate, dissolve. When he turned back, his face had taken on an expression Vindt couldn't read. "I don't know."

An odd answer, given Asche was obliged to tell the truth. Odder even given that—after all Vindt had just heard—he was even more convinced the Singer didn't do so much as breathe without a plan and purpose.

"What about my eyes?"

Asche's gaze flicked to them. They must be gray now, the variation the Singer preferred. "I told you already: nothing but a whim of nature."

"Then why did Ru... He was shocked when you mentioned them."

"I fear you'll have to ask Ru."

Vindt was sure there was more to this. However, he let it go for now, a far bigger mystery hovering between them unsolved. He took a breath. "The woman who rescued you —who is she?"

Asche didn't smile, but the glint in his eyes ignited. "Your goddess."

"You swore an oath to tell the truth."

"And here I sit, still alive. To succeed, I need all the support I can get. I cannot afford to be picky. I also take gods as my allies."

"Dina said gods don't exist."

A tiny smile played about Asche's lips. "Did he say exactly that? But whatever. Look, Vindt, I have answered all your questions truthfully. That doesn't mean I will reveal my entire plan to you. Perhaps one day. That depends on you."

Vindt still felt the impact of the oath, the universe listening. Again he wondered how big the gap between the truth and the full truth was. Offered voluntarily or not, the sincerity plucked at the tight knot of his resolve.

Which was exactly the Singer's intention.

"I know you think I'm telling you all this because I can't force you by singing anymore," Asche said as if he had read his thoughts. "But I want you to be aware I don't need to sing to make you my Thyd again. I'm not even talking about the humans at my command. Firstly, you are immune to *my* song because you carry a part of me in you and I can't fight myself. Other Singers can do all they want to you. But far more important, secondly—" He took off the bracelet on his left arm and held out his naked wrist.

Vindt wasn't prepared for the reaction of his body. Need erupted in every cell at the same time, an army of soldiers having lain dormant, waiting for the call to arms. It was all he could do not to launch forward and grab the bared wrist.

"The drug Ru gave you will keep you from dying when you go without blood—yes." Asche bored his gaze into

Vindt's. "But you're a Thyd, Vindt, and always will be." He put the bracelet back on. "Until I suck my part from you."

Vindt gave a mirthless laugh as he tried to will his racing heartbeat to slow. "Thank you for the demonstration. Quite apparently, the choice you seem to be giving me with all your talk isn't one."

"Yes, it is." Asche's voice took on the intensity from before. "Reisen was much more to me than my Thyd, Vindt. He was my ally. When I bound you, I had hoped... I wished..." His hand went to his chest in an apparently unconscious gesture. "It is possible, of course, to drag you through all of this against your will, but it would be very, very tedious. Success is going to take all my strength, my undivided attention. I don't know how long it will take for my part in you to loosen exactly, but it's a question of months, not years." The weight of his dark eyes increased. "Stay with me, Vindt. For whatever time it takes. Then, I promise, I will let you go. For good."

Stay with me. The sentence drew circles in Vindt's mind. "So, Ru, he never cared about the wrist Binding. It just gave him a reason to convict you. But you said yourself, you won't be able to stay hidden forever. Then what? Ru and the Council know what you're up to, they will—"

"They don't know. It's mere speculation. Ru is trying hard to convince them, but not everyone believes him. Yet."

"And why does Ru know?"

Asche hesitated. "It's not relevant for the matter at hand and, frankly, none of your concern. I have allies too, Vindt. I told you, I have been planning this for lifetimes. Besides, of those who do believe Ru, not everyone is a coward."

"Members of the Council?"

Asche smiled his small smile. "Perhaps."

Dina, yes, but he was its weakest member. From the others, Vindt had perceived nothing but hostility toward Asche. Unless they were talented actors. "Does that mean you will fight the First and your brethren?"

"Not for some time. They believe me dead for the moment, and I need time to recuperate, prepare and... become whole. But ultimately, it's possible."

Another war Vindt had nothing to do with, its outcome none of his concern. This time it would even transpire between creatures he despised, who he hoped would kill each other in great numbers. And yet...

"I understand you will need some time to think about this," Asche said. "I just beg you not to think too long. Demons might not bother me for some time, but I'm still a Singer. Every Verdur will know." He hesitated. "Also, if you want, I can..." His gaze flicked to a point somewhere on Vindt's face. His voice wavered almost imperceptibly as he said, "Do you want me to heal them?"

The muscles on Vindt's back clenched as his hand rose to his face. All of a sudden, the night was ablaze with scars, on his face, his back, and also... In the darkness, hidden beneath Asche's black hair, the marks his teeth had left on the neck wouldn't have been visible to his former human self. Now they were glowing, bright as the stars above. By now, he knew that the scourging had not killed the beast. Vindt felt it prowling and growling, craving to launch forward, to press the body before him into the sand and do with it what he had done once already.

He had not expected Asche to mention the scars, to make any allusion as to what had happened that day. Was this his way of apologizing? And if so, because he was sorry or because he thought it was what Vindt wanted to hear?

"I…" He cleared his throat. "Prefer to keep them for now."

"If you change your mind at any point," Asche said without meeting his eyes, "let me know." He rose, but stopped halfway, sliding back into a crouch. "And for the record: I didn't put the whistle on your saddle. I assumed you had one, but wasn't sure until you blew it."

"How can that be? Your entire plan hinged on—"

"Me being delivered. Not necessarily by you."

It took a moment for the words to sink in. "By who else?"

"The person in my retinue who had been spying for Ru for years."

"That's absurd. Who could that be?" Risi? Never. Narr and Kishoon? Neither. And then he remembered the conversation he had eavesdropped on. "Jun."

"Whoever. Everything was set up so that the person would have witnessed our next Binding."

"You knew Jun was spying on you, and you let him?"

The corners of Asche's mouth curled. "You should know by now I like games. Good night, Vindt."

"Wait." Vindt took a breath, trying to brace himself for the answer to another question he had to ask. "The others… what happened to them?"

"You mean did you condemn them to their deaths, too?"

"Did I?" Vindt's voice trembled.

For a long moment, Asche just looked at him, before he quietly said, "Jun and Layyad are back at The Haven. The others have gone missing."

"Missing? What does that mean? Please."

Asche's gaze hardened. "You should know by now I care for my servants. I planned this, remember?" He rose and disappeared into the darkness.

Vindt slumped onto the beach's warm sand. Alive. They were alive. Gaal. He let the relief wash over him, only now realizing how much the fear for the others, his guilt, had clenched his guts. One worry less. As for the rest…

The idea of a Singer's blood coursing through his veins had always discomfited him. Now, knowing he had been carrying a part of one with him all his life, from the day he was born, was… no, not discomfiting. Just strange. A part of Asche…

He closed his eyes, searching his body, trying to feel it. All he encountered, however, was the writhing emptiness.

Asche had never talked to him like this. Of course, he wouldn't have now, either, but for necessity. Still, the glow in his eyes, the fervor in his voice, the… passion.

Or was it obsession, madness even, as Ru had claimed?

Asche strove indeed for more power, but as a means to an end, to do what he believed was right, for himself, for his people. To free them. Was that noble, heroic even? The Verdurs, Thrithid, not being able to have a family—it was horrible. In Asche's place, would he do the same?

Vindt didn't know. He had never fought for something he believed in. In fact, he had never had a purpose other than to live. He felt almost… jealous.

Would it be so bad to give Asche what he asked for, his support? And later, the part that belonged to him anyway? A few months more.

He still felt the imprint of Asche's fingers on his wrist; the emptiness inside him circled around it like devotees around a shrine, desperate, hopeful, praying for deliverance.

Stay with me, Vindt.

He raised his eyes to the night sky, full of nameless stars, so indifferent to his fate.

* * *

Asche and Fahad were sitting on one of the mats when Vindt entered the hut. A brazier with glowing coals was the only source of light. The Singers' conversation died. Vindt briefly wondered what Asche had told the other. A second of silence passed, then Asche dismissed Fahad with a gesture. Vindt hardly noticed him leaving.

Asche's black hair, cascading down his shoulders, formed a stark contrast to the light fabric of his shirt. His gaze was intent.

"You said Reisen was your ally. That means you told him... things. Everything. I..." Vindt took a breath. "I want you to tell me too, the truth, at all times."

A subtle change rippled across Asche's features. Slowly, he said, "I didn't tell Reisen everything, Vindt. And I cannot promise to tell you. But... I can tell you as much as I deem safe for you to know."

Vindt considered that for a moment. "No more games."

"That's a... harsh condition. Not even chess?" When Vindt stayed silent, Asche sighed. "Very well."

"And I want you to swear another oath. That you will let me go when you get your part back."

The black eyes watched him for a long moment, before Asche took the dagger that Vindt was holding out to him. He sang, painting the writhing lines on the ground between them. With his usual practiced motions, he removed the bracelet and cut his veins. The universe announced its presence as black flames greedily consumed the blood dripping from his wrist. "I swear that as soon as I get my part back from you, I will let you go."

Blood fell, chiseling the oath into the world's consciousness. Asche made the flames vanish. Their eyes met. "I take it I can leave the bracelet off?" A slight quiver at the end of the sentence.

Vindt dropped to his knees. Asche extended his wrist. On the pale skin, no trace of the cuts the Singer had made with his dagger remained. The marks of Vindt's teeth were all the more obvious. The Binding seemed ages ago. The vein pulsed fast, in rhythm with Vindt's own heart. Asche no longer reigned in his aura. It coiled around Vindt, caressing, writhing in joyous anticipation. He grabbed Asche's arm with both hands.

Am I being a fool again?

His teeth found their destiny without Vindt taking his eyes from Asche's. Skin split; blood gushed over his lips, ran over his tongue, filled his mouth. He swallowed, slowly, deliberately. His blood rushed in his ears, pushed along by the beating drum of his heart, as he noticed what he had before: the Singer's eyes were not entirely black. A fine silver line encircled each pupil, making the iris look like a dark moon which had slipped in front of an ice-white sun, shielding its blazing glare. If it moved away some day, everything in the Singer's field of vision would burn to embers.

And Asche spoke:

"With my blood, I bind you. I bind your body and your soul. My blood will fulfill your destiny. You will be my shield and my sword. You will be my voice. You will depend on me as I will depend on you. You will defend my life with yours, and I will do the same for you. This Bond is sacred.

It shall only be broken by death."

GLOSSARY

Ak: The sun god in Risi's world of beliefs. He has different "forms" with changing names corresponding to the time of day (morning, night, etc.).

Binding, the: Ritual establishing the Bond between a Singer and a Thyd, repeated at monthly intervals.

Bloodstone: A translucent object made primarily of blood, created by a Singer. Its main purpose is decorative, and whether it holds magical properties is unclear.

Bond, the: The magical, blood-enforced connection between a Singer and a Thyd, lasting until one of them dies.

Demon(s): The term "demon" holds different meanings for different people, blending facts with superstition. Humans often refer to Singers as "demons," using the term synonymously with "evil creature." "Real" demons, however, are translucent creatures emitting a tart, metallic smell and a cacophony of noises. They randomly attack humans and animals but sometimes also lead concerted attacks against Singers.

Demon eyes: Human eyes turning white when their owner reaches puberty, regarded in Pel as a sign of demonic possession. According to Asche, it's merely a whim of nature.

Door(s): An invisible magical portal Singers use to travel to different places.

Eith: A truth oath sealed with blood, used by Singers to prove their sincerity.

Eternal Hunting Grounds: A concept in Pel's religion describing the supposed afterlife people go to after their deaths.

Faroosi And The Seven Whistling Spiders: A cast of characters in Risi's mythology.

First, the: The beings who created Singers. Their nature is unclear, even to Singers.

Gaal: Goddess worshipped in Pel.

Gift, the: The rare "trait" that turns humans into Thyds. It allows Singers to take over a Thyd's voice and use it as a weapon against Verdurs.

Ginsha: A harp-like instrument played by Singers.

Guzzar: Name of a country and its inhabitants, located on a continent across the First Sea from Pel.

Hatlú: A metal ring that magically prevents Singers from singing when placed around their neck.

Haven, The: The Singers' capital, perched on top of a mountain.

High Council, the: Ruling body of the Singers, comprising the seven oldest Singers.

Khesim: A bug rolling excrement over the ground, probably a dung beetle. A sacred symbol in Risi's religion, meant to bring luck and potency.

Kvahad-thed: The title Singers require to be addressed with, meaning *superior being*.

Ler: Language spoken in Leruv.

Leruv: The country Vindt was sent to for education during his youth.

Liut: Narr's and Kishoon's homeland.

Lord Tehered: A fictional evil character in "The legend of Sikandem/The legend of Tehered" who eats human souls.

Lyskú: The Singers' language.

Mandyrka: Term in Pel for a moonturner, translating to *moon worshipper*.

Messenger bird(s): Rust-colored birds, slightly smaller than ravens. They can retain a few phrases of Lyskú and replay them at the place they are sent to.

Moon child: A person with moon eyes.

Moon eyes: A rare human condition making the color of the person's eyes change with the cycle of the moon.

Moonturner: A plant whose leaves change color with the cycle of the moon from green to red.

Pel: Vindt's homeland. It's also the name for the language spoken there.

Pethal: Morning form of Ak, Risi's sun god.

Pledge, the: A ritual performed by the Singers at The Haven.

Sansýr-thed: Honorific title used between Singers.

Schiida: Lord Tehered's demonic horse in "The legend of Sikandem/The legend of Lord Tehered." Also the name of Asche's mare.

Seneschal: The most important of a Singer's human servants. He supervises the other servants and plays a crucial role in The Binding.

(Note: The term is used differently in this book from its actual meaning in medieval Europe.)

Sikandem: A human hero in "The legend of Sikandem/The legend of Tehered."

Singer(s): A species of ethereally beautiful, androgynous, human-looking beings, endowed with song magic.

Song: The magic inherent to Singers. Its concept isn't well understood among humans.

Svika: A derogatory term in Pel for a person with moon eyes, meaning *deceiver*.

Sylians: The people of Sylia, at war with Guzzar.

Thrithid: A kind of hell where Singers and their Thyds end up after their deaths, a place of eternal torture. Literally translated from Lyskú, it means *the place of the purified mind*.

Thyd(s): Humans with a special "trait," also referred to as *the Gift*. Thyds are crucial for a Singer's defense against

Verdurs but are very rare. Singers try to find each Thyd as soon as possible after their birth. Since this is a complicated process, some Thyds—like Vindt—slip their notice and grow up as normal humans.

Tsjuka: A flower common in Liut, Narr and Kishoon's homeland.

Växling: Word in Pel for a person with moon eyes.

Verdur(s): A shape-shifting creature that attacks Singers. Sometimes (wrongly) referred to as a demon. Their voice is the inverse of a Singer's song. Singers can only defend themselves against them with the help of their Thyds.

Weighing, the: A ritual between Singers determining the hierarchy between them.

Xixit: A human people whose culture died a thousand years ago, who worshiped the sun and the moon.

A PERSONAL REQUEST

A few personal words at the end. A lot of love, but also blood, sweat and tears went into this story until it reached its present form. Many times I was on the brink of giving up, doubting myself and my writing. But something deep down believed in it, believed in Vindt and Asche, and always made me continue.

Since you've reached the end, I do entertain the hope that you enjoyed this story. If you did, please talk about it with your friends and on your social media channels. Also, it would be wonderful if you could leave a review on Amazon and/or Goodreads. It helps a ton! Links below.

This story was written for you!

Amazon/
B&N

Goodreads

https://mybook.to/OBL

https://www.goodreads.com/book/
show/202799914-ocean-s-blood

ACKNOWLEDGMENTS

Dear reader, since you're here, you're apparently someone who reads acknowledgments. I do too, though I'm not sure why, because they always make me sad. Every writer seems to have a family who always believed in them and their work, a loving partner, cooking meals and giving neck massages, writing buddies with whom the author had inspiring phone calls all through the night, not to mention the long list of supporting professionals at their agency and publishing house.

I had none of that. I have no family, no partner, very few writing buddies, of which only one was permanent, no agency, no publisher. To the contrary, my "writing hobby" was often smiled upon; I was told I was crazy to write in English (which is not my mother tongue). I had countless crises with this book, for one reason or another. Besides, I have a chronic disease, ME/CFS, which not only keeps me from writing (or any activity, really) increasingly often because of the physical symptoms; it entailed a huge depression. If I should give the period in which I wrote

OCEAN'S BLOOD a theme, it would be: struggle.

And so, honestly, the first person I want to thank is: myself.

For always standing up when life kicked me down, for crawling back to this manuscript after having (literally) tossed it into a corner a hundred times, for turning a deaf ear to people who wanted to talk me out of it.

So. Great. I needed this.

Getting that out of the way, now to the few people who did support me in one way or another during the course of the three years it took from the first words of this book until its publication.

First, I want to thank Laura Lukitsch, who hates fantasy but has been an emotional pillar for me that I don't know how I could've done without. Thanks for (almost) daily WhatsApp messages, inquiring how I am, for listening to my rants, for sharing all the good and bad news, for bearing with all the versions of my cover and my book trailers, for all the picnics and wonderful excursions to medieval towns.

A heartfelt "thank you" also goes to my local chapter of the "Shut Up and Write" meetup group. During corona their online sessions were almost my only connection to the world, and even afterward, when we could meet in person again, their meetups remained my major form of social contact. Attending them was often my only reason to get out of bed.

Lyra Thornton has been my one constant critique partner, and my major source of professional feedback and encouragement. We read each other's manuscripts through various drafts, and her remarks have greatly improved this story. She's writing queer fantasy herself. Check out her books!

I also want to thank all the people who have read parts of or the entire manuscript and given their input, notably Michael Reardon, whose enthusiasm helped me through some of the major crises. Thanks also to Rafa for the many smileys left in the comments, and for being the weight tipping the scale for making me dump and rewrite 70k words...

Many thanks to my BIPOC sensitivity readers, Johanna Greenslade and T. Wu, and their invaluable comments.

Thanks to @loriciawrites_, who was the first to suggest a glossary and provided great help in creating it.

Thanks to Nuka and Lisa, my very first readers. Though we fell out at some point, their enthusiastic feedback in the beginning made me continue this story in the first place.

The last persons I want to thank, honestly, without any sarcasm involved, are: Asche and Vindt. They have always been at my side, sometimes compliant, sometimes sassy, but always there. Thinking of them, beaming my mind into their world, was at times the only thing keeping me sane.

ABOUT THE AUTHOR

My curriculum is a motley patchwork. Holding a degree in psychology, I've never worked in the field, but instead wriggled my way through different jobs across many countries. Traveling has always been my passion, though I prefer to stay in one place for extended periods of time, getting to know people and cultures in depth, rather than roaming around. I love languages and speak some.

Before I became addicted to writing, I drew cartoons whose dark, dry humor only few people got. My first writing years I dedicated to literary fiction and short stories; some are published in literature magazines. One foggy day, favorable circumstances involving Harry Potter on TV steered me back to the path of my teenage and early adult love: fantasy. Blood, swords, magic—I don't know how I could've missed out on that for so long.

These days, my life is sadly dominated by my chronic illness (ME/CFS), and writing is one of the few activities I can still pursue. I live in Berlin.